HOMECOMING RANCH

ALSO BY JULIA LONDON

HISTORICALS

The Devil's Love
Wicked Angel

The Rogues of Regent Street

The Dangerous Gentleman
The Ruthless Charmer
The Beautiful Stranger
The Secret Lover

Highland Lockhart Family

Highlander Unbound
Highlander in Disguise
Highlander in Love

The Desperate Debutantes

The Hazards of Hunting a Duke
The Perils of Pursuing a Prince
The Dangers of Deceiving a Viscount
The School for Heiresses (Anthology): "The Merchant's Gift"

The Scandalous Series

The Book of Scandal
Highland Scandal
A Courtesan's Scandal
Snowy Night with a Stranger (Anthology): "Snowy Night with a Highlander"

The Secrets of Hadley Green

The Year of Living Scandalously

The Christmas Secret (novella)

The Revenge of Lord Eberlin

The Seduction of Lady X

The Last Debutante

CONTEMPORARY ROMANCE AND WOMEN'S FICTION

The Fancy Lives of the Lear Sisters

Material Girl

Beauty Queen

Miss Fortune

Over the Edge (previously available as Thrillseekers Anonymous series)

All I Need Is You (previously available as *Wedding Survivor*)

One More Night (previously available as *Extreme Bachelor*)

Fall Into Me (previously available as *American Diva*)

Cedar Springs

Summer of Two Wishes

One Season of Sunshine

A Light at Winter's End

SPECIAL PROJECTS

Guiding Light: Jonathan's Story, tie-in to *The Guiding Light*

ANTHOLOGIES

Talk of the Ton (Anthology): "The Vicar's Widow"
Hot Ticket (Anthology): "Lucky Charm"

HOMECOMING RANCH

JULIA LONDON

Montlake
Romance

Copyright © 2013 DINAH DINWIDDIE
All rights reserved.

Printed in the United States of America.

Published by Montlake Romance
PO Box 400818
Las Vegas, NV 89140

ISBN-13: 978-1611099577
ISBN-10: 1611099579
Library of Congress Catalog Number: 2013936908

For Nancy
My hero, my best friend, my big sister

ONE

Pine River, Colorado

I'll tell you this story because my brother, Luke, won't. Even though it is more his story than mine. But you know how it is, the firstborns bask in the adoring light of being first, while younger brothers like me have to figure out where we fit in right from the get-go. Which means we tend to see the big picture while the firstborns see themselves. You younger siblings know what I'm talking about—we're the glue and they're the glitter, right? Although I can be kind of glittery, too. I'm an artist—I paint the canvas, I fill in the background of this family. I'm not bragging—it's just fact.

Okay, so two words for how *this* story started: Grant Tyler.

He was a fun-loving, adventure-seeking, hard-driving, cigar-chomping, skirt-chasing kind of guy. He'd lost as many fortunes as he'd made in his sixty-plus years. He liked the idea of being married more than he liked being married, and, trust me, he didn't get high marks from the ladies. Not like me, anyway—I've got *killer* game.

But Grant Tyler, he could always smooth things over somehow, because he was always hooking up with women. I know that from Dani Boxer. She runs the Grizzly Lodge and Café, and she comes around sometimes to have coffee with me and Dad. She's *awesome*.

So anyway, Grant could smooth over the ruffled feathers of pretty birds, but he couldn't smooth over the fact that he sucked at being a dad. I knew he wasn't much of one way back because I went to school with his daughter, Libby Tyler. She sort of looks like him, but a whole lot better. She's got these deep blue eyes and crazy curly, dark hair I always liked. I sat behind her in third grade and accidentally touched her hair and accidentally left some half-chewed Chiclets in it. Libby picked up her scissors and cut off a big lock of hair with the gum in it and put it on my desk. I think I kept it till fifth grade.

Anyway, I knew about Libby, but I didn't know about the kid in California or the one in Florida. That's right, ol' Grant Tyler had three kids by three different women. All girls. And he forgot to pay his child support more than he remembered. He swore he never saw a recital or a soccer game. I bet he didn't know what their favorite color was, or the name of the first boys to break their hearts, or what their dreams were, either. Not like *my* mom, who knew everything about us. My mom was the greatest mom *ever*. Except for the breast cancer, which was a deal-killer on the Mom of the Year award. That made her, like, *not* the best mom of the year because she checked out way before any of us were ready for her to go.

So when the end came for Grant Tyler—and it came at him fast and hard, just like he'd lived—he got a little religion and decided he needed to do right by his kids. Maybe he hadn't been a good dad, but by God, he'd leave something for those kids to hold onto. Except his Porsche. He wanted to be buried in that Porsche. Can you believe that? Imagine yourself on your deathbed, and what you're worried about is being buried in a car instead of what you were going to tell the Man Upstairs about all the stuff you'd done.

I know all of this part, because Grant Tyler announced it all to my friend Jackson Crane, his fourth and final business manager. Jackson claims he told his big corporate law office in Denver to screw it one day and came this way. He got on with Grant and worked nine months before the doc said Grant wouldn't make it. Grant told Jackson to leave everything he had to his kids. Jackson was confused, and he said, "What kids?"

"*My* kids," Grant said. "Madeline, Emma, and Libby."

Like me, Jackson knew only about Libby, and he said he honestly believed Grant was confused with all the drugs they were pumping into him, so he repeated, "Madeline and Emma?"

Grant, who had tubes coming out of every orifice, cocked his head to one side and studied Jackson as if he couldn't make out how he could be so slow, sort of the way I look at Dad's old pickup truck. He said, "Do I look like I want to do a lot of explaining right now? Listen up—I want to leave everything to them. All of it. Why the hell are you looking at me like that?"

I can picture Jackson futzing with the knot in his tie like he does when people talk about things he doesn't get. He also swallows a lot. He doesn't have much of a poker face, if you know what I mean. He said, "That's . . . admirable." Admirable! Ha! "But as you know, your divorce from your fifth wife is pending. And it's costing a lot of money."

"Yeah, tell me something I don't know," Grant scoffed. "What about it?"

"It's complicated," Jackson said.

To which Grant laughed and said, "I hope you look that sad at my funeral, Mr. Crane. You ever been married? I'll let you in on a little secret: It's always complicated." I guess Grant thought he was imparting the wisdom of the world, like he was the first guy to ever figure out that women are crazy and impossible to understand. "Go on, now, give it to me straight," he'd said to Jackson. "Tell me how complicated it is. But don't say the Porsche, 'cuz I ain't leaving it. Have you found out who can bury me in it yet?"

"Not yet. I'm working on it."

"You must think I got all the time in the world. I need to get that nailed down. All right, so?" he'd said, and with his hand, he gestured for Jackson to speak.

I know this: Jackson doesn't like it when people tell him to hurry up and talk. But he didn't mind then because he said that the gesture of lifting his hand and waving it around wore Grant out, and Jackson knew then that Grant really was going to die. Jackson found his balls,

I'm happy to say, and he told him, "You're not going to have anything to give your kids when the divorce is finalized. You're broke, Mr. Tyler. The only thing you'll have left is Homecoming Ranch."

"That's all?" Grant asked, like he couldn't believe that being the financial genius he was, he could have screwed things up that bad.

"That's all," Jackson said.

That was not what Grant wanted to hear. Hell, it's not what *I* wanted to hear. The thing is, Homecoming Ranch is really complicated. It's my home. It's where Luke and I grew up. Dad believes Grant really meant to help him out when he gave him that piddling sum for Homecoming Ranch, but I don't think so.

"Well to hell with it, then," Grant said, and Jackson said he sank back against the pillows and that for once, he didn't look so big. He looked pretty small and frail. "It's the thought that counts, right?" Grant said, as if he was seeking some affirmation from Jackson that it was okay to totally screw over your kids. "Leave that to them."

That should have been the end of it, but Jackson must have been really bothered by it, because he said, "You know you are upside down on the ranch's mortgage. It's more headache than legacy. You're leaving them a big mess."

But ol' Grant chuckled and gestured to himself, lying in the hospital bed in one of those gowns that hardly covered him, with a bowl to catch his vomit on the table in front of him. "You think I ought to get out there and spruce the place up? Those girls will just have to turn it around if they want anything out of it, won't they? It'll be good for 'em. Builds character." He'd grinned at Jackson. "It's the best I got, Jackson. Now, write this down. Madeline Pruett, I think she's in Florida, but you'll have to do a little digging with that one. And then Emma Franklin or Tyler, I don't know what the hell she's going by these days. I'm ninety-nine percent sure she's still in L.A. I ran into her mamma not too long ago. That gal is still a *fox*." He'd actually paused to remember Emma's mother fondly for a moment because that man was a dog to his dying breath. "And then there's Libby," he'd said with a sigh, and had nodded at the door. "She's probably sitting outside the room right now."

"She is," Jackson said, and I think he was probably pretty pissed off at this point. He likes Libby. Hell, everyone likes Libby. Most everyone. I hear Ryan doesn't like her much these days, but that's another story for another day.

I digress.

Grant was annoyed that Libby was trying to be a good daughter. "Jesus H, can't a man just die in peace?"

"I think she'd like to offer you some comfort in that regard," Jackson said, and I can just picture his jaw clenched tight as his fist. "And it's not like you're going to die any minute."

"You don't know that," Grant snapped. "Tell her to come back later. I got my comfort right here," he said, and with some effort, fished a bottle of Jim Beam from beneath his pillow. He laughed at Jackson Crane's expression, but his laugh quickly dissolved into a painful cough.

Yeah, the end came pretty hard at Grant Tyler.

I know it did, because I know everyone in town. My name is Leo Kendrick. Don't let my good looks and charming personality blind you.

TWO

Orlando, Florida

Unreal.

It was the only word that came to mind, popping into her head in neon colors. A girl should never hear of her father's death quite like she did, Madeline Pruett would tell her best friend Trudi a few hours after the fact. Especially when she didn't even know she had a father. And what made it spectacularly unreal was that there were strings attached to her father's death. Big strings. Enormous, bungee-cord-jump-off-a-bridge strings.

There was a long silence on the other end of the phone as Trudi took this news in. Madeline could hear Trudi's two-year-old daughter in the background banging cups on the tile floor. Then Trudi said, "Are you going to soccer practice?"

It wasn't exactly what Madeline would call "practice." She volunteered with Camp Haven, an organization that mentored at-risk youth. Camp Haven sponsored afterschool soccer camps, and Madeline coached little five-year-old girls. Not that Madeline was an outstanding soccer player—she was mediocre. But the coaching challenge was getting the girls to run in the right direction. The payoff was spending time with them. "Yes, I'm on my way," she said to Trudi.

"Okay, so here's what you do. When practice is over, I'll meet you at Paco's Cantina. Order two gold margaritas. I'm calling Rick right now."

Thank God for Trudi Feinstein, because Madeline really needed to repeat back the things the man had said about her father, to hear it out loud again, to make sense of it. She needed some moral support, someone to gasp and exclaim that it was all so unreal right along with her.

Madeline had tried to find that moral support from her mother when she'd called her just a couple of hours earlier, but Clarissa Pruett had cheerfully announced that she and some guy named John were about to go and "party" and to make it quick.

"Okay. My father died," Madeline said.

"Huh? What do you mean your *father* died? Who are you talking about?"

In her mother's defense, it was a legitimate question in a family of exactly two. Not that Madeline had lacked for dads—in her life, she'd been subjected to four that her mother had said she should call "Dad," and that didn't even count a few men in between. And quite obviously, Madeline had been produced with the help of an actual father. Turns out the one who had died was the absent sperm donor, the deadbeat the state could never track down to collect child support. Madeline had only one memory of him: a stack of gold chains around a thick neck, the reek of cigars, and a beefy hand with an endless supply of candy he dispensed like a broken gum machine. There was only one fuzzy picture of her parents—her mother with long hair, big floppy hat, a cigarette, and cocktail, and a man, whose face was partially obscured by her mother's hat.

"My real dad, Mom," Madeline said. "My sperm donor. He died."

"Well, I'm sorry to hear that," her mother said. Madeline heard the pop of a beer can over the cooking show blaring in the background from the enormous flat screen TV some man had bought her mother. Clarissa Pruett never actually cooked anything that Madeline could remember, but she watched that channel religiously.

"So how'd he die?" her mother asked before slurping from the can of beer.

The bigger question to Madeline was how did he *live?* Where had he been? It had not occurred to Madeline, in the shock of hearing about him at all, to ask how he'd met his demise. "I don't know."

"They didn't say?"

"It wasn't a they. It was one guy. Jackson Crane."

Jackson Crane had shown up late to the realty offices where Madeline worked. She was the fairly new agent who always took the people who came in after the other agents had left for happy hour. It was a trick that had landed her a few good listings, including her prize, the DiNapoli house.

"Now who is Jackson Crane?" her mother asked. Madeline heard the sound of a lighter, the quick inhale of breath as her mother lit a cigarette.

"My father's business agent or something like that," Madeline said, and told her mother how the handsome, tanned man wearing a tailored suit coat and crisp white shirt open at the neck had walked into her office. He'd reminded her of one of those sitcoms where four guys live together in a loft and have hilarious girl troubles, and she'd even assumed he was looking for a new bachelor pad somewhere in Orlando. She told her mother how he'd shaken her hand vigorously, thanked her for seeing him, and then said, *I flew in from Colorado and came straight here,* and proceeded to announce that he had some unpleasant news about her father.

He'd said it with dimples and white teeth, as if his unpleasant news could be softened by a Crest toothpaste smile. Madeline had been suspicious of him—she was generally suspicious of all men—and had feared his was one of those awkward smiles people get when they hear bad news and they don't know how to take it in. He clearly thought she would be very upset with hearing her father had died.

"I told him I didn't have a dad."

"I wish you wouldn't say that, Maddie," her mother said disapprovingly. "You make it sound like I was sleeping around. You obviously had a father."

Madeline chose to skirt around the glaring truth that her mother had spent most of her life hopping from one bed to another. "Not everyone has a father, Mom. Some people only have a sperm donor."

The absence of a father was the singular crack in Madeline's life, the chasm she could never seem to avoid. It wasn't that she dwelled on it, quite the opposite—she had made herself forget it a very long time ago. But inevitably, when she met new people, they would ask about her family, and she would end up explaining that she never knew her father, and, no, she never saw him but one time, never heard from him (never mattered to him, did not exist for him)—and she would have to relive the whole no-dad thing again. She much preferred not thinking about him at all.

"Why'd this guy come all the way to tell you?" Mom asked. "Why didn't he send a letter or something?"

"Because my father left me something, Mom. He left me a ranch."

"A *what*? What do you mean a ranch? A *real* ranch?"

"A real ranch," Madeline confirmed. Just saying it out loud made her feel strangely annoyed. She ought to be, as Jackson Crane had pointed out, excited by the prospect. But she wasn't.

"What about me?" her mother asked.

"What do you mean?" Madeline asked, confused.

"I *mean*, did he leave *me* anything?"

Madeline didn't even know what to say to that. Why would she think he had? "I don't—"

"What about all the child support he should have paid me? I ought to go after that."

Madeline was not surprised that her mother would turn news like this around to herself. "Mom . . . no offense, but you probably should have gone after that when you actually supported me. I'm almost thirty. I've been on my own since I was seventeen."

"Well," her mother said with a sniff, "when you go, ask about that. I feel like he should have left me something."

Go? Go where? A big, heavy wrench had just been tossed into the middle of Madeline's neatly ordered life. She had the DiNapoli listing, a fifteen-thousand-square-foot monstrosity of Greek revival meets Jersey Shore. It was a huge challenge to sell, but one that would pay off in a major way when it did. Eight months ago, Madeline's fellow realtors had told her not to take it, that the sellers were unreasonable, that they wouldn't come down off the asking price. But Madeline was determined. She'd spent a lot of time and money to market that property—a *lot*—and she wasn't going to leave that hanging. Plus, she'd committed to another eight weeks of soccer, and neither was she going to leave those little girls without a coach. Camp Haven had saved Madeline from a bad situation one summer by daily removing her from her mother's dysfunctional orbit. She was indebted to them. Coaching made her feel useful. She didn't have time for a father she never knew popping up, uninvited, unwanted, into her life.

"Honestly, I never thought he was a ranch kind of guy," her mother said, and at the same time, Madeline heard the faint, but unmistakable tone of a male voice in the background. "Well, listen, kiddo, I've got to get going—"

"Wait, Mom! There's more," Madeline said quickly. "That's not all he left me."

"Oh yeah? What else?"

"Two sisters."

Her mother took a long drag off her smoke and blew it into the receiver. "I guess that doesn't come as a big surprise. Look on the bright side—you've always wanted siblings."

It was true that Madeline had always wanted siblings. Brothers, sisters, she didn't care, just someone to be there when she came home from school. Someone who would make Pop-Tarts and watch TV with her until Mom dragged in from wherever she'd been that day. To think that all this time, Madeline had had not one, but *two* sisters was a lot to absorb. She imagined an entire life of barbeques and ski trips and father-daughter dances that had not included her.

"*I'll be just a minute!*" her mother suddenly shouted, startling Madeline, and then said, "You look like him, you know it?"

"Who?"

"Your father! Those blue eyes and that dark brown hair. Let me tell you, thirty years ago, Grant Tyler was one good-looking bastard. We sure sowed some wild oats." She laughed, but it dissolved into a phlegm-filled cough. "We discovered our sexuality together."

"Mom!" Madeline exclaimed. "Don't even. It's not like you guys were hanging out at Woodstock."

"You think Woodstock was the only sexual revolution in this country?"

"I am *so* not having this conversation with you."

"You know what your problem is?" Mom continued, ignoring her. "You're too uptight. You like things to fit in neat little boxes and go certain ways and they never do."

"Oh, I know, Mom. You taught me that things weren't going to go my way," Madeline said with a twinge of bitterness.

"Don't start with me, Madeline. I did the best I could. Now when are you going to go and check out this ranch?"

"I'm not."

That gave her mother a slight bit of pause. "What do you mean, you're *not?*"

"I don't want to go. I don't want anything from him. I don't want a ranch and two sisters I never knew I had until today, and the only reason I know about them at all is because he must have felt guilty on his deathbed. I have way too much going on right now. I just listed the DiNapoli house. I'm coaching a new team. I'm really busy."

"John, goddammit, I am on the *phone* with my *daughter!* I said I'd be there in a minute!" her mother shouted. "I swear, the things I have to put up with. I have to go, Madeline. We'll talk later. But you think about what you just said. Because I think you want to understand more about the man who gave you life. And you need to go see what we got."

Madeline had wanted to understand more about her father a very long time ago. And when the answers didn't come, she'd stopped caring. How could her mother not realize that? "No, Mom. I don't care who he was, and I don't want anything of his." There was, Madeline had realized with surprise, so much resentment in her voice. *So much.*

She'd expected her mother to argue, but in a rare moment of maternal instinct, Clarissa Pruett sighed. "He cared about you, Maddie. He *loved* you. But he was a weak man. Now I really have to go. I need some help with my car payment this month and it's best to keep Big John happy." She hung up.

"I'm not going," Madeline said into the dead line. And she meant it.

She had no intention of uprooting her carefully constructed life, of dropping everything to fly out to Colorado.

>━┥━◇━•━○━•━◇━┝━<

Trudi was not satisfied with Madeline's response either. "Don't be stupid," she said when they met up.

Madeline had known Trudi since the first grade. They'd met in Mrs. Bever's class—Madeline, the skinny, dark-haired, dirty kid who was always late because her mother couldn't wake up after a night of partying. And Trudi, the overweight, red-cheeked redhead with sparkling green eyes. They were outsiders, the kids on the fringe. But as they grew older, Trudi's personality far outshone her weight, and she became friend to all and enemy to none. She'd still experienced crushing moments—mean boys, meaner girls—but Madeline was always there, on her side.

And Trudi had been steadfastly loyal to Madeline in return.

Madeline used to envy Trudi. She'd had the home life Madeline had always craved: a real house, a mother and a father and a sister and a brother. Her mother got her up in the morning and fed her breakfast, and she was there when Trudi came home from school. She washed Trudi's clothes and helped her with her homework and took her shopping and went to all her school events and made cookies for the class.

Madeline and her mother had lived hand-to-mouth most of her life, putting down roots with whomever would take them in, living off the men her mother met, and then, whenever her mother was offended, which had been often, pulling up from their shallow moorings and blowing away. Mom had held a dozen jobs or more, had relied heavily on her blue-collar parents long after it was decent to do so, and had bristled when Madeline would beg for a house like Trudi's.

Well, Mom finally had the house. She'd inherited it when her parents had died, long after Madeline had left home determined to make a life completely different than the one her mother had shown her.

"You *have* to go." Trudi peeled a nacho from an enormous plate of them. "I am not going to let you sit there like a geeky bump on a log with your highlighters and flat shoes and miss this opportunity." She tucked the guacamole-laden chip into her mouth.

"What's wrong with my shoes?" Madeline asked. They were ballet flats, purchased on sale from Kohl's.

"I've told you before, Mad," Trudi said in that patient, motherly voice usually reserved for her daughter, Esme, or her husband, Rick, "there is practical, and then there is *too* practical. Anyway, we're not talking about your shoes, we are talking about *you* and the little bubble you live in, and your unwillingness to step outside of that bubble."

"I don't know what you mean," Madeline sniffed. "I have too stepped out of my bubble." She ignored the nagging thought that she had turned off her cell phone so that she would not receive messages from anyone who could possibly pull her out of her bubble.

"Oh, really?" Trudi asked, and looked up slyly from her chip. She didn't come out and say it, but she was talking about Stephen, a man Madeline had dated a few times. Trudi's husband had introduced them. Stephen was a lawyer, a successful guy who could drape himself over a chair and look at you in a way that would make you melt inside. He was fun, he was respectful . . . but then he'd gone and ruined it all a couple of weeks ago when he'd said he wanted to take things "to the next level." That sounded vaguely like a video game to Madeline, and it made her uncomfortable. Since then, she'd been sort of dodging Stephen. She had her breakup speech all worked out. There was no sound reason for her reluctance. Madeline was acutely aware that a mature person did not stop dating another mature person because of one little thing he'd said. It didn't make sense, she got that. But she did not want to go to the next level.

"By the way," Trudi said, "Stephen asked me to tell you that he has your movie guide."

Shit. Madeline needed her movie guide; she was a film buff. She and movies had a standing Friday night date, right after soccer. "I know he does, Trudi," she lied. "I'm going to pick it up tomorrow."

"Tomorrow?"

"*Tomorrow.*"

"I hope so, because Stephen is hot, he's a great guy, and he *really* likes you. He told me."

Madeline did not believe that men *really* liked her. She believed Stephen said he did because he thought he was supposed to say it, or had said it to other women and scored with it. "Come on, Trudi," she scoffed. "I'm a control freak, my condo is so neat that it's a little obsessive—you yourself have said so many times—and I work all the time. How can he like me so much? He doesn't even know me that well."

"How can you say that? He knows you're pretty and funny and when he figures out how insanely organized you are, he might actually see it as a benefit. Not everyone is as annoyed by it as I am."

Madeline snorted and reached for a nacho.

"For someone so smart, you can be really dumb sometimes, you know it?" Trudi pointed a chip at Madeline. "You know what's going on here, don't you? The reason you don't believe Stephen could really dig someone like you is because you have so many daddy issues you're like a walking Lifetime movie. Which is all the more reason you have to go to Colorado and clear this up."

Madeline laughed. "It has *nothing* to do with my dad. Please." But she wasn't certain that was entirely true.

"This is textbook Dear Abby," Trudi said with a wave of her pudgy fingers. "Your father abandoned you and now you don't believe a guy would have deep feelings for you. Hello! Just go, Mad. Go and do yourself a favor and answer all the questions your ten-year-old self had. How can that be a bad thing?" She'd swatted Madeline's hand away from her nachos. "So what's it called, this ranch?" Trudi asked as she signaled the waiter and made a gesture to their empty margarita glasses.

"Homecoming Ranch." When Jackson Crane had told her the name, Madeline had laughed. A high-pitched, nervous laugh. She'd said, *this is a joke,* and he'd said, *no joke.* And as Madeline had tried to take it in, to absorb such stunning news, Jackson Crane told her the Colorado ranch was about six hundred acres. Madeline the realtor had done some quick math in her head and had almost swooned with the possibilities.

"Wow," Trudi said approvingly. "Sounds like a place I'd like to visit. Another reason you have to go."

"It sounds to me like a place where Sperm Donor wore a ten-gallon hat and rode around on a big black horse while my mom hopped from one tract house to another."

"Could be some money in it," Trudi said, and wiggled her eyebrows. "Have you thought of that?"

"I don't want anything from him, Trudi. I mean, seriously, can you blame me?"

"No," Trudi said flatly. "But . . ."

"But what?"

Trudi frowned. She pushed aside her plate, planted her forearms on the table, and leaned across the table. "Okay, look, I wasn't going to bring this up," she said low. "But do you remember the box you kept under your bed in the fifth grade?"

Madeline could sense one of Trudi's "teachable moments" coming on. She glanced at the waitress, wished she'd hurry with the margaritas.

"You know, the one with the magazine cutouts?" Trudi pressed.

Something crawled up Madeline's spine. Yes, she remembered. She'd been ten years old then. She'd sit at the scarred Formica table in her grandmother's house with scissors and magazines, and cut out pictures of houses behind white picket fences, of families with cars and dogs and beach balls. There were always beach balls in those pictures. She'd cut out pictures of women with babies, of children on Slip 'N Slides, of happy, smiling people. She'd made up the life that she'd wanted so desperately and had saved those pictures in a shoebox under her bed.

"How in God's name to do you remember stuff like that?" Madeline asked.

"How could I forget something like that? So here's the thing—I remember that skinny kid with the freckles and the blue eyes and those horrible tie-dyed Keds, and I think she deserves to know why her stupid-ass dad wasn't around. Mad, you *have* to go. For that ten year-old kid."

Her ten-year-old self was a compelling argument, but it still didn't change Madeline's mind. But what did change her mind a few days later was soccer practice with a wiggling group of five-year-olds.

At the end of their practice—which consisted of a lot of running around and giggling about bouncing soccer balls—eight girls sat in a circle under a tree with Madeline and Teresa, the other volunteer coach. Teresa's husband generally attended, too, but that afternoon he'd been one of the volunteers dispatched to take two girls home.

The girls were drinking CapriSuns and eating apple slices that Madeline had brought. This was Madeline's favorite part of her day, her week, her month. She had been one of these girls once; she had sat under this tree, had wished that any of the coaches would be her new mom or dad. Madeline could not forget the yearning she'd felt then.

As a coach, she'd made up a game to play with the girls. They called it the Wishing Game, and they took turns announcing what they wished for. Madeline started the game that afternoon. "I wish, I wish, I wish," she said, pausing for dramatic effect, "that I had a pet unicorn!"

The girls squealed with delight, and around they went. Mostly, the girls wished for things: a Wii, a television. One wished her mom had a car. Another wished she lived in a castle with lots of cats. Another wished to be a princess with a Barbie car.

But Kenya had a different sort of wish. "I wish, I wish, I wish I was a boy."

Madeline and Teresa looked at each other. "A boy?" Madeline asked, smiling.

"Yep. If I'm a boy, my daddy will come home."

"Why do you have to be a boy for your daddy to come home, honey?" Teresa asked.

"I don't know," Kenya said. "Mommy said if I was a boy, he'd come home." She said it as if it were perfectly natural for a mother to tell her young daughter that she was the wrong sex, that her gender was the reason her father was missing from her life.

Two girls sitting next to Kenya dissolved into giggles. "Your daddy ain't coming home."

"Yes he is," Kenya said with the full confidence of a five-year-old. "He can't come home right now because he's a superhero. He's fighting bad guys."

The girls giggled, and Kenya looked to Madeline for support. "He's friends with Batman," she said, and the girls laughed again.

How could Madeline deny that child? How many times had *she* wished for a superhero dad? "I know," she said, smiling at Kenya. "I saw him."

Kenya's eyes rounded. "You saw my daddy?"

"With Batman," Madeline said. She could feel Teresa's frown of disapproval, could see the other girls staring at her with excitement. But that all faded in the light of Kenya's big grin.

So in the end, in a roundabout way, it was Kenya who made Trudi's argument for Trudi. Kenya deserved a better explanation of why her father was missing from her life. So did Madeline.

Later that night, when Stephen called, Madeline settled on the perfect excuse to end things with him: She told him she couldn't date him right now, because she was going to take care of some personal business.

"What kind of personal business?" he asked.

"My father died and left me some property in Colorado," she said. "Shared with siblings I haven't met." She gave him a brief explanation of what she knew.

"Wow," Stephen said. "You know, I have a friend in Denver who handles property cases. I could get in touch."

Madeline agreed to it if for no other reason than to end the call. She guessed a lawyer in Denver would probably tell her what Jackson Crane had already told her.

Over the next two days, she arranged everything at work. She made color-coded files with all her listings, prepared task charts for the realtor's assistant, Bree, to follow in case something should come up in the few days she was gone. She even prepared some automated e-mail reminders on the slim chance that her plane went down. She'd left explicit instructions for when and how the office was to contact her, and, please God, if she got an offer on the DiNapoli property, how they were to text her *immediately*.

Madeline had everything covered.

She always did.

Trudi had taken her to the airport at the last minute. Madeline's mother had forgotten to pick her up much like she used to forget to pay rent or buy milk or come to Madeline's school functions. Trudi chattered the whole way, something about rodeos, which normally would have caught Madeline's attention. But her mind was a good thousand miles away, the little knot in her belly beginning to morph into a watermelon. She didn't like stepping into the unknown, didn't like uncertainty in any shape or form.

At the airport, Trudi got out to hug her good-bye in front of the departures terminal. "I'm really proud of you, Mad. I think it will really help if you know more about him."

"Help what?"

"God, you're hopeless," Trudi groaned. "*Everything!* Oh, and one last thing. I feel that as your friend, I should point out that you might enjoy the trip a little more if you'd worn some jeans or something a little more casual." Trudi glanced down at Madeline's suit. "You look so . . . official."

Madeline was wearing her best suit, the one she'd worn to the closing of the Freemont Drive property, her first really big property sale. She had a briefcase-slash-purse slung over her shoulder, a neck pillow hooked onto the handle, and Jackson Crane's number in her pocket. She had one small carry-on bag containing a couple of mix-and-match separates, because she did not expect to be gone more than a couple of days.

"It's a business meeting, not a family reunion," she said, and swallowed down another attack of nerves.

"Right," Trudi said, seeing right through her as usual. "Just keep an open mind, okay?"

"I have an open mind!"

"No you don't. When it comes to Sperm Donor, you are locked down like Fort Knox." Trudi hugged Madeline tight, then let go, and walked around to the driver's side of her car. "Call me!" she shouted, and disappeared into her car and drove away.

Madeline would be calling her, all right. In about two days, from this very airport.

⤞⊶⊷⊙⊶⊷⤛

Madeline had to admit that Colorado was a lot cleaner looking than Florida, what with its dark blue mountains, its crisp, cool air, and the bright blue sky with fat white clouds above shimmering gold plains. It looked a lot better in person than it did in the pictures she'd found online. Apparently, she'd have plenty of time to study the breathtaking scenery, because her usual high standard of planning every moment of the day had not exactly meshed with the logistics of getting to this ranch. To say that she did not like surprises was a gross understatement. Madeline liked symmetry in her routine and to know what to expect and when to expect it.

What she did *not* like was to hear phrases such as "lost your rental reservation" or "four-hour drive from here." She liked to believe people when they said, "I'll meet you," as Jackson Crane had said, that they would mean the most obvious and most logical, "I'll meet you at the airport," instead of, "I'll meet you in Pine River."

But Madeline had regrouped, because that was the other thing she did extremely well. Her mother had gone through boyfriends like cheap dish towels, and they'd moved many times. When Madeline had to attend a new school, or miss a party she'd looked forward to because her mother woke her in the middle of the night, throwing clothes at her, telling her to pack, Madeline had learned how to regroup when it mattered most.

She had a map of Colorado in her right hand, the keys to her rental car in the left—the *last* rental car, the chubby-cheeked chatterbox behind the counter had said after cheerfully informing her they'd lost her reservation.

She marched out into the vast open that surrounded the Denver airport, determined to be undaunted by a few early bumps, and above all, to *not* freak out.

And she was not going to mope because the car was only a little larger than a circus clown car.

With her jaw clenched, Madeline wedged her carry-on into the backseat, then spread the map of Colorado on the hood. She reached into her handbag and pulled out a yellow highlighter—not to be confused with the pink highlighter, which she kept for work-related documents—and traced it along the route she would take to Pine River. She folded the map so that she could see the entire route at a glance, opened the passenger door, and arranged the map on the passenger seat. She put herself in the driver seat, put her phone in the seat console for easy reach, and dug out a bottle of water from her bag, loosened the top, and set it into the cup holder.

She was ready.

Madeline put her foot to the gas and pointed south. Or maybe west. Her sense of direction was not great.

THREE

Denver, Colorado

Luke was lost well before his date ever mentioned Q-forms. He'd met Jennifer at a barbeque and had liked her blond hair, her expressive brown eyes, and her earnest way of speaking. This was only his second date with her, and while talk of Q-forms and office politics was a little on the boring side—okay, a lot on the boring side—he was making his best effort to listen attentively and commit to memory some of the names she was tossing out.

But the vibrating of his cell phone was making it very hard to pay attention.

He'd surreptitiously glanced at it moments before he'd asked how work was going for her, and saw that it was his Aunt Patti. Patti never called unless something was wrong.

Ignore, ignore, ignore.

"I mean, I don't get the big deal, you know? We're all grown-ups. We ought to be able to work these things out, right?"

"Right." It could be his dad. It could be his brother, Leo. It could be anything. Or maybe nothing at all. *Ignore, ignore.*

"But Mallory, she's . . ." Jennifer paused, and pushed a thick lock of blond hair over her shoulder. "I don't like to talk bad about anyone, but Mallory is kind of arrogant, you know? She thinks her way is the only way. She drives me crazy."

"Ah," Luke said. *Remember Mallory.* He had a feeling her name would come up more than once if he continued to see Jennifer.

His cell phone vibrated again. *Ignore.*

"I mean she's really smart, and she has great ideas, but sometimes, I just want to say, 'Look, Mallory, you're not the only with great ideas and sometimes, you might want to listen to other opinions.'"

It had to be an emergency. Patti would just leave a message if it wasn't an emergency.

"Does that ever happen to you?" Jennifer asked.

The question startled Luke. "What?"

A look came over Jennifer's face that Luke read as annoyance. "Is that your cell phone buzzing?" she asked coolly.

"It is," he said truthfully. "Jen, could you give me one minute? I don't think I can ignore this call."

"Since when am I Jen?" she said, and sank back. "Sure," she said, flicking her hand at his phone. "Do what you need to do." She picked up her house specialty drink. The Nightingale, the waitress had called it. It was about two feet tall and blue.

Luke phoned his aunt. Patti answered on the first ring. "Patti?"

"Hi, Luke, thank God. I'm worried sick about Bob and Leo," she said in that pragmatic way she had of speaking, skipping over any standard greeting. It reminded Luke of his late mother, Patti's sister. "I drove out to the ranch today and it's closed up tight as a drum. They haven't been there in days, Luke, and I can't get hold of Bob."

Luke closed his eyes and resisted the urge to drop his forehead to the table. *Not now, not when I have three new builds lined up.* They were big jobs. Construction jobs for custom homes in a tony part of Denver.

"Where are you? It sounds like a party. Am I interrupting?"

"No, you're not interrupting," he said, and noticed the slight narrowing of Jennifer's eyes. "I'll call him and let you know what's going on."

"Please do. I don't do anything but worry about those two."

So did Luke. He clicked off and smiled at Jennifer. She arched her brows in question. "I've got to call my dad," he said apologetically. "My aunt can't get hold of him."

"So Patti is your aunt?" she asked, watching him closely.

"Yep. Listen, I'm just going to step out and make this call. It will be quick, I promise. Why don't you order us an appetizer?"

She shrugged and picked up the menu. "I don't even know what you like."

"Anything," he assured her, and made a quick retreat out onto the street.

His father did not pick up the call. Luke didn't read too much into that—Dad couldn't hear his cell phone half the time. But then again, there had been times in the past that Dad hadn't answered the phone because he was avoiding Luke.

Luke called his brother.

"Romeo speaking," Leo answered cheerfully after one ring.

Luke couldn't help but smile. "What's up, Romeo? Everything okay?"

"No, everything is *not* okay. I just found out that the Broncos traded the only cornerback we have that's worth a damn. We are seriously going to have to put the pass defense on every milk carton in America and hope to Jesus we find it before training camp. What's up with you?"

"Not much. So what else is going on, Leo?"

"Are you trying to get in my business? I've been beating off the hot babes as usual. I could use a new bat."

"I didn't know there were so many hot babes in Pine River."

"You'd be surprised, bro, you'd be so surprised."

"Leo—what's up with Dad?"

"Dad? Nothing," Leo said. "Hey, I think we might have a chance at getting that free agent defensive back out of Miami. Holgenstizer, or something like it."

Stalling. No one knew Leo like Luke, and Luke knew when his little brother was stalling. "Nothing, huh? So why did Aunt Patti call? Why does she say you guys haven't been out at the ranch in days?"

"*Shit*," Leo muttered. "Look, everything is going to be fine," he said, the cheerfulness gone out of his voice. "We've got it all under control."

Now Luke worried. "Got *what* under control?"

"We found a place in town that works just fine. Little house, and I can roll right out onto the park—"

"A place in *town?*" Luke exclaimed, and his heart caught. "What the hell, Leo? Why aren't you at the ranch? Where's Dad?"

"Look Luke, I'll be straight. It's not the end of the world, but Dad did something kind of stupid. Well, not kind of. Definitely."

No, no, no. The thirty years of Luke's life went skipping by him. All the times his life had been derailed because of his family, all the plans shot to hell because of them. He closed his eyes, sinking his fingers into the corners, rubbing hard. "Do I need to come home?"

Leo didn't say anything for a moment, then said quietly, "Yeah, I think you should."

FOUR

The only good thing about the drive to Pine River was Luke's vintage 1975 Ford Bronco, a fully restored jeep with leather seats and a Hemi engine Luke had rebuilt by hand. It was a sweet ride, and until only recently, it had sat unused, untouched, in the Kendrick family garage. Luke had bought it four years ago on a whim during one of the many times he'd had to uproot his life and come home to fix things. Only that time, he couldn't fix things. That time, his mother had called to tell him she'd been diagnosed with Stage IV breast cancer. She said she'd never noticed the lump until about three months prior, and then, she was so busy, she couldn't get around to seeing a doctor about it.

"Why didn't you tell me?" Luke had helplessly demanded.

"I didn't want to bother you," Mom had said. "You're right in the middle of classes."

Mom had done the best she could for as long as she could, but Dad and Leo were hopeless, and she'd finally been forced to call Luke home. "I'm so sorry, honey," she'd said, wearing the scarf around her head to hide what the chemo had done to her. She'd been sorry that she was dying and interfering with his school.

Of course Luke had come home. He'd come home to pay the bills and to cook for Dad and Leo and to make sure everything was running on the ranch when his mother couldn't do it anymore. He'd come home to keep track of her meds and help her in and out of bed and drive her to her oncology appointments in Durango.

The Bronco purchase had happened during one of those trips to Durango. The doctors had wanted new tests, and they'd kept his mother longer than either of them had anticipated. The waiting was the worst part about his mother's illness, all that time spent standing around, feeling helpless. So Luke had left the hospital and had ended up buying the Bronco on a whim.

With Dad's help, he'd managed to get it home. The truck had given him something to do, something to take his mind off the fact that his mother was dying and there was nothing he could do to stop it. He'd spent long evenings working under a single bulb in the garage, restoring the hell out of the Bronco. He'd even hand polished the lug nuts.

Two years ago, Luke had finished restoring the truck. Three weeks later, Cathy Kendrick finally gave in to the pain and the loss of dignity cancer had inflicted upon her. It seemed almost as if she were waiting for him to finish the Bronco, to come to terms with the fact that he couldn't fix everything. She'd died, leaving a husband of thirty-two years, two sons, four dogs, and a void in the lives of those who knew her.

For two years, Luke thought of that void every time he saw the Bronco in the garage.

After a time, when he was sure Dad and Leo could make it on their own, Luke had left the Bronco and his family behind and had returned to Denver for a third time. He'd finished school, earned his architecture degree, started his own fledgling business. He'd quickly realized that he needed to know how to run a business, and had enrolled in graduate school to earn an MBA. He was in his second semester.

A few months ago, on a cloudless, blue-sky afternoon, he'd come home to see his dad and Leo, and he'd looked at the Bronco in the garage and thought, okay, it's time. The pain of his mother's death had receded into a shallow, slow-running stream. He didn't think of the void now, he thought of her laugh and her smile, of the way she tucked her hair behind her ears and ran her hand over his head, even when he stood several inches taller than her.

The Bronco purred along today, a testament to Luke's great skills as a mechanic and Leo's greater skills at coming up with ideas of how to repair the old engine.

It was a beautiful day, the sort of crisp, clear mountain-air day, with a deep blue sky and a breeze so slight that it scarcely moved a leaf on the cottonwoods. Luke took a short cut over an old mining road called Sometimes Pass. In the winter, the state put big metal gates across it, as there was no money to keep the road cleared. That meant in the winter, if you were driving from Denver to Pine River, you had to swing down to Colorado Springs and over, adding an hour to the trip.

The road wound its way up past hiking trails and forest service roads. As Luke came around one turn, he noticed a small car parked on one of the many shoulder pull-offs. A woman was standing beside it. He squinted; it looked as if she had taken the spare tire and tire kit out of the trunk. She was leaning up against the bumper reading a book that looked like a manual. And holding a highlighter.

Luke slowed down as he passed. She was dressed in a dark suit and her hair was held up by one of those hair claws that looked like the hand of Grok. But what really caught his attention was that highlighter. It seemed like an odd thing on the side of a mountain road.

At the next point in the shoulder where he could pull off, Luke turned around and drove back to where she was.

The woman quickly straightened up as he pulled up in front of her little car. She eyed him warily under dark bangs as he got out of his truck, shifting backward to the railing, presumably to get a better look at him.

"Don't jump," Luke advised.

Beneath those dark bangs, eyes the color of a Caribbean sea rounded with horror. "No!"

"I'm kidding. Looks like you're having some car trouble."

She folded her arms across her middle and glanced irritably at the car. "Flat tire. This car is a cheap tin can."

Luke looked at the car. "I wouldn't give it that much credit."

The woman smiled. She was pretty when she smiled; her eyes seemed to glitter. Yeah, very pretty.

"Want me to change it for you?"

"I . . . do you mind?" she asked. "I have Triple A, and I called to make sure that I had coverage here, but my cell isn't working." She held it up to him as if to prove it. She definitely didn't look like the sort of person one usually saw on these roads. Typically the women tromping around here wore hiking boots, backpacks, and bandannas tied around their necks. This one wore a thin gold chain around a slender neck.

"You're just below the tree line here," he said. "You have to be in Pine River, or a little higher in elevation to get a cell signal. I'd be happy to help."

"I can pay you," she suggested.

"Not necessary. I'm happy to do it." It wasn't often that he got to help good-looking women, and this woman was very appealing to the guy in him. Yes, she looked a little too much like a headmistress in that dark suit and primly buttoned shirt, but he could see that she had some shapely legs and some very nice curves.

"*Thank* you." She sounded relieved. "That's really nice of you. I thought I was going to have to walk!" She laughed.

He glanced at her shoes. "I don't know—it's a long way to town in heels."

"Oh, I wear them all the time. I have Dr. Scholl's inserts."

Was she kidding? Walking in the mountains was a little different than walking down sidewalks.

Luke stepped past her in the narrow space between the car and railing. He noticed the gold chain around her neck was holding a little letter *M* in the hollow of her throat. He opened the driver door and reached in to pop the trunk, and saw the map spread out on the passenger seat. He couldn't help noticing the yellow highlighted roads from Denver, or that two of the highlighted roads had been x-ed out with pen. "Where are you headed?" he asked as he shut the car door.

Blue Eyes blinked. She folded her arms over her middle uncertainly.

Luke smiled at her. "You know the marauding mountain men up here usually have long beards and dirty clothes, right?"

Her eyes widened slightly, but then she slowly smiled, producing a dimple in one cheek. "Is *that* how I spot them? Thank you—that's information I need to have."

He grinned. "No offense, but you look a little lost. I'm from around here, and can probably point you in the right direction."

"Pine River," she said, dropping her arms. "The guy at the gas station told me to take Sometimes Pass road. He said it was straight up the road I was on, but I can't find it."

"You're on it." Luke casually flicked his gaze over her. Definitely a nice figure. Not too thin, curvy in all the right places. He wondered what business she had in Pine River. "The problem is, only the locals call it Sometimes Pass. It's only a pass after the snow season. Hence the name."

"No wonder I couldn't find it! Would you mind?" she asked, and crowded in beside him, brushing against his arm as she leaned into her car—way in—affording Luke an excellent view of her derriere. He had only a moment to admire it before she emerged holding the map. She spread it on the hood of her car and clicked her highlighter for action. "Where am I?"

Luke pointed at the county road that was Sometimes Pass on the map.

"*Aaah*," she said, and highlighted it.

She stood back, admired her highlighting for a moment, then glanced up. She seemed surprised to find him still standing there and peered up at him with those Caribbean blue eyes. "So which way is Pine River?" she asked.

A man could definitely lose his way around those eyes, Luke thought. "West."

"And that would be . . . ?" She pointed north.

Man, she really *was* lost. He pointed down the road. "That is west, the direction you're headed. Pine River is about ten miles down."

"Great. Thank you." She picked up her map.

"Welcome." He looked at those sparkling eyes again and moved to the safety of the back of the car. He discovered she had taken out the spare, the change kit, and had laid out the tools in a neat row. He took a look at the back tire that had gone flat. "Probably a nail or something like it," he said.

"I worried about that when I drove into the construction site," she said.

Where the hell was there a construction site around here? Luke paused to look down at the tools lined up.

"Oh, ah—I've been reading the manual," she said, and hopped around him. "It says to loosen the lug nuts first."

"Does it?" He reached for the Mickey Mouse car jack. "Not to worry. I've changed a lot of tires in my life."

"Sure, sure," she said, looking at the jack in his hand. She didn't look as if she fully agreed with him. "I just thought maybe, since it's a small car . . . you know."

No, he didn't know. He stepped around her, going down on one knee to slide the jack into its little sleeve beneath the car. He started to jack it up, but she was standing too close. He paused, looked up. "It's probably better if you stand back."

"Right," she said, stepping back. But her feet, stuffed into her heels, were in his peripheral vision.

He removed the flat tire, then fit the spare donut onto the rim. He noticed her turn the page of the manual, as if she was following along. He secured the spare and stood up. "You'll want to get that tire fixed as soon as you can." He began to toss the tire change implements into the trunk. "Those donuts are definitely not made for the roads up here." He shut the trunk, put his hands on his hips. "Anything else I can help you with?"

"I think that should do it." She shut her manual. "I didn't catch your name."

"Luke."

"Luke," she said. "Luke, thank you, so much. I'm Madeline." She smiled gratefully, and extended her hand to be shaken.

That smile knocked Luke back a step or two. It changed her face, made her softer somehow. Her eyes shone, and her mouth—well, there were a lot of fantasies floating in his head at the moment. He suddenly wanted to take Grok's claw from her hair and unbutton the top two buttons of her blouse. . . . But instead he took her hand. It felt weightless in his.

"Thanks," she said again, still smiling, and backed up to the rail again. "I won't keep you any longer." She carefully pulled her hand free.

"Welcome," Luke said, and with a weird little touch of two fingers to his brow—what the hell was *that?*—he added, "Take care."

"Thanks!" She clasped her hands behind her back and stood next to her car like a cheerful little armed guard.

Luke couldn't help but smile with amusement as he passed. He walked back to his truck, started it up again. He pulled out onto the road, drove up the road a little bit until he could turn around, then headed in the direction of Pine River. He waved as he passed her. She waved back.

A moment later, he glanced in his rearview to see what she was doing.

Blue Eyes had her map on the hood of her car and was folding it into a neat little square.

FIVE

The little town of Pine River sat at the very center of the valley, on the edge of the river for which it was named. One could see it on the descent down from the mountains, sitting in the middle of the valley like an oasis in a mountain wilderness. The town had begun as a hub for miners and ranchers, but as the mining operations had shut down, and larger ranches had consumed small ranches, Pine River had morphed into a tourist town. It was a little too far from the slopes to be a ski resort. Summers were the draw here. Hiking, white-water rafting, horseback riding, cycling, camping. Any outdoor sport a person wanted could be found here.

Luke had grown up in and around Pine River. It was where he'd gone to school, played football, fallen in love.

He pulled onto the shoulder at the intersection of a rural road that led to the family ranch. He debated driving the eight miles up, but thought it was probably more important to talk to his father first. As Luke pulled out onto the main road, a little Honda turned onto the ranch road, and behind it, a truck hauling Port-a-Johns. Odd. There was rarely any traffic on this road—just the ranchers who lived out this way. Maybe old man Kaiser was finally going to build that new house his wife had talked about for years.

He drove on down to the valley floor, coasting into Main Street. Two rows of western-style wooden buildings faced each other along one long strip. The business names were all designed to appeal to tourists: Grizzly Lodge and Café and Rocky Creek Tavern.

Luke stopped at the Blue Jay Grocery and Tackle Shop.

The grocery portion of the shop was small and close, and carried only essentials like toilet paper and milk. If a person needed more than basics, they could drive out to the Walmart on the old Aspen Highway.

Luke walked back to the junk-food aisle and squatted down to have a look. Cookies, that would do. He grabbed two boxes. What he didn't eat, he knew Leo would. He picked up some tortilla chips and salsa, then swung by the cooler to pick up a twelve pack of Coors, because he had a feeling he was going to need it.

With his booty paid for, Luke walked outside, his keys jangling in his hand. He hadn't quite reached the Bronco when he heard someone call his name.

He turned around, felt the shock and glance of pain at once.

"Luke Kendrick," the woman said. She smiled, and it went through Luke like it always had, sloughing off the years that had passed as it sank deeper into him.

"Julie Daugherty," he said. How long had it been since they had split? Three years? Maybe not quite. Julie was the woman Luke had intended to marry. She was the woman he'd bought the ring for, had gotten down on one knee for, the whole nine yards.

She was the one who had broken his heart.

"What a surprise," she said, walking cautiously forward.

She looked as gorgeous as ever, her blond hair cut stylishly short, her figure trim and athletic, only a few months past bearing her first child. "How are you?" he asked.

"Good," she said, and stopped at his bumper, her gaze flicking over the Bronco. "Still running, huh?"

"Better than ever." Luke turned to look at his Bronco, but a movement caught his attention. It was a tiny car with a donut spare driving slowly past. Blue Eyes was leaning forward, squinting up at the signs above his head.

"You look good," Julie said, not noticing the car. "But then, you always did." She laughed, and touched her earring. It was a simple but familiar gesture that took Luke back a few years. They would sit on the porch swing out at the ranch, talking about everything and nothing, and she would idly play with her earring.

"Thanks," he said. He didn't know what more he should say. All he could think was that if everything had gone according to plan, he and Julie would be married, and her child would be his. If it hadn't been for Mom and Leo—

"Are you still in Denver?" she asked.

"Yep. I just came home to check in with Dad and Leo."

Julie nodded. She smiled coyly. "Girlfriend?"

He hated that she felt she had the right to ask. He shrugged. "Sometimes."

She laughed. "I bet you have them falling at your feet, Luke. So how is Leo? I haven't seen him around."

Luke's breathing hitched a tiny bit. "He's good," he lied. "Doing great. And Brandon?" he asked, referring to her husband, although he could care less how that ass was doing. Did he hope it, or did a slight shadow glance over Julie's face when he asked about her husband?

She shoved her hands into the pockets of her jeans. "He's a proud papa." She didn't say more than that. They stood there, looking at each other, maybe looking past the weeks and months and years since it had ended between them.

Fortunately, Luke was saved from saying something stupid or inappropriate by the little car, which caught his attention once more. It drove by again, but in the opposite direction.

"Well," Julie said. "Tell your Dad and Leo I said hello, will you?"

"Sure."

She smiled warmly. "It was really good to see you, Luke. Really good."

There was something in her voice, something he didn't quite understand, but that he felt in his gut. He stood there a moment too long;

he could feel himself softening. Luke made himself move first. "You, too, Julie." He turned around, walked to the driver side of his Bronco.

Julie Daugherty had let him down in the worst way, and somehow, Luke had picked himself up and gone on with his life. He wasn't going to go backward now.

He looked back over the hood of his truck. She was still standing there, her hands tucked into her back pockets, biting her bottom lip, almost as if she was trying to keep from speaking. Her gaze was full of yearning and it sent a shiver of disturbing familiarity down Luke's spine. He got into his truck and turned the ignition before he made the mistake of asking her why she was looking at him the way she was.

If Pine River had a backwater part to it, Elm Street was it. On this street, the houses were smaller and a little more run-down than elsewhere in town.

Luke found the house where his dad and Leo were staying easily enough—it looked just as Dad had described it when he explained he and Leo were temporarily renting a place. It was a little green clapboard that sat in the middle of a square patch of manicured lawn, surrounded by a chain-link fence. The detached garage was only big enough for one car. A doghouse that looked new sat under a towering elm tree in the yard, but there was no sign of any dogs.

The house was tiny. Luke guessed two bedrooms, one bath. And there was no wheelchair ramp.

He parked outside the fence, grabbed his things, and walked up the gravel drive, hopping up onto the porch and knocking twice before walking inside.

"Hey, hey!" Leo called out as Luke stepped into the front room. "You took your own sweet time getting here, didn't you? Look at this, Luke, I am about to blow the *top* off this game!"

It always amazed Luke that Leo could operate a game controller with hands that curved in like lobster claws, the fingers useless. But Leo was a master at making do as his body slowly deteriorated. His head was bent slightly to one side, and his legs collapsed in on each other. He was only a shadow of the man he used to be.

Like Luke, Leo had played football, a big strapping nose tackle with a scholarship to the Colorado School of Mines, and dreams of making the pros. But the spring of his freshman year, his left arm started to shake in a weird way. He couldn't seem to grip a ball. Their parents took Leo to a slew of doctors and finally, to the specialists. That summer, Leo had earned the dubious distinction of being one of the younger people to be diagnosed with a motor neuron disease.

None of the Kendricks had known what that was, but Luke knew it was bad because of the look on his mother's face when the doctor said it was closely akin to Lou Gehrig's Disease. Her face went ashen and she gripped the arms of her chair as if she were fighting to keep from sliding off and melting onto the floor.

The doctor had tried to make it better by telling them that the disease didn't progress in exactly the same way as Lou Gehrig's disease, that everyone with motor neuron disease progressed differently. To Luke, that meant there were no rules; it could go fast, it could go slow. But there was nothing that doctor could say that would change the fact Leo's disease was devastating and deadly.

As far as Luke was aware, Leo had only let the grim change to his life put him on the floor once. After a night out with the guys, Luke had awakened to the sound of his brother sobbing. Leo was on the floor, sobbing for what was lost, for what the future held. He was only twenty years old. But then, in true Leo Kendrick fashion, he'd picked himself and his useless arm off the floor, wiped his face and had said, "Okay. Change of plans."

There was no greater hero than Leo Kendrick to Luke's way of thinking.

About a year later, Mom was diagnosed with cancer, and Leo never showed his feelings about his debilitation again. Now, having just turned twenty-six, he liked to joke that his was a different sort of disease that only happened to geniuses—counting himself and the physicist Steven Hawking.

Luke walked over and had a look at the TV. There were dragons breathing fire and a guy that looked like the quarterback Peyton Manning darting around them. Luke put his hand on his brother's shoulder. "Is that supposed to be you?"

"Dude, it *is* me!"

Luke leaned down, kissed the top of his brother's bent head. "Here," he said, and put the bag of cookies on a table next to Leo. He dropped his things, opened the bag, and shook a few of the cookies out. "Oreos."

"Thanks, man. I'm not supposed to eat anything like that, so don't let the warden see it."

"Are you having trouble swallowing?" Luke asked, a balloon of fear swelling in him.

"No, you moron—they make me fat." Leo laughed as he reached for one, managing to pick it up in his almost useless hand. He tucked it into his mouth and chewed crookedly.

"Where is Marisol? Hiding from you again?" Luke asked, referring to Leo's daily in-home care.

"Marisol adores me, what are you talking about? She's off today. Dad's here. He's out back, building a workbench. He's got grand designs for this place. A gym, a guest suite, a media room, you name it."

Luke chuckled. "You've been watching the house and garden channel again, I see. I hope Dad is planning on building a ramp."

"The fastest ramp in Pine River! Hey, Luke," Leo said, and turned his head slightly, as much as he could. "Go easy on Dad, okay? He does the best he can."

Luke smiled sadly. Personally, he didn't know how their father managed to do what he did; it all seemed so overwhelming to Luke. "I know, man. I know."

He walked on through the little house, his nose wrinkling at the musty smell. There were water stains on the ceiling, and the rust-colored carpet was threadbare in places. The wall paint was peeling around the window frames, and where there wasn't paint, there was a garish, seventies-era gold paper on the walls.

Luke paused in the kitchen to deposit the chips and beer on the tile counter. The kitchen was a small galley type, but it had the requisite appliances for an all-male household: a microwave and a dishwasher. The dirty dishes stacked in the sink looked as if they had the remnants of pasta clinging to them, and the handle of a ladle stuck out of a pot on the stove. Since Mom had died, this was how the Kendrick kitchen looked—like a giant Petri dish of experiments gone wrong.

Luke opened the back door onto a small, bi-level deck. There was room for only one folding chair and a table on the upper deck. On the lower deck, Dad had draped a two-by-four across the railing and was busy running a belt sander across it. When he paused, Luke called out to him.

Startled, Luke's father jerked upright. "Luke!" he said, his face one big grin. He turned off the sander, rubbed his palms on his jeans and walked up the steps, his arms outstretched. He was an affectionate guy, and gave Luke a tight bear hug, slapping him on the back a few times before letting go. "You look good, son. Real good," he said.

"Thanks. Are you all right, Dad?"

"Right as rain," he said.

"And how's the world's best armchair quarterback?" Luke asked, referring to Leo.

"Oh you know him," Dad said. "He's always good. Got him a new video game and that's all he's talking about this week."

"Marisol is still coming every day, right?" Luke asked, fearing that for some insane reason, his dad wouldn't tell him if Leo's in-home care stopped coming. Luke worried about it—he paid Marisol what he thought was a pittance, but it was all he could afford.

"Oh yeah, yeah, she comes around every day, like clockwork. She had some personal stuff today, that's all. Leo loves her."

Luke snorted. "I can imagine—Marisol is a good-looking woman."

His dad smiled a little. "She is that." He looked down at his hand, stretched the fingers wide, and said apologetically, "Sorry you had to come all this way, son."

He looked tired, Luke thought, and as usual, a wave of sympathy coupled with a stronger wave of guilt swept through him. "I *wanted* to come. I haven't been home to see you guys in a while." It was only a small lie; Luke hadn't wanted to come. He liked being in Denver, where he didn't have to think about the perpetual sea of trouble on which his family seemed to bob around like little buoys. "How about a beer?" he suggested.

"Love one," his dad said.

In the tiny kitchen, Luke tossed his dad a beer and helped himself to one.

"A party and no one invited me?" Leo called from the living room. A moment later, he and his chair crashed in through the narrow doorway. Luke tried hard not to grimace, but the marks on the door indicated Leo was having a difficult time getting around this tiny house.

"Have you been keeping up with baseball?" Leo asked as he maneuvered himself into a spot at the table. "Dude, you won't believe the pitching depth the Rangers have this year. . . ."

The three men talked about sports—well, Leo did most of the talking there—and about life in general. Dad and Leo asked Luke about his work in Denver. Leo expounded about Marisol's finer qualities without mentioning her mind, and Dad and Luke laughed along like pigs. It felt like old times, when they'd all lived on the ranch where Luke and Leo had grown up. Back before Leo got sick. Before Mom died. Back when they'd been three guys hanging out, talking about guy things. Before Luke got calls at night saying Dad and Leo weren't at the ranch anymore.

But then Dad reminded Leo that he was not supposed to eat cookies, only soft foods, and reality roared back into that little kitchen on a freaking freight train.

Leo, God bless him, just grinned. "That means you're going to have to put my pizza in a blender, bro," he said to Luke. "Be sure and get a big straw because I like lots of cheese."

"Noted," Luke said. "So," he said, popping the top off another beer, "what happened with the ranch, Dad?"

"On that note," Leo said, backing away from the table, "I've got a date with the Hounds of Hell." He scooted back with his remote control, banging into the little bar, then scraping against the door as he pushed his way through.

Luke's father sighed. He rubbed his face with his hands, rearranging his features and, for a moment, looking younger than his fifty-eight years. But then his flesh slid back into familiar sags and folds. "I got myself into a deal."

"Oh yeah?"

"Cooked it up with Grant Tyler. You remember him?"

"Vaguely," Luke said. What he remembered was a rotund guy with a booming laugh, nothing more.

"Grant knew that I needed cash to pay for Leo's expenses that aren't covered by Medicaid. Like that fancy bed in there. My credit is maxed out, Luke. I couldn't borrow enough to buy a shovel. The only thing I had was the ranch. So Grant, he'd done pretty well for himself in some deal, and he said, 'Look, let's just do a sale. I'll give you the cash you need and hold on to the title until you're able to sell some cattle or whatnot and get on your feet. Then I'll sell it back to you for the same price.' It was sort of like a second mortgage, a way to get me some cash. So we did the deal, and everything was good. I sold part of the livestock and paid off some debt. I was building up again, getting ready to get the ranch back when Grant up and died."

"Okay," Luke said. So far, nothing earth-shattering. "So there was a deal, and he died, but you have all the paperwork on it, right?"

"I've got paperwork for the sale. But we didn't have a written agreement that I would buy it back for the same price he'd paid." Luke must have looked as shocked as he felt, because his dad said, "We were friends, son. We had each other's word, and that's all we needed."

And there, in the distance, was the sound of the earth shattering. Luke's heart sank. "Dad, you always need a written agreement."

"Well I know that now," his father said a little irritably. "But I didn't think so at the time. He was a good friend and he was doing me a tremendous favor."

Luke looked at the dingy window above the kitchen sink. "Why didn't you tell me you were having trouble?" he asked calmly. "I could have gotten a loan. I could have helped you."

His father sighed. "Come on, Luke. You're in the middle of starting your own business. You're in school. You have your own problems, your own credit to worry about. You've got people backing you up that you have to think about. And you already pay for Marisol—you don't need my problems on top of that."

"But I've got some money put aside," Luke argued. "I'm doing pretty good. Dad, we're family—"

"Luke," his father interrupted sharply. "I know you mean well, son. But I already have one child who can't fulfill his dreams. I'll be damned if I'm going to have two."

Luke clenched his jaw. He stared down at the table, away from his father's gray eyes. "I still don't get why you left the ranch to come to this cracker box."

"Because a fellow named Jackson Crane came to see me. Said the estate had passed on to Grant's kids, and they were coming in for a powwow, and he suspected they'd want to sell. He said given the circumstances it was probably best we get out of the way while everyone decides what needs to be done. He knew about this house and I rented it for dirt cheap."

Luke could believe that. "What about Ernest?" he asked, referring to their long-time cowboy. For all of Luke's life that he could recall, Ernest had lived in the bunkhouse and taken care of things when Dad couldn't.

"Oh, Ernest just went down to Albuquerque to see his mom. He'll be back. Jackson Crane is keeping him on."

At least there was some good news. Ernest had been with them so long that Luke suspected he had no place to go. But the rest was more than Luke could absorb in one sitting. He stood up and walked to the sink, staring out at the patch of back yard. "So who the hell is this Jackson Crane guy, anyway?"

"He was Grant's guy. A business manager."

"He had a business manager, and none of this was written down? Grant essentially loans you money and you put up the title, and nothing about the loan agreement is recorded?" Luke turned to his dad, but Dad's head was down as he pushed thick fingers through his thinning hair.

Luke's shoulders sagged. His father was a good man, a great dad, a steady provider. But what he knew was ranching. Not real estate. And Mom had always been the one who kept their finances in check. "Okay, look, Dad, I am going to talk to this Crane guy," Luke said. "I'll talk to the heirs, too. I think we can all be reasonable about this. We'll work something out."

"Maybe," his father said with a shrug.

"Have faith—"

"Luke, look," his father said sharply, and suddenly came to his feet. He was an inch shorter than Luke, but just as broad. "I don't like that I had to borrow money against the ranch. I don't like that Grant died and left me in a bind. But the fact is, I got the money I needed for Leo," he said, pointing to the front room, where they could both hear Leo shouting at his game characters. "That's what matters. Leo's problem ain't going away, either. He's not getting better, he's getting worse, and the ranch . . . the ranch takes a lot of work."

Luke glanced at the doorway and hoped to hell Leo wasn't hearing this. "I get it," he said low. "Hell if I know how you do it all, Dad. But Leo isn't always going to be here. Homecoming Ranch is his home—not *this* place. More than that, it's *your* home—you've lived there all your life! So did your parents, and their parents. Ranching is what you *do*. What are you going to do when you don't have Leo anymore?"

Luke's father clenched his jaw. He put his hand on Luke's shoulder and squeezed it. "It's time you faced the fact that things have changed for us. And what's done is done. Now, I've got to give Leo his medicine." He turned away, stepped to the counter next to the fridge where three rows of dark brown pill bottles were lined up. A chart was taped to the front of the fridge, which his father consulted.

What about me? Luke thought. What about *his* life at the ranch, his memories, his hopes for it? He felt the hard kernel of resentment sprouting in him—resentment at how life had turned out for his family, all of it. "It's not done," he said tightly, but his father ignored him.

SIX

In a village where flannel ruled and elkhorns seemed to be mandatory décor, Jackson Crane looked as fresh and as Hollywood as he had the first time Madeline had met him. She'd found his office easy enough in this postage stamp of civilization that was Pine River. It was a low gray building that looked like a bomb shelter.

Jackson—who did not have a receptionist, Madeline noted—showed her into his office. He had a gunmetal gray desk, a squeaky office chair. On the wall behind him was a calendar with the picture of a man gleefully kissing a big fish, and the 18th of the month had been circled with a fat red marker. Below the calendar was a montage of pictures of Jackson Crane. He was skiing, or wearing a big hat and riding a horse, or grinning at the camera from behind goggles on a snowmobile. But what Madeline found odd about the pictures was that Jackson was the only person in them.

This man was an enigma to Madeline. He was a personable guy; he'd greeted her warmly, shaking her hand earnestly. "So glad you made it," he said, as he moved some papers around on his desk, obviously seeking something. "I don't have much time before my next appointment, but I wanted to get you the particulars of our meeting."

"I thought this *was* our meeting," Madeline said as he thrust a file folder into her hands.

"This?" he asked, his eyes widening slightly with surprise. "No, no, I asked you to come here so I could give you some basic information. We'll be meeting this afternoon at the ranch. We're on for three." He suddenly smiled. "You'll be meeting your sisters!"

A shudder of trepidation ran through Madeline. Of course she knew she would be meeting her sisters, but with it suddenly so concrete, Madeline did not feel prepared. She needed more warning than this, she needed time to mentally gear up. She felt like something was missing, like a flowchart, dossiers, pictures, *something*. "Just like that?" she blurted. "I fly out here and meet them just like that?"

Jackson chuckled until he realized she wasn't kidding. "Sorry—did you have something else in mind?"

No, Madeline didn't have anything else in mind. She just needed time to prepare, she always needed time to prepare. Meeting new people was never easy for her, and for two new sisters, she needed to collect herself, to tamp down unnecessary feelings about how these "sisters" had had a father, and she hadn't, that sort of thing. She assumed that they had been the recipients of the fatherly love that she'd been denied, that the reason she had never heard from him was because he'd been completely satisfied with his other two daughters.

"In the file I gave you is a copy of your father's last will and testament, as well as some information about the ranch," he said, and began to recite some statistics that flew over Madeline's normally tidy and organized head. "I've included a map." He looked at her curiously when Madeline didn't speak. "So we'll see you there at three to go over the details." He stood. "Okay?"

No, it was not okay. It wasn't remotely okay. Madeline really needed someone to hold her hand right now. But she stood reluctantly. "Yes," she said, and tucked the file into her purse. "Thank you."

Jackson walked her to the door like he had some place to be, and as Madeline walked down the gravel path to the parking lot, she heard the door shut behind her. She had just reached the parking lot when an orange jeep barreled up, coming to an abrupt halt. She barely had time to register that she'd seen the vehicle before when the man who had changed her flat stepped out of the Bronco.

Madeline tried to ignore the little thrill she felt sweep down her spine. She'd been standing on the road yesterday trying to convince herself that she could change a tire, to not panic, when he'd driven up in an old jeep-looking thing. A modern day knight in shining armor in his trusty orange steed. Not only was he almost unconscionably good-looking, he had changed that damn tire in about two seconds.

But now she felt a shiver of trepidation. What was he doing *here?*

He was wearing a white shirt tucked into skin-tight jeans, and a dark blue hoodie and boots. He'd combed his dark hair back so that it brushed his collar. He was tall and muscular, more than what she remembered. He fixed his gray eyes on her; she saw a flicker of recognition, and her pulse ticked up a notch.

She would have been very suspicious had he not seemed so surprised to see her. How was it possible that a man who looked like that, whom she'd met briefly on the road to Pine River, would end up outside Jackson Crane's office?

He looked at her, then at Jackson's office, then at her again, and his eyes narrowed slightly. Something changed in his expression. It seemed to tighten somehow. "You're the highlighter—"

"The what? I'm Madeline. The flat, remember?" she said, and fluttered her fingers in the vague direction of where the flat had occurred.

"I remember," he said, and pointed in the opposite direction of where she had fluttered her fingers.

She smiled. "Luke, right?"

"Right. Are you here to see Jackson?"

"Do you know him? I mean, I guess you do, seeing as how you are here. You do, right?"

"Sort of," he said, and looked at the office again, like maybe he wasn't in the right place.

"What a coincidence!" she said, feeling a little off kilter. "Are you from Pine River?"

"I was," he said, his gaze settling on her again. Now he looked at her as if he was seeing her differently. "I'm in Denver now. I'm here visiting family."

"Oh." She laughed nervously, her gaze flicking between his eyes, his shoulders, his mouth. Holy smokes, but the air felt weird. Sort of electric. She needed a script, something to follow. But since she didn't have one, she blurted, "So tell me, is there anything to do here? I have a three o'clock meeting and I am looking for something to do until then."

Luke shifted, peered closely at her. "There's a *lot* to do in Pine River."

"Like what?"

"Well," he said, his gaze sliding down to her shoes and up again, "Do you fish?"

Madeline snorted. "No."

"Hike?"

She'd never even *contemplated* hiking, much less done it, and shook her head so that a strand of dark hair escaped the claw and bounced down on her face. His gray eyes were fixed on hers, making her feel just the tiny bit woozy.

"What about riding horseback?" he asked.

For some reason, that made Madeline laugh. "I don't have a horse."

He arched a brow. "You don't have to have a horse to know how to ride."

"But if you don't have a horse, how would you know how to ride?"

He studied her curiously, as if he'd just discovered a dinosaur bone. "So basically, you came to a mountain town, but you don't do mountain stuff."

"Yes. I mean, *no.* I'm only here for a couple of days to tend to some business."

He nodded, almost as if he knew what her business was. "Well," he said, "there are a couple of souvenir shops in town. If you aren't here for recreation, I'm not really sure what else there is."

Souvenirs? He was telling her to go buy a souvenir? "Oh. Okay. Thanks."

"You bet. If you will excuse me, Madeline, I'm a little late for an appointment," he said, and stepped around her, all six foot plus, impossibly broad shoulders of him. Had she missed his shoulders yesterday? "I'll see you around, okay?"

What did that mean? *Would* he see her around? "Okay," she said, trying to sound airy and unconcerned. She walked on, got in her ridiculously tiny car, and surreptitiously watched him walk into Jackson's office. This much could be said—that man knew how to fill out a pair of jeans.

"That is enough of *that*," she muttered to herself, opened the file Jackson had given her, and removed the hand-drawn map to Homecoming Ranch. "Get a grip, Madeline. You are not here for fun and games. Or ogling."

She would start, she thought, by comparing the map Jackson had given her to the map of the area she'd picked up at the visitor's center. She certainly hoped this map didn't include any "sometimes" passes over the mountains. In her humble opinion, roads should be clearly labeled and marked on all maps.

SEVEN

Luke almost kicked my *ass* on "Hounds of Hell," but I came back with a surprise assault and pulled it out. I like it when Luke is home. Dad tries, but sometimes, a guy just needs his brother home so he can *totally* annihilate him on "Hounds of Hell."

I know Luke and Dad argue a lot. Dad says things aren't like they were before and we have to face that they aren't. Luke says there's no reason they can't be like they were, except without Mom, and without me on a horse driving cattle down the mountain, but I'm pretty good at directing traffic from the back of the pickup. Luke rigged up a deal where I can ride back there. It's cool. I don't tell him that it hurts like hell because I like getting up on the mountain. I miss it.

But last night, Dad and Luke had this big argument about Homecoming Ranch, and this morning, Luke was in a mood. He put on a good shirt, a go-to-Sunday-meeting shirt, and went down to Poplar Street to have a "word" with Jackson. I told him that Jackson's an okay guy, but Luke wasn't buying it. He said anyone who worked for Grant Tyler was suspect. I had to remind Luke that my muscles may not work, but my brain is still a functioning miracle of exceptional genius, and I'm serious, Jackson's okay. He had an asshole for a boss. Luke's had a couple of bosses like that, so he ought to be a little nicer about it, right?

He came back from the meeting all pissed off because Jackson told him what I *knew* Jackson would tell him—it's up to the heirs. It's not as if Jackson can rewrite all the Colorado state laws to make Luke happy. Still, that made Luke *super* annoyed because apparently he met one of the heirs. He said she was coming out as he was going in, and he was pretty sure she had to be one of the heirs, because why else would she be on Poplar Street? He's got a point there. Dani said Jackson took up space in an old gray building that looks like a morgue, only it isn't, but the story would be a whole lot more interesting if it was a morgue, wouldn't it? Dig it—Jackson Crane holding meetings in the middle of a bunch of dead bodies covered by sheets. What if they started rising up, one by one, and it turned into Zombieland?

Okay, so anyway, Luke sees this woman coming out of the incredibly ugly building and he didn't really know her, but he'd changed her flat yesterday on Sometimes Pass. I was like, "What the hell was she doing up there?" And he said he thought she was lost, and then today, she's coming out of Jackson Crane's office and that she was a highlighter. And I was like, *highlighter*, what's that? I mean, I know my way around the ladies, and I have *never* heard one called a highlighter.

"She highlights things. Maps. Car manuals." Luke said the first thing that popped out of his mouth when he saw her again today was *Highlighter*, and she was all *Whaaat?*

If it were me, I'd have been a little smoother, but Luke, he's got those gray eyes and dark hair, and he's really tall and built like an NFL quarterback, so he can say pretty much whatever he wants to a woman and she melts all over the floor. Trust me, I've seen it happen a thousand times. But this one didn't melt, and I bet that ticked Luke off. He's not used to having to work for it. Neither am I. I used to be like him, had women falling at my feet. Now I've got a disease that I can milk for attention. What, you think I'm above using it? No way. Women are very sympathetic about debilitating conditions, and if you look at them with cow eyes and a smile, it works like a charm.

So then the Highlighter smiled, and Luke said she had a really nice smile. And I said, "Maybe you should tap that," and Luke gave me one of those looks and said, "What is the *matter* with you?"

I just wish Luke would get over Julie Daugherty, that's all. He says he has, but she calls once in a while with her "problems" and there he is, ready to talk her through it. Anyway, back to the Highlighter. Luke said she announced she was only here for a couple of days, and then she walked away.

I can just picture how that walking-away view was for my brother. If he's like me, and I think he is, he appreciates the walking away as much as he does the walking toward. We Kendrick boys are connoisseurs of beautiful women.

Luke talked to Jackson, and Jackson told him there wasn't much he could do, but he was meeting with the heirs this afternoon, and maybe Luke could come out and make nice, that sort of thing. He also gave Luke the name of a lawyer, and he said, *You're going to need one if you can't work this out with the ladies.*

I have faith that Luke can work it out with the ladies. He said he was going out to the ranch to scope things out, get a feel for them. I said, "Are you going to tell them their dad stole the ranch from our dad?"

He looked at me like that was a dumb question and said, "Well yeah, Leo. That's the whole point."

Boy, I'd like to be a fly on the wall for that one. Women are super-hot when they're mad.

But then I got to thinking about it, because that's what I do, I *think*, and I said, "You know, you ought to invite them to dinner."

Luke said, "Now I know you're crazy. I don't even know them. I'm not bringing them here," he said, and honestly, I wasn't sure if it was because of the house or because he didn't know them.

I said, "No, think about it, Luke. They have no reason to make a deal with you. They don't know you, they don't care what Dad did, right? But maybe if they see that we are living in reduced circumstances," and I sort of gestured to my chair, but I can't really gesture anymore, so I had to knock my hand against it, "they might be more sympathetic." If you think that's a totally *sick* idea and a gross manipulation of emotions, you are right. I think someone should pay me for my great ideas.

But Luke, he just shook his head and said, "Sometimes, I really worry about you, Leo."

He doesn't need to worry about me. I know where I am and where I'm going. He needs to worry about himself because his path isn't so clear. That's why he needs a certified genius in his corner.

EIGHT

With a carefully highlighted map, Madeline started for the ranch later that afternoon, driving cautiously on a narrow two-lane road. It wended up through a forest so thick with pines, spruce, and cottonwoods that the trees were forced to bend over the road, creating a canopy. Roads seemed treacherous enough, but they were made worse by the ground squirrels that sailed out of the underbrush and onto the road before her car, crisscrossing in crazy patterns and narrowly avoiding death beneath her wheels.

She finally reached a plateau where the road ran alongside a meadow bursting with daisies and sunflowers. A handful of horses grazed, their tails swishing away flies. It seemed to Madeline she'd driven miles and miles, when in fact, according to her speedometer, it had been only seven. She found the turn she was to take at mile marker 243, just as Jackson's map said (kudos to him for accuracy) and turned onto a gravel road. The grade was steeper here, the curves around the mountainside longer. She drove through towering spruce trees until the road began to straighten out as it crossed another meadow. This meadow was much larger than the one she'd passed, and ahead, she could see the entrance to the ranch. It couldn't be missed—two thick wooden posts held up a sign, faded by weather, that said HOMECOMING RANCH.

Madeline coasted to a stop. Jackson had said the gate would be unlocked, but it was closed. She stepped out of her car, landing awkwardly in her pumps on the uneven road. The gate, all iron, came only to her waist; she gave it a healthy shove, and it swung back, clanging against the stretch of iron fencing that marked the entrance.

So this is where her father had lived? Madeline turned to look back down the road she'd driven. The forest, the mountains and meadow, all so breathtakingly beautiful. And so vast. *Too* vast. In Florida, one could hardly drive ten minutes without encountering another community. Madeline could get lost very easily out here without markers, without signs, without something to say where she was. Was that what her father had done? Put himself so far off the map that she couldn't possibly find him and the family he'd had that didn't include her?

Speaking of family, if only loosely, made the knot in Madeline's gut tighten. She'd come this far, she told herself. There was no room for nerves now.

She got back into the car and drove up a lane lined with cottonwoods and spruce trees, all of which seemed to grow out of a carpet of black-eyed Susans and daylilies. Through the trees, Madeline could see another meadow fenced in by split rails. It was coffee-table book perfect, save one jarring sight—in that lush meadow, a line of portable toilets that had been set up next to a split rail fence. She could not imagine what purpose those toilets served in a place where there were no people, besides marring an otherwise perfect mountain vista.

As her little car bobbed and bounced along the rocky road, she could see a glimpse of the house through a stand of alder trees. It was set back against the mountain and tall Ponderosa pines, situated next to a red barn with a steep A-line roof.

Madeline's heart began to beat a little faster. She didn't know what she'd expected, really—when someone said ranch, she'd thought of dusty rodeos and low-slung houses baking in the midday sun. She hadn't thought of *this*. It was impossible that her father had left her this. Impossible! Things like this did not happen to Madeline Pruett. She didn't possess a single thing that she hadn't worked hard to get, hadn't put in long hours of study or work to have.

When she pulled into the small circular drive before the quaint house, she could see the wear on it, but it was charming. The roof was a collection of steeply angled pitches over various rooms and floors. The ground floor of the house was built with stone, and the second story, which looked to have been added on at some point, was made of tongue-and-groove logs as big around as the wheels on her rental car. Large, plate-glass windows lined the front of the house, looking out at the vista of mountains rising up from the opposite edge of the meadow.

The realtor in Madeline appreciated the charm. But the realtor in her also understood the remote location would be a huge obstacle to overcome. It was as far from anything as it could possibly be, far from the world, and it would take a feat of marketing genius to sell it.

On the right of the house was a large room that had been added on to the original structure, judging by the difference in wood. It had a flat roof and crankcase windows, most of which were open.

Madeline opened the door of her car and stepped out. In between the house and the barn was a grassy area enclosed by cottonwoods and alder trees. Faded Chinese lanterns had been strung through the trees, and three picnic tables were situated under the branches. From one tree, a tire swing spun lazily. She could picture her faceless sisters, growing up in this idyllic setting with toboggans and hayrides and sleepovers.

The knot in her belly tightened again. And now, her head hurt.

Madeline walked around the front of her car to the flagstone walk. That was when she saw the four dogs lying under the porch, their heads up, their eyes locked on her, She could just see them through the leggy daylilies that decorated the front of the house.

Her heart began to pound with panic. Madeline had never had a dog. As a realtor, she'd had her fair share of bad encounters with overly protective dogs. Her standard checklist when showing a house included some guarantee from owners that their pets had been removed from the property or put into proper crates.

The dogs lifted their snouts, sniffing the air, as if she gave off some sort of scent, and she wondered wildly if it was dogs or bears that one should not look in the eye? Slowly, Madeline began to ease back, hoping to get around her car and in before they attacked, when the screen door opened and a woman with curly hair bounded out. "Hey!" she said.

All four dogs leaped to their feet and headed directly for Madeline. Madeline shrieked and raced around the car to the driver's side, crashing into the bumper and stumbling in her shoes as she reached for the door handle.

"They won't bite!" the woman shouted at her, following the dogs to her car. "Back to the garage, you beasts! Garage, garage!" she shouted at the dogs, and swung her arm out, pointing at the garage Madeline had not noticed until this moment. She had one hand on the car door, another gripping her bag, prepared to use it as a weapon. But the dogs suddenly pulled up and lazily trotted in the direction of the garage with peeling paint, disappearing between two cars parked there.

"Are you all right?"

Madeline jerked around. Across the top of her car, the woman with the crazy curly hair was staring at her with blue-gray eyes.

"I'm sorry if they scared you. They're just mutts. Harmless mutts."

"I'm fine," Madeline said, breathless. She wasn't fine—she was terrified. She straightened the jacket of her suit, pushed her hair behind her ears, trying to gather herself. She smoothed down her jacket again and glanced at the woman.

The woman was grinning.

The mess of curls was held off her face by a bandeau. She was wearing jeans, Converse sneakers, and a red-checkered shirt. She looked a little like a carhop, and Madeline guessed she was a caretaker or housekeeper.

"You must be Madeline," the woman said, her expression hopeful as she walked around Madeline's car to the driver's side.

"Yes," Madeline said, and extended her hand. "I'm here for the meeting. And you are . . . ?"

The woman's smile deepened. "I am *so* excited to meet you! I'm Libby!"

The name did not immediately register.

"Libby Tyler. Your *sister*," she said, as if Madeline hadn't heard the news that she had inherited two sisters. And she walked right past Madeline's extended hand and threw her arms around her, hugging her tight.

Madeline had tried to prepare herself for meeting sisters, but nothing could have prepared her, not really. A thousand questions danced through her head as Libby hugged her, such as how old Libby was, and where did the hair come from, and were there more like her? But Madeline couldn't speak. She was momentarily overwhelmed by the actual, physical proof of a sister. Someone who shared her DNA.

Libby was not what Madeline had imagined—she couldn't even say *what* she'd imagined, really, but she supposed she thought her sisters would look like *her*: medium height, brown hair, a butt that was this side of bouncy. Madeline had not thought once about curly hair, or boyish hips and a toothy smile.

"You're suffocating her, Libby," someone said, and Libby laughed, her breath in Madeline's hair, then let Madeline go.

"That's Emma. Your *other* sister," Libby said, and turned her head.

Madeline followed her gaze. Not only did Emma look nothing like Madeline, she looked nothing like Libby. She was tall and thin, almost painfully thin. Her hair was golden blond, sleek and hanging to her waist, the sort of hair Madeline knew cost hundreds of dollars to possess. She wore a flowing skirt that danced around her knees and a short brown leather jacket that matched the brown leather boots that were loose around her calves.

Emma eyed Madeline suspiciously, as if she'd caught her trying to make off with a cow. She casually perched one hip on the railing as she gave Madeline a good once over, and said, "You should probably know that we never heard of you until a couple of weeks ago."

Madeline appreciated straight talk, but in this case, she didn't care for the accusatory tone. "Same here," she said. She didn't add that she hadn't heard anything about her father, either, until a couple of weeks ago.

"Isn't this exciting?" Libby said again, looking between the two of them. "I mean, how often is it that you find out you have a *sister*?"

"Never," Emma said and stood up from the railing. "Leave it to Dad to omit that detail."

Dad. That casual reference did not escape Madeline's notice. It suggested Grant Tyler wasn't just a sperm donor to them, he was a *dad*, just as Madeline had assumed. A tiny bubble of resentment pressed against Madeline's thoughts, making her head hurt worse.

"Come in!" Libby said. "Come in, come in, I have so many things to ask you!" She hopped up on the porch steps as Madeline moved carefully in her pumps on the gravel drive, watching the garage in case the dogs renewed their interest in eating her.

"So you live in Orlando, is that right, Madeline? Do you go by Madeline? Or do people call you Maddie? I knew a Madeline once and she went by Linny."

Madeline couldn't even begin to explain how far removed she was from a Linny. These questions, fired at a rapid clip, in a cheerful manner, made Madeline feel uncomfortable and exposed. Outside of her bubble as Trudi would say. Moreover, she was mystified and a little alarmed that she should feel so panicky. Control freak, yes, she was definitely that, but she didn't generally *panic*.

"It's Madeline," she said. "And I live in Orlando." Was that the question? She stepped up on the porch, noticed the sag in the steps. The roof looked old, and she could see evidence of rot around a couple of window frames.

"Have you always lived there?" Libby asked. "When I heard about you, I wondered if you were from there, or moved there?"

"I've always lived there." Madeline didn't think this meeting was supposed to go this way. She thought surely there would be some introductions, some facts presented. She didn't think she would be questioned on the steps of the porch. *Order*—that's what Madeline needed. But for once, Madeline's curiosity won out over her need to shelter herself. "And you've lived here?" she asked, gesturing vaguely around her.

"Mostly," Libby said.

Madeline could picture Libby here in this charmingly quaint house in the mountains. She could picture her swinging on the tire swing, or standing at the window and watching it snow.

"When I was little," Libby said, "I lived in California for a while with Emma and her mother."

Whoa. Well that was a curve ball tossed out of left field—*Emma and her mother.* Did that mean there were *three* mothers? Good God, Grant was a serial monogamist! Hell, she didn't know *what* the man was. "In California—with Grant?" Madeline asked carefully.

Libby paused on the top step next to Emma, who was casually studying Madeline. "Is that what you called him? Grant?"

Among other things, Madeline thought wryly. "I didn't really call him anything," she said with an uncertain shrug.

"What do you mean?" Libby asked.

"I didn't know him."

"Ever?"

Madeline resisted the urge to rub the nape of her neck. "I never met him. I mean, there was once, when I was a toddler. But I don't really remember anything about it."

"Sounds fishy," Emma said.

"No it doesn't!" Libby said, looking horrified by Emma's remark.

But Emma's gaze flicked over Madeline, lingering on Madeline's briefcase before lifting her eyes to Madeline's face again. She said nothing, but turned around and walked inside without a word, letting the screen door bang shut at her back.

Madeline looked at Libby.

Libby gave her an anxious smile. "Just ignore her. She may not be the warm and welcoming type, but that doesn't mean she doesn't like you."

"It doesn't mean I do, either," Emma called matter-of-factly from inside the house.

Madeline suddenly felt like the little girl with an envelope stuffed full of magazine cutouts all over again. This moment reminded her of one of the many times she'd been transferred to a new school. It was her third class that year because Brad hadn't worked out for Mom, but David had. At the new school, Madeline had told some girls that she liked the Backstreet Boys. They'd looked at her as if she'd said something really wrong, and Madeline could recall how awkward she'd felt in that moment, like the only person not in on the joke. She felt that way now, as if she'd said something to keep her standing outside their little circle.

She didn't quite know how to proceed—how did she go about addressing the issues at hand under these circumstances? Okay, well, generally she found that it was best just to get down to business. Madeline decided the best course of action was to skip over the getting-to-know-you phase and go directly to the necessary business. The quicker the issue of this ranch was resolved, the quicker she could get out of here and go back to her safe world. *I wish, I wish, I wish.* She gripped her briefcase tighter. "You were saying you lived in California?" she asked, marching up the steps with resolve.

"Yep. With Emma."

"Only a year," Emma's voice came at them from an open window. "Libby is from Colorado. Pine River if you want to get right down to it. *I* am from California."

Libby smiled at Madeline and shrugged. "Emma's always right," she said airily, but Madeline heard the twinge of sarcasm in her voice.

Madeline followed Libby inside, her pump hitting the yellow pine floor with a resounding clap. The walls were covered in dated wallpaper, green vines of ivy meandering to the ceiling. The ceilings were tall and the windows cased with dark, polished wood.

She could see Emma sitting on a rose-colored camelback sofa in a room to her right, her arms folded, her legs crossed, and one foot swinging anxiously. Or with tedium. It was difficult to know.

The potbellied stove on the interior wall of that room made Madeline wonder if that's how the place was heated.

"Let me show you around," Libby said.

"That's okay, I—"

"No, no, Madeline, you should see what we have here. Emma and I have had a good look." She glanced at Emma over her shoulder. "Are you coming?"

"I'll let you do the guided tour," Emma said, and yawned.

Madeline followed Libby around the ground floor. She chatted incessantly, asking questions that only made Madeline tenser. *How old are you? Do you like Orlando? Have you ever been to Colorado?*

Madeline answered sparingly and kept her focus on the house. The kitchen was straight out of 1968, complete with what had to be the most ancient microwave she had ever seen. A sunroom overlooked a garden and what Libby called a river, but looked more like a creek to Madeline. It turned out that the room with the flat roof, added to the original house, was the dining room. But what made the ground floor spectacular was the views. From every room, big windows framed another slice of big sky, mountains, and meadows.

Libby led Madeline upstairs, to a surprisingly wide second floor corridor. There were four bedrooms in all, and even a sewing room, which Madeline guessed was originally a nursery. The sewing machine and a few bolts of cloth were still there, some of the cloth spread across an ironing board, as if someone would appear at any moment to iron.

Throughout the house, a lot of the furniture had been removed. But the remains of a family's life had been left behind in bits and scraps. In one room, on a dresser, was a family photo of twenty or so people, dressed in the trappings of the sixties. On the hallway floor was a photo of two young boys in baseball uniforms.

When they had completed the tour, Emma had peeled herself off the couch and was standing at the door of the living room, her shoulder propped against the frame. She openly took in Madeline's clothes as she and Libby descended the stairs. Trudi was right again—Madeline felt conspicuously overdressed in comparison to these women. Wardrobe had always been the bane of her existence—she never understood how to dress for different occasions. She couldn't latch on to ideas like Casual Friday, as there was nothing remotely casual about her Fridays.

Today, what she'd wanted—what she always wanted—was to present a professional, polished image. It was her shield of armor. But in that moment, looking at a comfortable Libby and a chic Emma, Madeline chided herself for thinking these shoes and this suit were a good idea.

"Well!" Libby said cheerfully, as if they were having a grand old time, "we've had the tour! Madeline, would you like some tea?"

"What? Oh, no. No thank you."

"Water?"

"I'm good," Madeline said.

"Are you hungry? I have some—"

"God, Libby, *stop*," Emma said. She sighed, and Madeline had the impression that this wasn't the first time Emma had told Libby to stop.

"Okay." Libby smiled. But it was not the grin she had met Madeline with. It was much tighter. "Maybe you could tell us a little bit about yourself while we wait, Madeline," she suggested. "I'll be honest—I haven't been able to stop thinking about you. I mean, it's so exciting to find out I have a *sister*. I want to know everything there is to know about you."

Too much, too soon! Madeline wanted to say. "I wouldn't even know where to start."

Libby was not one to take hints, because she suggested, "Well, what sort of things do you like? Do you have any hobbies?"

Hobbies. Her hobbies were work and taking care of her mother. She once had tried to learn to knit, but had put it down and never picked it up again.

"Scrapbooking?" Libby offered helpfully. "Sports?"

"Scrapbooking or sports?" Emma snorted disdainfully.

"What about siblings?" Libby asked, taking another tack. "Do you have any siblings?"

Surely she meant besides the two of them. "Ah . . . no. Just me," Madeline said.

"I have two younger brothers. Twins," Libby said. "Emma has a sister."

"*Step*sister," Emma clarified as she studied her nail.

"Is your mother still alive?" Libby asked.

Madeline's head was beginning to pound. Why was *she* on the hot seat? Why wasn't she questioning them? She hated this, not knowing what to do. And she wanted to sit—her feet were beginning to hurt. "She is," Madeline said. "Mind if I sit down?" She didn't wait for a response. She walked into the living room and sat heavily in a chair.

"So when is the last time you saw him?" Emma asked without looking up from her nail.

"Who?" Madeline asked, confused by all the questions and the mention of siblings.

One of Emma's carefully sculpted brows rose. "Your *father*. The reason we are all gathered here today like a litter of puppies. I am curious how well you knew him, because like I said, he never mentioned you."

There was no reason that statement should bother Madeline, not after a lifetime of never being mentioned. But it did, and in a surprisingly strong manner.

"God, Emma, you make it sound like she's making it up," Libby sighed.

"Maybe she is," Emma said. "I just find it very hard to believe that Dad could keep his mouth shut about her because God knows he couldn't keep quiet about anything else."

Something inside Madeline tipped, and out poured years of carefully controlled feelings about her absent father. "Are you kidding?" she asked.

Emma merely shrugged.

"Are you always so blunt?" Madeline asked.

Oddly enough, that made Emma chuckle with amusement. "Blunt is the *least* of what I am."

"Don't mind her—"

"I swear, Libby, if you tell her not to *mind* me one more time, I'm going to kick you. I have nothing to apologize for. I'm not the one who invited her here."

"Wow," Madeline said, truly taken aback. "Just to put your mind at ease, I didn't ask for sisters, either. Like I said, I never knew Grant, so if you think I am here to rip your inheritance out of your hands, think again. I never asked for it, never wanted it." She folded her arms, waiting for them to challenge her.

But Emma suddenly looked interested. "So this is really out of the blue?"

"Yes," Madeline said, angry that she suddenly had to justify her appearance at a place she'd never wanted to come. "It was a complete shock when Jackson showed up in Orlando. I obviously knew I had a father out there in the world somewhere, but I never knew him."

"*Wow,*" Libby said thoughtfully. "I assumed that you didn't know him as well as we did," she said. "I mean, Emma's right, your name would have at least come up, but still . . . I thought you at least *knew* him. Why didn't you? Did your mom keep you from him?"

Madeline snorted. Her mother had never kept *anything* from her, not even the things she should have kept from her. It made Madeline angry with herself and with these women that she suddenly felt guilty, as if she *should* have known Grant. That not knowing her father should feel like a failure as a daughter and a human being. "Let's just agree that you are both better acquainted and leave it at that."

"More than I wanted to be, that's for sure," Emma said, and moved deeper into the living room, her skirt swinging jauntily around her knees.

It occurred to Madeline in a moment of sheer insanity that she'd never had a skirt swing around her knees like that. Even her skirts were controlled.

"Emma, don't say that," Libby chided her as she followed her into the living room and took a seat on the couch.

"It's true," Emma said as she sat next to Libby. "It's not like he was a good father, Libby, you of all people should acknowledge that. Don't worry, Madeline. You didn't miss out on much."

Madeline wondered why Libby of all people should acknowledge that he was a lousy father.

"Emma!" Libby cried, and glanced sheepishly at Madeline. "He was an okay dad. I don't know what Emma's problem is, but he wasn't *that* bad." She looked at Emma again. "I know you didn't like him, but he was still your *dad.*"

"If that's what you want to call him," Emma muttered.

"Could you, just once, be *nice?*" Libby demanded.

"What, like you?" Emma said casually. "So people can take advantage of me?"

Libby gasped and gaped at her sister.

Emma groaned and held up her hands. "*Sorry.*"

"That was mean," Libby muttered.

"Yeah, I know. Sorry, Libby."

Madeline wanted to run. Endless questions were one thing, but conflict was the worst. Conflict was messy. People said things that they could never take back—she'd heard her mother say enough to know. Madeline didn't understand what Emma had meant, but judging from Libby's face, Emma couldn't take it back.

And yet, Libby only sighed and sank back against the couch. "Well, I guess I knew Dad the best then," she said crisply to Madeline.

Best, how? Had Grant Tyler taken Libby skiing, or to a father-daughter dance? Had he attended her soccer games and waited up for her when she came in from a date? And why did Emma say she knew him more than she'd wanted? What had he done to earn her disdain?

But the questions stuck in Madeline's throat. She wasn't certain she wanted to hear the answers—they wouldn't change anything. She was still the one he had never bothered to know, and Madeline would still feel awkward and out of place here. She suddenly wanted nothing more than to agree on what was to be done and go home to her ordered world where her so-called father did not exist. Where she didn't have sisters and no one argued around her.

"Maybe we should discuss what to do with the inheritance," Madeline suggested.

"Jump right to it," Emma said.

"We are going to discuss it," Libby said. "Just as soon as Jackson gets here, which should be any minute." She suddenly hopped up and went to the window to peer out.

"Right," Madeline said, and opened her briefcase. She pulled out a file folder.

"What's that?" Emma asked.

Madeline opened the file. "I jotted down some notes and ideas about how to proceed."

Emma frowned. "Proceed with what?"

Madeline glanced up; she was sitting much lower than Emma and scooched to the edge of her chair. "With the disposition of the ranch."

Libby whirled around so quickly that she startled Madeline. "What do you mean?"

Was it not obvious? "Well . . . to sell it," she said.

Libby's mouth dropped open.

"You are jumping to a very presumptuous conclusion, Madeline," Emma said calmly. "What makes you think we want to sell?"

Oh no. No, no, no. "Jackson said you live in California, Emma. I'm in Orlando. And Libby, I . . . it's so far out here."

"I don't care, I don't want to sell," Libby said. "I want to live here. I want to make something of it. We could make this into something huge. We have an incredible opportunity here."

That was crazy, full-on crazy. There was nothing they could do with this place in the middle of nowhere. "Make it into what, exactly?" Madeline asked as politely as she could.

"Exactly like *this*," Libby said, gesturing to the windows. "Most people would be very happy to have landed in a spot as gorgeous as this."

"Oh my God, I knew it," Emma said, and stood up. "I want a drink."

"Okay," Libby said, watching Emma move across the room. "What do *you* want, Emma?"

"I don't know what I want," Emma said with a shrug. "But it will take more than a letter from Jackson Crane and meeting a supposed sister for the first time for me to decide what I want." She tossed a wry smile over her shoulder as she walked out of the room. "Maybe we should turn it into a *spa*."

"Spas are very hard to get off the ground and become successful," Madeline said.

"Are you a spa expert?" Emma shouted from the other room.

"It's a ranch. A working ranch," Libby said firmly. "Why would we mess with that? Look, you two don't have to be involved if you don't want. I just thought that maybe. . . ." She shook her head and looked out the window. "Never mind. You don't have to be involved. I'll do it. I'll take care of everything."

"I know what you thought," Emma said, appearing in the doorway again. "You thought this would turn into a chick flick where we bond as sisters and discover we have all these things in common and we root for each other and marry brothers and raise each other's children. But that's not happening, Libby." She disappeared into the other room again.

Libby looked so wounded by what Emma had said that Madeline couldn't help but feel sorry for her. "Libby, I'm sorry . . . but I don't . . . I don't think this is for me," she said honestly. "I don't know why a father I never knew left me anything. My hope was that we could wrap this up as soon as possible."

"Wow," Libby said, her effervescent smile gone. "You *just* met us. Can you take a moment to decide if you want to know us? Have you considered *why* Dad left us this place? Maybe it was his way of reaching out, of giving you sisters, Madeline. Of giving me a purpose. Of giving Emma . . ." she trailed off.

Emma appeared at the door again. "Go on, Libby. Give Emma what?"

Libby frowned and looked away from Emma, declining to answer.

Madeline's head was pounding. This was not going well at all—she'd never guessed they would want to somehow make this forced partnership work.

"Here's what I think, if anyone is interested," Emma said, and pointed at Madeline. "I don't care if we are friends." She cocked a brow, almost daring Madeline to challenge it, knowing that she wouldn't. "And I'm going back to L.A. in a couple of days."

"But we need to make some decisions," Madeline said.

"I don't." Emma disappeared into the kitchen again.

Emma, Madeline thought, was a bitch. And Libby was too . . . eager. But of the three of them, Madeline was the one who had no real business here at all, no ties, no feelings, no history, not like these two apparently had. She wanted only to do what had to be done and leave before Grant could mess up her life any more than he already had. He could have left everything to Libby and Emma, and Madeline would never have known, would never have been the wiser.

"Then *go*," Libby called out to Emma, her feelings clearly hurt. "How stupid of me to think that maybe three sisters could make something of this place. *Together.*"

Madeline felt awful. She hadn't come here to hurt anyone's feelings. "I'm sorry, Libby. I am. But I don't know how we can be . . . partners," she said, discovering that she couldn't even say *sisters*. "We don't know one another. Grant must have known it would be a difficult situation for us, so I don't know why he left it to us like this."

"There is nothing here!" Emma shouted, and that was followed by the banging of a cabinet door. "Nothing!"

"Because he was our father," Libby said. "Isn't that what parents do? Don't they leave their worldly possessions to their children? And besides, he couldn't sell it, not with the contract."

"The what?" Madeline asked.

"What contract?" Emma asked, appearing again with a glass of water.

"Jackson didn't tell you? There's a contract Dad's heirs must honor, and we can't do anything before we meet the terms of it."

Madeline's pulse began to quicken. If she'd come all this way to find out it was even more complicated and impossible . . .

"The Johnson family reunion," Libby said, enunciating a little more than was necessary, looking at them both. "The contract has been signed. The deposits have been paid and applied to the event. Two hundred Johnsons are going to show up in a matter of days and they are expecting one long weekend of happy family reunion, and we have to honor that commitment."

For some reason, Emma actually laughed. "Well if that's not the topper on the cake."

Madeline thought she might pass out. She preferred to know what to expect, and she did *not* expect a family reunion. "I don't understand," she said, and rubbed her temples against the pounding in her head.

"I can't believe Jackson didn't tell you. It was Mr. Kendrick's idea, a way to make some money. He and Dad were setting this ranch up to host family reunions. The family will camp here, and they will use the kitchen, and the showers in the bunkhouse, and they will do all the things that make Pine River so attractive in the summer, only on private property with private guides. That's why the Port-A-Johns."

Two hundred Johnsons. And just like that, Grant Tyler had complicated Madeline's life even more.

Emma laughed again. "He's dead and he's *still* a prick. God, I need a drink."

NINE

Luke felt a surprising swell of nostalgia when he turned into the ranch's entrance. He and little brother Leo, separated by three years, had spent their childhood in a patch of heaven. In the winter, they would ski and snowboard, or, if necessary, use trash-can lids to careen down the grassy slope behind the house. Their summers consisted of hiking, fishing, building forts, and bear tracking, the latter much to their mother's chagrin.

When they were older, they'd joined their father in working cattle. It's what the Kendricks did—they were, and had long been, high altitude cattle ranchers.

But the rhythm of their lives had revolved around Luke's mother. She'd been there to feed them home-cooked meals after a hard day of play or work, to remind them to bathe when they had more important things on their mind, and to soothe the injuries, both emotional and physical, two boys tended to suffer. She kept the books for the ranch, sang in the church choir, and never missed a school event.

Dad didn't miss one, either. Mom had been their anchor, but Dad had taught them how to be men. He taught them how to cast a fly-fishing line, how to saddle a horse, and chop wood. To build things, to breed cows, to respect women.

Maybe Luke had taken all that for granted. Maybe he'd thought that even after Mom died, when the ranch had started to look and feel different from the one of his youth, it would always be there for him. He never saw this coming, never dreamed it would all slip from their grasp. He'd always believed that one day, when Dad was gone, he'd be here, carrying on the tradition.

He'd not realized how much it would hurt to lose the ranch. It felt as if the blocks of his life were being kicked out from beneath him, one at a time.

It still looked the same as the magical place of his childhood—with the exception of the Port-A-Johns, and Luke was sure he didn't want to know what that was about. He stopped just inside the gate, got out of his jeep, and walked across the meadow to the hillside. He studied the trees a moment, then walked straight for a Ponderosa pine. He pulled away the vines that had grown up onto the rocks beneath the pine, and smiled when he saw it—the fort he and Leo had built with river rocks, its entrance carefully concealed for spying. Luke had learned about the importance of proper engineering in building that fort. It had taken several tries and consultations with Dad before they got it right, but there it stood, maybe three feet by three feet, the best fort in America.

He and Leo would hide here, watching cows meander by, watching Dad and Ernest work. They brought pellet guns and shot at grouse and pheasant . . . until Mom found out what they were doing and took their guns away that summer. One Christmas, they'd made Dad a toolbox, and they'd hid it in here so he wouldn't find it.

Luke re-covered the entrance with the vines. He'd always assumed that he would bring his son to this fort. Then again, he assumed his mother would be here and Leo would be healthy and Julie would be his wife. . . .

"*Anh,*" he muttered, silently chastising himself. There was no point in reliving that heartache again.

He drove on to the house, bouncing over the little bridge Dad and Ernest had built over the mountain stream that ran through their property. The stream eventually widened and met up with Pine River, where they used to shoot the rapids.

As he pulled into the drive, Luke noticed things were looking a little worn, a little weathered. Repairs to the place had begun to suffer when his mother had gotten sick, but what he saw was nothing that he couldn't fix up in a couple of weeks. He would do that, Luke thought. He would fix things for Dad. He would make some wheelchair-accessible entries—there was only one at present, in the back of the house—maybe modify one of the rooms downstairs for his little brother so he wasn't living twenty-four-seven in the den. On the weekends, he could come up here and turn this into a home again.

Luke was used to seeing Dad's old pickup and Mom's Pontiac in the drive and was not used to seeing strange cars parked there. Mom's Pontiac was a beast of a car that could have ascended Pikes Peak. It still ran. It was in the garage, gathering a new layer of dust. The cars in the drive were the cars of strangers, of people who had slipped in and stolen his childhood right out from under him.

That little car with the donut spare in particular made him irrationally crazy. It was front and center, the car of the woman with long dark hair and blue eyes and a yellow highlighter. A woman who wore Dr. Scholl's inserts and suite to the mountains. She was definitely cute. And definitely quirky. And she was now, officially, on his shit list.

Luke pulled around, sliding into a spot beneath a canopy beside the garage. By the time he'd gotten out of his Bronco and returned to the drive, Libby Tyler had walked out onto the porch as if she owned the place.

She was another one on his list.

He had known Libby most of his life—or known of her. She was younger than him, Leo's age. Luke guessed everyone in town knew that she'd broken up with Ryan Spangler and then shortly after that lost her job at the sheriff's department. Leo said there was some trouble with Ryan after they broke up, although he didn't know what. But never mind all that. Libby Tyler was in his house. Not *her* house. His.

"Luke?" she said, her voice full of surprise as he walked toward the house. "Wow! It's been ages since I last saw you!" She smiled and extended her hand. "How *are* you? How's Leo?"

"We're all doing great, thanks," he said. He held her hand a long moment, looking into her eyes for any flicker of understanding, any recognition of what her father had done to his. He saw none.

"What brings you out?" she asked cheerfully, conveniently forgetting, perhaps, that this had been his home. Maybe that helped her to settle in.

"A little unfinished business."

She looked confused by that. "Jackson didn't mention anything."

"No?" Luke said as amicably as he could.

The screen door banged; Libby jumped a little as a woman with long blond hair and brown boots sauntered out onto the porch. She was as pretty as Libby was cute, sultry where Libby was fresh. But there was a resemblance between them, around the eyes. The third heir, he supposed.

"Well hello," she said, eyeing him, a hint of a smile on her face.

"Luke, this is my sister, Emma Tyler," Libby said, and to Emma, "This is Luke Kendrick. He and his brother, Leo, used to live here. I went to school with Leo."

Emma's smile deepened. "Hello, Luke Kendrick."

Luke knew women like Emma—she was the type to know exactly what affect she had on men and how to use that to her advantage. But he wasn't biting. "Hello," he said.

Emma deliberately flicked her gaze over the length of him, but Luke was distracted. Behind her, Blue Eyes walked out onto the porch in her conservative suit, her hair clipped to the back of her head. She was staring at him, clearly trying to work out why he was here. "It's *you*."

Luke smiled. "It's me."

"You guys know each other?" Libby asked incredulously.

"No!" she said quickly, firmly. But she was blushing and her fingers fluttered nervously around that little *M* at her throat.

"We met only briefly," Luke said. "Up on Sometimes Pass. I changed her tire."

Madeline's blue eyes were fixed on Luke, and she pointed in the general direction of her car and, presumably, the spare. "It was a nail.

Construction site." She cocked her head to one side to peer at him. "Why are you here, again?"

"Yeah, why?" Emma echoed curiously.

"Jackson Crane invited me. Is he around?"

"He's late," Libby said. "No, wait—there he is."

The four of them turned around to see a four-wheel drive F-250 truck barreling up the road. It slid into the drive and Jackson hopped out, all smiles. He'd changed clothes since Luke had last seen him, preferring hiking boots and cargo pants for the trip out to the ranch.

"Sorry I'm late," he said to them all, and held up a six-pack of diet coke and a bag of potato chips. "I brought snacks."

The four of them stared in disbelief at Jackson.

Jackson grinned, unfazed by them. "So, did you gals—and Luke," he amended with a nod, "have a chance to get acquainted?"

Luke wanted to kick him. With the point of his boots, right between the eyes. It wasn't as if they'd signed up for a class, here—they had some serious issues to address.

"Jackson, what is going on?" Libby asked.

"I'm sure you have a lot of questions, and I'll answer them all, I promise. So what do you think, Madeline?" Jackson asked breezily. "Not as bad as you thought, right?"

The other two women jerked their gazes to Madeline, who looked startled. "What? I didn't think it was *bad*," she tried, but looked as if she were about to twist right out of her shoes.

"Hmm. From the look of things, you guys didn't get at as acquainted as I'd hoped," Jackson said, as if they'd somehow failed him. "No worries! Let's go sit at one of the picnic tables and discuss a few things." He began striding across the lawn.

Emma looked at Libby, then followed Jackson to the west lawn. Libby was close on her heels.

Madeline looked at Luke. "This is weird," she said.

"Tell me about it." Luke gestured for her to precede him. Madeline hesitated, but then reluctantly began to walk.

Jackson had chosen the longest picnic table, one that Luke's grandfather had built. Perhaps he wanted to make sure there was plenty of
distance between everyone in case the fists actually began to fly. He
passed out cans of warm Diet Coke, opened the bag of chips, and
tossed them to the middle of the picnic table. The only person Luke
knew who would be comfortable with such an approach to serious
business was Leo.

"Okay, so let me fill in some background information," Jackson said
as he popped the top of one of the Diet Cokes. "Ladies, when Grant
passed, he'd just ended his fifth marriage, and to put it bluntly, he lost
his shirt in that one. All he really had left was this ranch."

"When did he *get* this ranch?" Libby asked.

"He took possession about a year ago," Jackson said and took a long
swig of soda.

There was an interesting turn of phrase, *took possession*. As if Grant
had wrested it from Dad's grasp—which wasn't too far from the way
Luke pictured it had happened.

"At the time of his death, he was upside down on the mortgage,"
Jackson added.

That was so shocking, so impossible, that Luke spoke without
thinking. "There's no way," he said. "He bought it far under market
value. How could he owe more than it was worth?"

Suddenly, all three women were staring at him.

"Oh . . . ," Jackson said casually, ". . . I should probably have mentioned that Grant Tyler bought the ranch from Luke's father, Bob
Kendrick. And he did indeed get one helluva deal."

"Right," Luke said. "Some might say he took advantage of my dad."

"Well, that's one interpretation," Jackson said cheerfully. "But while
he was waiting for your dad to live up to *his* end of their agreement, he
divorced and he needed money. So he took out a second mortgage on
this ranch, and unfortunately, the real estate market took a hit, and he
found himself upside down by fifteen thousand dollars. Which, of
course, does not include realtor fees. Right, Madeline?"

Madeline blinked. "Well, I . . . I don't know—"

"Oh—Madeline is a realtor," Jackson added.

"No wonder you want to sell," Libby muttered.

"No!" Madeline protested. "My wanting to sell has nothing to do with that." She looked at Luke, but his heart had lodged itself in his throat. A *realtor*. There it was, no denying, no pretending that he wasn't going to face an uphill battle in which the odds were stacked against him.

"But you have to admit, your being a realtor could come in handy," Jackson observed casually.

Madeline didn't say anything. She slowly leaned forward, put her forehead on the table, and Luke thought he heard her suck in a long, deep breath. He also thought he heard her whisper something that sounded like *lunatic*.

"Can we backtrack to what he said?" Libby asked, pointing at Luke. "He said Dad took advantage of his dad. What does that mean? What's he talking about?"

"We'll get to that," Jackson said. "But first, let me tell you that Luke's dad had a *great* idea for how to make that money back and Grant was totally onboard. He had the idea to make this *the* destination in the Colorado Rockies for homecomings, reunions, and weddings. And he thought that you girls were just the team to make it happen." He threw up his hands as if the problem were solved.

"Jesus, this *is* a chick flick," Emma said incredulously. She stood up. "Do you have any bourbon to go with that Coke?"

"I wish," Jackson said apologetically. "Listen, I know this is all a bit of a surprise. But I think it could work. Before Grant died, he spent what he had left on advertising this great retreat. The Johnson family—they're out of Texas—was looking for a place just like this to have their family reunion. A place where they can camp, and the kids can raft and hike, and the men can barbeque, and honestly, I don't know what all. But I drew up a contract and they signed, and so did Grant, and they paid their deposit, and the estate must honor that contract. It would cost you more to try and get out of it than to just do it."

"Do what?" Madeline demanded, lifting her head.

"Now don't get upset, ladies. There is still a lot to be done," Jackson
said. He took another long drink of his soda and crushed the can, the
first outward sign that he was as uncomfortable as they were. "Ernest
will be back this week, and he can do a lot of it. But we might need to
hire some of the work out."

"Such as?" Luke asked.

"For starters, we have the bunkhouse showers—"

"Shower," Luke corrected him.

"Shower, right, at least at this moment. We need to build a separa-
tion for men and women and maybe add a few temporary showers.
Maybe a few. We need to round up horses for horseback riding, move
the cattle up to lease grazing, and hopefully make a deal with some
river guides for rafting. The good news is I've already done a lot. The
tents will be delivered tomorrow. Barbeque pits come next week. But
we'll need someone here to manage it all. Which could be one of you!"
he said, as if he were a game-show host.

"Where'd you get the money for that?" Luke asked.

Jackson shrugged. "I sold his Porsche. It was a classic. I got enough
to cover the initial improvements."

Emma slowly resumed her seat. "Is it just me, or does anyone else
notice how screwed up this is?"

"Me," Madeline said, raising her hand. "This is . . . this is not what I
thought, Jackson. I can't stick around for this. I have a life and a business in Orlando. There has to be another way."

"No," Jackson said quickly and firmly. "Unfortunately, no, at least
not in the immediate future. And there are a few other issues that
Luke alluded to we should probably discuss at another time. You
know, once you've had a chance to absorb this."

Madeline rubbed her temples. "This is crazy. *Crazy!* There is no
plan, no organization. . . ."

No highlighter, Luke thought.

"What other issues?" Emma asked. "Get them out. I don't want to
hear about them later, I want to know what the hell is going on here
now. All of it, Jackson."

Jackson looked at Luke.

So did the women, three pairs of suspicious female eyes trained on him.

Luke sighed. "There were some mitigating circumstances in the deal our fathers made. They were friends, supposedly—or at least my dad believes that they were—and he believed that your dad was helping him out." He shook his head. He was making it more complicated than it had to be. "So Grant gave my dad the cash he needed for some financial issues, and the deal was that when my dad repaid the loan, he'd get the place back. At the same price."

Libby and Emma looked at him blankly. But Madeline's brows dipped.

"It was a gentleman's agreement. Mine needed some cash. Grant had some cash and offered to help him out."

"He didn't have as much cash as he thought," Jackson muttered.

"Nevertheless, the agreement was that as soon as my dad could pay him back, Grant would sell the ranch back to him at the same cost. But then Grant died and left my dad in a bind."

"Is there a contract for that agreement?" Madeline asked.

"Nope," Jackson said, clearly knowing where she was going with it.

"Not to put too fine a point on it . . ." Luke said, "but this is my family's home. This is where I grew up."

Madeline suddenly smiled. "Well then, great! That solves our problem, doesn't it? You can buy it back."

Luke clenched his jaw. "Can't buy it yet," he said tightly and stared into Madeline's blue eyes. She held his gaze, but her expression went from hopeful to stoic. She understood. She was a realtor, a negotiator, she was used to this. And Luke guessed she was not the type to be swayed by sentimentality.

"Well!" Jackson said brightly. "Like I said, lots to sort out."

"For God's sake," Emma said, and got up, sauntering off with a Diet Coke in hand, apparently in search of bourbon.

TEN

It was almost dusk when Madeline made her way back to Pine River. She was exhausted, light-headed, her head pounding and her stomach rumbling with hunger almost to the point of nausea.

It was true that she did not deal well with stress. Not her own, anyway. She was great at talking Trudi off a ledge, and soothing little girls who felt slighted on the soccer field. But her own stress was a different matter entirely. She tended to internalize it.

She usually avoided it with careful planning. It was Madeline's experience that when things were planned, when events unfolded according to schedule, that expectations were managed. Yes, it was all about managing expectations, and Jackson sucked at it. For example, this day would have gone a *lot* smoother if he'd just put some thought into how to present the issues. But between his glib attempts to appease them, and Libby's enthusiasm for that damn reunion, and Emma's cool indifference, Madeline had felt like she was treading water.

At some point, they'd agreed to take a break—Emma was determined to find some booze in that house. Madeline had sat on the porch, rubbing her temples, and Luke had come to sit next to her. God, but that man was good-looking. He looked like he'd jumped right out of an ad for Dinty Moore stew. He sat closely, his leg lightly touching hers. Madeline was fixated on his leg. Thick and powerful, dwarfing hers, and oh, so sexy.

He'd bent his head to look at her. "Are you okay?"

Beside the fact that her head was exploding, her feet were numb, and she couldn't shake the feeling of fatigue or chill, she was perfectly fine. "I'm good," she'd said, and forced a smile.

He'd nodded, squinted out over the landscape and had said, "I gather this is a little like having a tornado touch down in your life."

"*Yes*," she'd said, relieved that someone understood. "Yours too?"

"A little," he agreed.

"Who was it who said, life is what happens to you when you're making other plans?" She smiled brightly, even though she was cringing inwardly. Not only did she *never* say things like that, she didn't believe it for a minute. Life happened when she *made* plans.

Neither did Luke believe it, because he'd smiled wryly in a way that had made his gray eyes shine, and he'd put his hand on her arm. His strong, big hand on her arm. It was a workingman's hand, with the little nicks and marks of his life. "John Lennon, I think. Hang in there, Madeline. Today is probably the worst of it." He'd squeezed her arm and let go.

Madeline had appreciated his assurance, she had, but she couldn't help but wonder if he knew what two hundred Johnsons would look like. Madeline knew—she'd worked enough of the office client appreciation days to have an idea.

What was very clear to Madeline at the end of the torturous day was that this situation would not be neatly resolved in one or two meetings.

She walked into the lobby of the Grizzly Lodge, with its rustic furniture carved from enormous tree trunks, a fire blazing in a cavernous hearth, and, naturally, the bearskin rugs. Yesterday, when she'd finally rolled into town, it was the only place she could find to stay. When she'd checked in, the proprietor of the establishment, Danielle Boxer, had asked if she wanted the Bear Cub or the Aspen Forest room.

Danielle was a large woman, probably six feet tall, with unusually bright red hair piled high on her head. She wore a pink Guayabera shirt—one of Madeline's "dads" had worn those shirts on Sunday when he kicked up the footrest of her grandfather's old recliner to watch football. "I'd give you the Mockingbird room, but someone had a bit of a party in there if you know what I mean," she'd said, and had waggled her brows.

Madeline didn't know what she meant and didn't want to know. She thought the Bear Cub room sounded like the smaller of the two and chose that one.

"How long will you be staying?" Danielle asked—or Dani, as she insisted Madeline call her, as if Madeline would be staying for a time, long enough that they would know each other on a first name basis.

"I'll be leaving first thing Monday morning."

"That, I can accommodate. But I've got a big group of snowbirds coming through next week. They like to take the bus tours when the spring thaw starts."

Madeline would be long gone before the mad rush to Pine River, that was for sure.

"License and credit card, please," Dani had said. She glanced at Madeline's license when she handed it to her. "Oh! You're one of Grant's girls!"

Madeline had been stunned by that. "How—"

"Jackson Crane," she said with a laugh. "He has his breakfast here most days. I should have known it was you—you look just like your father."

Madeline's hands had gone instantly to her face.

"He was a good-looking man, I always thought so. And such a flirt!" She had laughed at that. "I tell you, if Big Ben hadn't still been kicking, I would have considered it. But Ben and I were married for thirty-eight years." She'd offered that up proudly.

"Impressive," Madeline had agreed, but her mind was whirling around the idea that she somehow looked like the man who had abandoned her.

Dani had beamed and handed her the keys to her room. "Sorry about your dad, sugar. That must have been a blow."

Madeline had merely taken the keys and smiled.

This afternoon, however, Madeline walked into a deserted lobby. The door to the coffee shop that faced the street was closed, the interior dark. That was *not* a good sign, as Madeline had hoped to grab a bite there.

Dani appeared from the office behind the front desk, dressed in a blue Guayabera shirt. Her hair hung in a long red ponytail down her back. "Oh, hey!" she said brightly when she saw Madeline standing in front of the closed door to the coffee shop. "Did you have a good day in our little village?"

No, it had been a disaster of a day. The worst. "It was okay." She rubbed her forehead.

"Are you all right?"

Madeline dropped her hand and smiled. "I have a bit of a headache, that's all. And I'm starving. Where's the best place to get some dinner?"

"My coffee shop," Dani said proudly. "But it's closed." She reached under the counter and produced a bottle of Bayer aspirin. "Take two of these. You probably have a little altitude sickness."

"What?"

Dani smiled. "Sugar, have you never been to the mountains? You're up in thin air. There's less oxygen here than what you're used to. Don't worry, it passes in a day or two. You'll get acclimated and hear those mountains call to you, I promise."

Crazy old bat, Madeline thought.

"Take two of these, get something to eat, and get some rest. The Stakeout is open."

The Stakeout, Madeline assumed, was a restaurant. "Is it very far? My feet are killing me," she admitted as she accepted the aspirin bottle from Dani.

"Just pull on a pair of jeans. Living in the mountains is a whole lot easier if you leave the heels in your closet." She winked at Madeline.

But Madeline hadn't brought jeans. She had another pair of slacks in her bag. Slacks that went with these shoes and this blazer. She hadn't planned on recreational wear, she'd planned on three days of what she thought would be meetings. "It's okay," she said, and forced a smile. "I'm not staying long. Thanks for the aspirin," she said, shook two from the bottle, and made her way to her room.

The Bear Cub was definitely a lodge room, with low, beamed ceilings, an adobe fireplace, and a four-poster bed with a quilt cover. And, naturally, the obligatory bearskin rug. The room was certainly cozy, just as Dani had said when Madeline had checked in. Perhaps too cozy—Madeline felt as if she were sleeping in a bear's den.

She kicked off her shoes first, and one of them ended up on the snout of the bearskin. She took the aspirin, then collapsed back onto the bed, staring up at the ceiling.

She was exhausted. Emotionally, physically, all of it.

Madeline, who always had a plan, who had every moment of her day mapped out, didn't know where to go from here.

She did not like the way uncertainty felt.

She, Emma, and Libby had argued about what to do, punctuated by generally unhelpful advice from Jackson Crane. Luke hadn't said much. She could sense he wanted to hold someone responsible for his father's poor decisions, and she felt for him in that regard, she truly did—she was no stranger to a parent making bad decisions. But she'd been making up for bad parents all her life, and she didn't want, or even know how, to make up for his.

A faint beeping filtered into her thoughts. Madeline dug her cell phone out of her purse and noticed that she had missed two calls.

Both from Stephen.

She winced, tossed the phone into her purse.

She would call him, she would. But right now she was starving. Madeline sat up, looked at her shoes, and with a wince, stuffed her feet back into them.

She could hear the din of the Stakeout before she realized it was coming from the blue western building with the wooden porch and the swinging saloon doors. From the look of the packed gravel parking lot across the street, everyone in Pine River was here. Madeline dreaded going to restaurants alone; it seemed to give off a lonely, cat lady vibe. But then, she couldn't remember ever being this hungry before. Ravenous! With a little salt and pepper, she would eat the railing.

She stepped in through the swinging saloon doors to the hostess desk.

"Table for two?" the hostess asked without looking up.

"One," Madeline said.

The young woman glanced up, her gaze flicking over Madeline. "This way." She picked up a menu and started walking through the crowded room, past the bar where people stood shoulder to shoulder, past tables where food had been served family style.

She finally stopped at a small two-top near the back of the restaurant, just outside the kitchen and next to the wait station. "Drink?" she asked, and put a menu on the table as Madeline squeezed into a chair between the table and the wall.

"Wine," Madeline said. "A big glass of red wine."

"You got it," the woman said, and disappeared into the crowd.

Only a few minutes later, a young man appeared carrying a bowl of wine on a stem. "Would you like to hear the specials?" he asked. "We have buffalo steaks tonight."

As Madeline had been raised on cans of Chef Boyardee and ramen noodles, she was not particular about food—anything was good. And buffalo sounded wildly exotic. "I'll have that," she said.

The waiter whipped out his pad and jotted it down. "How would you like it cooked?"

"Umm . . . medium?"

"Sides?"

"Whatever you have," she said, smiling. "Thanks." She picked up the enormous glass of wine and sipped. She closed her eyes, felt the wine filtering down to her toes. She'd relaxed from the pent-up explosion of anxiety she'd felt building in her all day. Now, she felt nothing but a low-grade headache and a bone-deep exhaustion. . . .

Until the hairs on the back of her neck began to prickle.

Madeline suddenly felt as if someone was standing just beside her. She opened her eyes and let out a small gasp of surprise—there *was* someone standing beside her. His arms were crossed, and a beer bottle dangled from two fingers. His weight was all on one hip, and his gray eyes shone with a hint of amusement.

Madeline couldn't help herself; she smiled. Those eyes inspired a lot of internal fluttering. A lot. "Hello, Luke."

He gave her a lopsided smile. "Hello, Madeline." He lifted his beer bottle in a sort of half salute, then drank. "Seems like you and I had the same idea."

There was something about Luke Kendrick that made her feel quivery. Madeline definitely understood that he was the kind of guy who, under much different circumstances, could make a woman like her do backflips. But the circumstances weren't different, and Madeline dropped her head back and looked at the ceiling with a loud sigh. All she wanted to do was eat and then collapse into bed and nurse her head.

She slid her gaze to Luke again. He was calmly staring down at her, one brow cocked with amused curiosity above the other. Madeline wasn't a fool. Luke was, in essence, an adversary. This was a real estate deal—he knew it, and she knew it. He was standing here because he wanted her and her sisters to sign that ranch back to him for a fraction of its value. But Madeline had not flown all the way to Colorado to just hand it back to this guy—okay, well, the jury was still out on why, exactly, she had flown out here—but nevertheless, the realtor in her would not allow it, not without a few questions, a few understandings, a few beneficial agreements.

Luke gestured with his head to the empty chair at her table, then shifted, leaning over her so a waiter with a full tray could pass. "Mind if I join you?"

"I *knew* you were going to ask that."

"I will take that as a yes," he said congenially. He plopped himself down in the chair, stretching one muscular leg out alongside the table, effectively trapping her between the wall and his motorcycle boot. "Are you having dinner?"

"I already ordered," she said quickly, lest he have any ideas about dining together.

"Great. So did I." He lifted his hand; a waitress appeared from thin air. Luke reached for his wallet. "Would you do me a favor? Would you transfer my ticket from the bar over here? I'm going to have dinner with my friend."

"I wouldn't say we're exactly friends," Madeline pointed out.

"Not yet," he said confidently, and handed the waitress a five.

"Sure," the waitress said, all gooey-eyed as she smiled at Luke. "Let me know if you need anything else."

"I'll do that," Luke said, and he winked. *Winked.* As if he were some handsome lead in a romantic comedy movie. He watched the woman hurry off to do his bidding before looking at Madeline again.

"That," Madeline said, gesturing between him and the waitress, "will not work on me."

His smile turned into a grin. "Duly noted—a five-buck tip will not work on you." His gaze wandered over her a moment, lingering a little too long on the vee of her shirt. "So what does work on you?"

A stronger fluttering began to tease the bottom of her belly. "What are you doing here, Luke?"

"Me? I'm *from* here."

"You know what I mean. What are you doing in this restaurant? At my table? You keep showing up wherever I happen to be."

"Someone could say the same about you, Maddie—"

"Madeline—"

"No," he said, his gaze wandering over her face and hair. "You are definitely a Maddie parading around in Madeline's clothes."

Why would he say that? Madeline self-consciously glanced down at herself and then up.

Luke was grinning. "I can picture you in a frilly dress."

That caught her off guard because Madeline actually had a frilly dress at home. It was chiffon and it was blue, and she loved it. But she had never worn it anywhere. There never seemed to be a moment that she could be *that* Madeline. The Madeline of frilly, flirty dresses.

"And by the way, from where I stand, *you* are the one showing up on *my* turf. On the road to Pine River, in my town, and at my family home. But you're cute, so I'm not going to make a big deal out of it."

Madeline blinked. She laughed. "Are you *flirting* with me?" she asked incredulously.

"Nope," he said, but he was smiling.

Madeline laughed again. "You *are*."

"It's just an honest observation." He winked, took a swig of his beer. "I wanted a drink after the ordeal of this afternoon, just like you." He made a point of looking at the boat of wine at her elbow.

"Don't mind if I do," she said, and picked up her wine and sipped. It felt good. It felt warm. Or was that his smile and the fact that he'd just called her cute?

Luke leaned across the table, glanced around them and said low, "Between you and me—is Jackson Crane a little nuts?"

Madeline laughed. "Oh my God, *thank* you! He is *completely* nuts. Or very good at what he does." She paused. "What *does* he do, anyway?"

"Hell if I can figure it out."

"And then," Madeline said, leaning in, too, "he shows up to a meeting like that with Diet Coke and potato chips. Seriously?"

Luke laughed. "He should have at least come with chocolate and bourbon. As it was, I thought Emma was going to start building her own distillery."

Madeline laughed. It felt good to laugh after the day she'd had. "Do you know Emma?" she asked.

"Never met her before today," he said. "Don't you?"

Madeline shook her head. "I never met her before today, either. What about Libby?"

"I know who she is," he said with a shrug. "But I don't know much of anything other than she recently broke up with a man here in town she dated for a long time. But that's it," he said. He eased back in his chair. "So you're a realtor, huh?"

"I am. What about you?" she asked. "What do you do?"

"I'm a builder."

"*Here?* In Pine River?"

He chuckled. "By the disbelieving tone of your voice, I think that you are underestimating our charming little town. But no, not here—

in Denver. I went to school there and ended up staying for the time being."

Madeline had so desperately wanted to go to college, but her mother had blown through the small trust fund her grandparents had set up for Madeline's education. The jobs Madeline had held barely covered rent, much less tuition. "So what do you build?"

"Houses," he said, and helped himself to some bread the waiter put on the table as he breezed by. "I'm just starting out. I have an architecture degree and I'm working on my MBA. I was lucky enough to apprentice with a large builder as an undergrad, and now, in exchange for a share of the profits, they are partnering with me on three housing starts to help me get my feet and my business on the ground."

Madeline's interest was definitely piqued. She would not have guessed him to be a builder, much less an architect. Rancher, yes. Lumberjack, maybe. He had a muscular build, a virility that she did not associate with architects, at least none she knew. "Tell me about your houses," she said, earning a curious look from Luke. "No, really. I love the idea of a house."

"You love the *idea* of a house?"

"You know, what they represent." She thought about her ten-year-old self and the shoebox. In her imagination, the house was full of her children, and the pictures they drew were tacked on the walls, and the dogs they insisted on adopting were sleeping in the patches of sun on the floor, and their rain boots and sports equipment littered the entry.

"Well, let's see." He obliged her, describing a couple of houses he'd designed and was building. He was enthusiastic as he spoke, but not boastful. He laughed at some of the mistakes he'd made, admitted to trying some new design ideas and not being sure they would appeal. His eyes lit when he spoke, the shine of pride that Madeline found very appealing.

He talked until the food arrived. Madeline was a little embarrassed to see that the buffalo steak she had so cavalierly ordered was the size of a small dinner plate, and the baked potato, loaded with everything in the kitchen, was only slightly smaller.

"Hungry?" Luke asked with a smile, and accepted the small piece of fish with rice and steamed vegetables the waiter handed him.

So that was how he kept so trim. Madeline picked up a knife and fork. "I've never had buffalo."

"Not my favorite," he said as he forked some salad. "All right, we've talked about me—now tell me about you."

"Me?" She paused in the sawing of the buffalo to think. The steak felt like boot leather under her dull knife. "Well," she said, "I am trying to get into high-end properties. So I took a listing for the biggest, ugliest house I have ever seen."

"On purpose?"

"Not really. Well, sort of." She giggled at herself. "I view it as a challenge, a test of my realtor abilities." She drank more wine. "Some might argue it was more of a test of my intelligence."

Luke laughed. "So tell me about this house."

Madeline found herself telling Luke about the monstrosity of architecture that was that house, filled with marble and Greek statues and perhaps the ugliest gold spackling on the walls in the history of housing. She told him it was overpriced in a down market and had sat on the listings for a full year with no movement. She told him how her peers had called her crazy to take it on—out loud and often—but that she was determined. She'd staged open houses, had suffered through tourists and neighbors who had wanted to gawk at the overdone interior design. She'd advertised it on every Internet site she could find, taking calls as far away as Kazakhstan.

"So? Have you had any nibbles?" he asked, seeming genuinely interested.

"Loads! But not at the asking price of three point five million." She thought about her client, Mr. DiNapoli. He'd been suspicious of her, had questioned her credentials and her youth. She, in turn, had prepared a PowerPoint presentation to convince him that she was the woman for the job.

"My biggest problem is the owner," she said. "He did some of the more colorful work on the house himself, and he is adamant that it not be undervalued." She laughed and sawed at her steak again.

"Know the type well. I designed a house for a guy who thought he was an architect, too. Only the things he wanted to do had no basis in sound engineering. Trying to convince him of that was a second job." He took a bite of fish, eyeing her thoughtfully. "Sounds like you have a good life in Orlando. But not a lot of time for fun."

"Fun!" She said it as if she'd never heard the word before, she realized, but Madeline did not generally think about fun.

Luke looked up with surprise again. "You know—letting your hair down."

The mention of letting her hair down made Madeline strangely uncomfortable. "I know." She looked at her steak. "May I have the pepper, please?"

Luke picked up the pepper and handed it to her, but when Madeline reached for it, he didn't let go. "*Fun*, Maddie. Every girl needs a little fun."

"I *know*," she said, and tugged on the pepper, but he refused to relinquish it. "I have fun."

"Like what?"

"Like . . . I have to spell out all the ways I have fun?"

"You have to tell me at least one."

Madeline didn't really have fun. She had precisely the life she'd designed, built, and inhabited. It was carefully structured, no cracks, no possibility for failure. Nevertheless, his comment made her feel a little strange. Maybe it was because Trudi was always telling her she really didn't have much of a life outside of checking in on her mother and working. Or maybe because Madeline recognized that it was true. But that's the way she liked things: no complications. Nothing to go wrong. Nothing to uproot or lose.

She gave one last mighty tug, wrenching the pepper free from his grip. "Okay. I coach soccer."

Luke's eyes rounded. "Okay. Now we're talking. That's impressive—"

"No, no, it's not impressive. I coach little girls—most of them are only five years old. I volunteer and I run up and down the sidelines and yell at them to go the other way."

Luke blinked. His gaze wandered over her again. "You're full of surprises, aren't you? What's your record?"

Madeline grinned. "O and four," she said. "I'm not kidding, we have some serious challenges in the direction department."

Luke's laugh was soft and low. "I love it," he said, and polished off his fish. "Is it just you in Orlando?" he asked casually.

"You're nosy."

"It's called making conversation. You ride into my town on a donut wheel, and I want to know more. My guess is that you've got someone there since you won't say."

Madeline smiled at him, took another sip of wine. She was beginning to feel woozy. "My mom is there."

"Cheater," he said with a grin. "That's not what I meant, but okay. What about a dad?" he asked. "I mean, other than Grant, obviously."

Dad, Dad, Dad . . . Everyone had one but her. "Nope," she said, and looked at her steak. Her willingness to fight the good fight against the buffalo was beginning to evaporate. She picked up the fork and knife and sent to work again. "A stepfather here and there. But they never stuck around too long." She continued her attack another moment then sighed, resigned. She put down her utensils and glanced up—right into Luke's gray eyes. "And I never knew Grant," she blurted. That peculiar heat of shame instantly crawled up her nape following her admission. She always felt it when she admitted to someone that her father never bothered to know her.

To his credit, Luke did not look particularly shocked or appalled. "Well, I'd say that was his great loss."

Madeline didn't know what to say to that; she could only hold Luke's gaze. She could see his sympathy, and for a moment, it felt as if the world were sinking away from them. Madeline did not like to talk about her life; it made her feel uncomfortably exposed. Her experience was that people tended to make judgments about others when they met, privately assessing by whatever criteria they carried around with them. But in that moment, Madeline had a strange need to speak, to say the things that she had carried for so long and so deep, and Luke—Luke looked like someone she could talk to. "I couldn't pick him out of a lineup," she said softly. "I never laid eyes on him. I mean, not since I was like two or something, and I think that was only one time. I never had a card or a phone call from him. He could have been anyone. He could have been the president, and I would be the last to know."

Luke said nothing at first, just looked across the table at her with something swimming around in his eyes.

Well, if that hadn't effectively ruined an otherwise pleasant conversation—

Luke reached across the table and put his hand on top of hers. "I'm sorry, Maddie. You didn't deserve that."

Madeline was taken aback by his empathy. It was impossible to explain the wild range of emotions her absent father had brought up in her this last week. All her life, really. The emptiness, the hopelessness, the never-ending girlish hope that he would come and save her from her life, and the crushing disappointment when he never did. All of that welled in her now, and Madeline glanced blindly at her plate.

Luke's hand slid away from hers. "Buffalo is always tougher than beef," he said. When Madeline looked up, he gestured to her plate. "Buffalo is tougher than beef. And honestly, this place?" He glanced around and shook his head. "I'd stick to something a little simpler, if you know what I mean."

"Good advice," she said, grateful that he had changed the subject. She sipped liberally from her wine and eyed the bread on the table, her belly not satisfied with the few bites of steak she'd managed to chop off.

"I like you, Maddie. Maybe we got off on the wrong foot at the ranch, so let's start over. This is what I've learned about you," he said, and held up his hand. "You've got some guy in the wings," he said, folding over a finger.

"I didn't say that," she protested.

"I know," he said, with a wink. "You're an only child. Until today, that is. You take on ugly houses and losing soccer teams."

"That about sums it up," she said laughingly. "Okay. Is it just you here in Pine River?"

"Wow," Luke said, settling back in his chair. "You just jump right in with both feet, don't you?"

"You did!" she exclaimed.

"That was different," he said laughingly. "No significant other. I have a dad and a brother. My mom died a couple of years ago. What else?"

What else? Things she would never ask. Such as where he'd gone to school, what he did in his spare time, how many women had he slept with . . .

"Aren't you going back to Denver?" she asked.

His smile seemed to dim a little. "It's not that easy for me."

"Why not? You have a job, too. You have the houses you've started, your partnership—"

"I also have a father who has no place to live."

Madeline gasped. "What? No one said anything about anyone being *homeless*."

"I don't mean that," he said with a wave of his hand. "He's rented a little house here in town. What I mean is that this has all been pretty tough on my dad and my brother, and they can't live in that little house forever."

"I'm sorry," she said. *Don't feel bad*, she cautioned herself. They taught you that in negotiation school first thing—take the emotion out of it. "I'm really sorry that all of this has happened to your dad."

"Thank you. You know my great grandfather bought that place? He came here from Tennessee and raised a family there. Then my grandfather took over and raised his family, and then my dad, and now there is my brother and me to carry on the family legacy. My mother died there."

Yep. Madeline felt sorry for Luke. She could see how much the ranch meant to him, how much it hurt him now. How lovely, she thought, to have a home to feel that way about.

"My father made a stupid boneheaded mistake, there is no denying it," he sighed. "I'll be honest, Maddie—I am hoping you can see why it's so important to us to correct that mistake."

Madeline nodded. "I *do* understand. It must be very difficult for you."

"More than I can actually convey," he said. He leaned forward, his gaze locking on hers, his voice soft. "And I would be less than honest if I didn't admit that it's even harder because you . . . well, you get it, right?"

Madeline's belly did a queer little flip. "Get what?"

"Well, like you said, you didn't know Grant. You didn't know about this ranch. It makes it a little harder since it's been in my family for generations."

It clicked then. Things started to make sense to Madeline. She got it—she got why he'd sat down. Why he'd pretended to be interested in her, allowing her to believe that he wasn't one of *those* guys, that he was genuine. And the whole time, he'd been setting her up, just as she'd initially suspected. Oh yeah, she got it. He thought that since Madeline didn't know her father, didn't know about this ranch, hadn't done anything to warrant the inheritance, then therefore she didn't deserve it. While he, on the other hand, had suffered his father's horrible lapse of judgment and *did* deserve it.

He must have sensed that she was not onboard because he quickly said, "Listen, I don't mean that like it sounds—"

"You *don't*?"

"Look, I'm not exactly practiced at this sort of thing, okay? I just think we ought to be able to work this out."

"You and me," she said flatly.

Luke sighed. He pushed his hand through a thick head of hair. "Madeline, you are obviously the most reasonable of the three. Emma is—I honestly don't know what the deal is with her. Libby isn't thinking straight with this family reunion thing. But you seem to get it. And you don't want the ranch."

"Oh, I get it," she said coolly. "You think that your father did something really dumb, but he deserves a second chance. And you must think I am really dumb and that you can be nice to me, and feign interest in me, and I will just eat out of your palm. Well guess what, Luke? I think that because my father abandoned me, because he lived his whole life without knowing if I was okay or not and basically left me to the world to sink or swim, that I deserve everything he had."

She was aware, of course, that she had *never* thought that until this very minute, but that was beside the point.

"That is *not* what I was saying—"

"Luke, hi!"

A woman with honey blond hair had suddenly appeared, startling both Madeline and Luke. She had a baby on her hip, a little girl with beautiful blond curls and a car clutched tightly in her hand. Luke, Madeline noticed, looked shocked. He came awkwardly to his feet, his gaze flicking to Madeline and back to the woman.

"Hi, Julie. I didn't see you."

Madeline stood up, fumbling with her purse.

"I'm sorry, I've interrupted," the woman said apologetically. "I just thought you might want to meet Violet, Luke."

Madeline found her wallet easily in her bag, thanks to her superior skills of organization, and quickly pulled out two twenty-dollar bills. She tossed the bills on to the table.

"Madeline, wait—Julie, this is Madeline Pruett. She's here from Orlando. And this is Julie Daugherty. She and I go way back—"

"Lovely to meet you," Madeline said, and smiled as pleasantly as she could. "Thanks for the company, Luke."

"Don't go," he said quickly.

"Please!" Julie agreed. "Don't let me run you off."

"Not at all. I was just getting ready to leave. I've had as much buffalo as I can saw off and I have a horrible headache," Madeline said, and smiled at the baby to avoid looking at Luke.

"Oh dear," Julie said.

"Pleasure to meet you. Good night." Madeline had to pass Luke to get out, brushing against his hard shell of a body that only served to make her angrier. He put his hand on her arm as she passed, but Madeline walked briskly on, proud of herself for making a bold exit.

But she was fuming, her heart pumping, and she couldn't resist a small pause at the entrance of the restaurant to look back. Luke and the woman were still at the table, only Luke was now holding the little girl. And a gorgeous smile illuminated his entire stupid face.

ELEVEN

Luke's grip of the steering wheel was white-knuckle tight as he drove back to Elm Street. He was furious with himself—he'd handled that business with Madeline with about as much finesse as a toddler handling a fluffy white cat.

He had some very mixed emotions about that woman. On the one hand, there was something very alluring about her. All day long, she'd come across as the only truly reasonable one among them. She asked smart questions, was reserved and thoughtful. And she was *cute*, goddammit. So damn pretty with big blue eyes and dark shaggy bangs. She was a Maddie, definitely. Not a Madeline. If the situation were different, if it had been any other time, any other place on earth, he would be very interested in pursuing her.

But the situation was not different, and on the other hand, Luke thought she would be the toughest of the three in trying to negotiate some sort of deal on the ranch.

What difference did it make? He'd messed it all up. He had no intention of bringing up the ranch when he saw her in the Stakeout. He really had believed she looked as if she could use some company. He had enjoyed the meal, *really* enjoyed it. She was funny, sawing away at a steak big enough to feed a family of four. He'd found her charmingly quirky with her ugly houses and little-girl soccer teams. Then he'd gone and tried to make some sort of point, and *bam*, just like that, he'd messed up any goodwill.

But how was he supposed to know that Grant Tyler had been such a dick of a dad? He might have been able to smooth over his gross mishandling of a delicate situation, but then Julie had shown up with her baby.

Luke had always known that Julie would make some beautiful babies. He'd been so rattled by Julie's sudden appearance with that little girl and the way things had ended with Maddie that he hadn't been able to think what to say when Julie had invited him to dinner later this week.

He'd said okay.

Idiot.

What he found curious was that Julie was at the Stakeout without Brandon. It seemed to him like a lot of work to get a baby out the door and to a restaurant with the only happening bar scene in town. But when he'd asked Julie about her husband, she'd blushed and said he hadn't been around much lately. Work, she said. Luke really didn't know Brandon but in passing, but he knew this—if he, Luke, had that wife and that kid, he'd be around all the damn time.

Luke was lost in thought when he turned onto Elm Street, but then, his heart suddenly plummeted: a fire truck and an ambulance were in front of the little house, their flashing lights illuminating the night. A fear clutched at his throat, the fleeting thought that this was it, Leo's time had come. He sped up, flying up the gravel drive. He leapt onto the porch as two firemen came out, their bags on their backs, pulling off their latex gloves. "What happened?" he shouted, but didn't wait for their answer. He all but tore the screen door off to get inside.

Two paramedics were crammed into the tiny living room, shielding his view. "Leo!" Luke shouted, louder than he intended, but his heart was racing, his breath suddenly restricted.

"Dude, I'm okay," Leo called up to him from somewhere on the floor.

One of the paramedics turned around. "Hey, Luke!"

It was Greg Durbin, a big lovable oaf of a guy Luke had known from his high school days. He was a paramedic now, and he stood up, hoisting his bag onto his back. "How the hell are you, man? Back in town for good or just visiting?"

"I—what happened?" Luke asked.

"Oh, sorry," Greg said, and glanced over his shoulder. "It's all good now, but Leo had another seizure."

"I like to call it an interpretive dance," Leo said.

Greg shifted; Luke could see Leo on the floor, his useless legs bent at weird angles, his arms crossed like chicken wings across his chest. The other paramedic was checking his blood pressure. Luke's dad, with his jaw tightly clenched, was on the floor with Leo, holding his head.

Luke knelt by his brother, seeking a bent hand.

"I guess we need to get you to Durango, buddy," Dad bit out.

"Excellent! A road trip," Leo said. "Okay, okay, Dad, you can let go now. It's over. Fellas, as much as I've enjoyed this little party down here on a carpet that smells like cat piss, it's time for *Project Runway*."

With Greg and the other paramedic's help, they picked Leo off the floor and strapped him back into his chair. His muscles had atrophied, but he was still a big guy, and it was not an easy task, especially in a small, crowded room.

When Leo was secure, and the television was on, Luke followed Greg out onto the porch. "What do you mean, another seizure?" he asked Greg, dragging his fingers through his hair. "How many times have you been here?"

"Lemme think." Greg squinted across the yard. "Seems to happen about once every three or four weeks. It's a tricky thing, getting that antiseizure medicine right," he said, shifting his gaze to Luke again. "You really ought to get him to see someone in Durango about it. These doctors in Pine River, they don't deal with stuff as complicated as Leo." He leaned in and said low, "Between you and me? I'm not sure your old man gets it, you know?"

Yes, Luke knew. It wasn't that his dad didn't get it—but sometimes, he had a hard time facing the truth.

"You really have to get those meds straightened out, Luke."

Luke sighed. "We will," he promised.

They chatted for a few minutes, catching up. When Greg left, Luke went back inside the house. He could see his father in the kitchen at the tiny little table, his elbows on the table, his head between his hands.

"You are *not* going to send *that* down the runway," Leo said to the TV.

As Leo was clearly occupied, Luke slipped into the kitchen. He put his hand on his dad's shoulder as he walked by on his way to the fridge. He retrieved two beers, handed one to his father, drank from the other and said, "So that's been happening a lot? Grand mal seizures in the living room?"

"Some," his dad admitted. "It's a problem with his medicine. Some of what they are giving him for the MND can cause seizures. So then they give him antiseizure medicine. It's a balancing act. I don't know why they can't get it right." His father tipped the beer bottle back into his mouth. "Gotta get him to Durango, that's for sure." He stood up, pushing back his chair and moved into the tiny kitchen and began to clear a space in the sink. "Right now, I need to get him something to eat."

Luke stepped out of the kitchen and stood in the doorway, watching his father, waiting for him to say more, to ask for help. When he didn't, Luke asked, "Do you want me to take him to Durango?"

His father paused, braced his hands against the edge of the sink and stared down a moment. "No, Luke," he said calmly, and turned his head to look at his son. "I don't want you to take him anywhere. What I want is for you to go back to Denver. I want you to go back to your life. You can't fix things here. And I don't want us to feel like a burden to you."

A tiny but sharp twinge of guilt flashed hot through Luke. He looked at the back of Leo's head, just visible over the back of his chair. "You're not a burden." He said it without thinking, just as he'd said it many times before. Families weren't burdens. Families were the most important things in the world. They had each other's back. Okay, usually Luke had theirs, but still.

"Yeah, we are," his father said firmly. He turned fully around from the sink, folded his arms across his big chest and stared at Luke as if he was silently daring him to deny it. "You may not say it right to my face, but everything about you says that we are a burden."

"What are you talking about?" Luke demanded. He'd been so careful not let anything like that show—

"You know what I'm talking about. All your life, you've had to come home and save the day. When you were in high school, you missed the state title because we had cows stuck up at eleven thousand feet dropping from altitude sickness. Ernest and Leo and I couldn't get them all down by ourselves. We needed you. You had to drop out of college for a time when Leo got sick because God knows your mother and I couldn't deal with it. And then there wasn't any money to put you back in, so you had to get a job on top of your studies. Then your mother got sick, and here you came again, to clean up after me and make sure Leo was cared for. I was useless, I know it. Those are just the big moments that come to mind, but there have been so many other times in between that I can't even count them anymore. I just know that you have always been the one who had to uproot your life, leave your dreams and ambitions behind to take care of us. And the toll that's taken on you is beginning to show."

"I haven't complained," Luke said defensively.

"Maybe you should have," his dad said stubbornly. "Think about it, son. Because of us, it took you six years to finish your degree—a degree I couldn't even help you with. And now, you've started a business, you're working on your MBA, but here you had to come again, and it's in the tone of your voice, the way you carry yourself. We're a burden and it's starting to show on you. So I want you to go on home. I can get Leo to Durango. Patti will come around and help when I need her."

"Maybe *you* see yourself as a burden, but I never said that," Luke snapped.

His father sighed wearily and stood a moment as if he wasn't sure what to say. But then he walked to where Luke stood, put both hands on Luke's shoulders and said softly, "Look here, Luke, I don't need you here. Now don't get me wrong, son—I love you and I want to see you. But I don't want to see the resentment grow any more than it has. I don't need you to come down here and save the day."

Luke was stunned. His father squeezed his shoulders then moved back to the sink. As Luke watched, his dad found the bowl he was looking for in the sink and turned on the water, squirted dish soap into it, and began to scrub it down.

Luke was hardly aware that he had turned around and had walked into the living room. He found himself staring out the window, his mind whirling through all the times he'd dropped everything to come home to *save the day* as his father had said. Yes, Luke was angry. And he would have been a whole lot angrier had it not been for one thought: His father was right.

He *did* resent it.

It wasn't that Luke didn't love his family—God no, he loved them more than anything in this world. The resentment had more to do with what he'd missed because of them, with the fact that so much had befallen them and yet he remained unscathed. He resented that his aunt had called him while he was on a date, and he resented himself for having the balls to resent her for it. But mostly, *mostly* he resented the hell out of the fact that his family had been steadily disintegrating for the last ten years and the universe would *not let up*.

But the resentment that welled up in him was tamped back down when he looked at the back of Leo's bent head. Maybe life hadn't been fair to them, but Luke would do anything for Dad and Leo. He truly feared for his family, with the loss of Leo looming so large before them. It was like a dark shadow following them around, always there, spreading just a little more each day.

As if he knew Luke was standing behind him, warring with his conscience, Leo said, "Come on, Luke, you *have* to see this! Tonight is unconventional materials night. I *hate* the unconventional materials challenge, but you know what I love? Heidi Klum." He grinned as Luke walked around and sat in Dad's La-Z-Boy beside him. "Lay down on ze bed," he said in an awful German accent. "I will have my vay vith you."

"Is that supposed to be Heidi?"

"That's supposed to be Heidi with *me*," Leo said, and turned his gaze to a string of models strutting down the runway in what looked like glass dresses. "So how was the Stakeout?"

"Okay. The food still sucks."

"Any women?"

Luke honestly hadn't really noticed, which was unusual for him. "I saw one of Grant's daughters. The one from Orlando." Funny how she was still on his mind.

"Who, Blue Eyes?"

Luke looked at his brother. "How do you remember everything?"

"Dude, I keep telling you—my brain is a machine. Here's the way I see it—they sent the *attractive* daughters in to mess with our heads."

"What, you think they have some ugly stepsisters lurking in the background?"

Leo laughed. "You never know. So it was Blue Eyes, huh?"

Luke smiled. Leo definitely had a steel-trap of a memory. "Yes, Blue Eyes, also known as Madeline Pruett."

"So what does she look like?" Leo asked. "And don't leave out a single detail. Start with her boobs."

Luke playfully swatted his brother's arm. "You're such a damn pig, Leo."

"Calling me names will not remove the swagger from this swine! Okay, tell me—and don't hold out on me."

Luke sighed. He looked at his little brother's shining blue eyes. "She has a respectable rack and a nice ass," he obliged him. That much was true. Her derriere was heart-shaped and a little bouncy, just like Luke liked them.

"*Excellent!*" Leo said, his eyes lighting. "What else? Thin? Round mound of fun? What's her personality like?"

"She's average build," Luke said. "Pretty." She had dark, shiny hair that she had released from the death grip of Grok's claw. He'd had an insane urge to touch it tonight. But as to what she was like? He still didn't know. She was private. Maybe a little standoffish, but not in a bad way—more like a kid who didn't know which group to join on a playground. "She's a little uptight," he said.

"That's the best kind," Leo said instantly. "You get to peel back one delicious layer at a time. Fun for everyone."

"I'm not peeling any layers," Luke said, shooting Leo a look.

"What about the rest of her?"

"She's pretty," Luke admitted. She had intelligent blue eyes and an expressive mouth. But it was the eyes, shrewd and a little innocent at the same time, that he kept thinking about. When she smiled, they glittered. "She's obviously got some issues."

Leo snorted. "Don't we all."

"And I don't think she's letting go of the ranch without a fight. Neither is Libby, for that matter," he added with a shrug. "Emma? I think she could take it or leave it."

Just then, their father appeared carrying a jug with a big silly straw.

"Dinner is served!" Leo said happily. "What's it tonight, Dad? Liquid mac and cheese?"

"It's a protein shake," his father said, and attached the jug to a strap he'd rigged onto the side of Leo's chair.

"Bo-ring!" Leo sang out, but clamped his mouth down onto the end of the silly straw that looped and twisted right up to his mouth. He took a long drink as his father settled in on the couch, his gaze on the television screen as more models paraded down the runway.

"Anyone else there tonight?" Leo asked.

"As a matter of fact, Julie Daugherty showed up."

"Ho! There's a blast from the past!"

"Not a good one," Dad muttered.

"So? Did you check her hands?" Leo asked.

"What?"

"Her hands," Leo said again, and waved his lobster claw of a hand at Luke. "Her *ring* finger."

"No, I didn't check it—why?"

"Dude." Leo waggled his brows. "You mean you haven't heard? Word is that she and Brandon are on the skids."

Luke snorted. Brandon would have to be a complete moron to mess that up. "You are my sole source of information, Leo. So where'd you hear that? From Dani?"

"No, actually, from Marisol," Leo said, pausing to sip from his straw. "She says Brandon is a prick and was hitting on her at her son's Little League game. I want to withhold judgment, because every guy wants to hit on Marisol, right? But she seemed pretty adamant that he is a player and has something going on the side. And Julie isn't putting up with that. I hear she kicked him out."

Julie, free again? Luke's head began to spin with just the idea.

His father heaved himself off the couch, frowned down at Leo and said, "On that note, I'm going out to the shed."

"Thanks for the totally nutritious but boring dinner, Dad!" Leo called out after his father.

Dad muttered something under his breath; a moment later they heard the back door slam.

"We'll come back to Julie. What about the ranch?" Leo asked, his joviality suddenly gone.

Luke sighed and shook his head. "It's a huge mess, Leo. I think we might have to face the fact that it's a lost cause and move on. We haven't any legal leg to stand on."

"Move *on*? Who are you and what have you done with my brother?" Leo demanded. "You can't give up, Luke. What about Dad?"

"What do you mean, what about Dad?"

Leo groaned as Heidi Klum's face danced across the television screen. "Look, I'm eventually going to get sick of this house and *Project Runway* and the Denver Broncos, and that's it, man, I'm outta here. Dad can't live here, no way. He'd go nuts. You have to try again."

Luke's chest constricted at Leo's way of stating that he would not live as long as his father. He could scarcely bear to think of that day. "I'm doing the best I know to do," he said.

"You gotta mix it up then."

Luke rolled his eyes. "I want to mix it up all right."

Leo nodded in that crooked way of his. He turned his attention to the television. "Hey, do you remember that classic Super Bowl between the Cowboys and the Dolphins?"

"No," Luke said.

"The seventies," Leo reminded him.

"No, I don't remember a Super Bowl from the seventies. I wasn't alive in the seventies."

"Okay, so the Dolphins lost," Leo blithely continued. "You know what happened to the Dolphins after they lost that one, right?"

Leo had an annoying habit of changing directions midstream. He was also fond of reliving great moments in sports in minute detail. Luke shook his head.

"Okay, well, they had a decent running game, but the passing game sucked. They made it to the Super Bowl on the strength of their defense."

"That's great," Luke muttered.

"No, no, you don't get it. They were playing these teams that had sucky offenses and their defense was kick-ass. But then they got to the Super Bowl and went up against the Cowboys, and they found out what a really good offense was like. I mean, Roger Staubach, anyone? And when the Cowboy offense shut down the Dolphin defense, all they had left was this Mickey Mouse offense that wasn't working. So the next year, they said, wait, we're going about this all wrong! We have to do what *those* guys are doing and build an offense! We have to bow to a superior defense and learn to win with a new offense."

"Are we going somewhere with this?" Luke asked.

Leo sighed as if Luke were taxing him with limited intelligence. "Dude, they had to change their game plan if they were going to win the big one. They had to go on offense instead of defense. Hello—Homecoming Ranch? Now do you get it?"

"Did they win?"

"No!" Leo said. "But they had the right idea."

A slow grin spread across Luke's face. "You're bat-shit crazy, you know that?" he asked. "Yeah, I get it. In your own ridiculous way, you are telling me I need to change the way I am approaching the heirs. Why couldn't you just say that?"

"That's no fun," Leo said, grinning again. "Glad to see some sunlight got down in the weeds growing in your head. Okay, now shut up—Heidi's going to tell us who is on the chopping block."

As Heidi Klum announced someone would be out, Luke looked at his little brother.

Man, he loved that guy.

TWELVE

The ringtone of Madeline's phone went off so loudly and so close to her ear that her heart almost went through her chest. She fumbled with her black sleeping mask, tearing it off her head so quickly that she took what felt like a hank of hair along with it. She found the offending phone on the pillow next to her head, where she must have dropped it last night when she'd collapsed like a rag doll into bed.

"Hello," she said, her voice hoarse with sleep.

"*Mad!*" Trudi shouted. "What are you doing?"

"Sleeping," Madeline croaked, and sat up. She'd pulled the lodge draperies shut last night, and only a thin beam of light was breaking through the dark. She leaned over and flipped on the bedside light. "How did you get through? I couldn't get a signal all day yesterday."

"I dunno. I have you on speed dial," Trudi said, as if that explained the technology behind cell phones. "Are you still in *bed?*"

"Yes. Why do you say it like that?"

"It's *noon*, Madeline!"

Madeline gasped and threw the covers back. "It's *noon?*" They were supposed to meet at one o'clock at the ranch to pick up where they'd left off yesterday.

"Not where you are, silly! It's ten in Colorado. Why are you so out of it?"

"I don't know. I've been so tired."

"Stress, obviously! *Well?* I am *dying* to know—did you meet your sisters?"

"Yes, God yes," Madeline said, yawning.

"*And?*"

"And . . ." She absently scratched her thigh. "And they are nothing like what I thought they would be."

"Okay. Tell me everything," Trudi said.

"I'm not sure what there is to say. Libby is cute. She has this really curly dark hair, and she's nice. But she's kind of unrealistic. And Emma is . . . well, she's beautiful. She has long blond hair and dresses like a fashionista. And she's so thin." She paused, thinking about how thin Emma was. "I think she might be an alcoholic."

"Wow, really? Did you smell it on her?"

"No," Madeline said. "I actually never saw her take a drink. But she kept talking about wanting one."

"No offense, but I think I might want more than one in that situation. So what did you guys do? Did they bring pictures? Are they married? Kids?"

"I don't know, really," Madeline said. "We met and then basically, we argued about what to do with the ranch."

"No way! Why would you do that? Why didn't you *talk* first?"

Now Madeline wished she had. "There was a lot going on. It's really weird doing the get-to-know-you thing when you're sitting on a huge ranch you've supposedly inherited. My mind was elsewhere." Madeline closed her eyes. The moment she did, an image of Luke's gray eyes and slightly lopsided smile began to swim in her mind's eye. She quickly opened her eyes. "It's so damn complicated, Trudi," Madeline said wearily, and told her best friend everything she could remember about the meeting at the ranch—with Trudi interrupting often, demanding details of what the ranch looked like, a description of the house, the details of the women she insisted on calling Madeline's sisters, down to what they were wearing.

When Madeline had filled her in on everything she could possibly think of, including running into Luke at the Stakeout the night before, Trudi let out a low whistle. "Wow. What are you going to do?"

What *was* she going to do? That was the million-dollar question. Madeline didn't like this feeling of not knowing what to do, or whom to do it with. She wanted to be somewhere where she knew the rules and what the day would hold. Where she dined on chicken, not buffalo, and her shoes were perfect for running around town. "Come home, I guess."

The words had fallen off her tongue the moment they'd popped into her head.

"Are you *crazy?*" Trudi shouted. "What's the matter with you? Madeline, it is an *enormous* opportunity for you. First, it's the closest thing to paternal heritage as you've ever had. Second, has it occurred to you that they might need someone just like you to sort it all out?"

"Third, have you forgotten that I have a job?"

"You have a job where others can fill in for you for *days*. You have a savings account that could float the national debt. When's the last time you took a vacation, anyway?" Trudi demanded. "Don't think, I'll tell you—it's been three years. Three *years*, Madeline. What is one week going to do to your life? What is one week going to do to the DiNapoli listing, which I promise you isn't moving any quicker than when you left? What's one week to your mother, for Chrissakes? If you aren't there next week she'll find a new boyfriend and move on."

"Hey!" Madeline said. "Thanks a lot! You make it sound as if I'm not necessary for anyone or anything."

"You are very necessary to *me*. You are necessary to your office and to a couple of other people. But you are also someone who lives in a bubble—"

"God, not the bubble again," Madeline groaned.

"Yes, the bubble!" Trudi snapped. "You live in it, and you will die in it if you're not careful! You've had something really extraordinary happen and you ought to at least hang around for more than twenty-four hours before you run. Promise me you will stay outside that goddamn bubble for one week, Madeline. Stay long enough to at least know if your sister is an alcoholic or if the other one is as young and dumb as she sounds."

"You aren't giving me any credit, Trudi," Madeline snapped back. "I've checked it out. There is nothing for me here but a phantom dad, two women I don't know, and a huge mess of an inheritance. That's not something you can box up and put on the shelf in a couple of days. No," she said quickly when Trudi tried to argue. "I know what I'm doing."

Trudi sighed with resignation. "You always do this, Mad. You always run away."

"I am *not* running away!"

"Yeah, you are. You would rather let something like that ranch— which sounds gorgeous by the way—slip through your fingers than deal with the people involved because you are so afraid of rejection."

"*Ohmigod!*" Madeline cried. "Will you please stop psychoanalyzing me? I am *not* afraid of rejection. I am being practical!"

"Whatever," Trudi said dismissively. "I have to go. I don't have time to fix your life, I've got my own. Oh, before I forget—Stephen called Rick to talk about you. He really likes you, Madeline, and he doesn't understand why you stopped liking him. He said he's been talking to that lawyer friend in Denver and has some information for you. Call him!"

"Leave it alone, Trudi."

"No, I will not leave it alone. I love you that much, Madeline Pruett, I love you like a sister, and I am *not* afraid of rejection. I'll talk to you later." She hung up.

Madeline stared at her phone and muttered a few choice words about Trudi Feinstein's bossiness under her breath. She was not afraid of rejection, for Pete's sake. She was seventy-five percent sure she wasn't.

She called her mother to report in. Her mother was probably on pins and needles wanting to know what had happened. . . .

No one answered.

She frowned; she could hear Trudi's voice in her head saying, *I told you so.*

Madeline tossed the cell phone onto the bed and padded across the bearskin rug to the drapes. She opened them to a bright, clear day.

She had to admit, the sky was a different, richer shade of blue than in Orlando.

Below her, people were milling about on the main street, and Madeline's stomach growled. She would grab a bite in the café downstairs and then head out to the ranch to try and come to some agreement with Libby and Emma.

⊱┈◆┈○┈◆┈⊰

When Madeline made her way downstairs, she was surprised to see that Dani was not wearing a Guayabera shirt today, but rather, a sweatshirt that said *Pine River Eagles*.

"Hello!" Dani sang out as Madeline entered the small café. "I'd about given you up for dead. How's your head?"

"Better, thanks."

"You keep taking those aspirin and drink lots of water. You'll adjust to the altitude in a couple of days. Want something to eat before you head back out to Homecoming today?"

Madeline had been about to say she wouldn't be here in a couple of days, but was drawn up short by the fact that Dani knew where she was going. Dani laughed at her look of surprise. "I'll just bet you think I'm one of those small-town busybodies you read about in beach novels. Well, I'm not. It so happens that Jackson Crane was in for breakfast."

"Oh."

"Just take a seat where you like, sweetie," Dani said. "I'll be right back to take your order.

"Thanks," Madeline said, and turned around—and almost collided with a table inhabited by Luke and an older man.

She gasped; Luke glanced at his wristwatch. "Sleep in?"

"Wow, Luke, this is the fourth coincidental meeting in less than forty-eight hours. Did you think I wouldn't notice?"

"I'm having lunch with my dad. Dad, this is Maddie Pruett," he said as he reached into his back pocket for his wallet.

"Madeline," she said curtly.

110

"Madeline," he said with a polite incline of his head. "This is Bob Kendrick."

"Pleasure to meet you, Miss Pruett." He was an older version of Luke—his hair had grayed and dark circles shadowed his eyes, but they were the same gray, thick-lashed eyes as Luke's, the same strong chin, the same broad shoulders. "I don't know about the other meetings, but this is my favorite breakfast joint."

She eyed Luke suspiciously. "How did you know I was staying here?"

Luke smiled as he slowly stood up, towering over her, standing so close that she could see the pearl in the buttons of his shirt. He fished a couple of bills out of his pocket and tossed them down on the table. "I didn't. It's lunchtime. My dad and I came for lunch. Try the Cobb salad; it's the best thing on the menu. Dad, are you ready?"

"I am," he said, and stood up, too, also towering over Madeline. He fit a cowboy hat on his head and gave Madeline a nod as he walked out.

Behind him, Luke leaned in and whispered, "Pine River is a small town, Blue Eyes. People run into each other." He walked on. At the entrance to the café, he paused to pick up a toothpick. "Thanks, Dani!" he called toward the kitchen, and went out without looking back at Madeline.

Madeline watched him leave—okay, watched his hips leave—and feeling fluttery again, she sat heavily at a table next to the one he and his father had just vacated. As she tried to sort out his angle this time, she absently ordered the Cobb salad.

Luke was right. It was excellent.

On her way to Homecoming Ranch, Madeline tried her mother again, catching her on the third ring. "Mom! It's Madeline!"

"Hi honey," her mother said. "What's up?"

"I thought you'd want to hear about Colorado."

"Who?"

"Colorado! You know, the ranch I inherited?"

"Oh, that's right," her mother said. "Hey, that reminds me, I've been meaning to ask you about that. Did you ask them about the child support?"

Madeline's improving mood took a turn south. "No," she said. "We barely got past the fact that we had inherited the ranch. I met the sisters."

"Oh yeah?" her mother said, sounding less interested.

"They seem okay."

"I guess they're happy about the inheritance," her mother said with a slightly bitter tone.

Funny, but Madeline didn't know how they felt. "I don't really know. So far, we've only discussed the logistics."

"Well, you need to discuss with someone the fact that Grant Tyler never paid me more than a few bucks of child support. There has to be someone you can ask."

Mom made it sound like there was a bucket of money and all Madeline had to do was ask the keeper of the bucket for it. "Okay, Mom," Madeline said. She was coming up on the road to the ranch. "Listen, I have to go. I'm going to lose you in a minute."

"Well call me when you hear something."

"Bye Mom," Madeline said, and clicked off the phone, but she didn't let go of it. She continued to hold it. Tight. So tight that her hand began to ache. She wanted to crush that damn phone and hurl it out the window. But she settled it for throwing it in the passenger seat.

Why did she bother? It was always that way with her mother—it was never about Madeline, it was about Clarissa. It had been that way forever, and Madeline wasn't foolish enough to think her mother would ever change. Sometimes, she wished she could be free of her mother. Just . . . *free*. But the wish always disappeared in the reality of her situation, and the guilt would creep in. If Madeline was gone, who would take care of Clarissa? Who would go by and clean her house and make sure she hadn't drunk herself into some stupor, or know that she'd gone off with some man and worry about her?

Her mother's indifference was intolerable.

She stewed about it all the way out to the ranch.

At the house again, Madeline saw only one car in the drive. She got out, looked up at the blue sky and took a deep breath of pine-scented air. It was so fresh, so clean. So unlike Orlando.

With a sigh, she dipped into the backseat to grab her bag. When she emerged, she saw the dogs. They were coming out from beneath the porch, stretching long, shaking off their coats, as if they'd been waiting for her to arrive.

The biggest one, a black dog with an enormous square head, was the first to advance, wandering over, his snout in the air. Madeline stood very still, hoping he'd walk past. But he didn't—he stopped to have a good sniff of her shoes and trousers. "Nice doggy," she murmured.

The dog behind the big one began to wag his tail when she spoke, and trotted over, nosing in beside the larger one. The other two followed a moment later, and all four of them sniffed her, crowding her. "All of you. All of you are nice doggies, very nice doggies," Madeline said, backing up against the car as the dogs closed in. The smallest of them sat up and put his paws on her thigh, and the big one had the audacity to stick his snout in her crotch.

"Okay, okay," she said, stiffening. "That's it. Shoo. Shoo, shoo, shoo—"

"*Hey!* Get back to the garage!" she heard Libby shout.

Madeline's head jerked up along with the dogs' heads. Four tails began to wag, and the dogs bounded around to the corner of the garage, where Libby had just emerged, carrying a plastic bucket and a mop. She was dressed in cutoff jeans and a Grateful Dead T-shirt. Her hair was piled on top of her head, and she'd parked a pair of sunglasses there, too, as if she'd only just arrived and had rushed to the garage to get the mop.

"Go, get!" she said sternly, and the dogs loped off, their tails high.

Libby smiled sympathetically at Madeline, who was still plastered up against her car. "Their bark is worse than their bite, you know. You really don't need to be afraid of them."

"I'm not afraid," Madeline said, although it was apparent that she was. She relaxed a little, leaned down to brush dog slobber off her trousers. It didn't brush off. She glanced at the bucket and mop Libby held. "Was there an accident or something?"

"Huh?" Libby asked, and then looked down. She laughed. "No. I'm just helping out." To Madeline's puzzled look she added, "I told Jackson I would clean up. You know, for the Johnson reunion. That house hasn't been cleaned in I don't know how long."

"Can't he get someone to come and clean it?"

"I don't mind," Libby said, and started for the house.

"Are you by yourself?" Madeline called after her.

"Just me!" Libby said airily, and bounded up the stairs, disappearing inside.

Madeline looked around. Where was everyone?

She followed Libby into the house and found her in the kitchen. The tiled bar was covered with white plastic bags. Madeline peeked into one—it was full of cleaning supplies. From the look of it, Libby was preparing for a full-scale scrub down. Madeline knew all about that—she'd had to do it to her mother's house more than once. "Wow," she said. "When you clean, you *clean*."

At the sink, where she was filling a bucket, Libby merely smiled at Madeline's comment. Her sunglasses were on the counter beside her now, and next to them, a folded apron. When Libby had enough water in the bucket, she picked up the apron and wrapped it around her waist.

"This seems like a lot of work for one person," Madeline said. "Wouldn't you rather wait until we, you know . . . decide something?"

Libby's hands suddenly went to her hips. "I've decided. I'm staying."

Madeline wasn't sure what she meant. "In Pine River?"

"No, here. At this house." Libby looked at Madeline as if she expected her to argue. "I've made my decision just like you've made yours. Not that yours is wrong, Madeline. I am sure you are doing what is best for you. But I am doing what is best for me." She began to dig through the plastic bags as if she were searching for something.

"You're going to stay out here? Alone?" Madeline echoed incredulously. "How? Wait," she said, her anxiety kicking into gear. "Did you guys decide without me? Where is Emma?" she asked, glancing around, almost expecting her to slink in through some door with a highball glass in hand.

"On her way to L.A." Libby ducked the mop into the bucket.

"*What?* What do you mean? What about all of *this?*" Madeline cried, gesturing to the house.

"She called me late last night and told me she'd see me later. Her boyfriend was waiting for her in Durango and he wanted to get out of there." Libby did not seem particularly disturbed about it.

But it made no sense to Madeline. "That's crazy! And irresponsible!" she exclaimed.

"That's also Emma for you."

"What does it even mean? Why would anyone be so—insensitive?"

Libby thought about that for a moment. "I don't know. Maybe she's had too many disappointments in her life."

"We've *all* had disappointments," Madeline pointed out.

Libby shrugged. "I just mean that things haven't always turned out like Emma thought they would, and she puts up walls."

Madeline snorted, ignoring the niggling thought that she did the same thing. "Do things turn out for anyone like they thought they would?"

For some reason, Libby laughed at that. "God no." She wrung the mop free of excess water, clearly all right with Emma having decamped.

"So have you two always been close?" Madeline asked curiously.

"Who, me and Emma?" Libby snorted at that. "Not at all. She's in California and I'm here. . . ." Her voice trailed off as if that was explanation enough.

"What does she do?" Madeline asked.

"She's an event planner or something like it."

"An event planner! But that's *great*," Madeline said. "She could handle the Johnson—"

"No, she's not going to do it," Libby said firmly. "She's not coming back."

"But . . . but we agreed to meet with Jackson at one o'clock—"

"Oh, I forgot. Jackson had an emergency in Denver," Libby said, avoiding Madeline's gaze.

"Does no one call?" Madeline asked. "What are we supposed to do, clean the damn house for Jackson? I am sorry, but this is *not* how people act! You don't just take off and not show up without at least *some* warning."

"You're losing your temper," Libby said, as if Madeline hadn't figured that out.

"Yes, I am! Because I am really, really angry right now!" Madeline sat down on a stool, braced her hands against her knees. "You can't just leave people hanging," she said, her voice a little softer. She was short of breath, her heart beating with frustration and the feeling that things were spiraling out of control already.

"I don't disagree with you," Libby said as she began to mop the kitchen floor. "But one thing is certain—the Johnsons are coming. With or without us, the Johnsons are coming. So I am going to help Jackson get ready for that. You can help too, if you want. Whatever you want to do."

"What I want is to settle this and go home," Madeline muttered.

Libby paused and looked directly at her. "Nothing is keeping you from going back to your life, Madeline. You can leave now, like everyone else."

Madeline was shocked. She'd come all this way, and for what? She tried to read Libby. Why was this all okay with her? "Don't *you* need to get back to your life?"

Libby's smile faded. She turned around and resumed mopping. With a vengeance.

"You have a job, right?" Madeline asked.

"Not at the moment."

"Oh. I didn't realize."

"I know, because you didn't bother to ask anything of us yesterday. If you had, I would have told you that I left my job."

"That's not fair," Madeline said. "I'd just flown in from Orlando. It's all been a little overwhelming, to be honest."

"Yes. For all of us," Libby agreed. "But at least we tried to get to know you. You just weren't very receptive."

When Libby put it like that, it sounded so rude. "I didn't—I wasn't . . ." Madeline stopped. Any excuse she offered would be seen as that—an excuse. Madeline felt tired all of a sudden, and slumped on the barstool, her chin propped on her fist. "You quit your job yesterday?"

"Umm . . ." Libby seemed to hesitate. "No, I left it a few weeks ago. When Jackson told me I had inherited Homecoming Ranch, I decided this would be my job." She stopped mopping and brushed a stray ringlet from her brow.

"What job did you leave?" Madeline asked.

"I was a clerk in the sheriff's office. I went to work there right out of high school. A very long time ago," she said, and stabbed the mop into the bucket again.

To quit a job without another one lined up, for something entirely uncertain, was so far out of Madeline's world she could not even grasp it.

"My dad left me a ranch," Libby said. "And I intend to make something of it." She started to mop again. "If you don't want to do that, I totally understand. But I do."

"So that's it?" Madeline demanded. "You stay, Emma takes off without a word, and I do what, pretend I never heard of Homecoming Ranch?"

"If that's what you want. Look, Madeline, it seems pretty simple to me," Libby said, and paused, stacking her hands on top of the handle. "We are committed to the Johnson family reunion. You can stay and help with that, or you can go home. It's totally up to you. I really do understand where you're coming from, so go back to Orlando if that's what you need to do. No one is going to think any less of you."

So why then did Libby sound a little accusatory? "I'm not trying to ditch you, Libby," Madeline insisted.

"I didn't say that. It's just that . . ." She paused and looked at the window. "I have a different perspective. I've had a different life than you. This place," she said, looking around at the fading wallpaper and the decades of grime, "means something to me. It feels like a place where I could make a difference."

"By hosting reunions?" Madeline asked skeptically.

Libby's face darkened. "By doing something for me. I don't expect you to understand. But I'm not ready to throw in the towel just yet."

Okay. All right. Libby was not budging. Madeline watched Libby resume her work and debated what she should do. She could go, as every fiber in her body was screaming at her to do. Just go now, leave this absurdity. But if she left, that would leave Libby to deal with everything. That would mean Libby would scrub floors without anyone but Jackson Crane to help her.

Madeline stared at the wall, breathing deeply to quiet her heart, trying to decide what it was she should do.

"Hand me the paper towels?" Libby asked.

Madeline sighed. She searched the bags until she found them and handed them to Libby. "Okay," she said, and shrugged out of her jacket. She unbuttoned the sleeves of her shirt, and rolled them up. "I give in. What can I do?"

Libby eyed Madeline skeptically. "Are you sure?"

"Come on, before I change my mind," Madeline said impatiently.

"You're not exactly dressed for it," Libby pointed out. "Can you put on some jeans first?"

"I don't have jeans."

"You don't have *jeans*?"

"I *have* jeans. I don't have them here. I only flew in to—" Madeline stopped. "I don't have jeans," she said flatly.

"Well . . ." Libby glanced around, clearly flummoxed by the lack of jeans for Madeline. "You could dust the blinds and the baseboards if you don't mind a little dust."

"I don't mind."

Libby put her mop aside to dig into one of the Walmart sacks. She withdrew a stack of towels held together by a paper sleeve. She pulled one towel out and tossed it at Madeline. "There's some furniture polish in the garage. I can get it if you are worried about the dogs—"

"I'm not worried about the dogs," Madeline said pertly. "I'll get it." She walked out of the kitchen, very worried about the dogs.

THIRTEEN

Luke noticed that it looked like rain was coming in from the east as he drove up to the ranch house. He pulled into the carport, opened the door of his Bronco and stepped out, and heard a bloodcurdling scream from the garage. It scared the life out of him—he bolted inside, expecting to find body parts or something just as heinous.

What he found was Madeline, her back against the wall of the garage, wedged in behind the rototiller, the mowing tractor, and several boxes of old tools Luke had once meant to take into Goodwill. He looked wildly about for the intruder or bear or whatever had prompted such a piercing scream. "It's there!" Madeline shrieked, pointing across the garage to some shelves.

Roscoe, the beagle, had his nose in the corner. Reggie and Rufus, the littermates, were lying in the middle of the garage absently looking about, as usual. And Reba, his mother's little terrier, was behind Roscoe, barking fiercely.

Luke started for the corner.

"No, wait!" Madeline shouted. "It's huge! Don't get too close!"

What was it, a bear cub? Luke didn't like to think that, for where there was a bear cub, there was a mama bear close behind. But it seemed a little early in the season for cubs. He stepped over the dogs, moved some old paint cans aside, then a box of his mother's

Tupperware. A rat darted past him, to a hole in the siding, and out of the garage. Roscoe—by far the smartest of the canine pack—raced out the open garage door after it. Reba stayed behind to examine the hole with her nose.

Luke put the box down and turned around. Madeline's arms were splayed against the wall, her hair had something that looked like a cobweb in it, and she looked terrified. "It's okay," he said. "It was just a rat."

"A *what?*" she shrieked, and somehow managed to press herself even flatter against the wall with such a gasp that Reggie's tail began to wag.

Luke held up both hands. "Take a breath," he said, and Madeline tried to do that. "Take another one. Put your hands on your knees and bend over and catch your breath. And calm down—it was just a rat."

"*Just* a rat?" she said as she bent over. "What do you mean, *just* a rat! That was no rat, Luke! It was the size of a cat! Where is it? Where did it go?"

"Outside. You're safe. He wasn't going to bother you—you're a lot bigger than he is."

"That," she said between two gulps of breath, "does not make me feel better." She made a strange sound, a sort of choking sound. Luke took a step forward. She made the sound again, then slowly straightened, her chest rising and falling with each anxious breath for a long moment. She wasn't choking. She was trying not to laugh. "I almost *died.*"

Luke smiled. "I'm pretty sure you would have survived it."

"Easy for you to say," she said, and pushed her hair back. She looked down at the rototiller in front of her, the box of tools beside her. He could picture her leaping through the air to put herself there when she'd seen the rat, and he couldn't help but chuckle.

"*What?*" she demanded, still smiling.

"How'd you get back there?" he asked as he offered his hand to help her over the boxes of tools.

"I don't know," she said, and slipped her hand into his. "I was airborne, that's all I know." She looked around—but there was no easy way out.

"Step up on that box," he said, pointing to a toolbox. "I'll help you."

She did as he said, teetering on the unstable box before he caught her by the waist and swung her down. She landed awkwardly, brushing against him. Everything seemed to freeze around Luke when her body touched his—nothing moved. Not him, not Madeline. Her eyes were on his, her hands gripping his arms. *Tight.* Something rushed through Luke's blood. He couldn't help himself—he brushed a strand of hair away from her face.

Madeline drew a long breath; her grip seemed to tighten. She stared up at him, her blue eyes glistening in the low light of the garage. "Thanks for saving me," she said, her gaze flicking to his mouth, making the blood rush faster in his veins.

"You're welcome." He looked at her full, lush lips.

"But I'm still mad at you," she said softly.

"I know," he said. "But I swear I wasn't setting you up. That was never my intent. It just came up." Her hair fell again, and he pushed it away once more, his fingers brushing against her temple.

Madeline lifted her gaze to his again, her eyes narrowing slightly as she peered at him. "I don't know if I believe you," she said uncertainly.

"Fair enough," he said.

"Mmm," she said, and let go of his arms.

Luke reluctantly let his hand drop from her waist. "What are you doing in here, anyway?" he asked.

"I came to get some furniture polish. But the only thing I found was a freakishly monster rodent." She ran her hands down her pants then glanced up at him. "What are *you* doing here?"

"I heard someone screaming."

She smiled a little lopsidedly. "I mean *here*. Again. Showing up where I am."

"Well, today I am here to check on the cattle."

She laughed. "Nice try. I haven't seen any cows."

"That's because they're about a half mile up from here. Our ranch hand is in Albuquerque right now, and someone needs to look in on them." He couldn't help himself; he took in her messed hair, her dirty shirt and pants, and her heels, and chuckled again.

"Okay," she said, folding her arms. "What's so funny now?"

"*You* are. You're a wreck."

She looked down at herself and smiled sheepishly. "Well, I didn't get the memo that today was cleaning day." She glanced up at him; there was a soft flush in her cheeks. "Nothing goes according to plan around here."

"That's the mountains for you."

"Yeah, yeah, the mountains," she said with dubious playfulness. She moved away from him, brushing off her pants. She paused next to a box of things on the hood of his mother's Pontiac. The box looked new in that it was not covered with the grime of car parts or dust. There were some picture frames peeking out the top. Madeline leaned over and peered in. So did Luke. The box held bathroom items, like a flat iron, bottles of shampoo, soap, and tampons. But no furniture polish.

Madeline removed one of the pictures from the box and squinted at it. "Is that Libby?"

Luke glanced at the framed photo. It was Libby all right, around the age of twelve or so. She was standing on an oval hooked rug, and on the wall behind her, he could see someone's baby pictures. "That's her."

"Who is she with?" Madeline asked, and Luke looked a little closer at the man sitting in the easy chair behind her, smiling up at her. He'd only met Grant Tyler a couple of times, but he would know him anywhere. He was a striking man—tall, black haired, and blue-eyed. The photo was a bad one—a grainy resolution, faded colors. But that was Grant Tyler, smiling charmingly at his daughter. "That's Grant," he said.

He could feel the tension suddenly radiating off of Madeline. When he looked at her, he saw the color had bled from her face, and Luke suddenly realized what had happened. "Madeline . . . haven't you ever seen a picture of him?"

She shook her head, her gaze locked on the picture. "Where was this taken?"

"I couldn't tell you," he said apologetically.

She stared at the picture. "They look happy, don't they?" She returned the picture to the box. But she could not seem to take her eyes from the ghost of the man she never knew.

Luke wondered what that must be like, to be an adult and see a photo of a father for the first time. He felt for her, more than he wanted to feel. He should keep his distance from her, keep his head clear until the issue of the ranch was resolved, but he was having a lot of trouble doing that, obviously, and especially when he saw such vulnerability in her. He thought of what she'd said of her father last night, could see the look of bewilderment on her face now. It was heartwrenching.

He felt a sudden need to remove them both from this garage, from the box of Libby's things, from that picture of her father, and away from his mother's car. "Come on," he said suddenly, grasping at something, anything, to take them from this garage. "Let's go check on some cows."

Madeline lifted blue, shining eyes to his. "How do you check on cows?"

"We drive or ride up the mountains to find them and check on them."

She frowned at him. "I don't know how to ride. And besides that, I really am still mad at you—the saving my life part notwithstanding," she said, waving toward the wall.

He smiled.

"Don't smile," she warned him. "I don't trust you, either."

His smile only widened. "I know that, too. Come on. It will be fun." He moved toward the open garage door, hoping she would follow.

"I think this is a bad idea," she said. But followed him.

So did the dogs.

FOURTEEN

Madeline let it be known she was not thrilled that the dogs would be riding in the back of the Bronco, especially since the four of them insisted on hanging their heads over the front console next to her head. But she seemed to quickly forget them when Luke started up the bumpy road.

The Bronco still rocked the old logging roads. Luke didn't hold back, either—when it came to the mountains, he was still a kid. Madeline held on with one hand pressed against the dash, the other clenching the overhead grip, and made little squeals of alarm when they hit a big hole or rock.

Halfway up, they encountered a tree that had fallen across the old logging road.

Madeline said, "Oh, well. I guess we need to go back."

"Oh ye of little faith," Luke said. He got out, grabbed his dad's old chainsaw, and demolished the section of the tree that covered the road. He returned to the driver's seat with a good sweat and a smile.

"Wow," Madeline said, a little wide-eyed. "That was impressive."

He winked at her. "Hang on," he said.

They bounced up through ruts and over rocks, taking washed-out corners too close, until they reached ten thousand feet, where a dozen cows steadily mowed their way across a meadow toward snow that had yet to melt in the shadows on the north side of the next rise.

Luke stopped in the middle of the meadow, got out, and opened the back hatch for the dogs. They raced off into the trees.

Madeline walked away from the Bronco and slowly turned in a circle. "It's amazing," she said, taking in the views. "You can see for miles and miles."

Luke looked around at the white-tipped blue peaks, the dark clouds building in the east.

"It's so vast and so *quiet*," she said, her voice full of awe.

"Yeah, I love it up here," Luke said. "In the winter, you can hear the snow fall."

"I can't imagine what that is like, hearing snow fall," she said dreamily.

She turned around to him, her eyes shining with pleasure—until she noticed the cows lumbering toward them. Madeline started for the truck, but Luke caught her arm. "They think there is something for them in the truck. They're going to walk right past you," he said, and watched as the cows didn't spare Madeline a glance as they meandered by. Finding nothing in the Bronco, they moved on, into the forest, probably sensing the rain moving in.

And indeed, the wind was picking up; it lifted the end of Madeline's hair. She wrapped her arms tightly around her, shivering a little as the clouds overhead cast shadows across her face. From the first time Luke had seen her on Sometimes Pass, she seemed to get prettier every time he ran into her. Up here, with her hair loose around her, she seemed almost too pretty, the sort of pretty that made a man look again and again, as if he hadn't seen it all the first time.

She was looking around the meadow, but when she turned, her gaze happened to land on Luke. They stood looking at each other for a moment, and Luke could feel something flowing between and around them. It was a little unexpected, a little unnerving, and completely exhilarating.

"Want to see something?" he asked.

"Sure!"

He pointed to the trees, and Madeline walked, picking her way in her clumsy shoes, across the meadow. At the tree line, she paused, and Luke stepped up behind her, leaned down so that his head was on the same level as hers, and put his hands on her shoulders, directing her attention to a stand of aspens. "Do you see it?"

"See what?"

"The blue jay condo." He pointed at a dead aspen, its white bark turned gray. But in that bark were dozens of holes. As if on cue, a blue jay fluttered into their midst, perching on the edge of one hole, then disappearing inside.

Madeline gasped with delight. "Are they all nests?"

"Most of them. It was a woodpecker habitat at some point," he explained. "The blue jays chased them out and moved in. Voilà , instant condo complex."

Madeline rubbed her hands against her arms as she examined the aspen. The wind was picking up and the temperature had begun to drop as rain approached. Luke shrugged out of his denim jacket and put it around her.

Madeline tried to hand it back to him. "I can't take your jacket."

"You're shivering, but I've got a couple of shirts on. And it's going to get a whole lot colder when rain moves in." He held the jacket open to her.

Another strong gust of wind prompted Madeline to step forward. She put her arms through the sleeves and smiled at him over her shoulder. "Thank you. And thanks for showing me the condo. It's so beautiful here."

"My mom used to say these mountains were her garden," Luke said. "She hiked up into the forest most days, but she always came back to this meadow." He chuckled at a memory. "In the summer, she'd come up here on Sunday afternoons to read her books. We had strict instructions she was not to be found unless someone was bleeding."

"*Nice*," Madeline said approvingly. "A sanctuary from boys, but the cows can stay."

How lucky he'd been, Luke thought, to have these mountains as his backyard. Once, when he was twelve or so, he'd honed his tracking skills and had followed his mother up here. He'd found her on a blanket next to the truck. She was lying on her back, an open book across her chest. He'd raced across the meadow to surprise her, but she had surprised him—she'd had tears on her face.

Naturally, he thought something horrible had happened, but his mother had laughed and tousled his head. "Nothing has happened other than someone wrote a very moving book. Do you know . . ." she'd said, as she'd closed her book and pulled him down on the blanket beside her, "that sometimes I wish I lived a long time ago in a castle?" And she had folded him in her arms. They'd lain on that blanket, watching fat clouds float by, talking about all the things they'd wished for.

"She was a great mom," he said, and glanced down, surprised by the swell of emotion. He was long past the point of feeling sick to his stomach when he talked about her. Now, she was a collection of warm memories.

"How did she die?" Madeline asked.

"Cancer." He didn't say more than that. There was nothing more insidious than watching someone die from cancer, nothing more horrifying, more gut-wrenching than watching your mother slowly waste away. He rarely talked about it.

"I'm so sorry," Madeline said, and touched his hand.

That small touch reverberated through Luke. He wrapped his fingers around hers. He was at odds with his emotions; his head and his heart were responding to Madeline, but at the same time he felt a shadow of guilt, as if he was letting down his mother by giving into his body's yearnings and forgetting about the ranch. He looked away from Madeline. "The only thing I have left of her now is memories. Places like this, where she used to be. I stand here and almost see her." He didn't say more than that. He couldn't say more than that. He glanced at Madeline out of the corner of his eye.

She was looking directly at him. "Luke?" she said.

His eyes fell to her lips. "Madeline?"

She smiled, and for a moment of sheer insanity, Luke wondered if she intended to kiss him. Even more insane was that he wouldn't mind if she did.

JULIA LONDON

"You wouldn't use your mom to try and back me into a sentimental corner . . . would you?"

He couldn't help the grin that began to move across his mouth. He slowly lifted his gaze to hers. Hers were sparkling now—with ire, with challenge, and perhaps with a bit of amusement. "Would it work?"

"Maybe," she said. "But it would be really demented of you."

"The most despicable thing ever," he agreed. "But sometimes a guy has to do what a guy has to do. Wish I had thought of it," he said, squeezing her fingers, "I'll just have to rely on my powers of persuasion with you, huh?"

She clucked her tongue at him. "I'm a trained negotiator."

Now Luke smiled. He shifted closer, leaned down so that his head was next to hers and said softly, "I wasn't planning to negotiate."

She gasped—with a laugh or surprise, he wasn't certain—and poked him in the chest. "Do you think I will fall for *that?*"

He grabbed her poking finger and held it tight. "Don't know yet," he said. "But I'm gonna find out just what it is you will fall for, Maddie Pruett."

She laughed, a soft, silky little laugh. "It's Madeline, player."

There it was again, that feeling of something dancing between them, something with a very strong pull. But wherever that moment was headed was suddenly lost to a loud crack of thunder over their heads. It startled Madeline; she cried out and whirled about at the same time, stumbling into Luke's chest. Her heel sunk down on the top of his foot; he hissed at the pain, and caught Madeline with an arm around her chest before they both went tumbling.

"I'm so sorry! Are you all right?"

"Fine," he said tightly, testing his foot again, privately fearing that she might have broken a bone.

Another clap of thunder heralded the arrival of the rain; Madeline looked up at the very moment the skies opened. She cried out with surprise.

Luke threw his arm around her shoulder and they ran—or rather, they hobbled, because of Madeline's shoes and his near broken foot—to

128

the Bronco, diving in just as the rain began to pour. A white light exploded around them, followed the next moment by at crack of thunder.

"What about the dogs and cows?" Madeline exclaimed.

"They'll be fine, they've already gone for cover." He started the Bronco and gunned it, lurching across the meadow and down the road as far as he could go before he couldn't see through the deluge. He stopped the Bronco just as another bright light flashed through the truck and the world was split by the crack of the bolt of lightning. It was so close that Madeline cried out and dipped her head; Luke put his arm around her shoulder and dragged her into his side. "It's okay, Maddie."

"We're going to be killed," she said breathlessly.

"Lightning will hit the top of those trees first," he tried to assure her, but another crack did not help his argument. He held her tighter. "Relax," he said. "We'll be fine. I've done this dozens of times."

She lifted her head. "Really?"

Not even close—maybe once or twice he'd been caught up high during a storm. But he smiled reassuringly and said, "Well. Maybe not *dozens* of times."

Madeline relaxed into his side, and Luke liked the way she felt against him. "Wow," she said, looking out the window as rain whipped around them and trees swayed into one another. It was raining so hard now that they couldn't see more than a foot in front of the Bronco. Madeline twisted around to look behind them. "I think we're stuck," she said.

Luke didn't notice if they were or not—he couldn't take his eyes off Madeline. Her white shirt was plastered to her, and beneath it, he could see a lacy blue bra, which was holding up a pair of perfect breasts. When he didn't respond, she looked at him.

That thing dancing between them began to circle around, drawing them closer together.

"Stuck," she said again, her gaze sliding down to his chest.

He wanted more from this woman than he ought to want. "For the moment," he agreed. "When it stops raining, we'll go down, even if we have to walk."

A soft smile illuminated her face. "Bad shoes, remember?"

God, he wanted to kiss her. "How could I forget? Broken foot, remember?"

She laughed. "Too bad cell phones don't work up here. We could call Libby to rescue us."

Luke wanted to feel those lips against his, touch her skin. Madeline was talking, but he wasn't really hearing her, he was watching her lips move, imagining how soft they would feel against his . . .

Until she said, "I can't understand why she wants to stay here."

Luke mentally shook his head. "What?"

"Libby. She wants to stay at the ranch."

She said it so casually, and all Luke could do was stare at her.

"What's wrong?" Madeline asked.

"Does this mean you guys have decided?" Luke asked, trying to keep his anger in check. They had no regard for the family history here, of the family *displaced* from here. "She's going to move into my family's house?"

"No, no, we haven't decided anything. But Emma went back to L.A.—"

"What? When?"

"This morning," Madeline said. "I was surprised too. No word, nothing, she just left. And Libby—Libby is convinced she needs to be here to manage the reunion."

Loud thunder and a very bright bolt of lightning cracked overhead, and Madeline jumped. She rubbed her hands on her legs as if she was trying to create warmth. Luke sighed. He was angry, but he was still a gentleman. "Sit tight," he said, and opened his door. He heard her shout after him, but he had already dashed to the hatch. He pulled it open and grabbed his emergency bag, then dashed back to the driver's seat.

That short exposure to the elements had soaked him. He pulled out a blanket from the bag and spread it over her lap, then his.

"Oh my God, *thank* you," she said, and bent her legs, kicking off her shoes and pulling her feet up onto the seat beneath the blanket. "You're like a Boy Scout." Luke reached into the bag and pulled out a package of peanut butter crackers and opened the package, offering her one before taking one himself. "I'm sorry," she said between bites of cracker, "I didn't mean to upset you. I thought you knew Libby was staying."

Luke had been upset by the situation with Homecoming Ranch since he'd called home after Patti's initial call. He glanced at Madeline as he popped a cracker into his mouth. "I didn't know. But I guess I knew it was coming."

"I suppose Libby is right," Madeline said thoughtfully. "We *do* have to do something about that reunion, right? But at least it's not a permanent move. I don't think."

Luke feared that it was. He'd heard enough to know that Libby's life was in flux, and he feared that if she got her feet down at this ranch, she'd be impossible to dislodge. He thought that of all of them, only Madeline might have a chance of persuading her differently, and only because she seemed so determined to get the hell out of Pine River—

A thought suddenly occurred to him. Madeline was the key to his predicament. She was a shrewd little puppy and she wasn't going to let this drag out. He didn't want it to, either. He could use her help, and honestly, he wouldn't mind having Blue Eyes around for a few days. He liked quirky. He looked at her shoes, splattered with mud, her damp and tangled hair.

Yeah, he'd like her to stick around.

But how did he get her to do that?

By appealing to her ego, that was how. He didn't know a person on the planet who was immune to a little ego testing. He said, "You know, I think the best course of action is just to get on with it and settle things between us. Then, if you guys want to sell the ranch, then sell it. Let Jackson figure out the reunion."

Madeline blinked with surprise. "That's what *I've* been saying," she pointed out. "And I think it's a little weird that now *you're* suddenly saying it."

"Well, I've had a few wet minutes to think about it," he said with a smile. "Look, I know my dad has made it impossible. My only hope is to try and put the money together to buy the ranch back. I figure that while you and your sisters do the reunion thing, I have a little time to come up with the money, right? But I don't want Libby to get too comfortable, you know?"

Madeline nodded. "I know. I don't want that, either."

"So all I need is a little bit of time. And a fair idea of what the ranch is worth."

"Hmm," she said, her eyes narrowing on him. "This change of heart sounds a little suspicious."

"I'm being straight with you, Madeline," he said. "I know a guy, Danny Duffy, who lives up Trace Canyon Road. He used to be a realtor, among other things. I think he could figure out what the place is worth. I'll call him as soon as I get to town."

"Are you serious?" Madeline said quickly, "I'd like to do some research before anyone talks about hiring a realtor."

"That's okay, Maddie. I know you have to get back to Orlando. Danny can do it."

"Okay," she said slowly, and looked out the window. "But you have to get a good, reputable, knowledgeable agent if you want to get fair value."

He shrugged. "I'm sure Danny Duffy will do what he can. He's about all we've got up here."

"I can do the market research," Madeline said. "I can even help find a realtor."

"From Orlando?" Luke asked skeptically. "And anyway, what about your job?" he asked, his eyes narrowing. "Don't worry about it—Danny can look stuff up on the Internet if he's not sure. I'm fairly certain he has Internet up on Trace Canyon Road."

Madeline nodded. She looked out the window for a long moment, then suddenly twisted around, so she was facing him. One button of her blouse had come undone, he noticed, giving him a peek of that lacy blue bra. "Okay, look," she said. "It's true that I have a lot of work waiting for me. But the beauty of being self-employed is I can take a few days off if I need to, right? I can stick around and do the research on value. It won't take me long."

"How long?" he asked.

"A few days," Madeline said. "A week, tops."

Luke nodded. His gaze skimmed over her breasts. "So are you saying that now you're willing to stick around a few days and help figure out things?"

Madeline looked as if she had swallowed a lump of peanut butter. "Yeah. I guess I am," she said, and as if to convince herself, she gave him an adamant little nod. "But what about Libby?"

"I think if she wants to handle the reunion, she should do it," Luke said, his gaze wandering lower, to her waist. "As far as the reunion goes, I'll even help her. I just don't want her to get the idea that it's a done deal, because I am going to do everything I can to get the ranch back."

"What about *your* job?"

"I can do a lot from here and head over to Denver when I need to. After all, we're just talking a few days, right?"

"Right," she said carefully. Her gaze moved to his chest again, and Luke wished she wouldn't look at him like that. It was too damn *tempting*. "Just a few days," she repeated softly, and lifted her gaze to his.

The rain, the chill in the air was everywhere around them but in that truck. Luke could feel nothing but a smoldering fire between the two of them.

"In fact," he said, "I'll probably drive over to Denver on Monday to check on things." He shifted in his seat, too, moving closer. He casually pushed a wet strand of hair from her face, then another from her neck, letting his fingers graze her skin.

Madeline shivered slightly at his touch. "Okay, Luke, I'll help," she said. "But I'm watching you. This feels too convenient and tidy after yesterday."

"I thought that's the way you liked things," he muttered, shifting closer, his face near her hair. It smelled sweet. "Tidy. Uncomplicated. To the point."

Madeline turned her head slightly and looked at him sidelong. "You're right. The tidier, the better for me. I don't like to invite chaos into my life by taking little detours."

He grazed her temple with his mouth; Madeline gasped softly. "Sometimes the detours are the best part of life," he murmured

"Are you trying to kiss me?" she asked, her voice a little breathless.

"Yes."

"I just *met* you," she said reprovingly, but she didn't move away.

"That is not true. You met me two days ago on the side of the road," he said, and kissed her temple. "And then again at Jackson's," he added before kissing her cheek. "At the ranch," he said, and kissed the bridge of her nose, "and in town." He kissed her brow. "And now, on this mountain, in this rainstorm, in my truck. We're practically an item."

"You're outrageous," she whispered, but she did not turn her head when he kissed her lips.

Her response was restrained, funny, we-shouldn't-be-doing-this kiss, but yet one that felt electric to Luke. She angled her head and kissed him back, her lips, butter soft against his, her skin silken beneath his fingers. It was simple, so simple, but the promise of something far greater was there, and his body was responding rapidly. Too rapidly. He felt himself tumbling hard and fast down a path of desire, and lifted his head, his eyes on Madeline.

She looked alluring with her tousled hair and wet lips. She also looked stunned. Luke thought to apologize. But before he could form a thought, Madeline suddenly lunged forward, grabbing the collar of his shirt and kissed him back. She kissed him so ardently that he fell back against the seat, and Madeline came over the console with him. He caught her up with one arm, pressed his palm against her cheek and temple. Madeline nipped at his lips, swept her tongue into his mouth, shoved her fingers into his hair.

Good God, but that kiss was hot and dangerously arousing. His body was hardening with that uncontrolled kiss, that passionate, fervent, surprising kiss. He slipped his hand inside the jacket, and pressed against the side of her breast.

Madeline made a soft little moaning sound into his mouth, and that was it. Luke lifted up, determined to take them both to the backseat, when a crash startled them.

Madeline gasped and lifted her head, planting her hands against his chest and looking wildly about. Luke looked around her mess of dark hair out the front window and saw half a dead aspen lying across the lower branches of two pines just to the right of the Bronco. He also noticed that the rain had begun to let up. He looked at Madeline; she had already faded back away from him, and was looking at him now as if she wasn't certain what had just happened.

She wiped the pad of her thumb across her lower lip. Her chest lifted with a deep breath. "Sorry," she said breathlessly. "I don't know what got into me." But she didn't look sorry, not the least bit. She looked like a woman who could rip his clothes off of him then and there.

"I'm not," he said. He was downright confused, yes—but not sorry. Whatever had just happened, it felt strong and real. And wholly incautious. "I think we can start down now," he said, and turned the ignition. "Hold on."

But Madeline was already gripping the dash and the handle above the window, and honestly, Luke wasn't certain if he hadn't just said that to himself.

FIFTEEN

She was such an *idiot!* Madeline slammed the car door and stomped in her wet pumps into the lobby of Grizzly Lodge. *Why* did she agree to stay? A *week?* Who had a week? She had clients and listings. . . .

Okay. Maybe, just maybe, she was more intrigued with Luke Kendrick than she would ever admit to anyone, and especially *not* Trudi, who was guaranteed to make a colossally big deal out of it. But man, sitting in that truck, under the blanket with a guy as good-lookng as Luke, she let her mind wander to other things. White-hot things. She couldn't believe he'd kissed her. But she really couldn't believe that she had kissed him *back.* She didn't think she had ever in her life kissed anyone like that. It wasn't like her at all, so reckless, so out of control. And Madeline couldn't even say why she'd done it, other than she was up on that mountain in the rain, under a blanket, and with Luke, handsome, sturdy Luke, and something just began to thrum in her. She'd felt a little outside of herself.

She was still shocked and excited and *shocked.* But, Lord help her, she'd enjoyed that kiss, more than any other kiss in her life.

Crazy, crazy! It was the chaos around her, that was it. She was still wearing his jacket! She had completely forgotten it when they'd come back down to the ranch. . . .

Well. Maybe she hadn't *completely* forgotten it, but he apparently had—he did not ask for it back. It smelled like him. All salty and sexy and—

Madeline, what the hell?

Okay, logically, she'd had no choice but to stay. Luke had been so quick to jump to the conclusion that they ought to get Danny the I'm Fairly Certain He Maybe Has Internet to take a look at the property. What was it about men that they immediately assumed a man, no matter who the hell he was, was better suited than a woman for a job?

Madeline had seen red, she'd really seen red, red, red, and the next thing she knew, she'd opened her mouth and said she'd stay.

"Goodness gracious, you look like a cat caught out in the rain!" Dani said as Madeline marched into the foyer, ready to kill and maim someone with her bare hands.

"I am. I was. Dani, a couple of things have come up." She slapped her purse down on the counter top. "I'll have to stay for a week or so."

"Well that's great news!" Dani said, smiling brightly. "I *knew* you'd fall in love with Pine River."

"I didn't—"

"Now maybe you can pick up a few things that aren't quite as businesslike," she said eagerly, eyeing Madeline's clothes.

What was up with all the sartorial scrutiny in Pine River? Madeline glanced down at herself—in addition to the smear across her blouse, her slacks were a silk blend, and she could see the water spots on them.

"So where will you be staying?"

That brought Madeline's head up. "What? Here!"

"Oh no, sweetie. I'd love to have you, I would, but, remember, I've got that busload of snowbirds coming up from New Mexico on Monday. Want me to call and see if the motel on the Aspen Highway can take you?"

Madeline suppressed a shudder. She'd driven by that hotel on her way out of town this morning when she'd been momentarily turned around and headed in the wrong direction. There were several big, muddy trucks parked outside the rooms, a sign displaying the SUPER LOW RATE of $19.99 A NIGHT and the *L* in the word "motel" was half gone. "Umm, no thanks. I'll figure something out."

"Why don't you give Jackson a call?" Dani suggested. "He might have an idea. He's so smart."

Smart was not the word Madeline thought of when it came to Jackson. She looked longingly down the hall to her room. She was getting used to her little cub room and was reluctant to leave it. "When do I have to be out?"

"Tomorrow afternoon. I can give you till four if that helps."

Great. Twenty-four hours to dig herself out of the latest round of chaos. In the meantime, Madeline had a more pressing issue. She was not going back up to the ranch in these shoes, or anywhere for that matter. "Is there a store around where I could pick up a few things?" she asked.

"Walmart out on the Old Aspen Highway, of course. I get these shirts there," Dani said proudly, gesturing to a blue Guayabera shirt. "Fifteen ninety-nine, you can't beat that. But if you want something a little more suited for the mountains, you can go down to Tag's Outfitter."

Madeline's phone was beeping at her. She rummaged around in her bag for it. "Tag's Outfitter?" she repeated as she pulled her phone from the bag. *Stephen.*

"Just down the street, catawampus from the Stakeout."

"Outfitter," Madeline said again as she muted the ringing of her phone.

"Outfitter," Dani reiterated carefully. "You can get your camping gear there, too."

"Camping!"

"It's an option. I mean, if you don't want to stay out on the highway."

Madeline almost choked. "I'm not that desperate."

Dani chuckled. "Don't be too sure," she said. "You might be camping before you know it. The mountains have a certain pull to them. You'll be feeling it in a couple of days."

Madeline picked up her purse. "Actually, I think I'm more of a beach girl."

"Well at least go check out the clothes there. Because you can't keep going up to Homecoming Ranch like that." Dani winked at Madeline. "How's your head, anyway?" she asked as Madeline started for the door.

"Better," Madeline said. "Thanks. The aspirin really worked."

"Sure it did. Keep them with you. This altitude does all kinds of crazy things to a person."

Apparently that was true, because Madeline had just broken every rule she had about following all of her rules.

She headed toward the Stakeout, scanning the street for whatever Dani might consider to be "catawampus." She was fairly certain she had spotted it—a low-slung adobe building with miles and miles of brightly colored ceramic pots in front of it, as well as a crop of big iron chickens on springs. Every breeze made them dip toward the ground and up again. Above the chickens hung a large sun bursting with big orange rays and the words "Tag's Outfitter."

Madeline was so wary of the place and the type of clothes they might carry that she didn't exactly register the ringing of her phone and answered without thinking.

"Hey! It's Stephen."

Madeline stopped walking. "Hi, Stephen." She banged her fist against her thigh for being so incautious. She didn't need any more detours in her day.

"So how do you like Colorado? Pretty state, isn't it?" he asked.

"It is," she said. "Beautiful. Lots of pines and . . . trees."

"Whereabouts in Colorado are you?"

"A little town called Pine River."

"I know that town. Near Silverton, right? I used to ski in Silverton. So listen, I talked to my friend in Denver. The news is good. Without any written agreements or liens that haven't yet turned up, the property is yours, free and clear. Better yet, he said he has a buddy who is a broker who specializes in ranch lands. He said not only could he help you out with that, he's probably got some buyers who'd be interested in talking. I've got his number. I can text it to you."

"That would be great," Madeline said. "Thank you."

"So when are you going to be back?" he asked.

"Umm—I'm not sure yet. Indefinite right now."

"Indefinite," he repeated.

"There's a lot more to be done than I realized."

"So what are we talking, a week? A month?"

"A few days, anyway," Madeline said.

"Okay," Stephen said. "So listen, Madeline," he said. "There's something I'd like to say—"

"Stephen, now isn't really—"

"I like you," he said, cutting her off before she could stop him from saying anything. "I like you a lot. You're pretty and you're different, and I know you don't want to get into anything, but I'd like to date you. You know, you and me. I promise I won't push you, because I get that you're skittish about guys or whatever, but really, that's okay. I'd just like to see you and see where it goes. No pressure."

Madeline sagged against the outside wall of the Squeaky Clean Laundromat, where she happened to be standing. Stephen was a great guy, and any woman would be crazy not to be into him. But Madeline wasn't. This is what she always did. She would go out with a guy a few times and then disappear. The one time she hadn't done that, the one time she'd tried to be a "girlfriend" to a guy named Trystan, he'd dumped her. He'd said he wasn't feeling it, whatever that meant. Madeline hadn't felt as devastated by that as she'd felt validated in what she believed about men.

But now, an image of Luke jumped into her mind, which she tried to push out. She didn't understand herself, or the fist in her belly when she talked to Stephen or thought of Luke, and honestly, she was too exhausted to even try at the moment. "I have so much on my mind right now," she said.

"Sure, sure," Stephen said. "But I just want you to know, that whatever it is you are going through, I want to help. Or not. And everything can wait until you get back."

"Thanks, I just need to take care of a couple of things."

"I know. Do what you need to do. I'll text you the name of this guy."

She thanked him and hung up. She didn't want to think too much right now. And besides, her feet hurt. Madeline walked on to Tag's Outfitters.

She had to duck her head to step into the place, which looked as if it might have been an adobe barn at one point. The ceiling was very low, the wooden beams exposed. Someone had thought it a good idea to suspend billed hats from the beams. There were dozens and dozens of them, hanging only inches over her head. The windows were small and rectangular, and the only real light came from a glaring fluorescent tube that stretched across the ceiling between the hats.

An old man with long gray hair and a longer gray beard was sitting on a stool behind the counter. He wore a stained sun hat and in his hair a feather that looked as if it had been plucked from a very large bird of prey. He glanced up at Madeline only briefly, then lowered his gaze to what looked like a sudoku puzzle, his pen poised above it.

"Ah . . . Danielle at the Grizzly Inn said you might have some clothes and things?"

Without lifting his gaze he said, "Got everything you need for living in the mountains. Ladies' section in the back."

Madeline looked around the store. There was no clear "back" to the store, just lots of meandering aisles through stacks of boxes. She looked at the man behind the counter. He made a mark on his puzzle.

She started down one path through boxes piled to near the ceiling, some of them leaning precariously. But at the end of that row, Madeline was rewarded with six round racks full of women's clothing. There was a closet with a curtain pulled across it that she supposed was the dressing room, and a surprisingly cheerful little rug just outside of it.

She perused the racks, sorting through sundresses with skimpy straps and brightly printed fabrics, T-shirts emblazoned with inspirational slogans and mystic symbols, hiking wear, and jeans. Madeline was not much of a shopper. She did not enjoy spending the money she made. She was guided by the fear that something horrible would happen—like her mother would land in a hospital after one of her nights of partying, with no insurance and poor health—and she would need every penny she ever made.

But today, Madeline decided she could use a little retail therapy. She picked up two of the sundresses, some hiking pants, a pair of jeans, and some T-shirts. She stepped into the dressing room to try them on. They were not her usual style, but one of the dresses reminded her of her blue dress at home. This one was red with white polka dots, and it floated around Madeline's knees the way Emma's skirt had floated around hers. Why not? Madeline thought, and smiled at her reflection. Why not wear a frilly dress?

She tried on the other clothes, and happy with her picks, made her way to the front of the store to purchase the items, including a sweater with pretty beading on it she found on the way up the aisle.

She deposited her things on the counter.

"That it?" the man asked, putting aside his magazine.

"No," Madeline said. "I need shoes."

The old man perked up at that, clearly interested in the prospect of selling shoes. "What kind?"

"Something practical for walking."

He eyed her curiously. "What *kind* of walking? Pavement or trail? Improved or unimproved? Hilly or flat?"

She thought about that. "All of the above."

With a grunt, he pushed himself off the stool, picked up a cane, and wordlessly hobbled around the counter. He led her to a big stack of boxes, where he paused, turned around, and had a good look at her feet. "Pick up your foot, let me see the bottom."

Madeline did as instructed, presenting the bottom of her foot.

He turned back to the boxes, found one about halfway down, wrested it from the teetering stack and handed the box to her. "Try these."

Inside the box was a pair of hiking boots. Madeline instantly recoiled. "I was thinking something a little sleeker."

"Sleeker," he said, sounding annoyed. "You want good walking shoes, or you want sleek?"

"Right," she said with a sigh, and sat down to fit the boots on her feet. The old man stood by, watching her as she donned them, then instructed her to walk. He nodded, then made her walk up a little wooden hill, and down again. He didn't say a word, but then again, he didn't have to. Madeline *loved* them. After two days of stomping around in her pumps, she felt as if she were walking on pillows. Soft, cushiony, supportive pillows.

"I'll take them," she said.

"You'll be needing socks," he advised, and bent down, fished around in another box and held out some thick hiking socks.

"Perfect! Thank you." She was determined never to take them off. Never.

"Need a backpack? Flashlight? Camping gear? Guidebook?"

Madeline, whose mood had been miraculously transformed by supportive footwear, smiled at him. "No, thank you. But I will take this," she said, and reached above her head and pulled down a bright pink ball cap. She'd never worn a ball cap in her life.

She paid for her things, wore the boots out of the store, and clomped back to the Grizzly, a smile on her face. Funny how such a small thing like comfortable feet could change a person's outlook. For the first time in two days, Madeline felt as if she could tackle this thing. She knew what she had to do: Assess the situation, take control, and restore order. Simple.

SIXTEEN

So Dad came in while Marisol was giving me a rubdown, and like seriously, man, he is the *last* person I want to see when I'm with Marisol, but he always comes in like she's just part of the furniture and starts talking and he said, "There's a woman outside to see Luke." And then he looked at Marisol like he was afraid she'd figure out who and start talking it up around town. Well, first of all, Marisol already knew. I said, "Julie's been sniffing around my big brother," and Marisol said, "Yeah, she's on the hunt for a new baby daddy because word on the street is that Brandon is moving to Colorado Springs."

I really like the idea that Pine River has a "street," sort of like we're badass here instead of a bunch of yokels trying to make a living.

Anyway, I knew it was Julie outside because she'd already called the house twice today. Dad was upset about that, too, because man, she did a number on Luke a few years ago. They'd planned the whole wedding. I think she even had a dress, and then she dumped him because Mom was sick all the time, and dude, Luke moped around. I mean, Luke *said* that he got it, that the Kendricks had a lot of issues, and who would want to marry into issues? But he forgot that love is a two-way street, and he needed Julie the most about then, and she bailed on him. You know what they say, love is blind, and Luke, man, he could have used a white cane or a Seeing Eye dog. But dude, we've never seen him like that, and just between you and me and the wall, he was a total dick to all of us. And that wasn't the end of it! I think she's called him up four or five times since then, needing him for this or that, getting his hopes up, and then backing off.

That's what Dad is worried about, because we can both see that it messes with Luke's head. But I told Dad not to worry, and he said, "Are you sure? Maybe I should have a talk with him," and I said, "No, no, no, don't do that. No thirty-year-old man wants to have that kind of talk with his dad, and besides, I am *so* sure, because I know Luke better than anyone, and I asked him once, I said, 'so, are you over Julie?' And he said, 'so over,' and he wouldn't have said that if he hadn't meant it."

Listen, I know Dr. Phil wants guys to communicate better because he says it every day on his show, but if I ever met him I'd ask him why, because guys don't need a lot of words to get our points across. Luke said he was over her, and that means he is over her. Paragraph, period, close the book.

So Dad went away after that and Marisol said, "You think you know so much," and I said, "I know you are craving my body like a chocolate sundae with whipped cream and caramel, so go ahead, baby, have at it." And she said, "One day, Leo, you are going to talk too much," and pinched my butt. Hard, man. There's gotta be a bruise.

Later, after Julie left the pound cake she made for me, even though I'm not supposed to have stuff like that, and her baby pulled the tube out of my catheter, Luke came home from the ranch. He was a totally different man than the depressed one who'd left this morning. He said he took my advice—like who wouldn't, certified genius here—and he said he'd worked it out, he'd bought us a little time. And then he casually mentions that Blue Eyes might stick around a day or so, but he says it *so* casually that I'm like *ho*, what's up with *this*? I said, "What about Emma?"

Luke did one of those double takes like he had to remember who Emma was and said, "She went back to L.A."

I said, "So what do you think? Blue Eyes isn't going to sell us out after all?"

Luke kind of laughed, a little chuckle that said to me he had a secret, and he said, "Well, I don't know about that, but at least I've got a few days to work on it." I think he was going to tell me his plan, but then the phone rang, and Luke answered it before Dad could, and surprise! It was Julie. They talked and talked and I started to get a little antsy because man, Luke told me he was *over* her. But then I hear him saying he'll be there at seven, and the next thing I know, he's got on his good striped shirt and he's headed for the door.

I said, "Whoa, whoa—are you going out with *Julie?*" And I said it like she had three eyes and no boobs. Neither of those are true, by the way. "Are you sure about that, man?"

Luke said, "Don't make a big deal out of this, Leo. She needs some help with her car while her husband is out of town. It's no big deal." And he went out the door. Kind of vaulted out, like he thought I was going to ask some more probing questions. And I was. I don't watch *Dateline* for nothing.

I turned up the Rockies and the Padres baseball game and I didn't even notice Dad until he came around and stood in front of my chair with his arms folded and glaring down at me like it was *my* fault. "I thought you said no problem," he said.

And I said, "Okay, let's not panic. He hasn't pulled out the ring yet has he?"

Dad said something terribly unkind to someone with motor neuron disease and stomped off. I have to admit, I was a little confused, too, because I would have sworn that Luke was into Blue Eyes. It's just this vibe I've had.

Anyway, when he came home, I was still up, in my bed watching *Top Chef* and wishing I had some potatoes in a port-wine reduction. Luke looked pretty hangdog. He stood in the doorway of my room, leaning up against it, his hands in his pocket and he says, "What are you watching?"

"*Top Chef.* How do you feel about empanadas?"

He said, "Turns out, nothing was wrong with Julie's car. She wanted to tell me that her marriage is splintering apart."

"I've heard that," I said.

He looked at the stained carpet (I mean seriously, were they processing wild boar in here before Dad and I moved in, or what?), and he said, "You know what sucks? What sucks is that after she dumped me six weeks before the wedding, it took me a long time to get over it. I mean, I labored like a damn ox to get past it, you know? I don't like that she's coming at me now. I don't like it at all."

I said, "Yeah, I know. So what are you going to do about it?"

I was hoping he'd say he was going to Kung Fu her ass, but Luke shrugged. He said, "It pisses me off that she can just give me a certain kind of look and I actually start thinking about it. I think, what if?"

Well color me speechless. I could have sworn that would never happen. But I figure that even geniuses have an off day every now and then. Every now and then, I said. You can trust ninety-nine point nine percent of what I tell you, and I am telling you if the Rockies don't get some pitching talent this year, they might as well hang up their cleats because they won't even come close to winning the division. You can take that to the bank.

Anyway, I said to my brother, "Luke, please don't do something totally stupid. You know what Mom always said."

He looked up, interested in that. "What did Mom always say?"

"She said never wear white underwear and a leopard doesn't change its spots."

Luke sort of peered at me like he couldn't quite make me out, and he said, "So which one is a message for me this evening, genius?"

How obtuse can one guy be? I said, "*Both*. Just don't do anything stupid. Julie may look good because you've been in the desert if you get my drift, but once a coward, always a coward, and she's a coward. Mom didn't say that, I did."

He looked like he was chewing on that for a minute. He said, "Thanks for the advice. So what's an empanada?"

Seriously, you'd think the guy grew up under a rock.

SEVENTEEN

Bree, the assistant Madeline shared with two other realtors at her firm's offices, wasn't very appreciative of Madeline's checking in on Sunday morning. But Madeline couldn't wait until Monday; she had too much to do in a very short week. She went over some details of her workload with Bree, making sure that two closings and some market research were covered for the week.

"This isn't really necessary," Bree said when Madeline insisted she take notes. "You spent an hour with me going over all the details of your workload for the next month in case your plane went down."

"Just double-checking," Madeline said briskly.

"You also double-checked in case you were in a car wreck and incapacitated."

"You can't be too careful," Madeline reminded her.

"Yeah, Madeline, you can."

Madeline could hear Bree's kids in the background, the low voice of her husband telling them to be quiet, that Mommy was on the phone. Madeline felt a familiar but strange squeeze in her chest, the one she always felt when she was confronted with the evidence of an actual happy family and the glaring absence of same in her life.

"Any movement on DiNapoli?" Madeline asked brightly, trying to ignore the sound now of pots and pans being banged around Bree's kitchen.

"Nothing," Bree said through a yawn. "I told you I'd call you the minute I heard anything."

"Right. Just hoping. Okay, well—I guess I'll see you next week?"

"We'll all still be here," Bree said. "Madeline—don't worry so much. You're only gone for a few days. Everything will still be here, including your listings. You made sure of it, remember?"

"Yes."

"With your flowcharts—"

"Right, okay—"

"And your e-mail alerts."

"Okay, okay," Madeline said. "Sorry." It was no secret to Madeline that she had some control issues. It wasn't the first time she'd gone a little overboard with Bree. She had tried to temper herself, she truly had, but her anxiety of something falling through the cracks outweighed her need to try and not bury Bree with details. It was an ongoing battle for her.

"Just enjoy yourself for once, will you?" Bree said. "Breathe some mountain air and unbutton the collar of your shirt."

Wow. She was seriously going to have to address her wardrobe since it seemed to weigh so heavily on everyone's mind. "Okay, I will." She would certainly try, anyway.

She made one other call, to Teresa, her co-coach of the soccer team. "No problem," Teresa said cheerfully. "Guess what? Melania scored a goal! It was completely by accident, but still."

"That's fabulous!" Madeline said, wishing she'd been there to see it.

"The girls are asking about you."

"Tell them I'll be back soon," Madeline said.

"Will do. Have a good time!" Teresa said.

A good time. What a novel idea.

Madeline donned a new sundress and checked herself out in it. She liked what she saw—she had a good figure for the dress. She never wore dresses at home—they felt too casual, too loose. Suits and pumps, that fit her life in Orlando.

Was that true?

She was beginning to wonder.

Madeline carefully packed her things, checked her room and bathroom three times for any items left behind, and made her way to the lobby.

Dani whistled at Madeline when she came into the lobby, rolling her carry-on bag behind her. "Now you look like a mountain woman, sweetie."

Madeline glanced down at herself. She was wearing the red dress with the white polkadots, Luke's denim jacket, and her hiking boots. She'd braided her hair and donned the cap, ready to work, to do whatever needed to be done. At least *that* felt familiar. It felt natural. That was who she was, really—a take-charge, get-it-done kind of gal.

"So where are you going?" Dani asked as she printed Madeline's bill.

"I haven't worked that out quite yet, but I've got a couple of options."

Dani grinned. "Sure you do. Pretty girls always have options."

Madeline smiled. "Thanks, Dani." She paid her bill and tucked it away into the clear envelope marked "receipts" in her day planner. "See you around?"

"I hope so!" Dani said. "We have breakfast specials every day this week, so come on down and get some when you're ready."

Madeline walked outside into bright, crystalline sunlight. She paused to breathe in deep, felt the crisp air expanding in her lungs and making her feel instantly better. All right, then, the best course of action was to tackle the tasks at hand, which she had conveniently listed just this morning. Number One: Extend the lease on her car rental.

She stood on the covered sidewalk and called the rental company with her plan to keep the tin can for the week . . . until she discovered she would have to pay a fee for converting her weekend contract to a weeklong contract.

"That makes no sense whatsoever," Madeline insisted.

"Maybe not, but that's the rules," the man said.

He would not be argued out of it. The only option left to Madeline that did not entail forking over an extra one hundred and fifty bucks was to take the car back to Denver and get another one. It was one enormous loop of red tape, but Madeline was not the sort to let go of one hundred and fifty bucks without a fight.

"Fine," she said pertly to the car guy. "I'll return it tomorrow and check it out again. Will that make you happy?"

"Not particularly, but it doesn't matter to me. Would you like me to reserve that for you?"

She rolled her eyes. "*Please.*"

"Okay. Midsize or compact?"

"You already know what I want! I already *have* the car, which, I'd like to point out is a kind of a piece of junk."

"Sorry, but I can't guarantee it will be that car," the man said.

Madeline thought she was teetering on the edge of losing her mind completely. As she argued with the man about renting yet a different car, she noticed Luke walking down the street toward her, his hands shoved in his pocket, his gaze on the sidewalk in front of him. Her pulse instantly ticked up, and her mind was suddenly clouded with the memory of that kiss, that singularly spectacular and quite unexpected, delicious, knee-melting kiss.

As Luke walked past her, he glanced up briefly, took two steps, then stopped and took two steps back, dipping a little to better see her, a smile on his face.

Madeline gestured to her cell phone, then held up one finger to indicate she'd only be a minute longer. "Okay," Madeline said. "Thanks. I'll be there tomorrow." She clicked off the phone and smiled at Luke.

"So what did you do with Madeline?" he asked. "You know, the woman in bad shoes and stained shirt?"

"You should recognize me by now, as this is the bazillionth time you've 'run into me,'" she said, making air quotations with her hands.

"That's because you happen to be staying at the place with the best breakfast in town. So what's going on here? You decide to stay a couple of days and do a complete about-face?"

"You know what they say, when in Rome," she said airily.

Luke folded his arms across his chest and eyed her up and down. "I like it," he said, nodding approvingly. "I like it a lot. But I didn't have you pegged for the polka dot type."

Madeline laughed.

"I didn't think you could get any cuter, but you just did." He reached for the tail of her braid and playfully flicked it.

Madeline was thrilled with his approval. Absurdly thrilled. So thrilled that she set feminism back about two decades. "It's just a sundress," she said.

"It's a dress all right," he said easily, and Madeline could feel herself melting inside. "Before you were cute in a Madeline-work-no-play kind of way. Now you're cute in a funky, fun way. Like the jacket," he added with a crooked smile.

Madeline realized she was beaming. But no one had ever called her fun before, and she was surprised by how much she liked it.

"Heading out to the ranch?" he asked.

"Ah, yes. About that," she said, crossing her feet at the ankles, which was a little hard to do in hiking boots, "I've been kicked out of the Grizzly Lodge and I need a place to stay."

"That's not good," he said casually, his gaze sliding down her body to her boots, and slowly up her legs again.

"I'm sorry—I know you'd rather I stay somewhere else. But there isn't really any other place."

Luke shrugged. "What's one more at this point? Technically, it belongs to you. In fact, you should stay in my old room. Last one on the left," he said, and flicked his gaze over her. "The bed's pretty comfortable."

A tiny shiver slipped down her spine. "I promise it will be like I was never there. In fact, I *won't* be there much. I have to work, I've got it all lined up. And I have to go to Denver tomorrow—"

"Denver? What for?"

"To return that crappy little car and get a new one," she said. "It's a complication with the rental company that defies all logic and is too absurd to even say out loud."

"I know you don't like complications," he said, playing with the tip of her braid again, rubbing it between his fingers. "As it happens, I'm going to Denver tomorrow, too. I could pick you up and bring you back if you need a ride." He tugged on her braid, forcing her to take a step closer to him.

"Great idea . . . but then I'd have nothing to drive while I'm here."

"You could drive my mom's Pontiac. It's not the most stylish thing in the world, but it runs like a tank."

Madeline remembered the Pontiac in the garage. It *looked* like a tank. "I don't know how to drive a tank," she said. "And I don't have night goggles."

"You drive it the same way you do when wearing a pink hat," he said, pulling her one step closer. "It's just sitting there, collecting dust. It could stand to be driven around for a few days. And it's free." His gaze slid to her mouth.

Free definitely appealed to Madeline's frugal nature. "Are you sure?" she asked. "Seems invasive."

"I'm sure." He'd pulled her so close that she could see the flecks of blue in his gray eyes. "I should point out that it's also got a decent backseat."

Madeline had never known how arousing it could be to have a man look at her mouth the way he was looking at hers. "Are you going to kiss me again?"

"I'd like to," he said. "Are you going to kiss me again?"

"It's not a good idea," she said softly.

"I know," he responded agreeably.

"Yesterday was an anomaly," she said. "Bad storm and all that."

"Oh." His gaze lifted to hers. "We're going with the bad storm defense, huh?" He smiled, and let go of her braid.

That smile swirled around in the pit of Madeline, lighting her up. "So . . . does this mean you are okay with me staying at the ranch with Libby?"

Luke laughed at that. "*No*," he said firmly.

He stood so close that she could almost *feel* him against her. It made her feel warm. Too warm. *Hot.*

But Luke kept smiling as if he could see how hot she was feeling, just how out of breath. "See you at the ranch later?"

"Yep." She nervously crossed her feet at the ankles, put her hands on her waist. "Lots to do." She made a little circling gesture with her fingers. "To resolve things."

He nodded, his eyes shining with pleasure. "Okay. But stay out of my stuff, Blue Eyes," he said, and stepped around her. He started to walk away, and looked back over his shoulder. "By the way, I dig the boots."

Madeline instantly looked down, almost having forgotten them. When she looked up, he had walked on.

She turned around and stared at her tiny little car, her heart racing a mile a minute. Her palms were kind of sweaty. Good God, she had not come to Colorado to get involved with some . . . some *hunk* and then fly back to Orlando! What was she doing? She was kidding herself, that was what. Any attraction to that man was going to end badly. She was going to get all giddy and excited that a man as handsome as Luke would find her attractive, and then she'd leave Colorado for Orlando and her life. It was her way: She'd always let a guy get close to her, a perfectly wonderful guy, and then back off. Run. It was a habit she had never examined too closely for fear of what she might discover. But it was as she'd told Luke—not a good idea.

So what was bothering her? Ah yes . . . she hadn't wanted him to agree that it was not a good idea.

"Jesus, *stop* it, Madeline," she muttered. *Just. Stop.*

But as Madeline got in to her car, she wasn't sure if her head wasn't telling her heart to stop being her twisted self for once? Or stop toying with the idea of a hot affair with Luke Kendrick?

EIGHTEEN

This time, when Madeline's clown car puttered into the drive at the ranch, she was ready for the dogs—she'd picked up dog biscuits at Walmart.

She emerged cautiously, the open bag in her hand, biscuits ready to be handed out. She was mildly disappointed that only one of the dogs bothered to come out from under the porch. As the dog approached, she was quick to hold up a biscuit. That proved to be a mistake, however, because the moment she held it up, the other three leapt to their feet and rushed out from under the porch, straight for her.

"Stop!" she cried out. "*Stop, stop!*" Madeline tossed biscuits at them, which they were incredibly adroit at catching, their tails swishing furiously behind them. They crowded in closer, wanting more, and a twinge of panic sprouted in her chest. "*Stop!*" she shouted again.

"*SIT!*" she heard Libby bellow, and from the corner of her eye, saw her striding from the garage, carrying a box, and all four dogs sat instantly. "Garage!" she commanded as she marched forward. With a wistful look and sniff in the direction of Madeline's box of biscuits, the dogs reluctantly slunk away, trotting off down into the meadow, their noses to the ground.

Madeline sagged against her car. "I don't know how you do that."

"Haven't you ever had a dog?" Libby asked, taking the box of biscuits from Madeline.

"No. We moved too much when I was a kid."

"Oh, really? Was your mom in the Armed Services?"

Madeline laughed. "No. She was flaky."

Libby blinked. She handed the box of biscuits back to Madeline. "Well, for starters, you don't offer biscuits unless they follow your command. Otherwise, it's a free-for-all." She suddenly smiled. "Look at *you*," she said. "Cute dress."

"Thanks."

"Are you going to try hiking?" she asked, leaning back to have a look at Madeline's boots.

"Maybe, yeah," Madeline said. She hadn't thought of it before this moment, but she'd seen some well-worn trails leading into the forest and thought, why not? "First, I was hoping we might talk," she said.

She noticed Libby's slight hesitation, but she said, "Sure! I found a coffeemaker yesterday. Want some?"

"Yes, thanks," Madeline said. She grabbed her handbag and followed Libby inside.

The kitchen was starting to look inhabited. In addition to the coffeemaker, there was also a toaster. A green-checkered dish towel had been draped over the oven's door handle, and some fresh flowers were in the little window above the sink.

"I'll make a fresh pot," Libby said, and began to bustle around the kitchen as if she'd been bustling around it for years instead of days, pouring out old grounds and taking a can of fresh coffee from the fridge.

Madeline looked around, wondering if she should do something or sit and wait to be served. What was the protocol between new sisters? She stood there, clutching her handbag. "I hope you won't mind a little company," she said, trying to sound light. "Turns out, I need a place to stay this week. The Grizzly Lodge is booked."

Libby gave her a sidelong glance.

Madeline's grip of her bag tightened. "Seems like it is here or that old hotel out on the Aspen Highway."

She hoped Libby would say something like, "Oh *heavens* no, you can't stay *there!*" But she didn't. She said, "That's great!" in a way that made Madeline think it was not okay, not okay at all.

"Are you sure?" Madeline asked carefully.

"It's not up to me," Libby said. "Choose one of the rooms upstairs and make yourself comfortable. What else did you want to talk about?"

That did not sound very welcoming. But Madeline pressed on. "Well, I was thinking about how to organize all the work we have to do, and I made some notes." She took them out of her bag.

"Great idea," Libby said. "I was thinking the same thing. I was planning to—"

"I thought it would make sense if we divvied the work up," Madeline said quickly before Libby could disrupt her train of thought, or worse, object to order. Madeline really liked the idea of specific areas of work—it took out all the guesswork. And she needed a plan—that's when she did her best work. It was the only way she knew *how* to work. "One of us takes charge of the cleaning. One of us does the research on the house and the market, one of us heads up the people management, and one of us takes charge of improvements. You know, however we have to get it done. That way, all areas are being addressed as quickly as possible."

"People management," Libby repeated uncertainly. "What's that?"

"I made up that term," Madeline said sheepishly. "But I was thinking, the reunion is what, two hundred people? That will require some coordination of people and activities."

"I know!" Libby said, nodding earnestly. "I actually have a little experience with that. At the sheriff's office I organized some of our bigger events."

Madeline tried to guess what events a sheriff would organize. "You could take charge of the house," Madeline said, consulting her list. "You know, cleaning and things like that. I will speak to Luke about doing whatever building project we need. And, of course, I will handle all the research, etc. I'm going to look into this inheritance thing."

"What inheritance thing?" Libby asked.

"Oh, nothing really. I was thinking that we only have Jackson's interpretation of our situation with the ranch and that maybe we should double-check with an outside source to be on the safe side."

Libby regarded her stoically. "You don't trust Jackson?"

"No, I do," Madeline said. "I just thought it would be a good idea to make sure all bases are covered and nothing's left out. So we have our assigned tasks to make this reunion go off, and then my commitment to do the research necessary to sell if that's what we decide. So what do you think?"

Libby walked slowly toward the cabinet, opened it, and took out two coffee mugs. "What about people management, or whatever you called it?"

"Umm . . ." Madeline had figured she would do that, but worried Libby would be a little miffed. "We can decide later," she suggested.

"Well," Libby said. "Looks like you've done a lot of thinking."

"It's what I do," Madeline said. "My job requires a lot of organization and planning."

"Mine did, too," Libby said. She poured a cup of coffee and handed it to Madeline.

Judging by Libby's cool demeanor, Madeline thought it best to leave that remark alone. "Thanks," she said, for the coffee. "Did, ah . . . did Jackson happen to leave the contract for the reunion?"

"He did," Libby said without looking at her. "It's on the coffee table." She picked up a dish towel and began to wipe down perfectly clean counters.

Madeline picked up her coffee. "I didn't mean to step on any toes," she said to Libby. "I thought I was helping."

"You didn't upset me." Libby glanced at her. "But it probably would have been more helpful if we'd made the list together."

Madeline hadn't thought of it that way. She was so used to charging ahead, with no objections from anyone, that she hadn't really thought at all. "You're right," she conceded, earning a surprised look from Libby. "I'm sorry."

Libby nodded and went back to wiping the countertops.

Madeline took herself out of the kitchen before she stepped on any more toes.

The papers were where Libby said they would be, spread out, as if Libby had been studying them, too. Madeline read through the requirements, making mental notes of all that remained to be done. Fortunately, Jackson had taken care of a lot of it. The big party tent that would serve as shelter and a gathering point for meals was sitting down by the fence, waiting to be put up. They had portable toilets and camping tents. The barbeque pits would be delivered in a day or two. The big project left was the construction of temporary showers at the bunkhouse. Madeline would have a look just as soon as she brought the rest of her things in.

She went out to her car for her carry-on, and carried it up to the second floor. Libby, she noticed, had taken up residence in what Madeline thought was the master suite and attached bath; her clothes were spread over the end of the bed.

At the end of the hall on Madeline's left, she found Luke's room. There wasn't really anything inside, none of his "stuff" to go through, really. There was a stripped-down bed and a bureau.

Madeline rolled her carry-on into the room. She peeked into the closet, and was happy to see blankets and sheets, but nothing else. She noticed some marks on the bureau that looked like hatchet marks, as if someone had tried to chop the top of the heavy pine bureau. She ran her fingers over the scars before very tentatively opening a drawer to look in. She found a single athletic sock and a few yellowed pictures. She picked one up; it was a photo of a much younger Luke—she would guess him to be about fifteen—and a boy who looked very much like him. The boy was wearing an irrepressible grin and a blue football jersey. Luke's brother, obviously; they had the same eyes. She put the picture into the drawer and closed it.

Madeline walked to the window and opened the blinds. She was surprised to find a medal hanging there. *First place Roping,* it said. She looked down, noticed the low-slung red building on the other side of the garage. Too big for a shed, too rectangular for a barn. That had to be the bunkhouse.

She walked out of the teenaged Luke's room, leaving her bag just inside the door.

Outside, sunlight spilled over her, warming her. It was another gorgeously blue day, and it inspired Madeline to try and hike up one of the trails.

As she walked past the garage, Libby emerged carrying another box. "Oh, hey," Madeline said. "I'm going to have a look at the bunkhouse."

Libby paused and glanced back over her shoulder at the bunkhouse, then at Madeline. "Are you asking me?"

"No, I—I'm just letting you know. I mean, unless you want to come along. The more the merrier."

"That's okay," Libby said. "I have some cleaning to do." She walked on.

Madeline shook her head and continued, pausing at the open barn door to peek inside. The stalls were empty, but it smelled of manure and hay, and there were several hay bales stacked along the back wall. Horse tack hung just inside the entrance.

She carried on to the bunkhouse, passing through a small fenced area where it looked as if someone had tilled rows for planting at some point, but where weeds now grew. The place looked closed up. Madeline opened the screen door and tried the handle of the door, but it was locked.

She let the screen door close with a bang and stepped off the little porch, walking to the one picture window, and peered in. The light inside was dim, but she could see pages from a newspaper on a chair next to a worn-out lounger. There was a small, flat screen TV mounted to the wall. She couldn't make out anything else. She walked around the corner to the back and was surprised to find a large deck with built-in seating and two barbeque pits. The kitchen was clearly visible through sliding glass doors. It was much larger than Madeline would have guessed, with a huge fridge and a freezer. Like the main house, the wallpaper was fading and the Formica countertops looked worn.

She went around to the back of the bunkhouse. The weeds were tall here, and she had to stand on a rock to look in one of two windows, only to find that the blinds had been closed. She hopped over to the next window, righting an old gray bucket to stand on it. The blinds were open, and she could see through to a hallway with green shag carpet. This room had bunk beds.

Just then, a man suddenly walked by the open doorway, naked except for a towel wrapped around his waist. He had long, wet hair. With a gasp of alarm, Madeline ducked. She hopped off the bucket and squatted down, looking frantically about. Someone *lived* here? She'd been casually peering in the windows of someone's *house*? She half-crawled, half-ran from the bunkhouse, and walked briskly down the road to the main house, her heart pounding.

She saw Libby on the back porch of the main house and jogged toward it. "Libby!" she cried. "There is a *man* in that house!" She flung her arm out, pointing to the bunkhouse.

"Ernest Delgado," Libby said, a little too pertly to suit Madeline. "He's the ranch hand here."

Libby had known a man was in that house when Madeline had gone off to have a look, and had let her go. "Why didn't you tell me?" Madeline demanded.

Libby shrugged. "I thought you'd probably worked it out for yourself that he'd come back."

Madeline whirled around before she said something she couldn't take back.

"Where are you going?" Libby called after her.

"For a walk!" Madeline shouted back.

She walked for several minutes before she was able to unclench her fists and take a breath. She paused and looked around her, at sunlight sparkling through the trees, at the dense foliage and rich colors in the shadow of the forest. The scenery was truly beautiful. So serene.

She moved again, only much slower now, breathing as deeply as she could of the cool, clean air. The path was steep, but she moved slowly, pausing every now and then to catch her breath. She appreciated the steady effort, the stretch in calves as she moved up. If she lived here, she would be like Luke's mother and walk up the mountain, into the forest, every day. This experience, at least in Madeline's narrow world, was incomparable to anything else.

She was actually smiling as she climbed, and at first didn't notice the sound below her in the trees. When she did, she decided she'd imagined it. But when she heard it again, she stopped and looked back. She expected to see a dog, maybe even Libby.

Madeline realized she hadn't actually come up as far as she thought; she could still see the top of the house. She listened for the sound again, and heard nothing. She turned around to continue on when she heard it again, and this time, there was no denying it—something was in those woods. Something bigger than a squirrel.

Much, *much* bigger.

Whatever it was crashed through the woods, its footfall slow but so heavy that she could hear the snap of every limb and twig beneath its weight.

Bear.

Madeline's heart climbed to her throat. She was uphill from a grizzly bear; her only escape was *up*.

The beast moved again, drawing closer, huge and lumbering. Panic-stricken, Madeline tried to think of all the things she'd read in the Grizzly Lodge's local guide about what to do if one ran across a bear. She could not recall one word, and couldn't picture anything but being mauled by a bear, her face excoriated by its enormous paws, her limbs bitten off.

Madeline lost it. Every ounce of composure, every ounce of courage, every shred of common sense flooded out of her like a levee had broken. She screamed—a bloodcurdling, piercing scream that scared even her, and began to run down the path, sliding on rocks and tripping over limbs, all the while shrieking, *"Bear! Bear! Bear!"*

She rounded a corner and looked back to see if the bear was on her heels, and tripped, almost stumbling to her hands and knees but managing, by some miracle, to right herself and keep running. When she was almost to the point where the trail flattened out into the clearing behind the house, she saw Luke running up toward her. Madeline launched herself at him, her arms going tightly around his neck. Luke stumbled backward but held on to her without falling, then grabbed her arms. "Madeline, what the hell!" he demanded, pulling her arms from his neck, holding her firmly.

"*Bear!*" she shrieked frantically at him, her fingers digging into his arms.

Luke looked past her. Madeline's blood was pounding loudly in her ears, her skin crawling with fear.

Luke suddenly threw an arm around her, yanking her into his chest, holding her in his ironclad grip. Madeline could hear the beast coming toward them. She did not let propriety stand in the way; she buried her face in his chest.

"Brace yourself, girl," he said softly. "We might have to fight."

"*What?*" she cried, jerking her gaze up to him.

His lips were pressed together, his eyes squinting at something in the distance. She could feel his strength, could feel safety in his arms. It was insanity that Madeline should feel anything in that moment, much less something hot and fast glowing in her. It was absurd that she should look at his mouth and think of kissing him—had she lost her ever-loving mind? What the hell was the *matter* with her?

Luke suddenly lowered his head, his mouth next to her temple, and blood began to rush in her ears. "Here's what we do. You create a diversion and I'll rush it from behind—"

"Are you *crazy!*" she cried, and struggled against him. All thoughts of kissing him were out of her head now, and survival her only instinct.

But Luke held her tight. His mouth began to quiver; the squint of his eyes began to glint with amusement. Madeline twisted around—

A cow was meandering down the path, another one behind that.

The laugh Luke had been holding back exploded out of him. Madeline shoved hard against his chest and he took a step back, doubled over with laughter. "It's a *cow*," he said through gasps of laughter.

"I can see that!" Madeline shouted. "I thought it was a bear!" She doubled over, her hands on her knees, sucking in her breath, trying to ease her racing heart, to erase the tingly feeling in her skin. "This is *not* funny," she said. But it was—she was trying to contain her smile.

Luke was overcome with laughter. "You should have seen yourself, flying down the trail. I've never seen anyone run that fast!"

"But the cows are way up *there*!" she cried, pointing up the mountain.

"They were. But sometimes, they get on a familiar path and come down." He was still grinning as he held out his hand to her. "Come on," he said, and grabbed her hand, tugging on her. "You gotta move, Maddie. The cows are headed for the trough." He tugged her just off the path, pulling her back into his body to let the two cows pass.

Every inch of Madeline was aware of every inch of him. She was lit up, raw, a big fat neon sign pulsing with adrenaline, and a gravity pulling her into the man at her back.

Luke put his hands on her shoulders as the cows wandered by. "Take another breath and remember, that one day, you will think it was hilarious you thought a cow was a bear."

"That assumes I don't kill myself trying to run from cows in the meantime," she muttered breathlessly.

"I have to admit, it's sexy," he said. "Unpredictable woman afraid of mice and cows."

The word *sexy* sluiced through Madeline like warm butter. "I am not afraid of *cows*," she corrected him. "Let's just say I am unfamiliar."

"Yeah, you keep telling yourself that." He patted her on the shoulder and stepped around her, starting down behind the cows.

Madeline hurried after him in case another unfamiliar beast should make an appearance. "Wait!" She hurried to catch up. "Where are you going?"

"To build some temporary showers. Wanna help?" he asked, then bellowed at one of the cows to move, hitting it on the rump. The cow galloped around the one in front, and the two of them trotted to the barn.

"I do! I had some thoughts on how to proceed," she said.

"With what?"

"All the work that must be done."

They had reached an old pickup that had stacks of plywood and assorted lumber in its bed.

"I thought about dividing the work into quadrants."

Luke paused and gave her a puzzled look. "Into what?"

"Quadrants. It's my organization technique. I am going to work on the contracts and research," she said, holding up a finger. "Libby is cleaning. You will do construction." She held up a forth finger. "We can decide later who will handle the Johnsons. I was thinking maybe a bulletin board by the fence around the front yard, you know, for notes and Lost and Found—" She gave herself a quick shake of the head. "I am getting ahead of myself. The point is, someone needs to deal with the Johnsons."

Luke regarded her with a curious smile. "Quadrants, huh?"

"Trust me. It works."

"Are you always so organized?"

"Yes," she answered without hesitation. "Always."

"Why?"

"Why?"

"I'm just wondering if someone can really live a life in quadrants." He handed her a hammer.

"I don't live in *quadrants*," she said, as if that were ridiculous. "But organization is what makes the world go around. What's this?"

"A hammer."

She smiled. "I *know* it's a hammer. But why are you giving it to me?"

"Because we need to start building showers. And organization does not make the world go round, people do. Flawed, unorganized people. Do you ever just go with the flow?"

"No," she said, watching him strap on a tool belt that hung low on his hips.

"Well *that* was definitive. Why not?"

"In my experience," she said with a small incline of her head, "in the absence of organization and planning, there is only chaos."

"I would argue—" he paused with a slight grunt to hoist lumber onto his shoulder from the bed of the truck "—that in chaos, there is often the joy of discovery."

"Oh no," Madeline said with a laugh. She knew chaos, and she had never known there to be any joy in it. Madeline had only to think back on her life, at the many times her mother's lack of organization had left them living in a car—

"What about yesterday?" He winked at her and started toward the bunkhouse.

Madeline blushed deeply at the reminder. "I'm just trying to avoid a big chaotic disaster here!" she called after him, and heard him laugh.

"You can't control everything, you know. Up here it's okay to go with the flow. The mountains have their own energy. You'll see what I mean. But for right now, Blue Eyes, we need to organize some showers."

He had a point. Madeline followed him down to the bunkhouse. There were three men there, two of them digging a trough. Madeline cringed a little at the sight of the man with long damp hair.

Luke surprised her, speaking to the men in Spanish. The four of them began to work, building a platform from slatted wood. Luke made Madeline help, standing behind her, showing her how to hold the hammer and set a nail when the four men hoisted a sheet of plywood.

It was hard work, she quickly realized, but exhilarating. They managed to erect the back of what would become three temporary showers. But when her arm began to burn with the exertion, and the hammer grew heavier, Luke took it from her. "You're fired," he teased her, and made quick work of the two nails she'd been assigned to hammer. "We'll finish up here."

She wouldn't argue and stepped back. "I'll go . . . organize something else," she said.

"Still need the ride tomorrow?" Luke asked as she began to back away.

"Still offering?"

"Of course. I could use a passenger who carries a map and a highlighter. I'll pick you up at the airport rental at five?"

Madeline could feel that ridiculously broad smile appear on her face again. "See you then," she said, and turned around, striding away before she turned to goo.

She looked back only once. Luke was still watching her. She smiled and turned around again.

Yep, she was right. That man looked awfully good in a pair of jeans. Madeline walked back to the house, feeling the pull of the mountains—or something—through her. She felt good. Airy. As if wind chimes were tinkling deep inside her.

Libby walked out onto the porch with a basket of laundry as Madeline stepped into the yard. She wasn't even perturbed with Libby anymore. "Need some help?" she offered.

"Hanging laundry?" Libby asked.

"I happen to be an expert laundry hanger," Madeline said.

"Okay," Libby said. "Come on."

Madeline followed Libby into the trees and a clearing she had not seen until now. There was a deck here, a couple of old Adirondack chairs among pots that had obviously been full at one point, judging by the dead leaves and stems. And a table made from the stump of an old tree. A pair of mushrooms was growing from a crack in the middle of it. A frayed hammock swung between two trees, next to the clothesline.

"This is pretty," Madeline said.

"I think it was Mrs. Kendrick's garden," Libby said, and planted the basket at her feet. She picked three clothespins from the line and pulled a floral chiffon blouse from the basket.

"That's lovely," Madeline said, and picked up a towel.

"Thanks. I bought it for a wedding."

"Whose?" Madeline asked idly as she pinned the towel.

Libby gave her a funny look. "Dad's," she said after a moment. "His last one. What was it, five? Six? I lost count."

"Wow," Madeline said.

"Yeah . . . I guess he got around."

Madeline wondered how Grant managed to attract so many women. Was he handsome? Sophisticated? She surprised herself by asking, "What sort of dad was he?"

"He was okay," Libby said, and shrugged. "He was decent to me."

Decent was an odd way to describe a father.

"You really don't know anything about him?" Libby asked as she picked up a sheet. "I mean, surely your mom must have said something about him, right?"

Madeline snorted. "My mom hardly remembers him. I don't think they were together very long. What about your mom?"

"They were together a few years after he split up from Emma's mom. I don't know this for a fact, but I think maybe something was going on between them before he ever left Emma's mom. My mom calls him her brain drain." She laughed at that.

So did Madeline. "Did he do things with you? I mean, like father-daughter dances, or softball, something like that?"

Libby tossed her head back and laughed. "God no," she said, smiling with amusement. "He wasn't that kind of dad. He was the kind of dad who sometimes gave me money and every once in a while would take me to dinner and ask how I was doing. And then I wouldn't hear from him for months." She paused, looking off for a moment. "He took Emma and me to Disney once. But even then, I remember he stayed in the hotel watching sports while Emma's mother took us to the park."

As a child, Madeline had been dragged to Disney World with her mother and her friends, usually left to fend for herself, loosely chaperoned by some teen, while her mother and her friends stayed behind in a seedy hotel and drank. Madeline hated Disney because of that.

"How did you end up in California with Emma, if he was married to your mom later?" Madeline asked.

Libby sighed. "Oh, the drama." She paused to pin a pillowcase. "We lived in Colorado Springs. When I was about eight, he and my mom broke up, and he went back to Emma's mom in California. It was like a soap opera. Anyway, Mom and Dad had this big, ugly custody fight and she lost the first go-round. Dad didn't want to pay child support." She smiled sheepishly at Madeline. "I guess that's no surprise."

Madeline smiled back. "Unfortunately, no."

"I was there a year or so with Emma and her mom, then Dad thought I'd be better off with my mom and shipped me home. My mom had met her second husband by then."

"Do you keep in touch with Emma?" Madeline asked.

Libby clipped a sheet on the line. "Not really. Emma's different. She's always out in the world doing things. And she's not very sentimental. Me, I'm more of a homebody. What about you?"

"It's just me and my mom," Madeline said. "She never married. And she wasn't very good at holding down a job, so we bounced around a lot."

"Looks like we have a few things in common after all, Madeline," Libby said.

Madeline wasn't sure why Libby said it precisely that way, as if she had already determined that they had nothing in common. Generally, Madeline would agree. But Madeline was beginning to warm to Libby. There was something about her that Madeline could relate to. As much as she hated to admit it, it was something sad.

"I'm going to Denver tomorrow," Madeline announced, turning back to business and the safety she felt in the midst of rules and tasks that needed completion, "I have to return my car to Denver. I'm going to catch a ride back with Luke. So I don't know how late I will be."

"Luke, huh?" Libby asked slyly.

"It's not like that," Madeline said. "He's just doing me a favor."

Libby looked as if she didn't believe Madeline for even a moment. "You have to admit that he's not too hard on the eyes."

"He's okay," Madeline said, but she could feel the telltale heat creeping into her cheeks and smiled self-consciously.

"Okay?" Libby snorted. "Most women I know would kill to have a shot with a guy like Luke Kendrick. But then, I hear he is still in love with Julie Daugherty."

Madeline's heart fluttered. "Who?" she asked coyly, knowing very well who. A pretty blonde woman with an adorable baby girl, that was who.

"Julie Daugherty. They were together for a few years. They were supposed to get married a while back, but then she broke it off."

That certainly had Madeline's attention. "Really? What happened?"

"I don't know," Libby said. "I just heard it through the grapevine."

This is what happened when attachments formed, Madeline thought. Disappointment. Deep rivers of disappointment. Perhaps this was a good thing. Madeline didn't want any attachment, so the rumor served as a reminder that she was experiencing nothing more than a little mountain flirtation that Trudi would congratulate her for. *Nothing more.*

As Libby chattered about something Julie did in high school, Madeline reminded herself that her life was in Orlando and she needed to concentrate on doing what she needed to do so she could go home. She really couldn't afford to be wandering around the mountains thinking silly thoughts about a man she would not know more than this week. Nor did she want to be on hand when the Johnsons began to show up.

In fact, when she left here today, she would drive to town and call Stephen, get the name of that realtor. No use putting that off, was there?

Yep, hearing about Luke and Julie was a good thing. It gave her perspective again. And Madeline would ignore that hearing it felt a little like being punched.

NINETEEN

So Dad and I are off to Durango today so they can stick more needles
in me. I wanted Luke to come, but he said, "No, man, I have to go to
Denver and check on work," which I thought was perfectly reasonable,
seeing as how he has a business there and didn't count on all this stuff
with Homecoming Ranch. But I was hoping he would come because
Make-A-Wish-Foundation is all over that hospital, and I've got a deal
with this kid, Dante.

Dante is sixteen, and he's got Stage IV cancer, and the Make-A-Wish
people want him to make a wish. He said he couldn't do Disney, he'd
rather die than do Disney. I don't think he meant it like *that*, but, you
know, like he really didn't want to go to Disney. So I said, "Dude, you
gotta shoot higher! Go big or go home! You gotta go for something
that makes you want to do the chemo every day, right?" And he said
he didn't know what that was. But I know this kid, he's always there
when I am. I know he's like me, and he *loves* sports. So I suggested,
"How about a Denver Bronco's game in a skybox?"

You should have seen Dante—he lit up like Rockefeller Center at
Christmas time.

So we've been working on a deal where we are trying to convince
Make-A-Wish to grant him that wish, along with a close, personal
friend. That's me, the color commentator. I can tell him everything

there is to know about every player on the Broncos' roster and then some.

I wanted to introduce Luke to Dante so Dante would add him to the list, too, because again, we're talking the *Broncos* in *premium* seats.

So anyway, Luke said he couldn't go, and then he said he'd be late because he's picking up Blue Eyes in Denver and taking her back to Homecoming Ranch, and I'm like, "The ranch? I thought you didn't want them out there!"

And he said, "I don't. But it's okay, we've worked it out for now."

Listen, I may be tied to a chair, but I am no slouch in the perception department. But lately, I can't read Luke at all. One minute he's "thinking" about Julie, and the next, he's got this funny look on his face telling me he's giving Blue Eyes a ride. I observed, and very casually I might add, "You seem to be running into Blue Eyes a *lot*."

Luke knows he is, because he didn't try to argue. He just laughed and said, "Don't wait up, loser."

Well, the joke is on buddy boy, because I *will* be up, because tonight is *The Walking Dead* marathon, and I am *not* missing that.

So okay, Luke went on his way, as happy as a kid in a bouncy castle, and I bet he hadn't even hit Sometimes Pass when Julie showed up. She stood at the screen door with her baby, all smiles, and yeah, her baby is supercute. She said "Hey, Leo, is Luke around?" Like she didn't dump him for Brandon. Like she hasn't called him every time she gets worried and then dumps him all over again. She's like one of those bounce back paddleballs, just keeps hitting him and waiting for him to bounce back, then hitting him again.

I said, "No. He went back to Denver." I didn't say he was coming back, and Julie looked kind of shocked, like, "What-am-I-going-to-do-with-this-baby" shocked, but then Marisol comes in with my medicine and she says, "What are you doing here, Julie?"

Julie said, "I'm looking for Luke."

Well, Marisol, she's not a fan of Julie, but she's also not a fan of lying, and she said, "He went to Denver, he'll be back later."

And I said, "*Way* later. Like next year later."

Marisol squeezed my shoulder really hard and she said, "Maybe you should come back tomorrow, Julie. It will be late before he gets back."

Of course Julie was all sweet smiles and thank-yous to Marisol, and she went bopping down the steps, her baby on her hip, looking back at me.

I swear, I think that baby gave me the stink eye.

Luke—I tried, bro, I tried.

TWENTY

Luke's day in Denver was not what he'd call a towering success.

The first thing he did when he arrived was to drive to his little two-bedroom bungalow in an older part of Denver. He'd bought the rundown piece of crap and had restored it with some money his mom had left him. Since then, the market had come up. Luke liked knowing that if anything ever happened, he had some equity in this house. Anything, like needing an attorney. The equity in his house was what he planned to use to fight the loss of Homecoming Ranch.

But before he spoke to an attorney, Luke had to see about his housing starts. He left the Bronco, switched to his work truck, and drove to the outskirts of Denver to check on the first three Kendrick Custom Homes. With the help of Stuart Homes, where he'd apprenticed the last few years, and who owned a minority share in his business, Luke had purchased three lots in a new subdivision. It had taken some time to get the deeds and permits set up, but in the last month, they had finished the site prep, had poured three slabs, and if all had gone well last week, the framing would have begun by now.

As he turned the corner onto Mountain View Street, he grinned at the sight before him. The framing on the first house looked almost complete.

He parked his work truck, hopped out. Refugio, the crew boss, met him on the sidewalk, and together, they walked through the framing so Luke could have a look. Satisfied that things were moving along, Luke was headed back to his truck when he saw Ben Stuart's king cab pickup truck glide to a halt next to the curb. Ben emerged with a wave for Luke. "Hey buddy!" he said cheerfully. "I wondered when you'd be back."

"I'm here today," Luke said. "Framework looks good."

Ben nodded, then looked back at Luke. "What do you mean, you're here today? Your dad's okay, right?"

Luke had told Ben that something had come up with his dad, but he hadn't explained what. "Dad's okay," Luke assured him. "He just needs some help with a couple of things."

Ben looked at Luke expectantly, wanting more.

Luke glanced at the two empty slabs. "Refugio said he could start framing this one next week." He glanced at Ben. "But I need to go back home for a week or two."

Ben's pleasant expression began to fade. "One week? Or two?"

Honestly, Luke didn't know long he'd be. He still didn't know exactly what he was doing in Pine River, other than trying to stick his fingers into a bunch of little holes in the dyke.

Ben guessed as much and groaned. "Come on, man! You have three starts, Luke. *Three.* Someone's gotta be here to manage it. These houses are clear across town from where I'm working right now."

"I know," Luke said apologetically. "I know the timing is bad. I know it's a pain in the ass. But right now, my dad's in kind of a bind, and I need to be there. No more than a couple of weeks," he assured Ben, and sent up a little bit of begging to the heavens that what he was saying was true. He'd worked too hard for this opportunity to let it slip through his fingers, and the way things were going, he would never have the scratch to do this on his own. He needed Stuart Homes, needed them more than Ben would ever know. "Believe me, I don't want to be in Pine River any more than you want me gone. I'll come in and check at least once a week."

Ben frowned. He glanced back at the men across the street hammering on the house frame. "Okay, Luke. I'll cover you for a couple of weeks. But I can't cover these houses forever—I've got my own work, and my wife is on my ass about the hours I keep as it is."

"I'm sorry, Ben."

"Yeah, well, sorry isn't going to cut it in a couple of weeks, okay? This was all about giving you a leg up, Luke," he said, gesturing to the housing pads. "We had this trouble with you last fall, always off to Pine River. We haven't even finished the first frame and you're doing it again."

"Come on, Ben," Luke said coolly. "It's not like I planned this. It's not like I haven't thought of every option and tried to come up with a better one. But you know the situation with my brother. I'm all my dad has."

That seemed to soften Ben a little. He nodded, turned his head and spit. "Yeah, I know. You've got a lot of talent, Luke. But maybe you ought to be using that talent in Pine River."

"There's no market for custom homes up there," Luke said.

Ben nodded. "Okay. Two weeks."

"Thanks, man," Luke said. He didn't tell Ben that not only was there no market in Pine River, but that he needed distance from Pine River. He needed time to himself, away from the constant pressure of disease and financial trouble.

Luke's day only got worse when he showed up at the door of his economic professor, who held once-a-week open office hours. Professor Whitehall was less friendly than Ben. "Mr. Kendrick," he said, looking at Luke over the tops of his glasses, "I thought you had withdrawn from school."

It went downhill from there. Luke had missed too many classes. Professor Whitehall told him that he didn't know if it was possible for Luke to catch up, but that he had one opportunity in the form of a test the following week. A test that covered material Luke had not even read yet.

His last stop before picking up Madeline was with the attorney Jackson had pointed him to. Dan Broadstreet was a big guy who wore a bolero tie and a short-sleeved shirt. He took Luke's hand in his beefy one, shook it vigorously, and then invited him into a conference room. He had a pad of yellow legal paper and pencil, but he made only one note as Luke explained the situation to him.

"This is a bad deal. We might be able to argue coercion or something like it, and at least keep a sale tied up long enough that any potential buyer walks away. That way, you'd have time to get the money together to buy it," he advised. "But there's really nothing to fight. If you do, you won't win. The laws around real estate protect the buyer. Even dead ones."

In essence, Luke had to make his new company work in order to generate enough money to buy back the ranch. Because any other money he had would go toward tying up a potential sale, prolonging it long enough to give him time to raise the money—money he was in danger of losing because he kept getting called back to Pine River. It was a desperate circle.

When Luke came out of the attorney's office, he noticed that clouds had moved in over Denver, thick and gray, hanging low. The temperature had dropped ten to fifteen degrees.

Madeline was waiting for him at the Economy car lot, shivering in a little sweater that tied up under her breasts and a turquoise sundress with yellow sunflowers dancing around the hem. She had a small bag that hung across her body, looped over her shoulder. And she was holding two bags from Target.

After the day he'd had, it made him strangely happy to see her.

He pulled up alongside the curb and lowered the passenger window of his truck. "Everything squared away?"

She looked slightly taken aback by his question, which he thought was a little odd, but then she smiled and the dimples appeared again. "I think so. Are you ready?"

"I am. Climb in."

She opened the door, slung her Target bags behind the passenger seat, and climbed up, leaning over just enough to give Luke a nice view of her cleavage. She pulled the door shut behind her and folded her arms tightly across her and looked at him. "I'm freezing."

Luke turned on the heat. "We have to swing by my house and get the Bronco, if that's okay."

"Sure!" She huddled forward, her legs pressed together, her feet still in the hiking boots, but today, thick socks were pulled up to her knees. Her dark hair had been whipped by the wind, and spilled across her back in an appealing tangle of silky strands. "The clouds came from nowhere," she said. "I was so busy, I didn't even notice them."

"Did you finish what you needed to do?"

She smiled at him. "I got a *lot* done. I love days like this when I can tick off my tasks, one by one. What about you?"

"I guess I did what I needed to do," he said, pulling into traffic. He didn't care to elaborate. He was trying to forget it. "I don't feel like I left anything hanging, anyway."

"See? Organization. *You* don't know for sure, whereas *I* know I don't have anything left, because *I* made a list."

"And I bet you highlighted the tasks as you finished them."

Madeline laughed. "Am I that obvious?"

She was so pretty when she laughed that he couldn't help but smile back. "A little."

"You're obvious, too, Luke Kendrick," she said. "I bet you think no one can read you."

"Of course no one can read me," he said confidently. "I'm a guy. We are trained from an early age."

"I knew it!" she cried triumphantly. "And I bet you are one of those guys who shows up to work and looks around and thinks, I should do that," she said pointing into space. "And maybe that. And maybe that if I have time before lunch, but if I don't, oh well, I'll get to it one of these days."

Now Luke laughed outright. "Construction does not lend itself to tidy little tasks, Maddie. My days are spent keeping lids on boiling pots."

"And you think selling houses doesn't have pots?" She snorted at that, and dug one of the Target bags out from behind the seat. She was jubilant as she paused to examine the sack's contents.

"So in all that highlighting, you still had time for a little shopping?"

"No. I *made* time to pick up a few things I *need*." She gave him a pert smile. "Important things, like *underwear*," she said gravely. "And lotion. I'm turning into an alligator."

It sure didn't look like that from where Luke was sitting.

Madeline peered into her bag. "I picked up some extra socks, too. My feet have been so cold. Oh, and this," she said, and pulled out a bear whistle. A cheap, souvenir-type bear whistle that wouldn't be useful in any situation, except maybe calling a well-trained dog. But Madeline draped it around her neck, and the thing nestled between two mounds of cream. She looked so proud of herself that he didn't have the heart to tell her that her purchase was useless at Homecoming Ranch.

"And some hair thingies."

"Can't have enough hair thingies," he said.

"You really can't," she agreed, and chatted about her day until he pulled into the drive of his house.

Only then did Madeline stop talking. She squinted at his bungalow, which he'd painted a sunny yellow with white trim. "Wow," she said approvingly. "*Great* curb appeal."

"I should hope so. I've spent a lot of time landscaping." He opened the driver door. "I just need to grab a couple of things."

"Mind if I look inside?" she asked, her hand on the door handle. Luke hesitated, but she quickly added, "I like houses, I really do. I just want to see."

"I can't vouch for how clean it is."

"I won't judge," she said with a smile, and hopped out of the truck. The wind had picked up; she cried out with alarm. "It's *freezing!*" she shouted, and darted for the front door, the hem of her dress kicking up behind her, revealing some very shapely hamstrings.

Hamstrings. Luke was admiring a woman's hamstrings. He told himself to reel it in, to stop looking at dimples and hamstrings and the way bear whistles rested between two very excellent breasts. He walked up behind her, reached around, unlocked the door and pushed it open. Madeline hopped inside like a bird, with her arms wrapped tightly around her.

Just inside the door, Luke pulled one of his flannel jackets off a hook. "Here. You're making me cold just looking at you."

"*Thank* you," she said gratefully, and slipped into it. "I'm going to have all your jackets at this rate." The jacket dwarfed her, but she sighed with delight. "Heaven," she said. She glanced around, her gaze looking up, to the crown molding, and then down, to the hardwoods and window casings Luke had put in himself. He'd painted the living room sea green. It was the color he remembered the ocean to be when he and Leo and his parents had vacationed in California many years ago.

"Wow," Madeline said, slowly turning in a circle, nodding appreciatively. "This place is *nice*. Did you do it?"

"I did."

"While you were in school?"

He nodded. While he was in school, while he was working. He'd found that he didn't have to think about troubles at home if he kept himself occupied every moment of every day.

"It's gorgeous, Luke." She moved forward, leaning through the doorway to peer into the adjoining kitchen. "Oh, wow, *completely* upgraded. You did it all by yourself?"

"All by myself."

She turned around and beamed at him. "It's really fantastic. You could make a fortune in Orlando. I—" Her cell phone rang, startling her. Madeline fished her phone from the little purse that hung around her neck. "Oh," she said, looking at the number. "Excuse me," she said to Luke, then answered the phone with a "Bree? Is everything okay? It's after hours there—"

Whatever Bree said caused Madeline to gasp. "You're kidding," she said flatly. "Are you *kidding*?" She suddenly let out a shriek to Luke's ceiling and did a fist pump. "That's *fabulous!*" She pulled the phone away from her mouth and said to Luke, "I got an offer on the DiNapoli property!" She followed that with a bit of a Snoopy dance, then put the phone to her head again. "Okay, lay it on me. What's the offer?"

Whatever Bree said dimmed Madeline's smile a little. She stood up a little straighter. "Okay," she said, nodding. "Okay. We can work with that. I mean, yes, it's a million less than what Mr. DiNapoli wanted, but he has to be reasonable. Give me something to sweeten the pot— how soon can they close?"

She nodded as Bree talked, her brow furrowed in concentration. "Fabulous," she said. "Who's the realtor? Andy Griggs! *Gah*," she groaned, bending backward. "Okay, all right, so I will call and present the offer to Mr. DiNapoli and give Andy a call. Great. Thank you, Bree! Thank you! And wish me luck!" She hung up the phone and looked at Luke. She seemed almost to levitate off the floor. "I have an *offer*. Granted, it's a lowball offer, but still, it's an offer!" She squealed again, then took a deep breath, and another, and punched in the number of the seller.

"Mr. DiNapoli!" she said brightly when the client answered, and whirled around, her back to Luke. "Hi! It's Madeline Pruett, and I have *great* news." She walked into the kitchen, talking very quickly, laying out the offer.

Luke could tell from the way her hand curled into a little fist and how fast she began to speak that DiNapoli didn't like the offer. But he had to hand it to her, Madeline was selling it. It was as if she had compiled a mental list of all the reasons why this was a great deal for the seller, and she was rolling through them, one by one, marking them off. Luke walked to the front windows and looked out while she talked. The sky to the north was so black that it almost looked green. They needed to leave now, or risk getting caught in what looked like would be one very ugly storm.

"Just think about it," he heard Madeline say. "We will counter, and if it's the statuary you feel is undervalued, maybe we can talk about removing that— Yes, I understand that you built the house around the art. But, Mr. DiNapoli, I'll be frank. You've had the house on the market for two years. Perhaps you should consider the idea that not everyone appreciates the sophistication of your artistry, you know? I mean, if you think about it, most people aren't exposed to the kind of art education *you've* had. . . . Okay, great. I'll wait to hear from you, then. But we could close this deal tonight. Just saying. All right."

She clicked off and turned around, her expression exuberant. "He's going to consider it. He's actually *considering* it! Oh my God, I may sell that ugly pile of stones!" She threw her arms in the air in victory.

Luke grinned at her happiness. "That's great news, Maddie. I'm happy for you. Listen, we better get going before the weather moves in—"

"What? No!" she cried. "No, no, I can't risk losing reception in the mountains on the biggest deal of my life! No, Luke, I have to stay put until he calls."

"We don't want to be driving across Sometimes Pass at night and in the middle of a really bad storm."

"Please, Luke," she said. "This is a really big deal for me."

It was impossible to say no to that pretty face with the dancing blue eyes. "Okay," he said, and Madeline made that little sound of happiness again.

"Okay, give me two secs. I have to call Trudi. And my mom," she said, and punched her phone again.

Luke decided to build a small fire to warm the living room, and went about that as he listened to her chatter to the person named Trudi, who was, judging by the talk, a very close friend. He heard Madeline say in the course of the conversation that she was getting another call. He stepped outside for more wood—the wind was horrible now, bending the old elm in the backyard—and when he stepped back in, he realized she was speaking to Mr. DiNapoli.

"That's *great*," she said, sounding almost breathless. "You won't be sorry, Mr. DiNapoli. I am sure your beach house will be *stunning* with the statuary . . . Well, your wife didn't want it in Orlando, either, as I recall, so I am sure you can convince her again."

Luke could hear Mr. DiNapoli's deep voice on the other end of her cell, rattling on about Greece or something.

"Okay, well, I better get hold of the buyer's realtor and present the counter. Don't want them to get cold feet!" A few moments later, Luke heard her say, "Hello, Andy." Her voice had changed completely; it was low and professional. The voice of the Madeline who had shown up at Homecoming Ranch the first day.

"Madeline Pruett here. Thank you for the offer on the DiNapoli property—what? I've had the listing several months. Why?" A moment later, she said, not as smoothly, "Oh spare me, Andy. He's not going to give it away . . . Yes, I have a counter." She marched into Luke's kitchen, her boots clumping on the wood floors, and told him what DiNapoli would accept. "Hey! That's not nice. He is a very nice man, and he's going to put the statuary out in his beach house. So are you going to present the counter to your client? What do you mean, they won't take it?"

Luke helped himself to a beer and perched on a barstool, enjoying the wrangling between Madeline and the Griggs guy. Madeline was a persistent woman—she laid out every conceivable selling point, down to the superior quality of the stone in the garage. In the end, it must have been enough to convince the other guy, because when she hung up, she whirled around and said, "He's buying in to the counter offer. I think. Maybe." She beamed at Luke.

Her announcement was punctuated by a peel of thunder over their heads. Madeline jumped; she looked at her phone. "Don't lose a signal now, please, please, don't lose a signal."

Rain began to pelt Luke's little house, and quickly turned into heavy, gray sheets. Madeline beat a steady rhythm on the back of a chair with her fist, staring at her phone. "Hey," Luke said. "Take a breath. You're about to make the biggest deal of your life."

Her eyes sparked with delight; she grinned. "Do you know how long I've been trying to sell this house? When I think of the open houses, the events, the advertising! Everyone in real estate in Orlando laughed when I took that listing. Especially Andy Griggs, so of course it would be *him* to call with a lowball offer, but that's okay, I can deal with him. I mean, we countered with half a million off the asking price. A half million! I practically had to tie Mr. DiNapoli down and get him to agree to list the place for three and a half million, which I can assure you is *way* over market. So to get him to come down—and someone to offer! Sometimes, people don't care about price, they only care about location or amenities, and they—"

Her phone rang.

Madeline gasped. She stared at her phone. "It's Andy." The phone rang again. "What if they don't take it? What if I have to keep that stupid listing?"

"Maddie . . . answer it," Luke said calmly.

"Right." She answered the phone, sliding into a professional voice. "Hi, Andy. What's up?"

She traced a finger along the edge of his table. "Mm-hm," she said, "Okay." She paused, her hand coming to a halt on the table. "That's *great*. Your clients will be very happy. . . . Thank you, Andy! No, I can't get a drink to celebrate," she said with a roll of her eyes. "I'll have Bree draw up the paperwork and get it over to you first thing." She paused. And then she said softly, "Seriously—thank you, Andy." She hung up the phone. She whirled around as another crack of thunder rattled the windows. She threw her hands up in the air, bent backward and laughed. It was not a chuckle, not even a chortle. Madeline's laugh was deep, from the belly. It was a laugh of pure joy, of happiness.

"I *sold* it, Luke!" she cried. "I sold that sorry piece of expensive shit!" She suddenly threw her arms around him and did a little quickstep to one side, then the other, hugging him. Luke managed to hang on to his chair. He also managed to catch the scent of her hair. It reminded him of the lilac trees that grew in his mother's garden.

Just as suddenly, Madeline let go. "Do you know what this *means?*" she cried, and punched him in the arm. "It means I'm going to make a *huge* commission!" She gasped. "Oh my God, I *am*! And it means people will have to take me seriously! Oh! I almost forgot! I have to call Mr. DiNapoli!" She grabbed up her phone, punching the Call Return button as she walked out of the kitchen, away from Luke, her smile radiant, her eyes brilliant.

Luke stood up from the bar and turned around to the window. He stared at the deluge of rain, hardly seeing it. He didn't really hear Madeline in the other room, talking about closing dates.

He was thinking about lilacs. He really liked lilacs. He had no idea until this moment just how much he liked lilacs.

TWENTY-ONE

The rain was falling so hard that if Madeline could have reached her mother, she wouldn't have been able to hear her. She put her phone aside and turned around—and saw Luke beneath the arched entry into the kitchen and dining area. He was leaning up against it, holding a frozen pizza. He smiled at her. "Hungry?"

"Starving," Madeline said gratefully.

She followed him into the kitchen, watched him turn on his oven, then slide in the pizza. He then reached into his fridge and pulled out two bottles of beer. He twisted the top off of one and put it in front of her. "We should toast your great sale," he said.

Madeline stared at the bottle as he took the top off the second one. "Don't tell me you don't drink beer," he said.

"Rarely." She glanced up at him. "Okay, never. I drank it once."

"Don't like the taste?"

"No, that's not it. I don't drink very much. I spent too many years cleaning up after my mom's drinking."

"Fair enough," he said. "But this is good beer, and your big sale deserves a big toast."

He was right. If Trudi were here, she'd be yelling at Madeline to step outside her bubble, pick up the beer and *drink*. She smiled at the image of Trudi and picked up the beer. How ironic that of all the people in the world who should be here to share this moment with her, it wasn't Trudi, it was Luke Kendrick.

"To Blue Eyes Pruett," Luke said, lifting his bottle aloft, and nodding at her to do the same. "The best realtor in Orlando, Florida."

Madeline grinned. "Here, here," she said, and tapped her bottle to his. She drank hesitantly, but was surprised that the beer went down smoothly. "*Hey,*" she said. "It's good."

"Of course it's good," Luke said. "It's made right here in Denver with pure mountain water." He gave her a wry smile and turned back to the stove.

Ten minutes later, they were sitting side by side at his kitchen bar, eating pepperoni pizza, drinking beer, and chatting. Luke was great company, Madeline had to admit. He was easy to talk to, and seemed genuinely interested in her.

He asked how she got into real estate.

"Looking for something," she said picking at the pepperonis on her second slice. "I wanted to go to college. I had grand dreams of being a doctor or a lawyer. You know, something important," she said with a laugh. "If I could have figured out how to do it, I would have, but unfortunately, we didn't have the money for me to go to college." She bit into her pizza. The lack of money was a sore spot for Madeline. Her grandparents had saved for her college, but they'd made the mistake of leaving her mother in charge of it. It was the story of her life—her mother abused her parents' trust and their resources time and again, and time and again, her grandparents kept trying to pretend their daughter was a stand-up adult.

"So you went into real estate."

"Yep. I was looking for a profession where I thought I could make a decent living and one that I would like. One summer, my best friend's parents put their house on the market, and I just happened to be there when their realtor came to talk to them about listing it. I remember thinking she was so pretty, and so professional. But what really impressed me was that she was driving a BMW." Madeline laughed.

He smiled. "There are worse reasons to choose an occupation."

"What about you? Why did you choose architecture?"

"Same kind of thing," he said with a shrug. "I wasn't good enough at football to go pro after college. And I hated English." He laughed. "I didn't know what I wanted to do. Then my mom got sick, and college became a hit-or-miss kind of thing. I would go one semester, drop out the next. Enroll again. It took me almost six years to finish as it was." He tossed a crust onto his plate. "If that doesn't focus you, nothing will. I landed on architecture and didn't look back. I couldn't afford to look back. And I'm struggling for time," he added with a shrug. "I'm not sure I'll be able to finish the semester because I've missed too much. I have to redeem myself next week on a test, or I have to drop the class."

"Oh no." Madeline would be beside herself if she'd paid for a class and couldn't finish it. She looked at Luke's hands. They were strong hands, with thick fingers, a scar across the back of one, calloused across the pad of his right hand. He'd built his life with his hands.

"It's not the end of the world," Luke said. "If I have to, I'll just take it again."

"Are you glad you chose architecture?" Madeline asked.

"Yeah, I am. I discovered that I really liked the math and puzzle of it. You know, putting things together, making different designs work." He suddenly smiled at her, and—whether it was the beer or the moment, Madeline was dazzled by it. Truly dazzled. Warm and fuzzily dazzled.

She smiled, too, took another swig of her beer. "I would love to see your houses and designs sometime. Houses are my thing, you know."

"I know," he said watching her. "Ironic, huh?"

She smiled. "A little." They sat gazing at each other. Madeline could feel the tension swirling around them again, but then the lights over the bar suddenly flickered. She and Luke looked up at the same moment, and in the next, the power went out.

"Great," she said.

"It happens a lot in the spring. Hold tight," he said, and got up from the bar, disappearing into the living room. Madeline shivered; the kitchen and dining area were awash in the green, murky light of the storm. All around that little bungalow, the wind howled, and flashes of lightning illuminated the room for a few seconds before the rain swallowed up the light and made the room murky again.

A moment later, Luke reappeared. He had a flashlight. "Grab the beers, okay?" he said, and held out the light, pointing it on the floor where Madeline was to walk. He led her into the living room, where he had propped two floor pillows against his couch, just before the hearth.

"Fabulous!" she said. It was warmer before the fire. They could hear the storm raging, could still see the flashes of lightning, but the fire seemed to form a barrier between the storm and them.

Luke's legs stretched long in front of him, his arm casually draped across the couch behind her. "So who is Trudi?" he asked. "You've mentioned her a few times."

"She's the sister I never had," Madeline said airily, before she realized what she'd said. She smiled sheepishly. "I mean, until now."

"That must be strange, finding out about siblings at this stage of the game."

"It's surreal," Madeline agreed.

"What about your mom?" he asked. "She didn't know about them?"

Madeline snorted and settled deeper into the cushion. "No." She felt warm and fluid after two beers, and uncharacteristically trusting. "I'll let you in on a little secret," she said sagely. "My dad wasn't the only bad parent in my life. My mother . . ." She took a breath and let it out, slowly, thinking how best to describe her. "She's not very responsible. No, wait, let me rephrase that. She's totally irresponsible," she said, pointing with her beer bottle for emphasis. "I've always had to take care of her."

"I gathered," he said. He put his hand on her leg and squeezed softly. "Sorry."

"I'll break it down for you," Madeline said, feeling safe. "One, lots of stepfathers and stepfather wannabes. Two, she never held a job more than a couple of months. Three, she squanders everything anyone ever gives her, and four, she's kind of self-centered."

"Wow," Luke said. "Sounds like you've had a tough life."

"You have no idea." Madeline liked this, she thought. She didn't get any judgmental vibes from Luke. He made it easy to confess the truth about her family. "I had good grandparents," Madeline said with a shrug, as if that made up for the completely ineffectual mothering she had received. "I bet your parents were Ozzie and Harriet."

Luke gave her a rueful smile. "I won't lie—they were pretty damn good parents. I had a great life at the ranch."

"Until now," she said.

Luke didn't say anything at first. He turned his head and looked at her, his expression resigned. "Until now," he agreed.

Madeline felt bad for him, truly horrible. But she couldn't change what had happened to his family. She looked to the window; the rain was still coming down hard, but the wind had begun to die down. Her gaze fell on a picture on a shelf on the wall. She could see Luke and a man who looked a lot like him. Luke had his arm draped around his shoulder. But sitting just to his left was the blonde woman who had come into the Stakeout the first night she'd met him. "Hey," she said, pointing her beer bottle at the picture. "That's Julie What's Her Name."

Luke glanced up from the study of his beer label and seemed surprised. "I forgot that was there." He hopped up, walked across the room, and picked up the picture. He took it down, slid it onto a table inside the entry hall.

"Why'd you do that?" Madeline asked as Luke settled back onto the floor beside her. "Isn't she your friend?"

"More like someone I used to know."

Madeline felt as if she'd intruded on something very personal. It seemed obvious to her that Libby was right—he still had feelings for Julie. "She must be more than that if you don't want to talk about her," she said, and glanced at Luke from the corner of her eye. She smiled. "I'm just saying."

Luke smiled wryly at her attempt to elicit information about Julie from him. "You don't want to hear about it, trust me. It's boring."

"Yes I do. For one, I'm a good listener. Two, I am basically nosy."

"I don't believe that."

"You're right," Madeline agreed. "I'm not really a good listener."

Luke laughed outright. He tapped his fist against Madeline's knee as if he were considering it. "It's old news, Maddie."

"Not to me."

"*Ay yi yi*," he sighed. "I was engaged to her, okay? But then she called it off."

"Why?" Madeline asked before she could stop herself. "No, sorry, scratch that. I'm too nosy."

"It's all right," he said, and tapped his fist against her leg again. "My brother got sick. He has a nerve disease that attacks the muscles."

"Oh, I am so sorry," Madeline said, and pictured something like muscular dystrophy.

"Yeah, that was heavy, but we were managing to get on with it, and then my mother got sick. I don't think Julie could handle all the attention my family needed from us."

Madeline gaped at him. That seemed so callous to her. "I'm sorry, Luke," she said softly. "That must have hurt."

"Sure it did." He smiled ruefully. "But it was a while ago, and you know how those things go. You get over them." He tapped her knee once more. "You know what I mean."

"Umm . . ." She tried to think of something clever to say, but her hesitation led him to cock a brow.

"Wait—you haven't suffered a bad breakup?"

Madeline shook her head.

"Seriously?"

"I dated a guy a couple of years ago. He broke up with me."

"How long did you date him?" Luke asked curiously.

"I don't know exactly—four or five months?"

He reared back a little as if he didn't know what to make of her. "I am not talking about puppy love, baby. I'm talking about full-on adult love. You know, men and women, sex, rock and roll—a lot of emotions and things you wish you'd never said, more things you wish you'd said. Crazy love, crazy pain."

When he put it like that, heartbreak sounded almost desirable. But the truth was that Madeline hadn't experienced anything like that. She'd never allowed herself to get close enough for that. She was an expert at keeping a respectable distance from emotions, which was why Trystan broke up with her.

"You're kidding, right?" he insisted. "Never?"

"No," she said, her face flaming. "Don't make fun."

"I'm not making fun." He shifted around to face her. "But are you telling me you have never been in love? How old are you, anyway?"

"God, Luke," she said, trying to squirm away, but he stopped her with a hand to her leg.

"How old?"

"Almost thirty," she said, feeling slightly apologetic for it. "Don't look at me like that. It's not so unusual."

"Wait," Luke said, ignoring her argument. "What about the guy?"

"What guy?"

"The guy, the guy," he said, gesturing at her with his hand. "The one you sort of acknowledged at dinner the other night."

"Who, Stephen?" she asked.

"Ha! I knew there was someone. So Stephen, what about him? What's wrong with him?"

"There is nothing *wrong* with him," Madeline said. "He's a great guy. It just takes a lot for me to get emotionally invested."

"Aha," Luke said, eyeing her curiously. "I get it. Either this guy is beyond lame, or you've got some impossible standards. What does it take?"

She snorted. "Come on, Luke." She moved to stand up, but he was too quick. He caught her wrist and held her there.

"*You* come on, Maddie. Tell me what it takes for you to become emotionally invested."

A million things flitted through her mind. *Trust. Belief. Courage.* She had never really put actual words to the fears that tumbled around in her. "I don't know," she said impatiently, and tried to pull her wrist free of his grasp.

But Luke tightened his hold. "I think you do know. You can tell me, Maddie. I won't laugh, I won't judge. And in a few days, when you go back to Orlando, you can forget you ever said anything."

"What difference does it make?"

"I don't know," he said, and lifted her hand to his mouth, kissing her knuckles, his lips warm and soft on her skin. "But it does. I like you,

Blue Eyes. And I am curious to know what demons are hiding in that hot body of yours."

Madeline's pulse began to quicken, and she couldn't help but smile.

"So what is it that keeps you from putting yourself out there?"

She didn't want to acknowledge what had been rattling around in her for so long, shaping her, forming the hard edges of her life.

Luke's expression softened; he seemed to get that this had gone from a playful conversation to something more serious for Madeline. He cocked his head to one side, brushed his knuckles against her face, pushing her hair away. "I wasn't kidding, you know. You can tell me. Whatever you say is safe with me."

He said it so casually, as if it were a matter of course for him. As if someone off the street could tell him things and he would keep them safe. His voice, his expression, cloaked Madeline with a sense of security. "I have to know that they aren't going to leave me," she said, her voice barely above a whisper. She wanted to tell him that they'd all left, every one of them. Her father, the men who had traipsed through her life with her mother. It was weird—she had wanted them all to leave and for so long and had harbored some stupid hope that maybe her father would come back and rescue her. Eventually, when they all left, and her father never came, the girl in Madeline had convinced the grown woman that it was because she somehow deserved it.

She opened her mouth to say all those things, but couldn't find the courage. She closed her mouth. Luke's expression didn't change; he traced a finger under her chin. "But how will you know they will never leave you if you don't put your heart on the line once or twice?"

"I know, it's screwed up. Believe me, I know," she admitted. She'd said too much. She felt a little short of breath. She pulled her hand free of his grip and tried to wave it off. "No big deal," she said, wanting to erase her confession. She picked up her beer bottle, downing the little bit that was left, and peered into the empty bottle.

"No?" Luke said, and settled back, away from her, his expression dubious. "It seems to me that it's had a great effect on you. I mean, you just said you can't get emotionally invested with this guy."

She forced smile. "I just sort of suck at dating, that's all. Stephen is a great guy. But I don't have a lot of time for him." That was all she was willing to admit.

Luke chuckled.

"Why is that funny?" she asked, confused.

"Because you don't lie very well, Maddie. You know what you need?"

Madeline sighed dramatically and fell back against the pillows. "Go ahead, take a number. There is always someone waiting in the wings who can't *wait* to tell me what I *need*."

Luke was undeterred. "Maybe you should put down the highlighter and just let life happen."

"Ha," she said with a snort. "You think I haven't heard that before? News flash, I *know* I'm a control freak. But that doesn't mean I can just snap my fingers and make it go away, any more than you can make your attachment to a woman who dumped you go away."

Luke's smile suddenly faded, and Madeline felt horrible. "I'm sorry," she said quickly, and sat up, put her hand on his arm. "I'm really sorry. I shouldn't have said that. See? I suck at this."

Luke grinned. "You said you suck at dating. Does this mean we're dating?"

"No!"

With a laugh, he gracefully hopped to his feet. He moved to the bookshelves and turned on a radio.

"Hey," Madeline said as country music began to fill the room. "How did you do that?"

"Backup battery." He stepped across the pillows and reached out his hand. Madeline eyed it suspiciously. "Come on, give me your hand. Let life happen."

He smiled so charmingly that Madeline hesitantly slipped her hand into his and allowed him to pull her to her feet.

"I'm going to show you one very easy way to loosen up."

"I don't need to loosen up—"

"Madeline."

She sighed. "You sound just like Trudi, you know that?"

His smile deepened. He slipped his hand inside the jacket she was wearing, around her waist, and pulled her into his chest.

"What are you doing?" she asked, stiffening, panicking slightly. "My God, I don't *dance*, Luke."

"Yeah, you do," he said easily. "Everyone does. It's just that everyone has their own rhythm." He pulled her closer, tucked her hand and his between them, and put his chin against the side of her head. "Relax," he said softly. "It's just a dance." He swayed with her to the right, then to the left, and back again. "Move your feet." He guided her again, moving her slowly one way, then the other, moving just enough to force her to take steps.

"This is ridiculous," she said, but the truth was that it was nice. *Very* nice. She was moving on a cloud, her eyes closed, nothing but the strength and feel of Luke against her, the music washing over them and mixing with the sound of the rain. She could not remember the last time she'd felt so soothed, so mellow, so *relaxed*.

Around the room they languidly went, the music mixing in with the sound of the rain on that dark, fire-lit evening. Madeline let herself go down the path of desire that steadily built. She was floating along with very little thought; she didn't think about Julie or Stephen. She didn't think about DiNapoli. She didn't worry about complications or where this thing with Luke was going, or what it meant. She just allowed herself to exist in that very pleasant, slightly magical place.

She rested her cheek on his shoulder and allowed him to move her along until the song ended. Even then, he didn't stop right away. He continued to sway a little bit until Madeline opened her eyes and looked up at him.

His gaze was warm, shining from somewhere deep, mesmerizing her. She felt fluttery again, just like the first time she'd seen him on Sometimes Pass. Madeline didn't flinch, she didn't look away as was her nature. She knew he would kiss her again. She knew before he lowered his head, before she lifted hers, that she would forget her private vow not to let it happen again.

When he did kiss her, Madeline was not prepared for the kiss that it was. She would not have guessed that a kiss so warm and gentle on her mouth could be so arousing. Her reaction was purely visceral; her mouth opened, her tongue met his. He pulled her tighter against him, pressing into her, and Madeline's hands found his shoulders, his neck. His kiss was deliberate, and she found it to be devastatingly sensual, exciting to the point that it seemed to spill over its edges and splash around them, filling the space in that cottage, filling her lungs and eyes and ears and heart with it.

It seemed to last only moments before he lifted his head and left her wanting more. Her hands were still on his shoulders. Her lips were still wet. "I thought we agreed this wasn't a good idea."

"Did we?" he asked, his gaze traveling her face.

"I don't remember," she lied.

Luke smiled and lowered his head to hers once more, but this time, Madeline kissed him back. She kissed him like she had never kissed another man, like she had never imagined kissing anyone in her life. She could feel him in every pore, could feel her body soaking him up like a big ocean sponge. She felt full to bursting with want and hope and . . . and *giddiness*. Something in her snapped free and let go. Her inhibitions began to melt away like tiny little snowflakes. The blood in her veins began to turn to fire; she was erupting with desire so strong that she'd lost control of it before she realized it was there. It pushed against her, demanding release. The feel of his hard body beneath her hands was fanning the burn in her; she put her fingers in his hair, traced his ear, brushed her palm against his shoulders and chest.

His hands were moving, too, cupping her bottom, sliding up her ribs, to her breasts. She made a cry of surprise into his mouth when he lifted her off her feet and took them both down to the pillows before the hearth. He came over her, draping his leg across hers, and kissing her so fully that Madeline couldn't help but cling to him and inhale the heat from the fire burning through her now.

The fire was so bright and intense that she did not feel uncomfortably exposed when he dipped his hand into her dress and freed one breast. Her head did not fill with questions of what she was doing, of warnings to flee when he took her in his mouth. On the contrary, she ignored who she was and lifted one arm overhead and closed her eyes, giving into the lush sensation of his mouth and his hands and his body on hers.

When his hand slipped beneath the hem of her dress, she didn't fight the urge to close her legs as she had in the past. It was as if that Madeline had been left behind in the Grizzly Lodge, and this Madeline was letting herself go, letting herself ride this storm, letting herself openly forage in the garden of sex.

He stroked her between her legs, his fingers dipping inside her. When she thought he would plunge into her and take her like a man who could only be sated by a woman's flesh—and yes, she would have liked that very much—he suddenly slowed. He kissed her tenderly, his hand cupping her face, his lips pressing against her temple, her cheek, her mouth. He was almost reverent, certainly caring.

She understood why he was so careful with her. She was so uncertain around him, about so many things. But in this, she was surprisingly certain. In a few days, she might never see Luke again, so tonight, she was going to let the mountains pull her to them. She was going to let herself off her leash.

Madeline pushed Luke, forcing him onto his back. He laughed with surprise, but when Madeline straddled him and began to unbutton his shirt, his smile faded. His hands went to her arms, pushing the flannel jacket off of her. "Hey—" he started.

Madeline kissed his mouth before he could say anything, then traced a wet line down his chest, nibbling him. Luke's eyes darkened; she could feel his body responding, hardening and pressing against her. She felt completely outside of herself, as if she were someone else entirely—a sexy, desirable woman.

Luke sat up, his arms around her, holding her tightly and kissed her fiercely. She dropped her head back so that he could devour her neck. "You're driving me wild," he growled into the hollow of her throat.

"Then we're even," she said huskily.

He made a sound deep in his throat and easily flipped her onto her back, kissing her as he unfastened his jeans and kicked them off. He sat up and removed his shirt, then braced himself above Madeline, his arms taut. He gazed down at her, dark-eyed, his jaw clenched as if he was holding himself back. The fire cast shadows across his face that made him look even more powerful. Like a warrior, Madeline thought dreamily. She smiled and touched her fingers to his face. "You are amazing."

Luke groaned and lowered himself to her, kissing her, his hands on her breasts, on her waist, between her legs.

Madeline felt herself sliding onto a little raft, floating on her own private sea of sensation. He moved between her legs and entered her so fluidly that she gasped with the pleasure of it. She opened her eyes and did not shy away from his gaze as he watched her, moving inside her, stroking her hair, kissing her mouth, her face. Madeline kissed him, too, his shoulders and chest, her hands sliding over rock-hard hips, then touching her fingers to his mouth.

They made love before the hearth, their breath hot and hard, their caresses urgent, their bodies slick with the intensity of their lovemaking. When Madeline's body did at last erupt with the sensation of his touch, she felt herself showering down with the rain in that little bungalow.

He followed her, burying his face in her hair as he found his release.

Sex with Luke went beyond the pale of pleasure—it was New Year's Eve, Fourth of July, and the Super Bowl all wrapped up in one moment. It was spectacular.

She and Luke lay there together side by side afterward, her leg now draped across his, their fingers interlaced, a throw rug loosely covering them. They talked about silly things, about houses, laughing as they compared the strangest houses they had ever seen. It felt to Madeline as if they talked about everything and nothing. It was easy. It was familiar, comfortable. His body was warm, his hands strong, but surprisingly gentle in their caress and when he ran a strand of her hair through his fingers.

Madeline didn't know when the lights came on, because she had drifted to sleep. She didn't know that Luke had gotten up to stoke the fire and find a heavier quilt, which he tucked up under her chin. Or that he had a last beer, watching her sleep in the soft glow of the fire, her hair spilling around her.

Madeline didn't know anything except that it had been one of the most splendidly shimmering evenings she'd ever known.

And then came morning. Bright sunlight and chirping birds awakened her.

It took her a moment or two to remember where she was—oh yes, he'd awakened her in the night, had urged her to his bed. And then they'd made love again.

Again?

Madeline pushed up on her elbows and turned her head. Through her tangled hair, she could see Luke lying beside her, his body as magnificent in the morning light as in the murky darkness of a storm. He was sleeping soundly, one arm draped across his chest, the other above his head. He was gorgeous, magnificent. Trudi would drool if she saw him.

Madeline moved slowly, carefully disentangling herself from the bedsheets. When she stood beside the bed—a little sore and a little light-headed—she grabbed his shirt and slipped it on, and quietly made her way out. She darted down the small hall to the living area. There was her bag, her phone still on top. Madeline picked them up and stepped into the hall bath, locking the door behind her.

She sank down onto the edge of the tub, ran her fingers through her hair as she stared at the black-and-white tiles of the bathroom floor. She felt a little queasy. She wanted to believe it was hunger, but she knew herself too well. She had exposed herself, had lost control, and what she was feeling was anxiety, full-blown anxiety, that would lead to cracks in her façade and leaks in her foundation. It was unsteadiness and fear that came from letting any light in through those cracks, any light that could warm her, strengthen her, and ultimately destroy her if it was extinguished without warning.

Intimacy made Madeline feel ragged and chopped up on the inside, like a bunch of tiny nicks that were liberally salted when she was least expecting it. But this anxiety felt like a thousand knives dragging through her. She'd had bouts of anxiety, but she'd never felt it quite like this. It felt as if there was so much of her internal wiring at risk! It made no sense, she recognized that. She only knew that she couldn't *control* this. She couldn't organize herself out of attachment to him, or keep from getting hurt. She couldn't keep from being rejected and left behind.

This was why she didn't have casual sex, Trudi's advocacy of it notwithstanding. Sex was *never* casual for Madeline. That wasn't to say she regretted a moment of last night, God no, quite the opposite. It had been surreal, and she'd felt . . . she'd felt so *happy*. So damn free from all the rules and expectations she put on herself.

Which only meant the cuts would go deeper, and the fall would be that much harder. Because now she had to deal with the inevitable aftermath of last night. In spite of the feelings she had for Luke Kendrick, nothing had changed: Her life was still in Orlando. She'd spent time yesterday meeting with the realtor who would give her a valuation of the ranch and bring them clients, just so that she could go back to Orlando.

Luke's life was here, and his heart was still attached, in part, to someone else. It was true—Madeline had seen the look on his face last night when he realized Julie's picture was there. There was something about that woman that was still rattling around in him.

The trick, Madeline told herself, was to detach from an extraordinary night calmly, rationally, and without bothersome emotions. And she was the last woman who knew how to do that with any finesse.

TWENTY-TWO

When Luke awoke, he stretched long, ran his hand alongside him.

The bed was empty.

He lay there, his eyes closed and a lazy smile as memories of a very special night drifted back to him.

Madeline's voice filtered into his consciousness, trailing down the hallway to him like a ribbon of smoke.

Luke sat up, rubbed his eyes, ran his fingers through his hair. Last night had been beyond excellent, because something about Madeline had shifted off center. He'd always thought her pretty, but she'd been alluring on a whole other level. She'd let herself go, had let herself exist entirely in the moment, and it had been incredibly sexy. It had made Luke forget an otherwise awful day, forget everything but her.

He loved the charming vulnerabilities in her, but last night, he'd seen a glimpse, however brief, of a wounded little girl still lurking somewhere deep inside. It didn't take a degree in psychology to get that Grant's absence in her life had done a number on her.

Luke empathized with her. He guessed he had some issues of his own, because her vulnerability had made him want her something fierce. That first kiss had knocked him to his knees. Madeline had stoked an unholy yearning in him and then had responded so openly and passionately that he'd been completely undone by it. *Completely.*

She intrigued him—she was full of twists and turns and little surprises, and Luke hadn't been captivated quite like this in . . . maybe in forever.

He swung his legs off the side of the bed and stood, padded over to his dresser and rummaged around for a pair of boxer briefs. He donned jeans over them and haphazardly buttoned a couple of the buttons to keep them from falling off, then followed the sound of Madeline's voice down the hall. She was in his living room, standing at the picture window, looking up at the mountains in the distance. "I know," she said into the phone, "I was so excited. You know how big of a sale this is for me."

Luke smiled to himself and leaned a shoulder against the doorjamb. If they had a medal for selling difficult houses, he was pretty certain Madeline would have wrested it from the poor slob's hand to don it.

"That's what I was thinking," she said, and touched a finger to a raindrop that was stubbornly clinging on the outside of the window. "I should get some great listings now, don't you think? I mean if I can sell *that*, I can sell, right?" She laughed at her own interpretation of her skills, then quieted, listening. "Mm-hm," she said. "He turned out to be a great help. Thanks so much for setting that up for me. He's already got a couple of people he thinks would be interested." She turned around, saw Luke standing there, and Luke saw the change in her expression—it went from smiling to guarded.

He ignored that. He walked over, kissed her head, stroked her silky hair, and touched her face. Madeline smiled, but it was a nervous little smile, and a funny little shiver traced up Luke's spine.

"So listen, I need to go. I am going back to Pine River today . . . Yeah, sure," she said, and turned away from Luke again. She added softly, "Can I just text you later?"

He didn't like the way she was speaking—quietly, nervously, and maybe even a little cryptically. He didn't like it one bit.

"Okay. You too. Bye." She clicked off her phone and tucked her hair behind her ear, then smiled.

Luke didn't smile. "Let me guess—Stephen?"

Madeline bit her lower lip and nodded. At least she didn't lie about it.

Luke didn't know what to say. It wasn't as if he thought last night had somehow magically transformed them into a couple, washing away all the issues surrounding Homecoming Ranch. He was a big boy, he could take that she had some sort of relationship in Orlando, no matter how loose it seemed to be. But he thought he might be entitled to a little bit of courtesy—maybe she could have held off calling her boyfriend at least until after she'd left his house.

But Luke didn't say anything; he turned around and walked into his kitchen.

"I called him because he helped me with some stuff yesterday, and I knew he would want to know what had happened," Madeline said contritely.

She had to call him this morning? Before breakfast? "You don't have to explain, Madeline," Luke said, and flashed her a cool smile over his shoulder. "We're both big kids." He turned his coffeemaker on, and reached into the cabinet for two mugs. He didn't like that one moment he was feeling buoyant and more alive than he thought he'd ever felt in his life, and in the next, he was feeling like a chump. What really infuriated him was that logically, he didn't believe he had any right to feel that way. They'd had a spur-of-the moment, socked-in-by-a-storm sexual encounter.

But he'd *felt* something between them last night. Something big and thick with lots of roots that could, possibly, if tended, grow around them. Hadn't Madeline felt that, too, if only a little? If only enough to put off calling the boyfriend until Luke was out of hearing distance?

"I have to call Bree," she said apologetically. "I need to get the ball rolling on the DiNapoli sale."

And now, he felt like an ass. She was tiptoeing around him, practically asking his permission to call her office. He'd been on the other end of this scenario more than once, having sex with a woman who thought that came with a tether and ownership instructions, and now, here he was, wishing he had a tether so this one couldn't get away. "Yeah, of course," he said, and turned his head, flashed her a smile. "Cream in the coffee?"

"Black, thank you," she said.

Why did that not surprise him? Black was easy—no decisions, no judgments, no need to second-guess how much cream or sugar to use. Just black. "Make your phone call. I'll make you coffee."

"Thanks." She disappeared into the living room.

"God, grow up, Kendrick," he muttered under his breath. He brewed the coffee, one cup at a time. He left hers on the coffee table, next to the floor pillows where they'd thrashed around, completely into each other, then took his and headed back to his bedroom and his shower. He tried to wash the conflicting emotions out of his head. He tried to be a *guy*, to consider it a one-night stand as any guy would do, and for shit's sake, move the hell on.

But Luke couldn't do it. He wasn't that kind of guy. He never had been. He couldn't simply notch last night into his bedpost and forget it.

Hell, he would never forget last night.

Luke finally emerged, clean-shaven and dressed in jeans and boots and a Pearl Jam T-shirt. Madeline was sitting nervously on the arm of his couch as she watched him walk down the little hall. She had cleaned up, too, as best she could, washing her face free of any makeup, braiding her hair and donning the pink ball cap. Going through the motions of getting dressed was the only thing that felt normal this morning.

Madeline didn't know what she was doing. She knew Luke was unhappy with her—God, *she'd* be unhappy if she were him—but anxiety was making her crazy.

She stood up a little too eagerly and pasted a bright smile on her face. "Wow," she said. "You look great."

He looked down at his old T-shirt. "Are you ready to go?"

"I am." She picked up her bag, slung it over her shoulder. She was wearing the same clothes from yesterday, but had returned his flannel jacket to the hook next to the door. Her hiking boots were laced up and tied tightly in perfect bows. Gone was the woman who had let herself go last night, who had felt things, experienced things she'd never felt before. Old Madeline was back. Uptight, do-not-step-off-the-center-line Madeline.

Luke opened the door for her. Madeline smiled, but he had already turned away to lock up. She walked on, slipped into the passenger seat of the Bronco, her focus on her phone, texting Trudi fast and furiously, a stream of empty talk.

She desperately wanted to say something. But while she debated, he started up the Bronco and headed for Pine River.

The more time that passed, the emptier the words rattling around in Madeline's head seemed to be. She blindly e-mailed herself lists of things to do, exchanged two e-mails with Jackson. Luke turned on the radio, his eyes on the road. Madeline wanted to touch his arm, his leg. She wanted to lay her head on his shoulder and close her eyes and think, but she was frozen with anxiety. At last, she tried to break the silence. "Good news—the storm didn't do any damage," she said.

Luke looked at her, confused. Madeline pointed to the radio.

"Ah," he said absently.

"I had an e-mail from Jackson this morning."

"Okay," he said, waiting for her to continue.

"He's found someone who is willing to lead the horseback riding, and he said he gave Libby some names of rafting outfitters we could hire. I think I could make a deal with them. Oh, and I thought we should have the meeting tent erected next to the picnic area beside the house. We might as well make use of that space."

Luke's gaze flicked coolly over her, then returned to the road. "I thought Libby had suggested it be down near the campsites."

Libby had said that, all right. Madeline just hoped she'd be open to discussion about it. "She seems pretty flexible. So how long do you think it will take to finish the temporary showers?"

"Don't know."

Madeline didn't believe that for a moment. "I was going to add it to my spreadsheet," she said.

"What spreadsheet?"

"I set one up yesterday," Madeline said, and clicked over to an app on her phone. "I find things are easier to keep up with if you have them lined out." She held up her phone; Luke squinted at it. It was a miniature spreadsheet with tasks and bars of yellow sliding across the screen, marking how many days to completion of any task.

Luke looked up from her phone and met her gaze. Madeline had the distinct feeling he wanted to say something, but all he did say was, "I don't know how long."

Madeline lowered her phone. "Okay. Well, when you do, let me know, and I'll add it." She smiled.

"Sure." He didn't sound like he meant it.

Madeline could feel the anxiety filling her up like a balloon. Last night had been so great, *too* great. She'd been so free, so happy, and now she was struggling. She never meant to hurt him, or anyone. And honestly, she didn't understand why he was so angry. It was one night. And he didn't really *know* her. If he did know her, really know her, he would . . . he would . . .

He'd what?

Madeline's pulse began to pound in her neck. *Say it. SAY IT.* It was all she could do to admit her greatest fear to herself: that he would leave her. He would know her, and he would leave her.

So tell him you're sorry. Sorry? But that sounded so wrong. What exactly was she sorry for? Because she wasn't sorry, she was enthralled by him. *Then tell him that, tell him how you feel.*

How did she feel? Scared and a little crazy at the moment. What she needed was some space. Some time to think, to put everything back in place.

By the time they reached Pine River about an hour later, Madeline had worked herself up into a silent lather about it. She was droning on about chairs and cots—hell, she didn't know what all she said. Luke barreled down the main drag, pulling up outside Tomlinson's Feed.

"What are we doing?" Madeline asked, sitting up, staring at the specials shoe-polished onto the windows of the store.

"Dog food," he said curtly, and hopped out of the Bronco. He didn't look back to see if she was coming, just strode in.

And then he took his own sweet time.

Madeline got out to stretch her legs. She called Jackson with a question about cots. "Hey!" Jackson said. "Libby is here. We're just going over a few things. You want to join us?"

Madeline looked at the feedstore. "Let me see. I'll call you back," she said, and asked him to give her a few minutes before she clicked off.

"Madeline, right?"

Madeline whirled around and came face to face with Julie Daugherty. She was more beautiful than what Madeline remembered, with silky blond hair, a perfect figure. She was wearing a short skirt and heels, making her an inch or two taller than Madeline. "Hi," Madeline said.

Julie looked at the Bronco.

"He's inside," Madeline blurted.

"What?" Julie asked, startled, and looked at Madeline again.

"Luke. He's inside," she said, gesturing to the store. "Dog food."

"Oh, I . . . I wondered," Julie said.

Just then, the door of the store opened and Luke walked out, a bag of dog food on his shoulder. His step slowed a little when he saw Julie and Madeline standing there together.

"Hey!" Madeline said brightly the moment she saw him. She felt like she was shaking with nervous energy. "Look who's here!"

"I see," he said. "Hey, Julie." He walked around to the back of his Bronco, swung open the back gate, and dumped the bag of dog food into the bed. When he shut the gate, he said, "What's up?"

Madeline looked at Julie, who was blushing. "I was at the bank applying for a job, and I saw you guys pull up," Julie said.

"A job?" Luke asked curiously.

Julie smiled and shrugged a little. "Desperate times and all that. I was going to grab some lunch. Do you guys want to join me?" she asked, but she wasn't looking at Madeline. She was looking at Luke. "I thought I'd pop into the Grizzly."

"Oh, not for me, thanks," Madeline said quickly. "I have *so* much to do."

"And I need to take her up to the ranch," Luke added, just as quickly, his gaze on Madeline now. She could see the look of warning in his eyes. But it was her escape, and she was taking it.

"You know what, Luke?" Madeline said. "I was just talking to Jackson a minute ago and it turns out Libby came into town to get some stuff, and she's in his office! I can get a ride with her."

"You don't need to do that—" Luke started, but Madeline was already backing away. "It's no trouble! You two go ahead." She darted to the passenger side of the Bronco and grabbed her bag. "This works out for everyone."

"No, it doesn't," Luke said.

"Luke, thank you. For the ride, I mean, to Pine River. It was nice to see you again, Julie," she said, already walking, already making her escape. "I'll see you guys later?" She didn't wait for anyone to answer, but put her head down and hurried off, her stomach in knots, the image of Luke with angry eyes and clenched jaw dancing in her mind's eye.

Those images couldn't stop her. They only made her anxiety worse. If anything, her escape had backfired—she felt more anxious and uncertain than ever.

TWENTY-THREE

Libby was all smiles when she and Madeline arrived back at the ranch. She pointed to the tent pads as they drove up to the house, the bulletin board on the fence. "It's all coming together!"

"It is," Madeline agreed. She would not have thought it possible, but here they were, actually putting the reunion together.

"How was Denver, anyway?" Libby asked.

The question startled Madeline at first, as if she were giving off a vibe of having slept with Luke. But Libby was looking at her without judgment. "It was good," she said. "Productive." It was amazing, confusing, and so many things were on her mind that Madeline hadn't heard half of what Libby had said on the way up to the ranch. She wanted to tell Libby about the valuation, about the realtor. But she knew from experience that it was better to come to the table with a fully prepared offer. That seemed especially important with Libby, and Madeline thought it might be the only way to dissuade her from the idea that they all band together and do the reunion business.

"Great!" Libby said. "Oh, by the way," she added as she grabbed a bag from the backseat, "I spoke to Tyrone Johnson. He and his wife Linda are the two in charge of the family reunion. He said the Johnsons will begin arriving next Thursday."

"Oh wow," Madeline said. "I still need to negotiate a group rate for the rafting and horseback riding."

"Already done," Libby said proudly.

But that was Madeline's task. Negotiation was kind of her thing.

"You weren't here," Libby said, as if she had guessed what Madeline was thinking. "The phone service was restored and I had time." She laughed. "Our first phone call was from Jackson of course," she said, shifting the bag to her hip as she began to walk toward the house. "But he had some amazing news. Apparently, he's been contacted about using the ranch as a destination wedding venue later in the summer."

"Oh wow, he really needs to take the website down," Madeline said.

"Really?" Libby asked, pausing. "I thought it was a good sign. This place has great potential."

Madeline felt a squeeze of irritation and disappointment. Maybe it was great for Libby, but it sure wasn't great for her. "I just don't see how this destination thing is going to happen. I mean Emma has already checked out—"

"Not entirely. I talked to her yesterday."

"You did?" Madeline asked, surprised. "What did she say?"

Libby shrugged and walked into the kitchen, putting her bags down onto the little kitchen table.

"Libby?" Madeline prodded her.

Libby picked up a towel and began to wipe down the counter, making huge circles with her cloth, as if there was some horrible spill there. "She wanted to know what was going on, what we are doing with the reunion."

"So is she coming to help?" Madeline asked.

"No," Libby said. "We just talked."

"That was nice of her to call," Madeline said with not a little bit of sarcasm. "She's obviously not interested in keeping this place. And I'm going back to Orlando. I just sold this really big house that opens up a lot of doors for me. So how exactly are we going to pull this off?"

"I'll do it," Libby said, looking slightly offended.

Madeline sighed. "Come on, Libby. This is not a one-person job."

Libby didn't say anything to that. Madeline sensed Libby knew she was right and didn't want to admit it. But Madeline wanted away from this ranch, *especially* after last night's brush with true, deep emotion. Emotion that, if left unchecked, if left to grow, could mortally wound her. Right now, she wanted nothing more than to finish off her list and get out of town, as far from Luke Kendrick as she could get. She wanted to go back to Orlando and finalize the DiNapoli deal. She wanted to get her movie guide from Stephen and make popcorn and stay socked away in her condo, and venture out only to the soccer field. Just . . . away from things that would hurt her.

"I know it won't be easy, Madeline," Libby said. "But I want to try and make it work. If nothing else, for Dad's sake."

Something about those words detonated inside of Madeline. Maybe it was the stress of having felt something so profound with Luke, or maybe just the notion that here she and Libby were, taking days and weeks from their lives to fix some colossal mess their father had made before he'd died, but Madeline exploded. "For *Dad's* sake?" she loudly exclaimed. "We don't owe *him* anything, Libby! He was a horrible father. He was absent, he was cheap, and he was self-centered. This isn't a *gift*, it's a burden, it's another damn burden he's heaped on me. He left me with nothing but the burden of my mother, who was no mother at all, and now *this?* This stupid ranch with this stupid reunion has taken us away from everyone we love just so we can fix it for *him*. What do you think will come from this, huh? I'll tell you what—a lot of aggravation and hurt feelings and more misery, *that's* what."

Her chest was heaving, Madeline realized. She'd been shouting, too, and she suddenly realized what she'd just said.

All the blood had drained from Libby's face. She was gaping at Madeline. "Wow," she said. "Just go then, Madeline. No one is asking you to stay, least of all me."

"Libby, I am sorry. I didn't mean—"

"Don't," Libby said curtly. "Don't apologize again. Please." She whirled around and strode from the kitchen.

"Libby!" Madeline shouted after her, but it was no use. She sank down onto a barstool and buried her face in her hands. She hated herself in that moment. She hated that she could hurt Libby and hurt Luke. That was not what she wanted, and she hated that she couldn't seem to stop herself, either. There was a vortex of resentment in her, swirling around, faster and faster, sucking her into it, colliding with the tsunami of fear that was always, *always* cresting through her.

Madeline heard the sound of a car and sat up. She rushed into the living room just in time to see Libby's little car bouncing over the road, away from Homecoming Ranch.

Great.

Madeline returned to the kitchen. Her belly rumbled with hunger. She looked around for something to eat, but it was all food that Libby had brought to the house. But there, on top of the fridge, was what was left of the bag of chips from that first meeting with Jackson. She took the bag down and opened it, ate a couple of chips. With the bag in hand, she walked into the dining room.

Libby had left some papers and the reunion file next to the phone. There was a pad of paper onto which she had made some notes. Just below those notes was another one that said *Emma*, with a phone number following it. Madeline ate a few more chips, pondering that number and debating. She ate a few more, dusted off her hands, and dialed the number.

It rang several times.

Madeline was about to hang up when Emma answered. "Hello?"

The raspy, hoarse voice sounded just like Madeline's mother— rough and hungover. "Emma?" Madeline said, just to be sure.

"Who's this?"

"Madeline."

"*Who?*" Emma demanded.

"Madeline Pruett. Your, ah . . ."

"God, what now?" Emma groaned.

"Thanks," Madeline said pertly at that warm reception. "I called to speak to you about the ranch problem."

"Shit, first Jackson, then Libby, now you—"

"We inherited it, Emma," Madeline reminded her.

"Yeah, I know. I was there, remember?"

"So we have to do something with it. Are you coming back? Libby wants to make this some reunion Mecca, but I need to get back to Orlando."

"So go. Why is that my problem?" Emma asked.

Madeline could hear things like plates and glasses banging around in the background of the call now. Her pulse began to ratchet up. "Listen, Emma, I didn't ask for this any more than you did. We have to come to some conclusion. Libby thinks you might want to keep the ranch, too."

"Sometimes Libby hears what she wants to hear," Emma said through a yawn.

"But what about you? Do you want to keep the ranch?"

The banging suddenly stopped. Emma said nothing for so long that Madeline thought maybe she'd lost the connection. But then she heard Emma sniff.

"Are you there?"

"I'm here," Emma said. "Okay, listen, Madeline Pruett. I don't give a *shit* what happens with that ranch. Can I be any clearer than that? I told Libby the same thing. You guys decide—sell it, keep it, I don't care. Just don't bother *me* with it. Okay?"

"Wow," Madeline said, truly taken aback.

"Hey, don't you try and read me!" Emma snapped. "You don't know me at all. You have no idea what my life or Libby's life has been like, and I don't owe you any explanation."

"I'm not asking for one," Madeline shot back. "And you don't know my life, either, Emma. All I want is to have this thing resolved. And since it appears as if neither of us wants to be here, it seems to me we should try and work together to get rid of it."

"Libby wants it. Why not let her have it? What difference does it make to you?"

It seemed so very obvious to her, and Emma . . . Emma was crazy, that's all there was to it.

"If Libby can't turn a profit, then we sell it. But if she can, don't sweat it. Just calm down and let people do what they want."

"Now who is trying to read *who*?" Madeline said angrily.

"It's not hard," Emma said. "You're a one-way street. I just can't figure out what you're so afraid of."

"I am not afraid—"

"Whatever," Emma said, cutting her off. "I gotta go." And she hung up. Just like that, the line went dead.

Madeline gasped with outrage. She glared at the receiver in her hand, then slammed it down. That was the last-ever consideration Madeline was going to give her. If this was what being sisters was all about, Madeline would take a pass, thank you.

She marched into the kitchen, looked wildly about. Okay. She was out here on her own. Out of her element. Drifting on a life raft. First Luke, then Julie, then Libby and Emma—*What are you so afraid of?* Emma's words echoed in her brain.

"Forget that," she muttered. Busy. Be busy, that's what she had to do. There was still quite a lot of work to do, starting with the erection of the big party tent. First things first, she needed to know if the spot she had in mind was big enough. She needed a tape measure. She'd seen one in the garage a couple of days ago.

Madeline marched out to the garage, sidestepping the dogs, who rushed out from under the porch to greet her, her hands up. "Garage!" she snapped, and all four of the dogs obediently fell in line behind her, trotting along as she rounded the corner and stepped into the dusty garage, where they fanned out to sniff things as she surveyed the workbench. She found the tape measure and as she was turning away from the bench, she saw the keys hanging on a hook on the wall.

Madeline looked at the Pontiac, which was covered with grime and a few boxes on its hood. She looked back at the keys. She put the tape measure down and grabbed the keys.

The door to the car was not locked. She put herself into the driver seat and looked around. The seat was pushed so far back that she could barely reach the pedals. The car was old; the console between the two front seats was enormous and the faux wood detailing was peeling around the radio dials. A dried-up Christmas tree air freshener dangled from the rearview mirror. Madeline fit the key into the ignition, scooted up in her seat, and tried to start it. The car wheezed and coughed; from the corner of her eye she saw the dogs flee from the garage.

One of her mother's boyfriends had been a mechanic, and he'd once told Madeline to prime her mother's old car by pumping the accelerator a few times. Madeline tried that, then turned the ignition. The car started and began to shake, vibrating so badly that one of the boxes slid right off the hood. Madeline cried out with alarm and turned off the car and got out to pick up the box.

"Madeline!"

She cried out and whirled around, the box in her arms.

Luke was standing at the door of the garage, his legs braced apart, his hands on his hips. He looked so virile, so sexy . . . and so *angry.* Madeline instinctively backed up, knocking into the car.

"What the hell?" he snapped, and suddenly dropped his arms and came striding forward.

"You said I could use it!" she cried. "I wasn't going anywhere, I swear it. I just wanted to see if it would start—"

He came to a halt before her, standing between her and the only exit out of this garage. "I don't mean the goddamn car," he said. He took the box from her hands and practically tossed it onto the bench.

"What's wrong?" Madeline asked breathlessly.

"What's *wrong?*" he echoed incredulously. "What the hell was that in town?" he asked gruffly, gesturing behind him.

Madeline looked to where he pointed.

"*Look* at me, woman," he commanded her. "Look right here, right in my eyes. *Look* at me. You haven't looked at me all day. I don't know what's the matter with you!"

"I don't know what you mean—"

"The hell you don't. You couldn't wait to push me off on Julie. You couldn't wait to run off. I can't figure out what the hell you *want.*"

She could feel herself tensing, a vise squeezing around her chest. *I want you. You, you, you.* "I thought . . . I thought—"

She couldn't explain the depths of her anxiety.

"I know what you thought," he said, not quite as loudly. "You thought you would push me off on Julie and then you wouldn't have to deal with it. Thanks a lot, Madeline. I never felt so damn inconsequential in my life."

He was standing so close, his gaze so intent. Madeline thought of those eyes last night, watching her, and felt a tremor deep inside. "I'm sorry. I didn't mean for you to feel that way—"

He took her head in his hands, forcing her to look at him. "You know, I always thought I got women. I thought I understood what they needed, and I've always been there, good ol' Luke, to pick up the pieces. That's okay," he said. "I have big shoulders. But I discovered this morning that I damn sure don't like it when the pieces that need to be picked up are mine."

"Oh Luke," she said. "I never meant to leave you in pieces."

"Then what *did* you mean?" he demanded softly.

She blinked. Luke suddenly pulled her away from the car, kissing her. It was a hard, determined kiss. His fingers splayed across her cheek and jaw, and he snaked an arm around behind her, pulling her into him, anchoring her there. He demanded entrance into her mouth with his tongue and kissed her until her knees began to give out on her, and Madeline melted right into him.

Only then did he lift his head, gazing down at her, caressing her cheek. Only then did Madeline realize she had caught hold of his wrist and was clinging to it.

"So I didn't imagine that we made love last night," he said roughly.

Her cheeks instantly bloomed. "No, of course not."

"What's the matter, Maddie? Why are you working so hard to pretend it didn't happen? Why are you pushing me off on Julie?"

Madeline's heart was beating so wildly she could hardly breathe. He pulled her closer, and Madeline's pulse began to pound in her neck. She was panicking, wanting to disappear, but Luke held her so easily, there was no escape from him.

"Just talk to me," he said. "That's all you have to do."

Her mind was whirling, her thoughts pressing painfully against her head. "Last night was . . ."

He surprised her by slipping two fingers under her chin and forcing her to look up at him. "It was what?" he demanded, and stroked her arm, his palm sliding slowly down, his fingers wrapping around her wrist, then sliding back up.

She closed her eyes. "*Incredible,*" she whispered, and slowly opened them as his hand moved around to her back. "But this morning, I think I had a panic attack. I know that sounds crazy, but I realized that I'm going back to Orlando, and I have baggage, and you have baggage, and probably—it can't work, Luke. It's not a good idea." She winced, hoping that didn't sound too harsh. "I don't think I can do this."

"Do what, exactly?" he pressed, his hand caressing her hip, sliding up her ribs, the heel of his palm on her breast, igniting another fire in her, causing her to catch her breath.

Be left. "You know what," she said, and drew an unsteady breath as he moved his hand across her breast, his fingers grazing the fabric covering her nipple.

"Well first of all," he murmured, "no one said anything about this going any place. No one mentioned commitment or marriage or even being pen pals."

"But . . ." *But he was right.*

"I'm not saying that it couldn't ever be more. I wouldn't mind it one bit if you decided to stick around Pine River. But I think maybe you jumped the gun a little." He leaned down to kiss her neck.

Madeline's eyes fluttered shut. She imagined this was what a thousand butterflies winging against her skin must feel like.

He dipped his head to the hollow of her throat. "At the moment, it was one night. We both enjoyed it and we don't have to hide from it. Where we go from there, or don't go, is okay. Just don't do what you did today."

"Right," she said, closing her eyes once more as he kissed her temple.

"You don't get to put your nose in my business."

She sighed—he was right again.

"And you don't have to be afraid of whatever it is that has you so locked up—rejection, love, I don't know. I just know you don't have to fear it with me. Okay?"

"Okay," she said.

"So we're good?" he asked, pausing to lightly kiss her lips.

"Better than good." She was already swimming in pleasure; it was pooling between her legs.

"That's what I want to hear," he murmured, moving his head down, to the patch of skin in the vee of her dress while his hand first slid down her leg, then between both of them.

"Just one question," she asked as he caressed her. "When do we decide where we go from there?"

Luke paused in his attention to her, his mouth on her skin. He slowly lifted his head and looked at her, amusement in his eyes. "God you're a mess," he said. "A beautiful mess." He pulled her into his arms, kissed her sweetly, languidly, until Madeline's legs were melting beneath her. "You're definitely an enigma," he muttered against her skin.

"Enigma," she said, enjoying his attention to her neck, "is kind of a strong word. It's more like . . . like unpracticed."

He smiled. "I think that makes me like you even more." He opened the back door of the Pontiac. "You obviously need more practice," he said, and gave her a playful shove.

She fell onto the backseat. Luke followed her in, coming over her, forcing her onto her back in that seat.

"What are you doing?" Madeline asked laughingly.

"I am going to kiss you," he said, his eyes on her mouth. "We're making up now."

"Were we fighting?"

"Do I have to explain it all again?"

No, he didn't. Her heart was racing again, but it was different this time. It wasn't panic, or anxiety. It was hope. Madeline slowly lay back as he settled one knee between her legs. A million thoughts went through her mind as he unbuttoned her blouse, kissing her skin, his mouth on her breast, his hand caressing her leg and her hip and stoking her blood. Her mind said no, warned her, chastised her for allowing this to happen *again* . . .

But Madeline closed her eyes to her thoughts, and sank into the pleasurable onslaught of his body against hers, losing herself in the exquisite sensations, and allowing herself to let go, to let go of control, of organization, of being Madeline, and drift along with a gorgeous man in the backseat of an old Pontiac. A deep sigh of yearning escaped her; she dug her fingers into his shoulders and arched against him as he moved his attention to her breast. She could feel his erection and pressed against it, sliding her leg suggestively against it. Luke made a growling sound, and ran his hand down her body, over the flare of her hip, then slid in between her legs.

Madeline found his mouth as he moved his hand against her, stroking her, reminding her of the euphoria she'd experienced last night, of letting go completely. Her breath quickened and she squirmed against him, wanting more, wanting it all again. Luke obliged her, sliding his arm underneath her hips to lift her, then pressing his body into hers, burrowing deep.

Once again, Madeline was beyond rational thought. She caressed his body with her mouth and hands, wanting to taste and feel every conceivable inch of him. She could feel herself spiraling as he moved inside her, his hand still stroking her. She was coiling tighter and tighter, rising to meet every thrust, desperate for the release. It shuddered through her body, reverberating through every limb, every muscle. She caught her cry and her breath, arched her neck and pressed against him as she fell off the edge of desire into pleasure.

"*Maddie,*" Luke whispered in her ear. His strokes came quicker, harder. She could feel the tension of his body, in the tight curl of his hand around hers, in his breath, hot in her hair. She felt them together, their bodies breathing in unison. It ceased to be physical; it was purely emotion for her now, far bigger and stronger than a physical release. And when she felt him shudder into her, she felt tenderness, desire, and a release of the anxiety. She felt free.

He collapsed onto her, his heart beating wildly against her arm. She kissed his cheek. His eyes were closed, his breathing still ragged, but he gripped her hand like a dying man. And then he opened his eyes, kissed her softly for one long, insanely perfect moment. He lifted his head, lifted himself off of her, and pulled her up. As she adjusted her dress, he stroked her cheek and said, "Come to dinner."

She giggled. "What? Right now?"

"No, in a few days. We'll figure out when, but you and Libby. Hell, I'll even let Jackson in."

Madeline realized he was serious. "To your house? Oh, Luke, I don't know—"

"Why? Are you afraid?" he asked, watching her as he fastened his jeans, and smiled.

She sighed. "*No*," she said, acquiescing.

Luke grinned. "I didn't think so," he said, and kissed her again. "Trust me. It will be all right."

Funny how, in that moment, with the glow of their lovemaking still warm on her skin, Madeline could almost believe it.

TWENTY-FOUR

The news from Durango *sucks*, man! They are like total downers with their tests and bullshit like "you'll probably need a feeding tube in twelve to eighteen months," and crap like that. I don't listen to them. They're just a bunch of talking heads to me. It's like I told Dad, "If they say I have to get a feeding tube, they can kiss my ass. It's bad enough I have to sit in this chair all the time, but if I can't have Aunt Patti's brownies, what's the point?"

Seriously, what's the point?

But it upset the old man, and I advised him not to dwell on that, because we are having a *par-tay!* Luke cooked it up as part of his campaign to Save Homecoming Ranch. He told us the same day Jackson came over and told me there were some guys from Denver sniffing around the ranch, and they were asking him lots of questions about the deal Grant and Dad made. Jackson thinks one of the heirs lawyered-up. Dad said he didn't have the money for a lawyer, and Luke said he did, he had like a ton of equity in his Denver house. They had this *huge* fight about it, and it totally reminded me of Muhammad Ali and Joe Frazier fights. Remember how they just went round and round? You can catch those fights sometimes on HBO.

Anyway, Luke is way more stubborn than Dad and he said, "We're not letting go without a fight. I've already seen a lawyer." And then he said to me, "And we're having a goddamn party, Leo."

He said it like that because it was my idea to begin with. Luke rejected it when I first presented it, but he always comes around to my brilliant ideas. Think about it—it's going to be hard for the lovelies to totally cut us out of the ranch when they actually put names to faces and meet us. You probably think I'm going to use my chair for sympathy. Hell, yeah! It's got to be good for something, right?

But that's not why Luke invited them. He's always been the Dudley Do-Right between us. Still, I like that he's beginning to think like the apprentice of a certified genius.

I said, "You only want a party because you're totally into this Blue Eyes chick." I was just kidding around, but he acted all annoyed. Judge and jury, allow me to present the facts: First, he doesn't want a party. Then he comes back from Denver and he suddenly wants one. And he wants to invite Blue Eyes and Libby and Jackson to this party, which, you will not be surprised to hear, flipped Dad out.

Dad said, "We don't have the space and besides, we eat stuff like Chef Boyardee. How the hell are we going to have a *dinner* party?" So I e-mailed Aunt Patti, and she said she would make lasagna, and I said to Dad, "Next time, don't wig out, come to your Problem-Solver." That's me.

Fact number two: Luke is spending all this time in Pine River, it's like over a week now, and he's got to be sick of sleeping on the couch. But everyday he gets up and goes to the ranch, and every night he comes back—sometimes super late—and talks about what they did. So one day, I asked him, "What's there to do out there when the sun goes down?"

He said, "*What?*" Like I was speaking Greek.

And I said, "You're up there super late all the time. Are you building latrines in the dark?" I thought it was kind of funny but Luke said something about me being an ass.

So later, Dad told me to lay off, that we needed to work together to get Luke back to Denver because houses don't build themselves, and that Luke was letting this woman get under his skin. Only it was hysterical because it was clear that Dad thinks the woman under Luke's skin is Julie.

I *know* it's not Julie because Dani told me about "the lunch" Julie and Luke had. Dani heard half of it, heard Julie begging for him to take her back and Luke saying that wasn't going to happen. She said you could have driven a Mack truck through the gulf at that table and Luke would have been happy. She said he looked like he wanted to fold himself up into a little ball and bounce away. (Side note: It would be *awesome* if Luke could make like Rubber Man and turn himself into a ball and bounce away.)

To be fair to Dad, he has this misperception because Julie keeps coming around. She was here Wednesday night with that evil-eye baby of hers, and it so happened it was the same night Marisol got mad at me for suggesting she'd put on a few pounds (well she has, but it's not like I'm complaining. I like the way her butt looks). Anyway, Marisol let Julie in. So we sat in the living room watching *Castle* with that baby staring at me, and Julie was trying to ask me questions, like "has Luke said anything about when he'll get back to Denver?"

To which I responded with a succinct, "Nope."

I wasn't going to tell her that the guy he's working with has called him a bunch of times asking him this question that the other day, he told Luke that he had one more week, and then he was going to have to do something, because this guy couldn't handle all his work. I heard Luke tell him he'd be back by the end of next week, no problem.

I was about to tell Julie that, but then the baby started crying and she had to go, and I didn't try and stop her—the woman *talks* while my show is on. She was walking out of the house just as Luke drove up. I thought for sure he'd walk right around her and come inside, but no, they sat down on the porch steps and talked for like an hour. When he came in, he was sort of smiling, but not in a happy way, sort of in a "I can't believe it's butter" kind of way.

He took one look at me, pointed his finger, and said, "Not one word about her, Leo. Not one, or I will knock your block off."

Well, they don't call me Big Mouth at the hospital for nothing, and I said, "Agreed. Not one word about Julie. So what's up with you and Blue Eyes?"

Luke looked startled and said, "What the hell, Leo? Why are you always trying to create drama where there is none?"

I said, "Hold up there, Cowboy, I'm not creating anything. You haven't gone back to Denver, you spend every day at the ranch, and the only person you talk about is Madeline Pruett, and for the first time in like a hundred years, you are not hot to trot after Julie Daugherty. It doesn't take a *genius* to see what's going on here, but I *am* a genius, and I get it."

Luke folded his arms across his chest. He had the same expression on his face that he had when we were teens and he found out I'd been smoking weed at lunch. He decked me and told me that was the best way to get kicked out of football and lose the scholarship I needed to go to college. Turns out the *best* way is to get MND. But that night, Luke looked like he was going to deck me again. He said, "No, Leo, you're wrong. I'm just trying to save the ranch so you and Dad have a place to live, okay? And in case you've forgotten, I'll remind you that Dad and Grant Tyler thought it would be a *great* idea to have a damn reunion there that *we* have to put together. So while I'm trying to figure out how to get the ranch back, I've been building showers and extra latrines. *That's* what I am doing out there. If you don't believe me, I'll put your lame ass in the van right now and drive you out there and shove your head down one. Now shut your damn mouth or I will." And he stalked off.

I shouted, "You and what army!" And stuff along those lines, and some choice words I will not repeat here. But for the record, Luke did not answer the fundamental question: How do you build latrines and showers in the dark? Because you can't. That's why he is not a genius. He does not think these things through. That's what I told Marisol, and she told me to lay off Luke. She said, "He does all that he can for you and your dad. He's always there for you. If he likes the girl's company, it's nothing to you."

Yeah, okay, she's right. But it's like I told her: "I kind of wish he wouldn't do so much for me, you know? I mean, I want him to get the ranch back, because Dad is going to need it. But I kind of like being in town. People come to see me. My good looks and winning personality have attracted half of Pine River to this door, and I even talked the Methodists into building the ramps Luke said he was going to build and didn't, because he's been out at the ranch all week making moon eyes at the Florida chick."

Marisol said, "You don't know that, Leo. You should really learn to keep your mouth shut."

Yeah, well that's not going to happen because that's all I've got left, you know? It's part of my magnetism.

TWENTY-FIVE

Luke gave Madeline the honor of hammering the last nail in the temporary showers. She cheered when it was done, hopping about in her shorts and hiking boots, and a skintight T-shirt that had been a distraction for Luke all day. She had smudges of dirt and grime on her face and arms, and an ugly scrape across her knee.

"I can't believe it," she said breathlessly. "I built a shower!"

"And a latrine," he reminded her.

"*And* a latrine. I'm just padding my resume left and right." She laughed again, the sound of it reminded him of the soft sound of morning birds.

"So how are we doing on your list?" Luke asked as he hitched the hammer onto his tool belt and tested the sturdiness of the wall once more.

Madeline removed the pencil she had taken to wearing behind her ear, pulled a grimy, crumpled list from her pocket, and studied it. She put it up against the wall and drew a line through it. "Done." Her face suddenly lit with a bright smile. "We're all done! We're actually and officially ready for the Johnsons!"

She stuffed the paper into her pocket and smiled up at him. She glanced around her, then stepped forward, put her hand on his abdomen. "You're a stud, you know that?" she asked, and rose up on her toes, kissing him.

"You are too, you know that?" he asked, and caught her around the waist, holding her there, kissing her a little more thoroughly.

But Madeline put her hand on his chest and with a nervous laugh, stepped out of his embrace.

It was a fact that they had been together a few times that week. And it was a fact while Madeline had begun to relax, to let her hair down, so to speak, she still managed to keep him at arm's length most of the time. It felt almost as if there were two Madelines: the wildy sexy, passionate one who showed up when they were alone, making love, and then the careful, controlled, anxious one who was around the rest of the time.

Luke tried to figure out why that was. He did not want to believe what Jackson had told him, that lawyers had been engaged. If that were true, why wouldn't she tell him? He didn't think Libby had hired lawyers—she was too intent on making the reunion a success and already planning for a wedding here to be engaging lawyers. He supposed Emma might have hired them, but that seemed unlikely, as she had no interest in the property that he could see.

It had to be Madeline. But the woman he was sleeping with was warm and passionate. She was funny when she let her guard down, eager to work. She had slowly come around to the mountain way of life—hell, she'd even fed the dogs this morning. He could not believe that she was plotting to sell Homecoming Ranch to complete strangers while she was with him. But then again, when they weren't in bed or stealing moments here and there, she was busy running through a list of things to be done. Was it for the reunion, he wondered? Or to prepare the property to sell?

Another thing that was eating at Luke was that while he understood Madeline was cautious and a little skittish when it came to men, he didn't get why she was so fearful that someone would discover they were . . . involved. Luke didn't know what else to call it: They were involved.

He looked at her now as she scrutinized their handiwork. "So," he said as he tested the water pressure in the last showerhead, "nothing left but herding Johnsons around now, is that right?"

"I think so," she said cheerfully. "We've got the horseback riding and river-rafting lined up. Ernest built a horseshoe court and cleaned up the—what did he call it, the washer pit? The cows are somewhere," she said, gesturing to the mountain. "Everything is set up and ready." She beamed at him. "I really can't believe that we pulled it off."

Neither could he. Two weeks ago, he would have sworn there was no way it would happen. "Now what?" he asked.

"Now what about what?"

He paused to look at her. "I'm talking about you and me, actually." He hadn't intended to ask that now; it had just come out.

The question obviously gave her pause. Her smile faded and she squinted off in the distance. "Well," she said, and flicked her hair over her shoulder. "I guess we'll be on hand to greet the Johnsons, right?"

That was the first time she'd mentioned being around when the Johnsons arrived. In fact, she had made it very clear she would *not* be around for that. He arched a brow.

She shrugged at his questioning look. "I mean, we've gone to so much trouble."

"What about the DiNapoli house?"

"I can . . . I can get someone to cover that," she said uncertainly. "We're talking only one more week, right?"

"I'm not really sure what we're talking about, Maddie."

Madeline smiled uneasily. "Why are you looking at me like that?"

"Because I'm wondering what happens after that."

She took a step back—unconsciously, consciously, he didn't know. "I don't know. I thought we didn't have to decide anything right now."

"We don't. But maybe we should talk about it. We don't talk, Maddie. We get together—"

"Right, right," she said, blushing, and looking surreptitiously over her shoulder.

"Is there something you want to tell me?" he asked, watching her for any sign of deception.

"What? Why would you say that?" She seemed truly taken aback, truly offended.

"I hoped you had given it some thought," he said, wiping his hands on a rag he had stuffed in his back pocket. *Tell me. Tell me you've involved lawyers to sell this ranch.*

She bit her lower lip. "Well . . . I thought maybe you could come to Orlando," she said timidly.

His heart sank a little. "And do what?"

"I know some architectural firms. I could find something for you."

"I've started a business in Denver," he pointed out.

She nodded, as if she'd anticipated this argument. "But you can build anywhere."

Luke sighed. So this was where it was going, then—nowhere. The last couple of weeks had been some of the best of his life. He'd felt things for Madeline Pruett he'd not felt for anyone else in a very long time. He could argue that she could do her job here, too, but he couldn't ask her to give up the life she'd built any more than she could ask that of him.

But she just had. And she clearly meant to sell Homecoming Ranch yet, even knowing what it meant to him. What really stung was that he knew, had known, the first night they were together in Denver, that this was one messed up relationship, judging alone by the circumstances of how they'd met. Worse, he couldn't even say to himself what it was he wanted anymore. He just knew that he wanted her. But he wanted her to want him in the same way. And even then, he didn't know what it meant for either of them.

Luke bent down and picked up the power drill. "So another week, huh?" he asked lightly.

She smiled, and she looked, he thought, a little relieved that he wasn't going to press it. "I think Libby could use the help," she said.

"Okay." He turned back to the work, but something made him look at Madeline again. "Maddie? Is there anything else you want to tell me?"

He would remember the look she gave him in the days to come. Her eyes shuttered and she looked, he thought, as if she was in pain. But she shook her head.

"Okay," he said, and turned around to gather his tools. *Okay.* She'd tell him when she was ready. He just hoped that he was ready when she did.

>─┼─◄►─⊙─◄►─┼─◄

When Madeline told Libby she was staying, Libby looked like she thought it was a joke. Madeline couldn't blame her—she hadn't believed it herself until the words actually tumbled out of her mouth this afternoon when Luke had asked her, what now?

"Another week?" Libby repeated.

"Another week," Madeline confirmed. She'd just come back from Tag's Outfitter, where she'd bought two more sundresses and two pairs of shorts. And some funky shoes she never would have worn in Orlando, would never have even looked at—but they felt so comfortable, and she imagined herself wearing them to tramp all around the ranch, leading Johnsons about.

"Why?" Libby asked. "Just yesterday, you told me you'd finished up most of the work you needed to do."

That was true. Things had been tense with Libby since Madeline's outburst. Madeline had tried more than once to apologize, but Libby would not stay in a room with her long enough to hear it. "I just thought since the Johnsons were going to start coming next week, I might stick around and help out. Is that a problem?"

"No," Libby said, eyeing her curiously. "It's just that you've made it really clear you don't want to be here. I thought you were miserable."

"I'm sorry about that," Madeline said. "I wasn't ready—"

"Stay if you want," Libby interrupted. "This is as much your place as it is mine." She walked out of the room.

On the other hand, Bree seemed very open to Madeline extending her stay. "I kind of need to stay one more week," Madeline said when she called. "Could you handle the DiNapoli inspection for me?"

There was a pregnant pause on Bree's end until she said, "Who is this and what have you done with Madeline?"

"I've still got some personal stuff I need to deal with," Madeline said, and wondered briefly what that even meant anymore. She only knew that she wasn't ready to give up this thing with Luke quite yet. Whatever this thing was. She'd spent a week working alongside him, watching him build temporary showers as easily as if they were Legos. He had a great sense of humor, he was careful with Libby's feelings, and most of all, *most* of all, he made her happy.

She was pretty sure what she was feeling was love. Not infatuation, not lust. *Love.* Real, true love for the first time in her life. That was the frightening thing.

"Of course I'll do it," Bree had said, always eager to get her fingers into the realty business while she studied for her license. "But I can't close the deal for you."

"No, no," Madeline had assured her. "I'll be back. I've worked too hard and too long to sell that place."

Which is precisely what she repeated to Trudi. She would be back. She had finally sold the DiNapoli property, of course she would be back. "I just need to finish up here," she said. "No big deal."

She probably shouldn't have said that, because Trudi latched onto it instantly. "Really? Because *everything* is a big deal to you."

"No it's not," Madeline said laughingly.

"Yeah, it is. Who are you kidding? I'm super, *super* surprised. I mean you couldn't surprise me more if you told me you were *moving* there. You're not going to *move* there, are you?"

"Of course not!"

"Seriously, you never step out of your bubble. A place for everything and everything in its place—"

"Trudi, okay!"

"What about Stephen?"

Madeline sighed. "What about him?"

"Mad, come on," Trudi chastised her. "You yourself said he's been so helpful. He told me that the broker has people who are excited about the property. What more evidence do you need that he really digs you?"

"I didn't know I was looking for evidence," Madeline said. But Trudi was right. Because of Stephen, she now had a pretty good ballpark of what the ranch was worth. She knew that the Kendricks had no real legal leg to stand on. And she knew that the broker, who specialized in ranch properties, already had a couple of clients who were interested in the ranch. The man said in a day or two he would have some concrete numbers for her to present to Libby and Emma, and then, of course, Luke. She tried to tell herself that she was giving Luke information he needed—that was, how much he'd need to buy the ranch back. But she was being less than honest with herself.

Just thinking of Luke made Madeline's face heat. She had lied to him today when he'd asked if there was anything she wanted to tell him. And while Stephen was calling in his friends to help her, she was making love to Luke on the hammock in his mother's garden, in the Pontiac, in his childhood bed. Madeline Pruett, who Trudi had labeled a Goody Two-shoes, had stepped out of so many bubbles she almost didn't know herself anymore. She loved Luke. Why was she working so hard to sabotage it?

"I know Stephen is excited for you to come back," Trudi continued blithely. "He said you guys had a long talk last week."

Madeline would not have called it a long talk, but they did speak about the DiNapoli sale and what it meant for her career that morning in Denver. There had been lots of "taking over Orlando real estate, rah-rah" talk. "He's been great," she agreed weakly.

"Then call him and tell him you'll be back in another week," Trudi said.

Madeline looked out the window at the mountains. They looked blue in the late afternoon light. She'd noticed that they changed color throughout the day. Sometimes a gold yellow, sometimes rust, sometimes blue. The mountains were always the same, always different.

"Hello?"

"I'm here," Madeline said.

"Have you heard from Clarissa?" Trudi asked.

Madeline had heard from her mother only once, and then it was to ask when Madeline would be getting the back child support. Madeline just let her think someone was looking into it—it was easier than arguing. "Not really. I'm a little worried about her. The last couple of times I spoke to her, she's been talking about people I've never heard of, and she sounds drunk half the time."

"So what else is new?"

"I'm not there to keep an eye on her, that's what."

"Mad, you've been gone a couple of weeks, that's all. Do you hear how crazy that sounds? You're a grown woman—you should be able to be away from your mother for a couple of weeks."

Tension began to stiffen Madeline. She was very familiar with Trudi's opinion of her mother, but that was her *mother* Trudi was dismissing, a woman who had no one but Madeline. "My mom isn't like yours, Trudi," she said quietly. "She needs constant—"

"Attention," Trudi interrupted. "Don't kid yourself, Mad—it's all about her."

Madeline's belly twisted dully. She didn't know who she was supposed to be anymore. "Listen, I have to go."

"Come on, don't be upset with me."

"I'm not upset with you, Trudi. Really, I'm not." That was true. Madeline was upset with herself, with the universe. She was upset that she'd lived so long by so many rules that when they began to snap like twigs around her, she didn't know what to do. "I really have a lot to do."

"Okay," Trudi said. "Well . . . call me."

Of course Madeline would call her. But not for a few days. She loved Trudi, but Madeline was beginning to think that maybe she didn't need Trudi's constant approval and advice.

But she wasn't going to think about that. Right now, she was going to think about the dinner party at Luke's house tonight.

Frankly, Madeline was a little nervous about the dinner. She didn't want to discover anything about Luke or his family that would ruin the luster of this thing between them. She didn't want to call this "thing" a fling, because it seemed so much more than that when she was with him: exciting, thrilling, perfect. But when she was alone, her head overtook her heart. She second-guessed herself and the things she was feeling and began to fear it was superficial.

Yet she couldn't let it go.

She decided on the yellow dress with blue cornflowers because it skimmed her body. Her hair was another issue. The air was so dry here that it wouldn't hold the least bit of curl. She'd taken to wearing it loose and long, and tonight, she tied a scarf around her head as she'd seen Libby do, to hold all but her bangs away from her face.

The one thing she didn't have was shoes. She was pulling on her hiking boots when Libby walked past her room.

"Cute!" Libby said.

"Thanks." Madeline smiled sheepishly and stood up. "I don't have the right shoes."

"I have some sandals that would go perfectly with that," Libby suggested, and Madeline was aware that it was the most Libby had said to her in a few days. "I'll get them."

"No, Libby, thanks, but—"

"I'll be right back," Libby said, and disappeared into the room she had been using. She returned a moment later with some fabulous sandals the same shade of blue as the cornflowers in Madeline's dress. "Oh, wow, they're perfect," Madeline said, "but I shouldn't."

"Why not?" Libby asked, looking at the shoes.

"I would feel funny wearing your shoes."

Libby sighed. "Man, you are tough, you know that? I can't figure you out."

Madeline sighed. "Honestly? I can't figure me out, either."

"Look, I know you don't want sisters, or this ranch, or . . . anything. But Madeline, we *are* sisters whether you like it or not, and borrowing my shoes is not a big deal. It's what sisters do," she said, thrusting the shoes at Madeline.

Is that what Libby truly thought? If only she knew how ironic that was, because Madeline had wanted sisters all her life. But the words, like so many other words in the last two weeks, stuck in her throat.

Libby was right. She acted as if she couldn't wait to get out of here. But was that really what she wanted? Could a person change so fundamentally in two weeks? She looked at Libby and smiled ruefully. "I'm sorry, Libby. I know I'm not very good at letting people in. You probably won't believe this, but I'm trying."

Libby looked at the shoes in her hand, then at Madeline. Her expression had softened. "Take the shoes," she said. "Please."

Madeline took the shoes. "Thank you," she said, and smiled.

It seemed that with every day that passed, Madeline was drifting farther and farther away from all the things she thought she'd known about herself.

She wondered, as she tried on Libby's shoes, if she could drift so far away that she might not find her way back to her safe harbor.

TWENTY-SIX

Libby and Madeline pulled up behind a sports car in front of a little green house on Elm Street where the Kendricks now lived. Madeline was surprised by how *tiny* the house was. Lights were blazing in every window, and she could see the forms of people moving around inside.

"How well do you know the Kendricks?" Madeline asked as Libby pulled down her visor and applied lipstick.

"Not that well. I was in the same grade as Leo, so I've seen them around."

Libby opened the driver's door and stepped out. Madeline juggled the flowers she'd brought, and climbed out a little less gracefully. She stood at the car a moment, looking at the green house. She thought of the stately ranch house high above town compared to this one. She knew how it felt to leave a comfortable home and move into something that was much less so. She was struck by a strong pang of guilt that the Kendricks had suffered it, too.

Libby had already walked through the gate and past the empty doghouse; Madeline hurried to catch up. She could hear laughter from inside, and her old nemesis, her fear of what people would think of her, began to get the best of her. Her stomach was in knots by the time she reached the porch.

Libby apparently had no such fears; she stepped up to the door and rapped loudly. A moment later, the door swung open. A woman with a short bob of gray hair and a barrel chest smiled out at them. "Well, Libby, I recognize *you*," she said. "You still have that beautifully curly hair."

"It's good to see you again, Mrs. Compton," Libby said politely.

The woman looked past Libby to Madeline. "And you must be Madeline. I'm the boys' Aunt Patti. You girls can call me Patti," she said, pushing open the screen door. "Now come on in."

Libby went through without hesitation. Madeline held out her handmade bouquet to Patti Compton. "I, ah . . . I picked these from Mrs. Kendrick's garden."

Patti gasped and put a pudgy hand over her heart. "Well," she said, "isn't that sweet? Oh Lord, but Cathy had the greenest thumb. She would have loved these." She smiled brightly at Madeline. "I'm Cathy's sister. So, thank you, hon," she said, and took the flowers from Madeline as she pushed the screen door open wider. When Madeline didn't move, she put her hand on her shoulder. "Don't be shy. You have to jump in with both feet when the Kendricks are together or risk getting run over. Especially if someone rings the dinner bell."

Madeline hesitantly stepped across the threshold, standing just inside the door. There were so many people crammed into the tiny living room that she felt claustrophobic. Libby had already made her way through the room—Madeline could see her leaning up against the doorjamb, talking to someone in the next room.

"Now that's my husband, Greg," Patti said, pointing to a man with a very large belly. "And that's my brother-in-law Bob—he's the one who owned the ranch, you know. Of course you know Luke."

Madeline had never been so grateful to see anyone in her life. Luke smiled, and she instantly felt lighter. He looked sexy in a gray button-up shirt tucked into black jeans. The shirt matched his eyes exactly. "Hi, Madeline," he said, as if they had only just met. "You look great."

"Thank you." A blush of pleasure was rising in her cheeks, and her smile broadened.

"Ex-*cuse* me!" a man bellowed behind Luke. "What am I, a piece of the furniture?"

Luke smiled. "Madeline, I'd like you to meet my brother, Leo," he said, and stepped aside.

Madeline froze. She hoped her face did not betray the utter shock she felt in seeing Leo, his body twisted unnaturally, his head cocked at a strange angle. Luke had said he had a muscular disease, which she'd interpreted to mean something like muscular dystrophy—nothing like this.

She realized she was staring. "I'm sorry," she said quickly. "Hi, Leo."

"Not to worry," Leo said cheerfully. "You're not the first to be caught off guard by my studly good looks. Wow. You really *do* have blue eyes."

A woman stood up from the couch. She said something in Spanish to Leo that made him grin crookedly. "Hello, Madeline," she said in an accented voice. "I am Marisol Fuentes. I am the zookeeper."

"Marisol helps us keep up with Leo," Luke said beside her. "You met my aunt and uncle, and you've met my dad," he said.

Madeline said hello to them, exchanging small pleasantries.

"And you know Jackson."

Jackson was sitting in the corner, looking dapper in his skinny jeans and leather jacket. He smiled, tilted his beer bottle at her. "Hey, Madeline!"

"Where's Libby?" Leo called out. "Where'd she get away to? Hey Libby, sweetcakes, I've been dying to talk to you probably as much as you've been dying to talk to me!"

"Leo has illusions," Luke said with a fond smile. "Want to give me a hand in the kitchen?"

"Sure." Madeline followed him into the kitchen. It was even smaller than the living area, and Luke had to inch in between the fridge and the little kitchen bar to open the fridge. He pulled out two beers, popped the tops, and handed her one. A shout of laughter went up in the front room.

"I didn't know," Madeline said. "When you told me that Leo had a muscular disease, I had no idea—"

"Yeah," Luke said, and looked down to rub his nape. "It's motor neuron disease. He's slowly turning into a vegetable." He tipped the beer bottle back and took a long drink. "Never seems to be a good time to say, hey, by the way, my brother is in a chair. And besides that," he leaned forward, glanced to the doorway. "We don't do a lot of talking." He stole a kiss from her.

Madeline jumped back. "*Don't*," she whispered, a tiny moment before Luke's aunt and uncle came tromping through the kitchen and out the back door.

"You look fantastic," he said, his gaze skirting over her. "Gorgeous."

Madeline blushed again. "Thank you."

Luke stepped away from her and opened the fridge. "We're going to eat outside," he said, and took a big bowl of salad from the fridge, kicked it closed, put the bowl on a tiny little breakfast bar and grabbed some tongs to toss it.

"How long has he been like that?" Madeline asked.

"Five or six years," Luke said. "He was playing football for the Colorado School of Mines and started to notice that he couldn't grip a ball with his left hand. It took about a year before they finally figured out what was going on, and then, things started happening pretty fast. He's been in a chair for about three years now."

Madeline could not imagine the devastation for Leo, for his family. The wasted potential was heartbreaking. "What will happen to him?"

She saw the hitch in Luke's shoulders. He turned partially away from her to grab salt and pepper and said, "Eventually, he won't be able to breathe or swallow. Nothing will work."

He didn't need to say more than that. Madeline could feel tears building in her. "Luke . . . I am so sorry."

"Thank you," he said. He turned back to her, composed, but distant.

Madeline could not fathom it. She'd never endured anything so painful. And to think his mother's cancer had come in the midst of it! How did one family find the strength to go on every day? How did Luke hold them together?

"May I do something to help?" she asked.

"No, you sit back and relax," he said, and began to toss the salad.

Madeline didn't know how she was supposed to sit back and relax. In the living room, she could hear Marisol's lilting accent and Libby's laugh. The back door suddenly banged open, and Patti came in. "Excuse me, hon," she said, and squeezed her ample hips past Madeline into the kitchen, next to Luke. She bent over at the oven, bumping Luke aside, and brought out two pans of lasagna, stacking them on the stovetop.

She was peeling back the tin foil when Libby came in to the kitchen. "Want me to get the drinks?" she asked.

"That would be great," Patti said. "Glasses are there."

"There" was just above Madeline's head, and she had no choice but to step back into the living room where Jackson and Leo were sitting together.

The two men abruptly stopped talking when they saw Madeline.

"Come in, Madeline," Jackson said. He gestured to a chair on the other side of Leo. It was set slightly back; she wondered if she was supposed to pull it up and join the conversation.

She sat, looking at the back of Leo's head, wondering how he'd found the strength to endure what he had. She turned her attention to the peeling wallpaper, and noticed a big framed collage of photos on the wall behind him. It was the only adornment in the room. They were various pictures of a happy family—a broad woman who looked like Patti, who Madeline assumed was Luke's mother, Leo with a cane. Luke, Leo, his mother and father sitting on a picnic bench that she recognized from the west lawn at the ranch, laughing. Pictures of a happy family before their lives were decimated.

Jackson suddenly hopped up, interrupting Madeline's thoughts. "I'm going to get another beer. Anything for you, Madeline?"

She glanced down at the beer she was holding. She'd taken one sip. "No, thank you."

"I'll be back," he said, and walked out of the room, leaving her alone with Leo.

"Hey," Leo said. "I can't see you." His chair suddenly lurched forward, then stopped and lurched backward, and again and again, until he had maneuvered it around to face her. He smiled crookedly at her. "You like football, right?"

"Ah . . . not really."

"What, are you kidding? You have three professional teams in Florida! Dolphins, Buccaneers, Jaguars—you've gotta find *one* you like."

"I never really got into football," she said apologetically.

"Tragedy of the first order. Basketball? Baseball?" he asked hopefully.

Madeline shook her head. "Soccer."

"Wow," Leo said, wincing. "That is the *one* sport I could care less about. All that running around for a point?" He shook his head. "Okay, how about video games? I have a new game, 'Hounds of Hell.' It's *dope*, man. You have to kills these giant dogs before they kill you. Come on, let's play."

"I don't know how," Madeline said quickly.

"You don't have to know how," he said. "You're playing a guy with useless arms." He grinned crookedly. "The controllers are over there."

Madeline stood up and collected two controllers and placed one in his lap as he instructed. Leo did a quick little tutorial about how to work the controller as the game booted up. "Remember," he said. "Kill the hounds. Ready?"

"I guess," she said uncertainly.

The game started, and the hounds were released from their cages, galloping right at them. "Okay, *fire! Fire!*" Leo shouted. In a moment of panic, Madeline had to study her controller again, remembering which button was the Fire button. By the time she punched it, the hound had leaped at her.

"Oooh, you're *dead*," Leo said sympathetically, and somehow managed to fire and kill several of the beasts in the next minute. "I've never seen anyone die so *fast*," he said, impressed. "You know what that means, right?"

"No, what?" Madeline asked.

"A guy with useless arms in a chair *beat* you." He laughed gaily.

His laugh was infectious. Madeline grinned at him.

Leo moved his crippled hand from the controller. "So what do you like, Madeline? There has to be something you like."

"Movies," she said. "I like movies."

"Now we're cooking with grease! What kind? Sci-fi, thriller, dram-edies, period films?"

"I lean more toward romantic comedies."

"A fine genre and one that happens to be my favorite, too," he said loudly. "Let me guess—you're a *Love Actually* kind of girl."

"Nope," Madeline said, smiling. "More like a *Knocked Up* kind of girl."

"Ack! That was going to be my second guess. Get this, *Knocked Up* is Luke's favorite, too."

Madeline must have looked as surprised as she felt because Leo said, "It's a little known fact that Luke Kendrick loves a good *looooove* fest." He waggled his brows at Madeline.

"You're kidding me."

"I would *not* kid about something as unmanly as that. He also cries at baby and puppy commercials, too. Loves the little buggers."

Madeline laughed. "I don't believe you. I don't think he has time to watch movies."

"Well maybe not in Denver. But when he comes here, we watch a lot of tearjerkers, believe me."

"Does he come to Pine River a lot?" she asked.

"Probably a whole lot more than he wants to. I mean, it's not hard to figure out that Luke is the Kendricks' go-to guy."

She nodded. "I can see that."

"Yep. I'll let you in on a family secret. Dad and I aren't the most ef-ficient team in the world. If it weren't for Luke, we would have either killed each other by now or be living on the streets with our pet mon-key. Luke's always pulling our bacon out of the grease, you know? And the great news is, he's a good sport about it. I mean, think about it—it took him about six years to finish his architecture degree because he had to keep dropping classes to come home and fix this or that prob-lem. Yep, that's my brother. He comes home to save the day, then he watches movies with me and plays 'Hounds of Hell.' And he's *way* better at it than you."

Madeline smiled. She liked Leo, very much. He had a great person-ality, and he was a straight shooter, which she appreciated. "He *must* be good if he's better than me."

Leo laughed. "I think I like you, Madeline from Orlando. And in case Luke hasn't said it to you, he likes you, too."

"Leo, Madeline, time for dinner!" Patti called, popping her head into the living room.

Luke squeezed around his aunt into the living room. "Okay, genius," he said to Leo. "Time to strap on the feed bag." He smiled at Madeline as he stepped up behind Leo's chair. "He hasn't told you any wild and unbelievable tales, has he?"

"Not a single one," she said honestly.

"That's because I haven't even *begun* to talk," Leo said as Luke took hold of his chair.

"He's not kidding," Luke said. "Consider yourself forewarned. We'll meet you out back." To Leo, he said, "No hot-rodding, buddy."

Madeline watched him roll Leo out. She stood up and walked to the collage of pictures that hung on the wall. Yes, it was plain to see that Luke was the cog in this family wheel, trying to right his dad's mistake, taking care of his brother. He was a good man, Madeline thought, and she felt a yearning unlike any she'd ever felt in her life—for that. For family. For a hero.

TWENTY-SEVEN

When Luke and Leo were kids, the whole family would come out to the ranch, and beneath the Chinese lanterns his mother hung on the trees, they would have big dinners on one long table. His mother had always dressed it up with a tablecloth, flowers, and fancy dishes. The kids would play on the lawn while the meal was prepared, and again, afterward, when the adults would sit around with their homemade pie and coffee.

Tonight, they were missing the backdrop of the mountains and the fancy dishes, but Patti had put up Chinese lanterns and had brought her own tablecloth. And the lasagna was as good as anything Luke's mother had ever made. It took him back to a simpler, happier time. Could it be like that again?

He looked at Madeline. To him, she was gorgeous. And tonight, so different from the woman he'd met up on Sometimes Pass. She was laughing at something Leo said, her eyes crinkling in the corners. They could be this, he thought. They could be this couple, living this life.

Leo was entertaining them all with his grand schemes to win tickets to a Denver football game. Patti was appalled—and rightfully so—that Leo had convinced his young friend Dante to try and get the tickets through the Make-A-Wish Foundation.

"Come on, Aunt Patti," Leo had scoffed as Marisol mashed up his lasagna to a pulp. "He thinks it's pretty cool. He *wants* to go. And he wants to take me. But just in case that doesn't fly, I am working on backup plans. I *will* see a game at Mile High Stadium if it's the last thing I do!"

No one said anything for a long moment.

Leo laughed. "Okay, it won't be the *last* thing I do. Better now?"

"I think it's great," Greg said, and pointed his fork at Patti. "You know Cathy always said this kid was going to be something someday," he said, winking at Leo.

"I *am* something," Leo said. "I'm a chick magnet. Just look how many I've got around me right now." He grinned, trying to turn his head to look at Libby, Madeline, and Marisol.

"The only thing you have around you now is flies," Marisol said casually. "Just like the rear end of a horse."

"You love me, Marisol," Leo said cheerfully. "Just admit it. Come clean. We all know it and it's embarrassing."

"Do you boys remember the lasagna Cathy made for my Tyler's birthday?" Patti asked.

Dad laughed. "That thing was a *brick*. Could have been the cornerstone of a new house." The Kendricks laughed while Patti explained to their guests that Luke's mother had overcooked the lasagna a wee bit.

Luke remembered that day very clearly. Mom had been beside herself—with fifteen people for dinner, the lasagna burned to a brick. Under the table, he put his hand on Madeline's knee, and she turned a brilliantly warm smile to him. Yes, he could see her at this table for years to come. He could see them, dining under a Colorado sky, their children playing on the lawn while the two of them ate pie and drank coffee.

"Libby, you have a pretty big family, don't you?" Patti asked.

"Me?" Libby said, looking surprised. "I have a lot of cousins. My mom has four sisters. There are a lot of them, but we don't get together like this. It's usually my mom, her husband, and my twin brothers."

"What about you, Madeline?" Patti asked.

"Ah . . . it's just me and my mother," Madeline said politely, but Luke could feel her tensing.

"Where's your mom, in Orlando?"

"Yes."

"Well, this must have been a great surprise," Patti said.

She was only making small talk like any good hostess would, but Luke knew Madeline well enough now to know how uncomfortable these questions would make her. Her fist curled in her lap, and she glanced at Luke. He smiled reassuringly. On some dusty, remote level, he understood the anxiety that she seemed to live with. In moments like this, he felt sorry for her. Madeline had not had an easy life.

Madeline suddenly sat up. "It was a huge surprise," she said, and laughed a little, looking at Libby across the table. "Of all the things I imagined about my dad, this wasn't it. Two sisters and a ranch? I was not expecting that."

"I'm really glad you came out, Madeline," Jackson said. "When are you heading back to Orlando?"

"Next week." She said it without hesitation, so easily, that Luke realized her mind was made up.

"What?" Leo exclaimed. "But you can't. You have to stay and redeem your piss-poor performance on 'Hounds of Hell.'"

Madeline smiled warmly at Leo. "I would love to, but I have a lot of active listings. And my mom needs me." She turned that warm smile to Luke.

He did not smile back, and he saw something flicker in her eyes. Guilt?

"Time for dessert!" Patti announced, and stood up. "Madeline, would you help me?"

"Of course!" she said, and hopped up, picking up hers and Luke's plates.

Luke watched Madeline walk into the house behind Patti, looking pretty damn gorgeous in that yellow dress that hugged her hips. He thought of how her hair felt in his hands, how she felt beneath him, and he wondered if he was crazy for feeling like he did about her.

The woman had issues. Serious issues.

He wished he knew the first thing about how to fix those issues.

>—◆>—○—<◆—<

Madeline was assigned drying dishes while Patti washed. Patti chatted gregariously about life in Pine River. A new Applebee's was going in on the Aspen Highway, which excited her because she'd heard they printed the Weight Watcher point values on their menus. She was sorry to see the Piedmont Tire Store close up in town, but it couldn't be helped because old Mr. Piedmont had emphysema.

Marisol joined them, bringing in food to be put away, fitting it into a tiny little fridge that seemed absurdly small for three men.

"Did you hear?" Marisol said to Patti, pausing to bend sideways and look outside, where the men were now engaged in a game of poker. "Julie Daugherty has split from her husband."

"Oh no," Patti said. "I so hate to hear that. I thought she and Brandon were a cute couple. I mean, obviously I thought she and Luke were cuter, but if that couldn't work out, I was happy to see her with a good man."

"He is a dog," Marisol said emphatically. "He has his thing in any woman who will bend to him."

"Marisol!" Patti said, her face going bright red. She gave Madeline a sheepish look. "Sometimes, you just have to ignore her," she said, with a pointed look at Marisol.

"I say only what is true," Marisol said with a shrug. She covered a bowl of beans and said low, "Now, she wants to be again with Luke."

Patti stopped washing and turned around. "What?"

Marisol nodded furiously. "She comes here, two, three times a week. Leo, he has heard this from Luke, that she wants to be together again. They sit on the porch and they talk long time. *Long* time."

"Well, that's their business, Marisol," Patti said primly.

"Yes, of course it is their business," Marisol said with shrug. "But I do not like to see her with him again, do you?"

"It's none of our business," Patti said firmly. "I want whatever makes Luke happy. That's all." She turned back to her washing.

Marisol frowned at Patti's back. "Very well, pretend you do not hear me," she said with a flick of her wrist. "But if they come together again, she will hurt him again. I know this woman. I know how she is." Her gaze shifted to Madeline, and then to the plate Madeline held.

Only then did Madeline realize that she was not moving, that her towel was stuck to the plate, her body going cold. She slowly resumed drying, her thoughts racing now. She'd known when this affair with Luke began that it could never be more than it was, in spite of any fantasies she might have harbored that it could be. And now it felt as if her instincts to protect her heart, to cocoon it, had been right. Luke liked her, she knew that he did. But he didn't love her, not like she was beginning to love him, she was fairly certain—how could he love her and Julie at the same time?

She took her time finishing up, stacking the dishes neatly on the bar, as there was no place in the two cabinets to put them. By then, everyone was eating pie and playing cards.

Madeline wrapped her sweater tightly around her and walked outside. Mr. Kendrick apparently had bowed out of the game and was sitting on the steps of the little porch.

"May I join you?" Madeline asked.

"Come on," he said, and patted the wood step next to him.

She sat down on the step and fixed her gaze on a Chinese lantern.

"You don't want to play?" Mr. Kendrick asked.

"No." She smiled sheepishly. "I'm horrible at games, and there is nothing I hate more than losing money."

He laughed. "Me, too."

It was ironic for him to say, given how much he'd lost in selling Homecoming Ranch. He seemed a good man, and Madeline couldn't help but feel sorry for him. How did one man bear so much loss? She looked at his creased face and imagined him striking his deal with her father, the devil. "May I ask you something?"

"Shoot," he said.

"What was he like? Grant Tyler, I mean."

Mr. Kendrick studied her for a moment, his gray eyes—Luke's eyes—regarding her with the same casual interest. "Well, I can say that he wasn't any good with women, but I guess you knew that."

Madeline smiled. "That is the one thing about him I knew."

"He thought he was some hotshot, some business brain, but I think he made more messes than anyone I ever knew. When Grant was on top, there wasn't no one higher. But when he fell, he landed with a bang."

Madeline glanced down, wishing she would hear something about Grant that she could honestly admire. Just one small thing that would make her feel as if she hadn't descended from a long line of losers.

"He wasn't all bad," Mr. Kendrick said, as if she'd voiced her thoughts out loud. "I mean, he really was trying to help me out. He thought he was a wheeler-dealer and was probably just shy of the law, but his intentions were good. He knew I needed the money for Leo."

"For Leo?"

"Yep. Insurance only covers so much, and that was back when I could get insurance for my son."

Madeline bit her lower lip. He'd sold the ranch for so much less than it was worth so that he could take care of Leo.

"I take it he wasn't much of a dad," Mr. Kendrick said.

"You'd have to ask Libby," Madeline said with a shrug. "I never knew him."

Mr. Kendrick nodded. "I won't make excuses for him," he said. "But I'll let you in on a secret—Grant himself told me he was never the same after his son died."

Madeline started. "What? What son?"

"Hadn't heard about that? He had son with his first wife. To hear Grant tell it, he doted on that kid. They had a little house out in Florida somewhere. He'd just gotten out of the military, was doing something with aviation equipment. Said he was really happy then. But that kid, somehow he got out from under their watch and they found him in the pool. He was about two when he drowned."

Madeline's stomach dropped. She'd had a brother? A baby who had drowned? She suddenly felt sick to her stomach. "I didn't . . . I never . . ."

"Well I guess he kept that ache to himself then," Mr. Kendrick said. "I don't think he would have told me, but when this last wife left him, he came over one night, just as drunk as he could be, and he poured it all out."

"Oh my God," Madeline murmured.

"Now I never approved of the way Grant handled his kids, I can tell you that much. But after he told me, part of me always wanted to cut him a break. I just know how crazy I'd be if I lost one of my two."

They sat in silence for a long moment. Madeline swallowed down a lump in her throat. She had never thought of her father as anything other than slightly less than human. She could not imagine the pain of his loss. And here she was sitting next to a man who had sacrificed so much for his child. A child he would lose.

She felt guilty for something she hadn't done, guilt by association. "Mr. Kendrick, about the ranch—"

"Now Madeline, you do what you need to do about that," he said, cutting her off. "We'll be fine. We've made it this far and we'll keep making it, no matter what. One thing I've got is two strong sons. We can weather just about anything." He smiled, then surprised her by squeezing her knee. "You take care of *you*. Do what you need for you."

She appreciated his sentiment, but the little green house was scarcely big enough for Leo's wheelchair. How could she worry about only herself?

Libby appeared before them, her purse on her shoulder. "There you are. Are you ready?" she asked brightly.

Luke walked up behind Libby. "You're not leaving, are you?"

"We have so much to do tomorrow," Libby said. "The Johnsons will be here on Thursday."

Madeline stood up and looked at Luke. He said, "Are you leaving?" She had the feeling he was asking her something else entirely, something much deeper, and Madeline didn't have an answer for him. She could feel a sea change in her, as if everything she had ever known, everything she had ever been, was turning over, bottom-up. It felt big, overwhelming. This time, she couldn't reason everything out, couldn't chart it and follow a predetermined path. She felt strangely paralyzed by the life she'd worked so hard to achieve.

She looked at Luke. He deserved some explanation from her. He deserved the best the world had to offer, not some woman from Orlando with a trunk full of emotional baggage. She wanted to tell him how she felt about him and what she meant to do, but honestly, standing there, she didn't really know what she meant to do. "I have to go," she said simply, and smiled sadly.

She could see in Luke's pained expression that he understood her.

Luke walked Libby and Madeline out to their car after they'd said their good-nights. He stepped back inside the fence and watched until the red taillights of Libby's car disappeared around the corner. When he turned back, he was surprised to see Jackson with one hip perched on the railing of the porch, watching him.

"So what's up, Luke?" Jackson asked shrewdly. "You look a little like a sick puppy."

"Funny," Luke said.

"Hey, I got a call from your attorney, Dan Broadstreet. He had a few questions for me."

"Did he?"

"I guess he was looking for something to help you out. But he told me it didn't look good, that case law won't back up the deal your dad made, and that it would be a big waste of money to try it." He shrugged sympathetically. "But I guess you knew that."

"I knew it," Luke said. "My goal is to fight it long enough that I have time to get enough money together to buy the ranch back. I'm driving over to Denver tomorrow to go over things with Dan."

"Seriously?" Jackson said, surprised. "You guys don't have the money for that."

"I have the money," Luke said.

Jackson sighed. "Everyone appreciates your determination, Luke. But your dad doesn't want to go back to the ranch. Do you know that? I don't know if it's because his wife is gone, or it's too hard to handle Leo out there, but he's been pretty straight with me—he doesn't have any interest."

"Maybe so. But Leo and I do."

Jackson cocked his head to one side. "Leo, too?" he asked, sounding skeptical.

"Yes," Luke said. "Leo, too." He didn't know if that was true or not, and now he would make it a point to speak to Leo about it. "But definitely me, Jackson. Everyone seems to forget that Homecoming Ranch is my legacy, too."

Jackson nodded. "I thought you were sticking to Denver."

"I am," Luke said. "For now. That's where the work is. But one day, I'm going to have kids. And I want the ranch to be there for them, just like it was for Leo and me. Like it was for my dad. I'm not willing to say, hey, you know, my dad made a mistake, and move on. There is too much family history, too much of my life wrapped up there."

"I hear you, man. But it's happening all across Colorado. Ranches are too expensive to run and maintain. We can agree to disagree about Grant's methods, but he was onto something. You've got to have twice as many cattle up there to pay for that operation. Your dad was sinking faster than a stone in a pond."

Luke folded his arms across his chest and stared back at Jackson.

Jackson groaned. "Okay," he said, throwing up his hands. "Okay. I'll help you however I can. Just promise me one thing."

"What's that?"

"Promise me you won't tell me how much money you lose in this deal. My tiny money-grubbing heart can't take it."

TWENTY-EIGHT

"This is going to be *great*," Libby said as she put the finishing touches on her own special project, a welcome sign for the Johnsons. She'd labored over it for several days, painting it onto some weathered boards that had come from an old shed the men had removed to make way for the showers.

"Looks great," Madeline said. She was reviewing the budget she'd made Jackson give her. If there was any money to be saved, she would find it.

Libby stood back and admired her handiwork. "If Luke would ever show up again, we could get this hung." She glanced sidelong at Madeline. "Do you know where he is?"

Madeline had to swallow down the bitter lump of disappointment. "No," she said as lightly as she could. "Haven't heard from him." She was puzzled by it, hurt by it. He hadn't come out to the ranch, and the one afternoon she drove into town for some things, she didn't see his Bronco on Elm Street, or anywhere else. There was a terrible ache in her heart where he had been these last weeks, and she wanted him to fill it back up.

Love. Love was doing this to her. Not anxiety. Now she understood what an incredible, physical yearning love was, and it was turning her skin inside out.

"The first wave of Johnsons is coming this afternoon!" Libby reminded her. "Did you see the little wagon I put coffee and tea on?"

"No."

"Come and see!" she said, beckoning Madeline up away from the kitchen bar. They walked out the front door, down the porch steps Luke had repaired. There, by the fence next to Madeline's bulletin board, was a miniature red covered wagon. Big urns of coffee and tea were placed on it, next to creamers, sugars, and Styrofoam cups.

"It's great," Madeline said. "Where'd you get it?"

"Dani. Oh, there's Ernest!" Libby said and flashed a smile at Madeline. "I bet I can talk him into hanging the sign." She scampered off, her curly hair bouncing behind her.

Their work was done; there was nothing left but the waiting for hordes to arrive. It was a glorious day, a great day for a family reunion. Madeline thought of the Kendricks, and how many reunions they must have had here. Her heart ached—they should still *be* here.

She decided to walk—it occurred to her that she might not have many more opportunities to do so.

It was funny how she'd taken to walking in the mornings, going a little farther each day. This morning, like most mornings, the four dogs were quickly behind her, settled into her new routine, their snouts to the trail, their tails high. Although she couldn't keep their names straight, she had warmed to them, too. They were good companions on chilly spring nights.

Madeline listened to the chatter of birds as she walked. She realized, about halfway up, that she didn't feel so out of breath as she had when she'd first come to Colorado. It was remarkable, that over the course of a little more than two weeks, she had been transformed. She felt the mountains in her now, felt the pull of them in the mornings, the desire to climb up, to see what nature had to offer. When she'd first arrived, Dani had suggested she would feel that way, and Madeline thought she was crazy. Turns out, *she* was the crazy one. Who could not feel the allure of this patch of paradise?

But this morning, Madeline felt so empty, too. She truly missed Luke. She missed him standing at the bottom of the trail when she came down, missed him building showers and latrines in tight T-shirts and jeans. She missed the way he smiled at her and the way he made her feel when they made love.

Where *was* he?

The despair she felt for him was so much more powerful than the despair she'd felt when other people had disappeared from her life. Before, she'd felt lonely and undeserving. This despair was something altogether different; it was abrading, chipping away at her soul. She debated driving by his house and actually inquiring, but then she thought of the conversation between Patti and Marisol, and the talk of Julie Daugherty coming around.

Maybe that was it. Maybe Luke had reconciled with Julie. She would hope that he would mention it, but then again, why would he? Madeline had made it clear—*too* clear—that this would end. She'd been so fearful of it she had done what she always did and backed too far away. She hadn't even found the courage to tell him. He must believe she didn't care.

Madeline was lost in thought when she heard the sound of heavy footfall. She stopped on the trail. The dogs stopped behind her, their snouts in the air. One of them, the big one, turned and ran down the trail.

How interesting, Madeline thought, that she didn't fear a bear. She felt for her whistle around her neck, but she didn't lift it to her mouth. She stood on the trail, waiting, listening to the sounds of the thing moving closer. And then, just ahead of her, an elk emerged from the woods. The animal was huge, standing as tall as she. The spread of its horns had to be five feet across. It snorted, lifting its head, and eyed Madeline. The smaller dogs began to bark, but the elk didn't notice or didn't care. It dipped its head, sniffed at the ground, then slowly, laboriously, moved on, stepping into the woods on the other side of the trail and disappearing into them.

It felt almost like a dream. A majestic, magnificent creature drifting through her morning, appearing from nowhere, disappearing into nothing.

Just like Luke.

She had the strange urge to run after the beast, to catch it. But she was frozen, looking at the point she'd last seen it, wishing she had done something different, had moved to touch it before it disappeared.

Madeline was so lost in the image of that elk, in missing Luke, that she didn't at first register the sounds from below. Several moments passed before she recognized her name. Libby was calling her.

The first wave of Johnsons had arrived.

TWENTY-NINE

The first thing Luke noticed was the sign hanging over the entry: WELCOME JOHNSON FAMILY REUNION. He couldn't miss it—it covered up the HOMECOMING RANCH sign that had hung over the gate for decades. He took a deep breath and drove up the road, over the little bridge and into Tent City, where pads, spaced precisely apart in the meadow, housed tents that looked like red alien pods. There were two RVs parked in the far end of the meadow, too, their awnings already extended. This wasn't camping. This was pretend camping.

Wandering in and out of the big circus tent erected for their meeting place, were Johnsons in matching red T-shirts that said JOHNSON FAMILY REUNION, THE ROCKIES.

Luke tried not to look at the invasion of tomatoes. It made him feel helpless, and he didn't need any help in that department—Dan Broadstreet had done a pretty good job of telling him just how helpless he was. "Why are you even here?" Dan Broadstreet had rumbled as he sat with him in his office. "Just this checking in with me is costing you money."

"Because I need to talk," Luke said.

They had talked, all right. "A written agreement, even on the back of a cocktail napkin, is one thing," Dan said. "It's defensible. But a verbal agreement? Unless there are a bunch of witnesses, that's a much tougher thing to sell. At first blush, I said I didn't think you could. Now, I've looked into it, and I'm going to tell you straight up—you're wasting your money. You can't stop this, Luke. You have nothing to file, no standing. Soon as the ranch is out of probate, it's theirs to do with what they want. You'd be better off dealing directly with them than trying to find some legal maneuver."

Deep down, Luke had known that. He'd known it the first night he'd sat with his father at the kitchen table. But when he'd left Dan's office that afternoon, he had accepted that he was truly defeated. He couldn't come up with the money. He couldn't stop a sale. It was done.

He'd also stopped in at his borrowed office while he was in Denver and learned there were problems with his house. The plumbing lines hadn't passed inspection. It had taken him a couple of days to straighten it all out.

And then he'd gone home to collect a few things, take care of a few things. In his mailbox, he'd found the usual stack of bills, but also a letter from his professor telling him that as he had missed the exam, he had no choice but to fail him. He was giving Luke the opportunity to withdraw from class.

Inside his house, things remained as he and Madeline had left them the last time he was in town. There were beer bottles on the hearth and the floor pillows on the floor. It was a stinging reminder of how foolish he'd been to believe that something magical had happened that night. God, he could be such a sorry sap at times.

He drove back to Pine River and Homecoming Ranch in a sour mood. He could scarcely bear to come up to the ranch and see strangers milling about. He'd meant what he'd said to Jackson—this ranch was the Kendrick legacy.

However, he had to grudgingly admit that Jackson was right, too. He knew it was becoming increasingly difficult to turn a profit up here. He knew Dad was between a rock and a hard place. And he knew that if he'd come home a year or so ago, he might have been able to help Dad turn it around. But what about his houses? What about the work he'd put into his degree, into making his brand-new company work? What about all the hopes and dreams that he'd had for himself, that had been steadily picked off, one by one, as his family faltered?

He didn't know what to do, and the fact that he'd scarcely been able to think of anything other than Madeline had made him crazy. It reminded him of his high school buddy Brad Levitt, a big nose tackle on the football team. When Allison Rangold broke up with him, Brad had moped around for days and had topped off the humiliation of letting a girl get under his skin by crying on the school bus after a big loss. The guys never let him live it down, and Luke had privately thought him weak.

Now Luke knew that he was weak, too. He still didn't get it completely, didn't understand how Madeline had managed to capture him like she had, but he had that woman firmly rooted under his skin.

At the ranch, Luke parked his Bronco in its usual spot. He got out and greeted the dogs, who seemed more excited than usual. They hadn't had this much activity since Mom died and streams of people had driven out for the memorial service, which was held in the meadow.

Luke walked up to the house, almost colliding with a little tomato that went flying by. Inside, he found Libby in the dining room with three middle-aged women. They were studying what looked like a map.

"Luke! Hey!" Libby said brightly when she saw him. To the women, she said, "This is Luke Kendrick. He's our . . ." She stumbled there, trying to think of the correct word.

"Hand," Luke said, and extended his hand to the Johnsons. That's what he was now—a ranch hand.

The ladies exclaimed about the property, how beautiful it was, how excited they were about the dance tomorrow evening—the first Luke had heard of a dance—and the shopping in Pine River. One of them warned Libby and Luke to be sure and keep an eye out for Uncle Belo, who was known to wander, sometimes without key articles of clothing.

Luke promised and excused himself. He walked into the kitchen and stopped in the middle, looking around. Something was different.

He finally figured out what it was—his mother had stitched four pictures of teapots, and had put them up between the cabinets and the back door. Those pictures—along with any pictures of the Kendricks, anything that would say this house had once belonged to them—were gone.

He had to get out of there, and strode out the back door, down the steps, and through the little herb garden on his way to the trail that led up into the woods. He passed the family picnic area, where three tomatoes were sitting at one of the tables with several beer bottles between them, laughing and talking.

Luke stepped onto the trail and turned into the little path that led to his mother's garden. The trees had begun to leaf out, covering the entrance, and once he stepped through them, he felt alone. He stood on the tranquil patch of earth, staring up at the sky. *Mom, what do I do now?*

His life was changing again, rushing down a new riverbed, carrying him along in its wake. The familiar, the places in his life where his soul found comfort, were dissolving and shifting out of sight.

Luke didn't fear the change. What he feared was that he would never recover from this blow. Julie, his mom, Leo's illness—from those blows, he had recovered. But losing Homecoming Ranch? That felt impossible to withstand.

"You came back."

Luke whirled around; he hadn't heard Madeline come through the trees. She looked prettier to him than she lived in his memory, her eyes glittering in the sunlight, her hair, heavy silk. "Did you think I wouldn't?"

She smiled wryly. "I didn't *think* so—I was certain you wouldn't. I'm really glad you did." She suddenly moved, running forward, leaping into his arms, her mouth landing on his.

Luke caught her, stumbling back one step to keep them from crashing to the ground. She kissed him with urgency, with the desire he had felt these last few days boiling in him.

Madeline lifted her head. "Where did you go?" she asked breathlessly, and kissed him again, arousing all his desires, all the demons in him that wouldn't stop until he'd had all of her. He twirled around, and fell with her onto the hammock, his hands skimming her body, the trim waist, the flare of her hips.

"You left and didn't tell me," she said as her hands explored him just as eagerly.

"Had to go, baby," he said, and kissed her again. He didn't want to talk—right now, he just wanted her. One last time, he wanted to be with her. He kissed her face, her neck, finding his way to her breasts. He'd just freed one from the bra beneath her T-shirt when voices reached them.

"Delores, you are *not* going into those woods alone!" they heard someone say sternly. "You know what kind of wildcats and bears are in there?"

Luke and Madeline swung in the hammock, with Luke's hand over Madeline's mouth as she shook with laughter.

"There are no wildcats up here!" Delores protested. "Maybe some bears, but not *wildcats*!"

A small laugh escaped Madeline, and Luke, trying hard not to laugh out loud himself, held a finger up to his lips.

"What do you think this is?" the first woman demanded. "Looks like a statue or something."

"Probably some Indian thing."

Luke realized they were talking about one of his mother's neglected craft projects. It was a fence post that she had tried some paints on, with the idea of carving something, or perhaps making a birdcage. But she'd lost interest and let it stand there, weathering away during the harsh winters and mild summers. He was overcome with laughter and buried his face in Madeline's shoulder. They struggled to stay quiet until Delores and whoever her companion was had moved away, and only then did Luke laugh so hard that he and Madeline rolled out of the hammock, landing on the soft grass just below them.

He gathered Madeline up in his arms, kissed her face. "God, I want you," he murmured.

"Me, too."

"Tonight," he said. "Come into town. We'll have dinner, find a place . . ."

"We will?" she asked hopefully.

"Leave it to me." He had no idea how, but he'd figure it out. He had to figure it out. He had to have one last moment with her before it all went to hell.

Madeline's smile was luminous. "I can't *wait*. I need to be with you, to talk to you—"

More voices filtered in to them and they stilled, listening. When it seemed that no one was coming, Luke said, "We better go and give Libby a hand." He rolled Madeline over onto her back, kissing her once more, before he grabbed her hand and helped her up.

Two vanloads of Johnsons, arriving from the Durango airport, descended on Homecoming Ranch at the same time that one of the extra ovens Ernest had installed was found to be malfunctioning. Luke and Ernest spent an hour repairing that problem, and when Luke was finally free of it, he walked outside and saw Madeline with a group of children. She was down on one knee and was actually introducing the dogs to them. Who could believe this was the same reserved, shy woman who had shown up in a suit and pumps?

The reunion was happy chaos; cries of delight at seeing relatives and friends after a long while echoed between the mountains. It reminded Luke of his own childhood. Homecoming Ranch was one of the most beautiful patches of earth.

More Johnsons arrived, pulling up in rental vans, cars, and pickups, gathering around the big bulletin board that Madeline had made him erect. He had to admit, it was coming in very useful. Two hundred people were a lot, even for a place as big as Homecoming Ranch.

One carload of Johnsons managed to get their car stuck when they backed off the road, which meant that Luke had to pull them out. He spent a good half hour with that, and had just pulled the car back on the road when a pair of Mercedes sports cars sailed by on their way to the main house.

He unhooked the Johnson car, stuck around to make sure they parked without driving into a ditch again, then headed back to the house. As he pulled up next to the garage, he noticed Madeline on the drive, speaking to a group of men. Specifically, to men in expensive suits and shoes. Those men hadn't come here for a reunion.

This was it, he realized. The moment of truth Luke had known would come, that he'd hoped would never come. He could feel painful resentment burning through him, the feeling of fresh betrayal slicing through him. He got out of the Bronco and walked up into their midst.

Madeline's expression was pained. "Luke, this is . . ." She hesitated, and Luke wondered if she had forgotten the man's name.

"Stephen Wallace," the man said, his hand extended, his gaze cool. *Stephen.* Good-looking Stephen in his expensive shoes and crisp white shirt. "I am Madeline's attorney," he said, a statement that seemed to surprise Madeline. "This is my associate, Jim Puryear from Denver, and the real estate broker we have consulted, Chip Danziger."

This was what Leo would call a full-scale assault. Madeline was going to end this between them with all guns blazing. He leveled his gaze on her.

"This is Luke Kendrick," Madeline said, her voice weak. To Luke, she said, "It's not what you think. I didn't know they were coming today."

"Maybe not today, but you knew they were coming," he said.

"Allow me to introduce Mr. Taranaku," Chip Danziger said, gesturing to the diminutive man next to him. "He represents some folks who are very interested in buying this place."

"What?"

The sound of Libby's voice startled them all. Libby was suddenly there, holding several rolls of toilet paper in her arms. She looked at Taranaku, then at Madeline. "*What?*" she demanded again. "What is going on here?"

"I will explain," Madeline said.

"It's great to meet you all," Luke said casually, and reached in his back pocket for a card to give them. "But if you want to speak about the ranch, you'll have to speak to my attorney."

He handed the card to Stephen and looked him directly in the eye; Stephen steadily returned his gaze.

Luke shifted his gaze to Libby. "Libby, if you've got a minute, there're a couple of things I think you and I ought to talk about." He put his hand on her elbow and turned her away.

"Wait!" Madeline said. "I'll come, too. I can explain—"

"I think you've explained yourself pretty well," Luke said, and looked past her, to the men there.

"What is going on?" Libby asked, her eyes wide with confusion.

"I'll fill you in," he said, and walked on with Libby. He did not look at Madeline as he walked away.

THIRTY

Madeline was appalled and ashamed, absolutely ashamed.

She never dreamed Stephen would fly to Colorado. She never imagined in her wildest thoughts that he would come out to see the ranch with the realtor, bringing a buyer along. She had believed these men would give her information—*only* information—that she could share with Libby and Emma and Luke.

She had completely underestimated Stephen. Completely.

"What are you doing here?" she'd demanded when she'd realized what was happening. "Why are you here?"

"I came to help," he'd said cheerfully, as if Madeline would be happy about such a blindsiding. "Turns out, a case I'm working on has some documents in Aspen I needed to look at, and I thought, why not kill two birds with one stone?"

Why not just kill *her*? He couldn't have done a better job of it, showing up like this, with these men. Luke . . . *Luke* . . . he'd looked at her with such disgust. And worse, as if he'd been expecting it. Libby, dear God, Libby—she looked so confused, so hurt.

"Mr. Taranaku would like to have a look around, Madeline," the broker said. "Would you mind giving him a quick tour?"

"Me?" she asked, incredulous.

Chip had looked about, and said, "I don't see anyone else to do it. Is it a problem?"

"Of course not," Stephen had said blithely. "I'd like to see it too." He spoke as if he and she were buddies, as if it was a perfectly sane thing for him to do, to fly out here to have a look around a ranch she'd inherited.

Madeline made quick work of the tour, showing him the house, the bunkhouse, and the barn. She did not feel obliged to show him the paths leading up to Mrs. Kendrick's garden, or anything else.

Nevertheless, Mr. Taranaku seemed quite interested and asked if there were more events lined up. "Weddings? Business retreats?"

She remembered Libby saying there'd been some interest in a wedding, but she said only, "You should contact Jackson Crane about that. In the meantime, we have so much going on, I am going to have to excuse myself."

"Of course," Chip said. "We've seen enough for now. Am I right, Mr. Taranaku?"

"Yes," he said. "It's quite impressive. I think this is exactly the sort of property my group is looking to find."

Chip Danziger gave Madeline a wink as he escorted his client back to his car. Madeline turned a murderous look to Stephen.

He grinned proudly. "See? Just a matter of knowing the right people. Looks to me like you're going to get a nice nest egg out of this."

Madeline didn't want a nest egg. She wanted no part of this. She could have kicked herself for ever having listened to Stephen in the first place.

"I'm at the Grizzly Lodge," Stephen said when it came time for them to go. "Can I see you tonight?"

Madeline thought of Luke, and his promise that he would find a place for them to be together, away from the prying eyes of everyone else. She wanted that, more than anything. But first, she had some business that she needed to finish once and for all. "Yes," she said. "I'll come when we are through here."

Stephen smiled happily. "Okay. See you later." He walked back to the cars and got in.

Madeline watched the two Mercedes drive down the road, then went in search of Luke and Libby.

They were not in the house. Nor were they in the big circus tent—at least she didn't think so, but there were so many people coming and going, she couldn't be sure. She walked over to the bunkhouse, but there were only women inside, cooking up pots of beans and brisket on two enormous pits on the patio just outside.

Where was Luke?

His mother's garden. She hurried up the path, the dogs falling in behind her.

But Luke wasn't in the garden. Nor was Libby anywhere to be seen. The garage, then. Madeline walked down to the garage, looking for the Bronco, some sign of him. Just as she reached it, Ernest strolled out, carrying a toolbox. "Hey!" she said brightly. "Have you seen Luke?"

"He left," Ernest said.

"He *left?*" Madeline stared at him. "When? Why?"

"Don't know why, but he left a half hour ago," Ernest said. "Don't mean to rush off, but we've got a broken table up under the big tent." He walked on, leaving Madeline to stand in the garage, staring out over the meadow.

Of course he'd left. Why would she expect any different? She had done this to herself. Luke was right—she may not have known those men were coming, but she had put the wheels in motion. If he'd done this to her, she would have left, too.

This hurt worse than anything she had ever felt in her life. She couldn't bear to think of how she'd hurt *him*; it threatened to bury her. *Go to him.* For once in her blessed life, she would go to him and lay the truth out to him. For once in her life, she would not be afraid to open herself up, because she could not risk losing the best thing that had ever happened to her.

She turned around—and gasped when she saw Libby standing there, glaring at her. "Libby," she said breathlessly. "I was looking for you."

Libby folded her arms over her middle. "Is it true?" she quietly demanded. "Did you just go off and find someone to buy the ranch without talking to me or Emma?"

"No! I mean, not exactly. I told you I was going to find out how much the ranch was worth. It just so happened the broker had a client who was looking for a place to build a new resort. So he brought him."

Libby's mouth dropped open. "I don't believe you," she said. "Are you seriously trying to sell Homecoming Ranch and make it into another damn *ski resort?*"

"No, not me. The broker mentioned it—"

"How could you?" Libby said, her voice trembling with rage. "God, I was stupid enough to believe that you and I had started to bond! But you just walked right over me. You've been walking over me since the day you showed up here."

Madeline's heart constricted painfully.

"Admit it!" Libby demanded. "You think you are better than this ranch. You think you deserve some special compensation because you didn't know Dad and you think you know what is best for everyone."

"I don't think that. Libby, please listen—"

"What, so *now* you want to talk? You know what the worst thing is, Madeline? The *worst* thing is that you don't give a damn what anyone else wants. All you care about is yourself, and all you want is the money out of this place so you can go back to Orlando! You don't really care that people like *me* need this place, and people like *Luke* need this place. I *know* you don't give a damn about me, but I really thought you cared about him."

Those words stunned Madeline. "I *do* care! I told you I was going to look into things! All I wanted was information!"

"That is not all you've wanted—you've wanted out from day one. And I guess you've found a way to do it without regard for me and Emma or Luke."

Madeline had nothing to say to that; it was true, all true. She'd been so concerned about protecting herself and keeping a lid on her anxiety that she'd hurt everyone else involved. "Libby, please let me explain."

"I don't want to hear it," Libby snapped. "Go back to Orlando and live your life, Madeline. No one cares. *No* one. Honestly? No one even wants you here." She whirled around and flounced away, her strides long and hard, carrying her as fast and as far from Madeline as she could take herself.

Madeline stared after Libby, but she couldn't move. She'd lost her breath. She finally put her hands on her knees and bent over as a vise of panic closed in around her throat, forcing the air from her lungs. She'd made a huge mess. *Huge.* And she'd just ruined the one chance she had in this life of having a sister. Libby would never trust her now. Madeline didn't deserve her trust.

She straightened up with a deep breath, and noticed several Johnsons standing there, watching her. "Is everything all right?" one of the women said. "Are you okay?"

"I'm fine, thank you," Madeline said. "Just a little sisterly spat." She smiled at the ladies and made herself move, one foot before the other. She had to fix things. She didn't know how, but she had to fix the mess she'd made. An apology felt too little and too empty, but she had to start somewhere.

Regret began to burn through Madeline, leaving huge holes in her heart where Libby and Luke had been these last few weeks.

She walked in to the house, heard Libby in the kitchen, banging things around in anger. Madeline jogged upstairs to Luke's room, gathered her things, showered and changed into a new dress, donned her socks and hiking boots, and headed down to the garage.

The keys to the Pontiac were still hanging over the workbench. She got in and started it up, and slowly backed out, careful so as not to hit any Johnsons.

The Pontiac rode like a big steamship down the road, gliding over the smaller pits that had felled the little rental car she'd had. Madeline turned a little too sharply out of the main gate, and the rear wheels spun out from underneath her, but with a shriek of surprise, she managed to straighten it out.

In Pine River, Madeline drove to Elm Street. She was disappointed that Luke's truck wasn't there. Neither was the van. Frankly, it didn't seem as if anyone was home; the house was completely dark.

Madeline drove on, to the Grizzly Lodge, where she took two parking spots because of an inability to park the tank with any precision. She was early yet, but stalked into the lobby nevertheless.

"Well hello there, stranger!" Dani called out to her. She wore a purple Guayabera shirt today. "How are things up at Homecoming Ranch? Heard you have a house full."

Things at Homecoming Ranch were a disaster, and Madeline still could not wrap her head around the damage she'd done. "We do," Madeline said. "Lots of Johnsons."

Dani laughed. "That's an interesting way to put it. Where is Luke?"

"Ah . . . I don't know," Madeline said. "I'm just going to sit over here and wait for a friend, if that's okay?"

"Well of course it is," Dani said.

Madeline sat in one of the big leather chairs, waiting for Stephen, going over what she would say, while Dani bustled about, in and out of the office.

At six o'clock, Stephen came down. He looked surprised to see Madeline there. She stood up and smiled at him, and from the corner of her eye, she noticed the curiosity on Dani's face.

"Hey," he said, taking her in. "Love the dress. Are you hungry?"

She wasn't hungry at all; she was a ball of nerves. "There's a decent restaurant up the road. The Stakeout," Madeline said, and walked to the door, pulled it open. "They serve buffalo steak."

Stephen laughed. He stepped behind her and caught the door, holding it so she could go through. "I don't know about buffalo."

"It's good," she said. "Tougher than beef. But I wouldn't recommend a steak there."

Stephen gave her a funny smile. "You've gotten all mountain-y on me."

Madeline considered that a compliment.

"It's cute," he said. "I like it." He put his hand on the small of her back to lead her out the door. Madeline felt uncomfortable, but then again, she always had with Stephen.

At the Stakeout, they settled in at a table and Stephen ordered wine. He seemed happy with himself, as if they were on a date. "I drove by the DiNapoli place," he said. "They were moving the stat-ues."

"Oh?" Bree hadn't told her that, and Madeline hadn't asked. She didn't have her list of things to check off, didn't have a schedule of all the things that needed to be done. She was flying naked as far as her job went, gone far too long to keep a handle on everything. "I need to get back in the next few days and wrap that up," Madeline said, more to herself than to him.

"Bree said that a woman called looking for the agent who sold the DiNapoli house. Apparently she's got a dog of a house, too." He laughed.

New shiny listings was exactly what she had hoped would happen if she sold the DiNapoli place, not ugly ones. Still, Madeline didn't care. That seemed so shallow, so unimportant compared to the hurt she'd caused here.

"Bree said she'd tried to get hold of you to let you know, but she was having a hard time reaching you."

"Cell phone reception," Madeline said listlessly.

The waiter brought the wine, poured it for them. Stephen swirled it around in his glass, then gingerly tasted it. Madeline watched him and thought about Luke, the way he popped the tops off beer bottles. She'd discovered she liked beer. She wished she'd had a chance to order one tonight.

Stephen nodded, and the waiter poured wine for the two of them.

"So," Stephen said when the wine had been poured. "Now that it looks as if we have this place sold, when are you coming back to Orlando?"

Madeline thought about how best to answer him. Her hesitation seemed to make Stephen a little nervous because he said, "You've had a great little vacation, right? A great experience. But your life is in Orlando, isn't it? Don't you want to get back to it now that you know Bree is holding a listing for you?"

"I do," Madeline said, and that was true. She had built her life there, brick by brick. She'd worked so hard to make it in real estate. She'd bought a cute condo in Winter Park, and she felt just on the verge of really making it, all on her own. But that all seemed so meaningless tonight. It *wasn't* meaningless, she told herself. Maybe empty.

Madeline pushed away the wine and signaled the waiter.

"Is something wrong?" Stephen asked.

"Yes," she said calmly. To the waiter she said, "I'd like a beer."

"What kind?"

"Any kind. In a bottle, though. I like it in bottles."

The waiter arched a brow. "I've got a microbrew you might like."

"*Great*," Madeline said, although she had no idea what a microbrew was. "Bring it."

Stephen smiled. "You should have said something," he said, gesturing to her wine. "We could have had beer."

She thought of Libby out at Homecoming Ranch by herself, and how hard she'd worked to make the ranch ready for the Johnsons, who were, if everything went according to plan, having a bonfire tonight. Libby was right—Madeline had been self-centered and fearful.

"Trudi said you might need a little nudge," he said with a chuckle. "I can tell you really like the people here."

Trudi. Her rock, her best friend. Madeline had relied on her so much that Trudi was now calling the shots.

"Madeline, what is it? You seem distracted."

She'd known from the first date Stephen wasn't her type, and yet she had allowed him and Trudi to persuade her. She had agreed with Trudi that her reluctance with Stephen had to do with *her* insecurities and fears, but sitting at the Stakeout, Madeline didn't know if that was true. She thought it was more likely that it was much simpler than that: Stephen was not the one.

"Madeline?" he asked, and sipped his wine.

"I'm a little distracted," she admitted. "The thing is, I'm coming home just as soon as the reunion is over. But . . ."

Stephen's smile faded. He put down his glass. "Here we go," he muttered.

Madeline took a deep breath. "But I can't come back to you, Stephen," she said. "I don't . . . I don't feel that way about you." There. She had said it as plainly as she could.

Stephen frowned thoughtfully, as if they were playing a little game. "I know that you've had a rough life and it makes it hard for you to trust—"

"No, wait," she said, and held her hand up. "Listen, I love Trudi. She has been the one constant in my life. But she is not me, Stephen. She thinks she understands me, she thinks she is in my head. But she's not. It's not that I am fearful of what will happen. It's that I don't *feel* that way about you."

He sank back into his chair, staring at her. He clenched his jaw and looked away, his hand curling around the wineglass so tightly she feared it would snap in two.

"I'm sorry," she said.

He looked at her as he sat up and reached in his back pocket. "I guess I should thank you for being honest," he said. "I hope you don't mind that I don't thank you, at least not right now. I just did you an enormous favor, Madeline."

"Not really," she said with an apologetic wince. "Actually, you caused a lot of trouble showing up like that."

Stephen glared at her. "Great. You're welcome for bringing you help and potential buyers." He pulled out some bills and threw them down on the table. "I'm sure Jim and Chip will do whatever you need them to do with the ranch. I'm headed to Aspen first thing in the morning."

Madeline swallowed.

Stephen stood up. He began to walk away, but he paused and looked back at her. "We're not going to see each other again, Madeline," he said. "But I hope you don't throw away all that you've worked to achieve to be in this little town. There's so much more to life than this."

"Actually," she said, holding up a finger, "my *life* may be in Orlando. But I've lived more in the three weeks I've been here than I did all twenty-nine years I spent in Florida."

Stephen rolled his eyes and strode out. Madeline felt bad for him. And sorry that she hadn't said this to him a long time ago. But she also felt lighter than she had all day.

And now, she had to talk to Luke. Madeline waited until she was sure Stephen was gone, and then she stood, up, too. The waiter looked confused. "Something came up," she said, and walked out, the keys to the Pontiac in her hand.

She was nervous when she turned on to Elm Street and saw that lights were on. Luke's Bronco was not in sight, but she could at least tell someone she'd come by. Maybe she could say hi to Leo, try that silly game video again. Madeline parked in front of the house, gripped the enormous steering wheel of the Pontiac and rested her forehead against it.

Her life had not prepared her for these moments, but for once in her damn life, Madeline was determined to tell Luke how she felt. She had to, if only for herself. She had been transformed by her time in the mountains. Part of her had been illuminated, and Madeline didn't particularly like what she'd seen: a coward. A closed-off, emotionally drained woman who hid behind tasks and schedules and anxiety. But there were other parts, stronger parts, that she did not intend to lose. So she would say what she needed to say, and if Luke didn't feel the same way, well . . . she would cross that bridge then.

She made herself open the door of the car. She made herself get out and walk through the gate. She was committed then, and quickened her step, jogging up the two steps to the porch. She opened the screen and knocked loudly, and steeled herself, her chin up when she heard the footfall of someone coming to the door.

As it swung open, Madeline smiled brightly. Until she noticed how puffy Marisol's eyes were. "Marisol!" she exclaimed. "Are you all right?"

She shook her head. "Leo. He is in the hospital."

Madeline stopped breathing for a moment. "The *hospital?*"

"A seizure. A very bad seizure."

Nausea began to spiral in Madeline. "Where? Here? Is there a hospital in Pine River?"

"No, no, Durango. They all go to Durango."

Madeline looked wildly about. She had no idea where Durango was. "Is there something I can do to help?" she asked, her mind racing. "I could take them some things if they need them, I have the Pontiac. Tell me what I can do to help."

"Julie, she takes their things. She's gone already with their things. You cannot help now. Now, we wait."

Madeline's heart sank to her toes. She stepped back from the door. "I am so sorry, Marisol. I hope everything is okay. You don't know how much I hope everything is okay."

Marisol nodded, but she was already pulling the door closed.

"I'm so sorry," Madeline said again, bending to one side as Marisol waved to her around the door and shut it.

Madeline stood there a long moment, staring at the door in something of a daze. Her mind was whirling with fear for Leo, with pain for Luke and his family. And with regret. *So much goddamn regret.*

She finally turned around and walked back to the Pontiac.

THIRTY-ONE

I didn't die if that's what you think.

I gave everyone a good scare, though, because according to Dad, my seizure was worse than normal. I don't remember a thing about it, except waking up and looking into the big brown Bambi eyes of Tiffany, my favorite nurse. It was sort of like waking up in the middle of a bunch of vestal virgins. Which, I should point out, is not all it's cracked up to be, according to PBS and their great series on the Romans.

Tiffany totally ruined the fantasy by telling me I had a seizure and that yes, she was married and happily so. Man, give a guy a break! I'm going to demand only single nurses from here on out.

But here is the interesting part about my seizure—who do you think showed up with overnight kits for Dad and Luke? (Dad and Luke, by the way, clearly thought this was It, the big Swan Song, seeing as how they were both racked out in my room when Tiffany brought me back to the land of the living). Anyway, who showed up but Julie Daugherty! I was surprised, and I was *super* happy she didn't bring The Stinker. She leaned over and whispered to Luke, and he sat up and said thanks, and then he looked at me. He said, "Leo," in this cracking voice, and I said, "Oh man, don't get all weepy eyed on me *now*, Luke."

C'est la vie. There was a lot of carrying on about my not-so-miraculous recovery, and Dad got especially verklempt, and put his head on my leg and he cried, actually *cried*, and then everyone was talking and laughing nervously like, whew, it didn't happen *yet,* and I was thinking, sheesh, tonight is the start of the new season of *Survivor,* so could we move this along a little?

The doctor came in and he said, "Well, I hate to tell you this, but Leo is going to be okay for now." Everyone's a comedian these days.

He said, "We've got a new seizure medicine that we think will work very well, given your symptoms. And we are also going to increase your intake of blah blah blah-di blah." Because everyone knows I am not taking enough medicine, right? I didn't really listen to much until he said, "But I think, if you remain stable, we can let you go home in twenty-four hours."

I was hoping that balloons would drop out of the ceiling and a naked Tiffany would bust out of a cake, but of course that didn't happen. But what *did* happen is that Dad asked if he could speak to the doctor outside, and Luke said, "Julie, can I talk to you?" And he put his hand on her elbow like they were a couple and led her out. And he didn't come back for a really, really long time. So long that Dad finally agreed to go down and find me something to eat besides gruel, which is what they serve you in hospitals if they think you can't swallow.

I was lying there, minding my own business, wishing Julie had brought "Hounds of Hell" because hospital TV is *boring* and here comes Luke, and I swear, he looked worse than me. I said, "So what's going on? Are you and Julie getting together? Am I going to have to put up with The Stinker pulling out tubes and messing with my TV?"

Luke gave me one of those looks and said, "I guess the seizure made you completely crazy, and not just half-assed crazy. *No,* we are not going to be a couple. In fact, I just told her it wasn't going to happen and to quit bugging me about it." That's not exactly what he said, but I reserve the right to paraphrase if necessary.

Anyway, bottom line is that he dumped her once and for all. Let me tell you, if I could sit up, I would have hugged him. But instead I said, "Oh, do *tell.*"

Luke said that he told her that he couldn't go backward, he could only go forward, which of course I took to mean Blue Eyes, and I said so, but Luke shook his head and said, "Stay out of it, Leo. She's got issues. Anyway, I need to get back to Denver. I mean, assuming you're okay. I've got houses to finish."

Between you and me, I would be the last person to tell Luke not to go back to Denver, because I mean, what's worse than that, asking someone to stay behind because you can't even pee by yourself, you know? Still, I was kind of hoping he'd stay. I like having him around. I know he and Dad argue a lot, but they argue about big important stuff, like what's going to happen with the ranch. I know he's got the house thing going, and he worked really hard to get his degree. So I said, "Great! Those houses won't build themselves, you know." Just like Dad.

And he said, "No, they won't. I figure it's even more important now, because the lawyer says that without some divine miracle or some great compassionate concession by the heirs, we can kiss Homecoming Ranch good-bye."

He looked so sad about that, and I felt really bad for him, because I know Luke is the sentimental kind. He likes the idea of big fancy ranches and big families. That's all I was thinking when I said, "Maybe you and Blue Eyes could work it out in the bedroom instead of the front yard."

I meant that in the nicest possible way. I wouldn't lie to you.

But Luke, he said, "You know, if you weren't lying there like a sack of beans, I would knock your block off."

And I said, "Go ahead, try it. I've still got some kick in me," which reminded me of the NBA season a couple of years ago, and I said, "Do you remember that game between the Spurs and the Mavericks where there was that big throw-down and they were ejecting players left and right?" And we started laughing about that.

I never got to finish up with my critically acclaimed thinking about Blue Eyes.

THIRTY-TWO

Exhaustion set in before Luke made it back to Pine River. Sitting vigil at a bedside for a couple of days was enough to exhaust the strongest person, but add to that, in the middle of it he had finally, at long last, told Julie to take a hike.

He felt a huge sense of relief now that he'd done it, now that he'd told her in no uncertain terms that he did not love her anymore, would not love her again, and to please stop coming around. He just wondered why it had taken him so long. He wondered why he'd never been able, until now, to let go.

He didn't want to think it had anything to do with Madeline. He didn't want to think about her at all.

He wasn't exactly angry with Madeline—he guessed that if the shoe had been on the other foot, he might have said and done the same things she had. He would like to think he would have been more straightforward about it, but really, he didn't know. It was all so screwed up to begin with.

Luke felt like he didn't know anything anymore. The only thing he knew was that he needed to get back to his life, to filling the hours and days with work and school. To keep all thoughts and feelings at a numbing distance.

He drove through Pine River and out to Homecoming Ranch to check on things.

The place was a wreck. Trash cans were overflowing, which was an invitation to disaster when wild animals roamed nearby. The Johnsons had trampled paths in the grass between the bunkhouse and house, which were now muddy thanks to afternoon rains. They needed gravel or, at the very least, straw.

Luke pulled in behind a multicolored bus from the rafting company. It was disgorging Johnsons like red bouncing balls. Libby was standing at the fence, wearing a sun hat, checking off names as they came off the bus.

He walked up behind her. "Hey Libby, how are you doing?"

She looked up at him, her expression harried. "Hey, stranger! I've learned a *lot*, Luke. A lot! Next time, we need some controls. Hey, Albie!" she shouted, looking at something over Luke's shoulder. He turned around, saw a boy who looked to be about ten trying to coax a barking Roscoe out beyond the fence. "What did I tell you about bugging the dogs? Leave them alone!"

"Like I was saying," she said, glaring at the kid as he skipped by, "I have a pretty good idea what we need to do."

Luke didn't think now was a good time to say that he wouldn't be part of any "next time."

"Is Madeline around?" he asked.

Libby frowned. "Not this morning. I guess she had things to do in town."

Just as well, Luke thought. He didn't know what he would say to her at this point. Good-bye and good luck, he supposed. "What can I do to help?" he asked.

"That shower is acting up again," Libby said. "No hot water this morning. And two of the cows came down and wandered into the campsite. You've never seen so many people scramble in your life. Like they were bears. Ernest drove them back up, but he hasn't been here to help with the two tents that were knocked off their pads."

"I'm on it," he said.

The repair to the shower took him a good hour, an hour in which he had time to think. He would explain to Libby that if she and her sisters decided to keep the ranch, they would need to build a real shower facility. The temporary ones were not built for this kind of use. He would suggest that if they were going to keep on with these events, they invest in some cabins. He would tell them to make sure that they kept the trash locked up and to check the hot water heater about once a week. The thing was old, and sometimes the pilot went out.

There were so many things he could tell them. *So many things.* That there was a fort down by the campsite, hidden in the bushes. That there was a little trail up the mountain, about five hundred vertical feet, where they could see a waterfall. That his mother's hummingbird mixture was the best for keeping hummingbirds around, that the rabbits would eat from the vegetable garden so to be sure and cage the plants. That they needed to oil the weather vane from time to time or the squeaking would drive them crazy.

So many things.

When Luke was ready to leave, he stopped in to see Libby once more. She was at the kitchen table, sorting over papers. "Hey!" she said brightly. "Do you want something to eat? They gave me a big tray of brisket and I can't eat it all—"

"No, I've got to get to town. Libby, I'm not coming back."

"What?" Libby studied him a minute, as if she was trying to make sense of those words. "You mean, ever?"

He shrugged. "I've got my work in Denver and I've left it long enough."

"But I thought . . ." She shook her head. "It doesn't matter. I hate to see you go, Luke. I hate how we came to know each other, too. I hate how this property came into our hands. I wish it could have been different for all of us."

"I appreciate that, Libby, but it isn't different, and I need to get on with my life. Ernest can help you with anything you need, you know."

"I know. Most of the Johnsons are leaving tomorrow anyway." She smiled wryly and stood up. Before Luke knew what she was doing, she wrapped her arms around him. "Thanks for everything, Luke. I know this hasn't been easy for you."

He hugged her back. "Take care, Libby."

He walked out to the garage and his Bronco. The Pontiac, he noticed, was gone. It seemed almost as if it was a sign from his mother—even her spirit had left the ranch. It wasn't theirs any longer. This wasn't where his family was anymore. His family was in Pine River. This was now just a place he'd once lived.

Luke drove back to town and the little green house on Elm Street to pick up a few things before heading back to Denver. He was grateful to find that Marisol had picked up after their panicked, heart-stopping flight to the hospital. Luke had a vague recollection of food on the floor, of Leo's nutritional drink spilling everywhere. Even in the best of circumstances, three men in a tiny house led to some pretty disgusting piles of stuff.

He found most of his clothes in folded piles, scattered between the living room and Leo's room. He stuffed them into his bag. In the living room, he searched for a pair of his shoes, and heard someone walking up the drive. He assumed it was Marisol.

"Luke?"

The sound of Madeline's voice slipped in and wound tightly around his heart. He slowly turned his gaze to the door. She was standing on the other side of the screen, looking pretty in blue. Heartbreakingly pretty.

"What are you doing here?" he asked, not unkindly.

"I need to talk to you."

The last thing he wanted was another emotional discussion—he'd had enough in the last forty-eight hours to fill a lifetime. "Maddie . . . now is not a good time," he said. "I've got to get back to Denver and I've had a long couple of days."

"I know. I heard. I'm so sorry about Leo. Is he . . . ?"

"He's okay," Luke said. "For now."

They stood, staring at each other. There was so much unspoken between them, so much that didn't really need to be said because it was palpable in that little living room.

"May I come in?" she asked.

Luke groaned softly to the ceiling. He didn't want to do this, not now, not after everything he'd just been through. But he couldn't find the strength to say no to her.

She took his silence for a yes and opened the screen door, stepped apprehensively over the threshold. "I need to explain something," she said, before he had a chance to speak. "I didn't know those men, or Stephen, were coming to Homecoming Ranch. I mean I knew the broker had a potential buyer, but I thought he would call me with some figures that I could present to all of you."

Luke arched a dubious brow.

"I swear it, Luke. I was expecting a phone call. Not an entourage. Not a buyer."

"Why didn't you tell me you were expecting anything? Or tell Libby for that matter? Why didn't you just say that you had hired a lawyer?"

"Because I had this idea in my head that I would have it altogether in one neat little package, so that all your questions would be answered."

"Sometimes, these things aren't so neat," Luke pointed out, and wondered how she could not know that.

"I know, I know," she moaned, her eyes fluttering shut for a moment. "I honestly thought I was doing the right thing, but the only thing I did was hurt you, and hurt Libby." She sighed, and he noticed that tears were pooling in her eyes. "It was stupid," she said with a shrug. "I really had no idea that they would come, that *Stephen* would come. I'm not with him, you know," she said. "That's the other thing I need to say. I am not *with* him. There was nothing there to begin with, but now I have made that very clear to him. And to you."

Luke believed that. But he had nothing to say to it. At this point, it just felt too late for this.

Madeline seemed to sense his apathy, because she said very earnestly, "And the last thing I want to tell you is that I told Chip I am not looking for a buyer right now. I told him that Emma and Libby and I have to decide what we are going to do, and that it was going to take a while, because we have just met one another."

Luke arched a brow at that. "Do Libby and Emma know this?"

"Yes." She smiled a little. "And we're still arguing about what it is we want to do."

"Well, I'll make it easy for all of you. The Kendricks are not going to pursue Homecoming Ranch. We don't have the money to buy it back, and honestly, I don't think Dad and Leo want to go back." It pained him to say it, but he had accepted the truth.

"But *you* do," she said.

He did. God, he did. But Luke swallowed down his disappointment for the hundredth time and shrugged. "Yeah, well, some things are not meant to be." He looked at her pointedly.

Madeline swallowed. "There's time, Luke. Really. We're not in any hurry to sell it. Libby really wants to do this wedding, and she is okay with me going back to Orlando and leaving her to do it. Like, *really* okay," she said, sounding a little sad about it.

"Well, I wish her luck." He looked at his wristwatch. He didn't want to prolong this. It had been hard enough as it was.

"I was hoping that maybe you would come, too."

Luke looked up.

"To Orlando." Luke started to shake his head, but Madeline quickly stepped forward. "Just hear me out," she said before he could speak. "Please just hear me out."

God, but she looked so hopeful. "Maddie, baby—"

"Don't talk, please don't talk," she said, and stepped even closer, her blue eyes locked on his. "I have to say this now or I will lose my nerve."

"So say it."

She took a deep breath and a rush of words came forth: "I love you."

Those words knocked the wind right out of Luke. He had wanted to hear them, and yet had believed he'd never hear them.

"I love you, Luke. I do. I love you, I think I loved you the minute you saved me on Sometimes Pass."

Her declaration slid right into his heart. But it did not make him feel all the things a man should feel when a woman professes love— they made him feel uncertain. Luke pushed his fingers through his hair and tried to process this. He wanted to trust her. He wanted to forget everything that had happened and sweep her up in his arms. But he couldn't bring himself to do it, because he knew, deep down, that nothing had really changed between them, except that her words now hung between them.

"That was *not* what I was expecting you to say," he admitted. "I don't even know what to say to that, Maddie. I'll be honest, I have felt so disappointed the last couple of days."

"I know. And you don't have to respond," she said quickly. "But I had to say it. Because, Luke, you opened up a whole world to me. You've shown me things I never knew—" She paused, like she wasn't sure what else she should say. "You taught me how to let someone in and it feels so perfect and right. Do you know for the first time in my life, I know what love is? I am full of it, full of love for you."

She looked so sincere, and Luke's heart went out to her. He touched her face, and she turned her head, kissed his palm, and pressed her cheek against it, her eyes closed.

Luke felt the same way about her, of course he did. But he couldn't say those words out loud, not now, not knowing she would go back to Orlando. He was afraid what those words opened him up to, afraid of what would happen if he actually said them a second time in his life. Especially to Madeline, *especially* her, because she meant more to him than anyone ever had. If he said *I love you* to Madeline, it should mean something more than good-bye. It should mean that this was it, they were going to be together forever, they were going to make it work. *It should not mean good-bye.*

And that was all it would be, because he was fairly certain that nothing would keep Madeline from leaving.

Madeline opened her eyes, big blue eyes gazing up at him, full of raw emotion like he'd never seen in her.

"If you feel that way, then stay," he said, testing her. And he held his breath, a tiny pinprick of hope in him.

Madeline's face fell. "I can't," she said softly, and all his hope evaporated. "I have to go back to Orlando. There's my work, and my mom."

He started to glance away, but she caught his arm. "Luke, I made a phone call to a guy I work with. He is willing to take you on."

"Take me on for what?"

"To be an architect. He has a firm there, and he said he would love to talk to you. He builds these big office buildings."

"I don't design office buildings."

"Right." She nodded. "But you could."

"And you could sell houses here," he pointed out. "Or in Denver."

She bit her lower lip.

He already knew her answer, he'd known it all along. At least she'd been honest about that. And he guessed that he'd known his answer, too. He put his arm around her shoulders and pulled her into his body and kissed the top of her head. "Madeline Pruett, you put the I in irony. For someone who fears being left . . . you sure do a lot of running."

"It's not that. You don't understand my work or my mother—"

"I'm not talking about just Orlando," he said. "I'm talking about your life. You run, Maddie. You ran from Stephen. You ran from me after we got together in Denver. You just told me you loved me, and yet you're about to run again."

"I'm not running, Luke! I'm trying to take you with me."

"But, Maddie, you knew before you asked me that I wouldn't come." He interlaced his fingers with hers. "Here's the thing, baby. You can't live on your little island waiting for things to be perfect. Relationships, families—they come with lots of flaws and nothing is ever going to be perfect. And if you are going to stand around, hoping that all the kinks and hurt and messy stuff will go away, you'll never know the joy of any of it. You'll be waiting alone for a very long time."

He suddenly realized that in his own way, he'd been doing that, too. He'd escaped from his less-than perfect family, from the issues that seemed to crop up like weeds, when in reality, he was needed here more than anywhere else. Maybe, Luke thought, he'd been searching for perfect when it had been right in front of him all along. He had a family who loved him and needed him, right here, in this ugly little green house.

That's why he couldn't go with her, Luke realized. Maybe he'd known it organically, understood it in his soul while his heart had longed for something else.

But whether he'd faced it or not, he'd always known that he loved his family too much to leave them behind again.

"Don't misunderstand me. I am grateful you told me how you feel," he said sincerely. "I know it took a lot of courage to say it. But I don't think you understand that saying 'I love you' and loving someone are really two different things." He was learning that himself. He let go of her, leaned down, and picked up his bag. "I've got to go. I'm going back to Durango to see about Leo, and then up to Denver." He caught her by her braid and pulled her to him, then leaned down to kiss her. "You're one of a kind, Maddie," he said softly, and kissed her again. "I am going to miss you something fierce." He kissed her one last time, dropped her braid, and stepped around her, walking out to his truck, leaving her standing in his family's house.

Madeline stared out the screen door and watched Luke walk across the yard. She couldn't catch her breath as she watched him get into the Bronco and leave. Her stomach roiled with disappointment and regret, and her vision blurred as his Bronco turned the corner onto Main Street.

She'd ruined it. She'd ruined the one true thing she'd ever known.

Madeline looked blindly around her, at the collage of photos on the wall, at Leo's wheelchair and video game console. She tried to catch her breath as she walked outside and carefully shut the door behind her, then moved woodenly down the porch steps.

Everything that had happened to her here, everything she'd felt, that she'd become, was churning inside her. Every moment with Luke, every moment at Homecoming Ranch, with Libby, with Leo—it all churned. In the middle of the yard, the churning brought Madeline to a halt. She suddenly fell to all fours and vomited in the grass, as her body tried to purge the pain and disappointment of losing the only true love she'd ever known.

When her body could not expel anything else, she stood up, dragged the back of her hand across her mouth, and walked to the car.

She had lost everything, but the dull, bone-aching pain of her loss had only begun.

THIRTY-THREE

On a stifling hot and humid day in Orlando, the DiNapoli sale closed. That afternoon, Madeline's brokerage firm gathered at the local watering hole to toast her. Madeline nursed a warm beer. It was the biggest payday in her life thus far, a milestone reached, and her broker predicted many more sales for her.

He based that on the fact that Madeline had picked up three new listings of big, ugly houses. That wasn't exactly what Madeline had hoped would happen in selling the DiNapoli property, but suddenly, owners of ugly houses were calling her to sell them.

"A sale is a sale," Bree said, when Madeline had taken another call for an ugly house in a bad location. "If you don't want it, I'll take it." Bree had just obtained her realtor license and was hungry for listings.

Madeline invited Trudi to her celebration happy hour. Trudi was in fine form, taking center stage and telling stories about Madeline as a girl that were only loosely based in fact. But they were entertaining, and Trudi had Madeline's office mates laughing. Madeline sat at the end of the table with her beer and quietly mused that it had always been this way. Trudi was the star in their relationship and Madeline was the support behind the scenes. The only time Madeline had shone on her own was when she stepped out from under Trudi's light, in Colorado.

When she and Trudi drove home afterward, Trudi, who had imbibed a couple of chocolate martinis, put her foot on the dash of Madeline's car and said, "You know who would have been fun to have there? Stephen."

"Oh my *God*," Madeline moaned.

"I saw him the other day," Trudi said. "He's selling his SUV. He bought a Lexus. That guy is going places."

"Trudi, *why* do you keep bringing him up?" Madeline asked. "We are over, we are done. It's like he's paying you."

"No, actually," Trudi said cheerfully. "He was pretty upset with me for bringing *you* up. He says a lot of the same things you do. But I can see how great you guys would be together."

Madeline rolled her eyes. She hadn't even thought of Stephen in the last couple of weeks. She rarely thought of anything or anyone other than Luke. Of course she hadn't heard anything from him, and she wasn't naïve enough to have expected that she would. The only thing she knew of him until recently was the one phone conversation she'd had with Libby since leaving Colorado. Before Madeline had departed Homecoming Ranch and Colorado, Libby had reluctantly accepted her apology, and Madeline suspected she had only because Madeline was leaving. When Madeline called a week or so ago, Libby mentioned, in the course of her spirited description of the wedding that would take place at the ranch next month, that Luke had been out to add some showers to the bunkhouse.

"Oh," Madeline said, trying to sound as casual as she could. "He's been home?"

"I think he moved home," Libby said.

"*Moved* home? Are you sure?"

"Yeah, that's what I understood," Libby said.

What about his houses? What about all that he'd hoped to accomplish with them, his dreams? "Well . . . how was he?" Madeline asked.

"He looked great!" Libby had said.

Fantastic. Luke was great while Madeline was splintering apart a little more every day, a little piece of this and that falling away from her.

She couldn't seem to shake the blues. She couldn't seem to find her happiness in Orlando, and she was beginning to wonder if she'd ever had it. Now that she had been out of her bubble, as Trudi would say, Madeline could see just how much she'd isolated herself from the world. The only friend she had was Trudi. She had no real life—she moved between work and late hours, and her mother's house, and back to her condo with her streaming movies.

Soccer was Madeline's only solace, and while she was excited to see the girls again, Teresa gave her the news that funding to Camp Haven had been cut, and the soccer league would be folded into the city park and recreation program.

"What does that mean?" Madeline asked as she handed out CapriSuns to the girls.

"It means that there is going to be one soccer league. A smaller one. And about twice as many volunteer coaches."

Madeline understood her. There would be less opportunity for girls to find soccer as an escape from their lives, and less opportunity for her to coach these girls. It felt like the final slash of the knife. Madeline looked up through the haze of heat and humidity on that sweltering afternoon and longed for mountains and crisp air. She missed having a purpose that was shared with others. Even if the other was Libby, a sister who could scarcely tolerate her.

Madeline could scarcely tolerate herself.

She'd done a lot of thinking about her three weeks in Colorado, and she would give everything she had for the opportunity to do it all again.

It wasn't as if her homecoming to Orlando was appreciated, either. When she'd arrived from Colorado, Madeline had gone straight to her mother's house to check on her. She found her mother in a caftan, smoking a cigarette. The place was littered with beer cans, and some man was sleeping in the back room.

"Who's that?" Madeline whispered.

Her mother glanced to the back room. "Ron," she said. "An old friend. So? What'd you find out about that back child support?" she asked. "I've got some things I'd like to fix up around here."

Madeline had looked at her mother—really looked at her. "It's going to be tied up in court for a long time."

Her mother took a drag of smoke from her cigarette and blew it at the ceiling, then shrugged. "Stupid bastard," she said.

Madeline had left her mother's house, resigned that she'd lost the best thing that had ever happened to her, and for what? For a job selling ugly houses? For a mother who cared more about child support for a thirty-year-old daughter? Yeah, *this* was the life.

But then, out of the blue, she got a text from Leo. He said he had a new texting machine, and that Libby had given him Madeline's number. He asked if she followed the Florida Marlin baseball team.

No.

The next day, she got another text from Leo asking if she had ever heard of Javon Walker, who once played for the Florida Marlins.

No.

Look him up.

That night, Madeline looked up Javon Walker. He was a talented athlete, she guessed, because he had played for the Florida Marlins before turning to professional football and playing for the Denver Broncos, among others. She texted Leo back. *Looked him up.*

Leo fired back almost instantly. *He thought he knew where he belonged, where his talents fit in best. Turns out, he was wrong. His talents fit a whole other game better. So he CHANGED GAMES. If he'd stayed with baseball he would have fallen into obscurity and would probably be shooting crack in some back alley by now. Get it?*

No.

You will.

Madeline shook her head.

But she kept thinking about it. What was he trying to tell her? That she shouldn't play baseball?

It so happened that Madeline was checking on her mother one afternoon when Leo texted again. *Are you still thinking about baseball?*

No.

Think about it!

"What's that?" her mother asked.

"Oh," Madeline said with a shrug. "Someone in Colorado."

"Yeah, who?"

Madeline looked at her mother. She had been complaining about Ron, and how she was ready for him to take a hike, but that she had an insurance payment coming up. She had not once asked Madeline about how she'd felt about Colorado. Not once. "He is the brother of someone I fell in love with," Madeline said curtly.

Clarissa's brows rose to her hairline. She was speechless for a moment. "Well, well, well," she said, a smile spreading across her face, "Maddie isn't a robot after all."

"Hey!" Madeline said.

"Well? It's not like you ever have boyfriends for more than a week."

"Thanks, Mom," Madeline said. "Maybe that's because I've seen how well you've done with them."

Her mother's eyes narrowed. "You watch how you talk to me, miss. I never said I was no saint."

"No, you never said that," Madeline agreed.

"If you love some guy, what the hell are you doing here?" her mother asked, waving her hand at her daughter.

Madeline gaped at her; anger surged like a tidal wave through her—she wanted very much to punch a wall. "Good question. What *am* I doing here? Oh that's right—taking care of *you*."

"*Me!*"

"Yes, Mom—*you*. I am always taking care of you! Someone has to, because you damn sure don't."

Her mother looked surprised. And then she laughed. *Laughed.* As if the joke was somehow on Madeline. "No one asked you to take care of me, did they? Look here, Madeline Grace, what are you, twenty-eight?"

"I'll be *thirty* next month, Mom."

"Okay, you'll be thirty. So think about how long you've been trying to make us into something we're not, some cutsie mother-daughter story. Don't you get it? I'm not going to change, I'm not going to miraculously turn into the kind of mother you've always wanted. I don't *want* you taking care of me. I do all right on my own!"

Madeline wanted to argue that point, but kept silent.

"I'll tell you this, though. I'm still your mother, and I may not be a very good one, but I love you, kid. I want you to be happy. So go be happy! Go be in love! Don't do what *I* did—find a good man, settle down, have kids. And stop feeling like you need to take care of me, because you don't."

It was the first moment of genuine clarity in her mother that Madeline could remember. She was shocked by it. Her first instinct was to argue, but a second, stronger instinct took hold. How funny was it that in that moment, she thought of Javon Walker. He figured out his talents fit another game better than the one he was playing. Maybe it was time Madeline figured out she didn't fit in so well taking taking care of a mother who didn't want her help. If she kept on this path, she might end up like her mother—entirely incapable of maintaining a lasting relationship. The thought made her shudder. Madeline *had* to change, and her mother was giving her the freedom to do it.

Madeline suddenly smiled. She stood up, kissed her mother. "Thanks, Mom. For the first time in my life, I can say with all sincerity, *thank* you."

"About time," her mother said, and as Madeline started for the door, she shouted, "Don't forget about that back child support!"

Madeline shut the door behind her, pulled out her cell phone and called Stephen. "Hey," she said when he answered. "I heard you were selling your SUV."

THIRTY-FOUR

At first, Luke's decision to stay in Pine River had caused a huge argument between him and his dad. When he realized he would not win, his father had said angrily, "You're throwing your life away, just pissing away everything you've worked for."

"Who says success is only in Denver? I'm going to pick up here, Dad. Family is more important to me."

"Does anyone care what *I* think?" Leo asked.

"No!" Dad and Luke had both shouted in unison, then looked at each other in surprise and burst into laughter. That was the last time they'd spoken of Luke's decision to stay in Pine River.

The next two months were a blur. Luke's heart hurt too much most of the time, and he covered it up with activity and, on occasion, a whole lot of beer. He sold his houses to Stuart Homes at a loss, which he expected. But he sold his bungalow for much more than he'd anticipated, which gave him a little nest egg to start a new business. Together, with Jackson's help, he and Dad had bought the little green house on Elm Street for dirt cheap. Luke added a larger living room, helped the Methodists add some wheelchair ramps, and was in the process of building a new master suite for his father. When that was finished, he would move off the couch and into his dad's old room.

It was a warm afternoon when the van they used to cart Leo around broke down again. Luke and his father were working to fix it, Luke on his back beneath the old thing, fighting a bolt beneath the oil pan. His dad was somewhere up top, directing him. He heard his father speaking to someone, but his attention was on his work. "Dad!" he called. "I need a different wrench."

When his father did not immediately answer, Luke turned his head. He saw a pair of hiking boots and some festive socks. Luke's heart stopped beating for one crazy moment—he would know those hiking boots anywhere.

He slowly rolled out from beneath the van and looked up. Madeline was standing above him. Two thick dark braids hung over her shoulders. She was wearing a wool toboggan hat on her head, in spite of the warm temperatures. And she was smiling. A brilliantly warm, happy smile. "Hi, Luke," she said.

"Maddie?"

"Yep. It's me. I'm back."

"Back . . . for what?"

She laughed. "For *good!*"

A small surge of hope shimmied down his spine. Was it possible? Could she have really come back for good? Luke stood up, dropped his wrench.

"I'll go check on the genius," his dad said, and stooped to pick up the wrench as he moved away from the van.

Luke hardly noticed; he was eyeing Madeline suspiciously. "What do you mean, for *good?*"

She laughed again, that deep laugh he'd once heard from her in his house in Denver. "I mean, I left Orlando in my rearview mirror. My *new* rearview mirror. Well, new to me, anyway. It's not a Pontiac, but it got the job done."

He followed her gaze, saw a Chevy Tahoe parked at the end of the drive. He could see the back of it was completely stuffed with things, and his heart skipped a beat or two on its way to racing. She wasn't kidding—she really had come back. "You drove here?" he asked incredulously.

"Yep." She rose up on her toes, clearly proud of herself, then settled back down and locked her blue eyes on him, blue eyes he had seen over and over again in his dreams and his thoughts. "How are you?"

He was an empty, working machine, that's was how he was. He had taken a painful heartbreak and had turned it into physical labor, the only thing he knew to do and the only thing that could drown out his thoughts and numb his pain. But to Madeline, he shrugged and said, "Okay."

Her eyes narrowed on his. "You haven't done anything drastic have you . . . like get married?"

"No."

"Girlfriend?"

He smiled. "No. You?"

She smiled, too. "No girlfriends *or* boyfriends. I've only got one person on my mind, and he is standing in front of me."

The hope beating in his veins, picking up steam. "Is that right?"

Her eyes were sparkling with happiness in a way he'd never seen in her. She looked different to him—more relaxed. That was it, he thought. He didn't see the worry, the anxiety around her eyes, and he realized that she was happy. He also realized he'd not really seen this side of her. "What's going on here?" he asked.

"Well," she said airily, "I don't know how to put it, exactly, other than I have determined that my talents fit another game altogether."

"What?"

She laughed at his utter confusion. "I'm not going to play baseball anymore, I am going to play football."

That explanation did not help, and she beamed at him as she slipped her hand into his. "I love you, Luke. I love you so much," she said, and pressed a free hand to her heart, almost as if to contain it. "I've thought of only you—well, and the mistakes I made, which were a lot, and how much I hurt you, which makes me sick to think about. But . . . my feelings haven't changed. I still love you so much, and I am not going to run anymore. From you or from anyone. I'm staying put, right here in Pine River."

"Maddie—"

"Wait, wait, before you say anything! I know that I'm taking a chance here. I know that *you* may not feel that way about *me*, and I am ready to accept that. But I would not be true to myself and my new outlook if I didn't tell you exactly how I feel. So, Luke, I am telling you that I love you more than I have ever loved anyone in my life, or ever will love anyone again, and whatever happens, I wish you much, much happiness in this life."

Luke was momentarily stunned into speechlessness. After dwelling on what he'd lost when Madeline had gone back to Orlando, he'd finally pushed down all those emotions, along with the love he'd felt for her, into a tight little ball. He squinted at her, unsure if he could trust her or not, unsure if he could allow that ball to uncoil and set those emotions free again. "So what are you saying?" he asked. "That you want to get back together?"

Madeline laughed. She gripped his hand tightly, and like he'd done once, lifted it to her mouth and kissed his knuckles. "I'm asking you to marry me, Luke Kendrick. But I will settle for getting back together, openly and proudly. I mean, if you will have me."

The ball exploded. Everything Luke had ever felt for this woman unfurled, filling him up. He couldn't believe this was happening, that at long last, someone was doing something for him, giving him what *he* needed. That Madeline had somehow found her footing and had leaped off the cliff into life. He couldn't believe how much he needed her, and with a fierceness that he'd never felt for another person. Nothing had changed for him—he still needed her beside him as he faced the uncertainties of the future. He needed her in his bed, at his table, and bearing his children.

Luke suddenly grabbed her up in his arms, pressed her cheek against his shoulder, closed his eyes and let the moment seep into him. "Yes," he said. "*Yes.* I love you, Maddie. I always did. And I never stopped."

She gasped with delight and lifted her head. "*Really?*"

"Are you kidding? *Really.*"

"Even when you knew how crazy I was?"

"Don't remind me and ruin the moment—but yeah, even then."

Madeline threw her arms around his neck, kissed his face, his mouth. "Thank God," she sighed into his ear. "Thank you God."

He pulled the cap off her head, closed his eyes, and buried his face in her neck. She smelled like lilacs.

He really liked lilacs.

EPILOGUE

Okay, Grant Tyler may have started this story, but it doesn't end with him. So much has happened, starting with the magnificent news that I got a *killer* new game, "Aliens Attack IV." I am the undisputed king. Many have tried and failed to best me. Guess who is my biggest competition. Guess! It's not Luke, it's Blue Eyes! Once that girl figured out how to use her opposable thumbs on the controller, she totally got into it, and now, Luke has to take the controller from her and put it away. She's like a cat with catnip, a jock with a lot of bold talk about how she's going to *beat* me.

Her trash talk needs a *lot* of work.

I know you're wondering about me, and who wouldn't be? I'm the spice in this pie! First, the new seizure medicine is working—I've only had one since the Big Kahuna. So forget that, because what I really want to tell you is that my brilliance has landed me a trip to the Denver Broncos home opener this fall! That's right, yours truly will be sitting in a skybox, *with* Dante, who—drumroll—is in remission! No, we didn't get the trip from Make-A-Wish Foundation, because apparently, they frown upon sending kids in remission with their color commentators to big fancy skyboxes. But Marisol and Dani worked it out with a local charity. I am so *stoked,* and so is Dante. The last two times I saw him he was wearing these really ugly Denver Broncos orange sweatpants.

We had a picnic at Homecoming Ranch so Dad and I could see the changes. I haven't been up there in months, but Luke goes every day. That's what he does now, he sort of works for Homecoming Ranch. Jackson figured out how to pay him a salary to keep things zipping along up there, which is really cool. I asked Luke if they were going to really build cabins for people to stay in and he said he didn't know, but it looked like there would be at least two weddings, and who knows after that? I wonder if one of them will be his. Because it doesn't take a genius to figure out if he marries Maddie, we're back in the ranch business, right?

Anyway, while we were up there, Libby told me she heard Julie Daugherty had divorced her husband and got a job at the bank, and that maybe she was dating Eric Kutzheimer. Look, the Kutz played football with me at Colorado School of Mines. Between you and me and anyone else who cares to listen, Eric had to be the dumbest right tackle who ever dragged knuckles across a football field. But then he went into business with his dad in some ore mining operation and now he's dirty, filthy *rich.* So good for Julie and her stink-eyed baby.

Jackson Crane was there, too, of course. Dani said that she'd heard some things about him, like maybe there was something shady in his past, which totally wouldn't surprise me, because Jackson knows way too many people and he just showed up in Pine River one day. Just showed up, rented that gray building, and hung out a shingle. But I dig Jackson. He has some really cool red pants that he rolls up at the ankles and wears with loafers. I think sometimes he thinks he is playing the lead in a movie in his head. Hey, it's better than the sound of crickets up there.

Dani also told me something kind of strange about Libby. She said that Libby was driving around Ryan Spangler's house in a sort of sneaky, weird way. I don't know what is going on with that, but Libby better be careful. Libby is awesome. But sneaking around is *not* awesome. It's weird.

Oh, I almost forgot! Marisol is pregnant. No, not by me! Not that I didn't try and talk her into a little *sumpin sumpin*, but she always uses that "I'm married," excuse with me. But, okay, that aside, you know what this means. It means another stink-eyed baby is going to be toddling around, messing with my controllers and probably gnawing on my feet. Not cool, man, not cool!

I'm going to set up a Facebook page for the little Stinker. Watch for it. It will be called, The Stinker.

As for Dad, he's all happy that Luke is home. And he's happy about Blue Eyes. She's been staying out at the ranch, and Luke is here, but still, it's like I told Dad, Luke seems super happy now that he has someone around to agree with him all the time. I finally just came out and asked Luke if they were going to get married, and he said something bogus, like "all good things in time, doofus." Like that means anything. But I heard Maddie talking about rings to Marisol. You heard it here first, kids—there's going to be some big damn deal around their engagement, like they are the first two people in the history of the world to get engaged. Which is totally okay with me, because I really like Maddie and it means another party. Hoozah!

That's it for now. *Moo latte* as we say up at the ranch.

ABOUT THE AUTHOR

CARRIE D'ANNA

Julia London is the *New York Times*, *USA Today*, and *Publishers Weekly* best-selling author of more than two dozen romantic fiction novels. She is the author of the popular Desperate Debutante, Scandalous, and Secrets of Hadley Green historical romance series, as well as the author of several contemporary women's fiction novels with strong romantic elements, including the upcoming *Return to Homecoming Ranch* and *The Last Homecoming*.

Julia is the recipient of the RT Book Club Award for Best Historical Romance and a four-time finalist for the prestigious RITA award for excellence in romantic fiction. She lives in Austin, Texas.